DEC 2 7 2010

DEATH AT AN EARLY AGE

A HARRY BROCK MYSTERY

DEATH AT AN EARLY AGE

KINLEY ROBY

FIVE STAR
A part of Gale, Cengage Learning

GALE
CENGAGE Learning™

Detroit • New York • San Francisco • New Haven, Conn • Waterville, Maine • London

GALE
CENGAGE Learning

LIBRARY OF CONGRESS CATALOGING-IN-PUBLICATION DATA

Roby, Kinley E.
    Death at an early age : a Harry Brock mystery / Kinley Roby.
    — 1st ed.
        p. cm.
    ISBN-13: 978-1-59414-895-8 (alk. paper)
    ISBN-10: 1-59414-895-3 (alk. paper)
    1. Brock, Harry (Fictitious character : Roby)—Fiction. 2. Private investigators—Florida—Fiction. 3. Murder—Investigation—Fiction. 4. Gulf Coast (Fla.)—Fiction. I. Title.
    PS3618.O3385D38 2010
    813'.6—dc22   2010030097

First Edition. First Printing: November 2010.
Published in 2010 in conjunction with Tekno Books and Ed Gorman.

Printed in the United States of America
1 2 3 4 5 6 7 14 13 12 11 10

For Mary

"For those who husbanded the Golden grain,
And those who flung it to the winds like Rain,
Alike to no such aureate Earth are turn'd
As buried once, Men want dug up again."
Rubaiyat of Omar Khayyam

1

Freed from his desk, Harry Brock stepped off his lanai into the heat and brilliance of a late spring morning and gratefully took a deep breath of the soft, spice-laden air emanating from the tangle of oaks, ficus, cabbage palms, trailing lianas, and riotous undergrowth crowding up to the sandy patch of cleared land surrounding his house and barn.

A solid man of medium height, deeply tanned, with short, thinning silver hair, he had once been a Maine game warden, a career that perished when he walked onto a man gutting a deer he had shot out of season. Seeing Harry, the man grabbed his rifle and began banging away at him. Harry shot the man in the hip to disable him, but the bullet shattered on bone, and a sliver of lead ripped through his body, piercing his heart.

Harry was arrested, charged, and tried for murder. The jury found him innocent; but, fed up with the loneliness and anxiety of being a warden's wife, Jennifer left him, taking their two young children with her; and the state, deciding Harry's notoriety would prevent him from carrying out his duties as a warden, fired him.

For the next two years he drifted in misery from job to job until he finally ran out of roads on Bartram's Hammock in Southwest Florida, where an old farmer by the name of Tucker LaBeau helped him to build a new life as a private investigator. A few years later in an ironic twist of fate, the Florida Fish and Game Department made him a game warden and put the Hammock and the adjacent Stickpen Preserve, a vast cypress swamp bordering the Hammock's north and east sides, under his care.

Having finished his paperwork for the day and delighted to be out of the house, Harry was setting off on the narrow, white sand road running in front of the house to check on the Hammock's wildlife. Wearing shorts and a tattered Tilley hat and carrying a light backpack and his CZ in a shoulder holster, he planned to walk to the north end of the road and return home along the edge of the Hammock while staying close to the water of the Stickpen Preserve, to make sure poachers and alligator-hide hunters were not at work.

Crossing through the shade of the very large live oak on the left corner of his front yard, he paused, through habit, to glance at the Puc Puggy Creek flowing southwest between the east bank of the Hammock and a mile-wide stretch of reed-covered floodplain through which the creek meandered on its way to the Gulf. When he turned away from the creek, he saw a man carrying a rifle approaching him on the sandy road, kicking up little puffs of dust as he strode along.

Aside from the fact that the man seemed to be in a hurry, Harry could draw no conclusions as to why he was on the Hammock or where he could have come from because the road behind him ended in the water of the Stickpen Preserve. As the man drew closer, Harry saw that he was dressed in dungarees, a blue work shirt, buttoned at the wrists, and a pair of dusty work boots.

"Toke Wylie," Harry said when the man stopped in front of him, shifted his rifle, and gripped Harry's hand. "It's been a while."

"Hello, Harry. You keeping all right?"

"Yes. What about you?"

"Good enough."

Harry recognized him as a man he had met. Harry had met

him several years ago when he had been doing some work that involved the casino on the Hierba Alto reservation. His full name was Tocqueville Emerson Wylie. He had told Harry that he considered it a great joke on his mother's part to have named him and his brothers after writers, and preferred to be called Toke, which was how he signed his name.

"Have you eaten this morning?" Harry asked, having noted that the man had been wading knee-deep in water, and his dungarees had not yet dried.

Wylie nodded.

"You'd better come with me," he said, then added, glancing at Harry's sneakers, "You'll get wet."

"That's all right," Harry said, knowing that when he was ready Wylie would tell him what this was all about and that he would not have come for him unless something was seriously wrong.

"You got a cell phone?"

"Yes. Is someone hurt?" Harry asked, thinking he might need to be calling for help now.

"Dead," Toke said as he turned and started walking back the way he had come.

Half an hour later Harry waded through a shallow tongue of water, pushed through a tangle of stopper bushes, and followed Wylie onto a narrow stretch of dry ground. Both men were soaked to the waist, and their shirts clung to their backs, soaked through with sweat. Wylie had stopped and was staring across an expanse of black water, dappled with shadows and fingers of sunlight falling through the cypress that rose around them like gray, leaf-topped pillars.

"There," Wylie said, pointing.

Harry blinked, rubbed his eyes, and looked again. To his chagrin, a foot in its rakish, red high-heeled shoe and some ten inches of tanned leg were still there, thrusting straight up out of the black, leaf-speckled water.

"Damnation!" Harry breathed, momentarily forgetting Wylie and addressing the foot, "How did you get here?"

The inappropriateness of the red shoe, looking as if it was on its way home from a dance, kicking up like that in the middle of the Stickpen, twenty-five miles from the nearest dance floor, offended him. He was also seriously put out by the complications the foot and its shoe were about to conjure.

"Rigor mortis," he muttered.

"What?" Toke asked, wearing a puzzled expression.

"That leg would not be sticking up like that unless rigor had set in. And if it had set in, why would whoever went to all the trouble of dumping her here leave it sticking out of the water that way? I assume the point of putting her out here was to hide her."

"Probably didn't," Wylie said, indicating the very large alligator, floating a dozen yards away in the shadow of one of the huge cypresses. "I expect he chivvied her around some, finding out if she was ripe enough to eat."

"I don't like this," Harry said, taking note of the alligator.

Only the animal's eyes and the tip of its nose were above the surface, but Harry knew it was large because the reptile's half-lidded eyes and his nose were about fourteen inches apart, which meant the alligator was about fourteen feet long. The fact it was floating there told Harry it considered itself a stake holder in the foot and what was attached to it.

"Waiting for her to soften up," Wylie said.

"She hasn't been in there long," Harry said, "or that leg would have flopped over."

"You want to pull her out?" Wylie asked.

"Got a canoe here somewhere?"

"Johnboat," Wylie replied. "The boy's with it."

It wasn't in sight, but Harry didn't expect it to be. Wylie

would have cached it before going in search of him.

"I want to take her out of there, but we can't," Harry said. "The police don't like having the crime scene disturbed."

Wylie nodded and said, "She didn't walk in here in those shoes."

"Dumped out of a boat?" Harry suggested.

Wylie shook his head and said, "Deeper here, but all around here it's too shallow for outboard motor or big inboard."

He held up a hand with his fingers spread.

"Nine, possibly ten inches," Harry said.

Wylie nodded. Harry pulled out his cell phone.

"You going to stay after you've called the sheriff's office?" Wylie asked.

"Got to," Harry said sourly. "I take it you're not."

Harry got the answer he expected, having guessed that Wylie had something in his boat he didn't want the police to see.

"The police are going to want to talk to you," Harry told him.

"You have to give them my name?"

Harry said he did, and the news did not seem to surprise Wylie.

"I'm easy to find," he said and shook hands with Harry.

"Thanks for telling me about this," Harry said. "You didn't have to."

Wylie nodded at the red shoe.

"Finding her gave me a bad feeling," he said.

With that he turned and gave a single, piercing whistle. A moment later a johnboat appeared among the cypress bolls, poled by a thin, dark-haired boy in dungarees and a ragged Harley-Davidson T-shirt. Harry judged him to be twelve or thirteen.

"Franklin. My boy," Wylie said when the boat touched the dry ground at his father's feet.

"No one could doubt it," Harry said, nodding at the young edition of Wylie.

"Mr. Brock," the boy said, returning Harry's nod.

Wylie stepped into the boat and switched ends with Franklin, inching carefully around something covered with an ancient piece of canvas that might once have been a painter's drop cloth, and exchanged his rifle for the pole.

"Take care, Toke," Harry said as Wylie, with Franklin sitting cross-legged in the front of the boat with the rifle across his knees, poled the boat out onto the dark water.

Wylie raised a hand in reply and soon slipped out of sight among the trees.

Harry made the call.

2

It was nearly noon by the time the body was hoisted into the helicopter with a lot of swearing on the part of the deputies who were wading thigh deep in the inky water and trying to do their crime scene work while at the same time looking over their shoulders, thanks to Harry's description of the big alligator, which had sunk from view at their arrival.

By the time Harry had slogged his way home and gotten cleaned up, it was nearly two. Reluctantly, he checked his answering machine, guessing what he was going to hear, and was not disappointed. Captain Jim Snyder of the Tequesta County Sheriff's Department wanted very urgently to talk with him. He called the sheriff's department and told the dispatcher he was coming in.

"The coroner's having trouble finding a cause of death," Jim said in a pronounced Eastern Tennessee accent, tossing the file onto his desk.

Jim, a tall, horse-faced man with cropped hair so blonde it was almost white, had been studying the contents of a file before he spoke.

"Do you know who she is?" Harry asked.

"Yes, her name's Lilly Rhinelander. It didn't mean anything to me, but from what we know so far, she lived down on Cat Boat Key and has more money than T. Boone Pickens," Sergeant Frank Hodges put in.

Hodges was a heavy, red-faced Floridian with short, sparse, sandy hair, whose uniform fit him like the skin on a sausage.

"I've heard the name," Harry said without much interest. "Relatives been notified?"

"John Edward Kringle, the oldest son. He lives in Boston," Jim said. "He said he had a brother and a sister and would take care of telling them. It turns out he and his brother and sister have been down here for more than a week. When I told him his mother was dead, he didn't express any surprise or grief or anything else."

Jim shook his head, reminding Harry that Jim never ceased to be painfully surprised by people's actions.

"How did you come to find Rhinelander?" Jim asked.

Harry had known these two men for years and regarded them as his friends, but he was aware that the friendship had fault lines and was maintained only with a lot of forbearance on both sides because his work frequently put him on the shady side of the law. This was, however, a situation in which Harry saw no likelihood of their being at cross purposes.

"Toke Wylie showed up at my place around six-thirty this morning and said I'd better go with him."

"Toke Wylie," Frank said, looking at Jim. "Do you know him?"

"No," Jim said impatiently, "but it's clear that Harry does."

"He's an Hierba Alto," Harry said. "You met him when I was helping that blackjack dealer. He lives on the reservation."

"I remember," Frank said with a loud laugh. "Toke was a long way from home, probably collecting a few alligator hides for fire water."

"For the Lord's sake, Sergeant," Jim said, his ears growing red as they always did when he was agitated, "don't you know better than to say something like that?"

"It was only a joke," Frank protested.

Harry grinned. Jim Snyder had come from the mountains of

16

east Tennessee. His father had been a preacher, a farmer, and a bootlegger. Harry remembered Frank once telling him that the father's combination of callings had made Jim a worrier, shy around women, and a straighter arrow than was altogether good for his health.

"I don't know what he was doing there," Harry said quickly, to put an end to an argument that, he knew from experience, could go on and on, "but I know he didn't have to wade for an hour through the Stickpen to get me. So I think we owe him one."

"We'll have to talk to him," Jim said.

"I told him that," Harry replied. "He answered that he'd be easy to find."

"About as easy as a mouse in a haymow," Jim grumbled.

"And when we do find him," Frank said with a happy grin, "he'll be about as talkative as a tree."

"How do you think she got out there?" Jim asked, standing up and stretching his long frame.

"She never walked out there in those spike-heeled shoes," Frank offered.

"And I doubt that she was carried," Harry said. "The place where Wylie found her is a long way from any road, and it's a steady slog through stopper tangles, muck, and knee-deep water," Harry said.

"What about a boat?" Jim inquired, coming around to sit on the edge of his desk. "Wylie got in there."

"There's too much undergrowth to use an outboard motor or oars," Harry said. "He was poling a johnboat, the narrow, flat-bottomed kind the Hierba Alto build. Not too heavily loaded, one of them will float in about four inches of water."

"Maybe the Indian dumped her in the water and came to get you as a cover," Hodges said.

Harry let that pass, not wanting to mention either the hump

under the canvas or Franklin.

"When I first knew him, Toke Wylie was a kind of medicine man and probably still is," Harry said, not wanting to believe Wylie had anything to do with Rhinelander's death. "He might have been on a collecting trip."

"Maybe," Hodges said a little harshly, "but I don't think there's a place anywhere in there where you could set a float-plane down."

Jim frowned at him, knowing as well as Harry did that in his spare time Hodges hunted wild pigs and like the rest of his clan wasn't too particular where they went looking for them.

"That leaves a helicopter," Jim said, "or an airboat." He was starting to say more when the phone rang.

He answered and said yes and no a few times in a stiff voice then hung up.

"Preliminary report from the medical examiner," he said, turning a little pink, but trying to sound casual. "No cause or time of death yet, and aside from some slight bruising on the chin, the body shows no evidence of trauma."

"Then they didn't drop her out of a plane," Hodges said.

"You might be able to get an airboat in there," Harry said.

"So it's that or a helicopter," Jim said.

Jim was unofficially engaged to Kathleen Towers, the Tequesta County Medical Examiner, and Harry, surprised to hear that it was Kathleen Jim had been speaking with, asked, "Things all right between you and Kathleen?"

"Kathleen who?" Hodges demanded in a mock-surprised voice.

"That's enough," Jim protested, his ears lighting up. "No, we're not having any trouble." He paused and stood up, his face growing longer. "At least, I don't think we are."

"I thought you were talking to an insurance salesman," Hodges said with a roar of laughter. "If I talked to Pauline like that, I'd be eating out of the dog's dish for a month."

"We're just trying to be professional on the job is all," Jim said loudly.

Harry regretted having asked the question in the first place, but he had asked it from genuine concern. Some years back, the woman Jim was going to marry was murdered. Love had come to him late and hit him hard. Against all the evidence, he blamed himself for her death; and it was years before he would look at another woman. Harry had brought Jim and Kathleen Towers together, but whether or not Jim could forgive himself, lay aside his grief and guilt, and marry Kathleen was still an open question. Harry knew that Kathleen was losing hope, and that if Jim lost her, it might break him.

"My fault," Harry said. "Do you need me any longer?"

"I think that's all for now," Jim said calmly. "Let's call it a day."

"There's somebody I think might have some information about this killing," Harry said, having a late thought.

"Fillmore Wiggins?" Jim asked.

"That's right."

"He wouldn't give the captain and me the scrapings off his boot," Hodges said.

"Right again. Do you mind if I talk with him?"

"Go ahead," Jim said, dropping a hand on Harry's shoulder, "but give him some warning you're coming or you might not live to say 'ello.' "

Harry laughed as he left, but knowing Wiggins made his laugh a little brittle.

An insurance surveillance in Tampa kept Harry away from the Hammock the next two days, and he crossed the small wooden humped bridge onto the Hammock from County Road 19, his link to the outside world, with a distinct lift of spirits. He was just settling into his return by putting away his groceries and easing the chore with a beer when his phone rang. He groaned at the interruption and reached for it.

A man's voice said, "This is Adrian Cooper. The name won't mean anything to you, but you may be familiar with the name Lilly Rhinelander."

The heavy voice, Harry noted, was calm and unhurried.

"I know the name," Harry said, intrigued why anyone knowing Lilly Rhinelander would be calling him. "Her body was found three days ago in the Stickpen Preserve and reported on television and in the newspaper since then."

"It's because of the nature of her dying that I'm calling you," he said. "She was my mother; and once that becomes known, I expect to be charged with her murder."

The man's voice conveyed no emotion. In Harry's experience, people expecting to be charged with murder were usually angry, frightened, confused, or all three at once. If Cooper was experiencing any of these emotions, he was keeping it well hidden.

"Why did you call me?"

"You are a private investigator."

"That's right."

"Then I want to hire you."

"What am I missing?" Harry asked, beginning to think he was talking to a nut. "From what you've said, you need a lawyer and not a private investigator."

"I want you to find my mother's killer."

"I'm meeting this Cooper tomorrow," Harry said. "Have you got a cause of death yet?"

He was sitting in Jim Snyder's office again, watching Jim flip through a file on his desk and thinking that the green paint on the walls and the rickety furniture were looking more wretched every day.

"No, and the family is howling about that, but if Adrian Cooper is Lilly Rhinelander's son, it's the first I've heard of it."

"And he didn't say why he wanted to talk with you?" Hodges put in.

"Only that it concerned his mother's death," Harry replied.

He did like not lying to these two men, but he knew that saying Cooper expected to be charged with killing Rhinelander would instantly make him a subject of the investigation. Until he knew more than he knew now about Cooper, he chose not to expose him to that kind of scrutiny.

"I went to the coroner's inquest," Hodges continued, "and most all of the hearings, and don't recall that name being mentioned. There were plenty of other names. That Rhinelander knew more people than Billy Graham, and most of them are pissed off at her . . ."

"Let's not get into that," Jim said, breaking into Hodges's loud laughter.

"From what I've read, the will is likely to be contested," Harry said, getting to his feet. "That means the carrion eaters will soon be circling. So I suppose Cooper could be a nut or a reporter looking for a story."

"Sounds more likely than Rhinelander's having an adult son no one's heard of," Jim said.

Harry nodded.

"Are you getting any outside help with the investigation?"

It was clear from the papers that this murder investigation was going to have national attention. Lilly Rhinelander's wealth guaranteed that.

"Not of the kind we either want or need," Jim said, his ears getting pink.

"The Feds," Hodges said, "are threatening to come in and

step all over our feet and be a general pain in the ass."

"They don't know the place or the people and will make all kinds of mistakes," Jim agreed with a frown, "and make people angry and uncooperative when there's no need of it."

"That must be giving Harley Dillard fits," Harry said, picking up his hat.

Dillard was the state attorney for the twenty-second district, and Harry planned to go straight to Dillard's office as soon as he finished talking with Jim and Frank, something else he was keeping to himself.

"Sheriff Fisher's ass is in a sling too," Hodges said with another loud laugh.

Jim winced. "You ought to think once in a while, Sergeant, before you speak."

"If I did that, I wouldn't be able to talk at all," Hodges responded, beaming.

"Got a suspect yet?" Harry asked.

"A whole barn full of them," Hodges replied before Jim could answer.

"Family?" Harry asked.

"Unfortunately, yes," Jim said gloomily. "Later I expect there will be others. It does seem that she collected enemies faster than clover blossoms draw bees."

"I don't envy you," Harry said and opened the door to leave.

"You talked with Wiggins yet?" Hodges called after him.

"Not yet."

"And Harry," Jim said, pointing a finger, "if you take this job, remember that any evidence you uncover comes to me."

"Count on it," Harry said, but neither Jim's frown nor Hodges's grin suggested they believed him.

The state attorney's offices were located on Oyster Street in a three-story white stucco building with a red tile roof. The office building was located in a quiet section of Old Avola where the streets were shaded by pin oaks and palms. Beginning to think he had made a mistake in taking Cooper at all seriously, Harry parked his Land Rover and stepped onto the dappled sidewalk, pausing to enjoy the cool breeze blowing from the Gulf, three blocks to the west, and the slow swaying and gentle murmur of the trees. The muted hum of distant traffic from Route 41 to the east added to the somnolence of the scene.

He would have liked to drop onto one of the teakwood benches arranged under the oaks and enjoy the unusual quiet but resisted the urge, pushed through the brass and glass doors into the dark marble lobby, and gave his name and destination to the young woman at the reception desk. She made a call and with a meaningless smile told him the floor number and location of the offices.

He was already chilled by the time he stepped into the elevator and thought it was a toss-up whether the greatest curse of Florida was the arctic air-conditioning or the bellow of lawnmowers and leaf blowers.

A tall, dark-haired woman strode out of one of the offices.

"Harry!" she cried, running toward him with outstretched arms and a smile that lit up Harry's heart.

She looked so much like a younger version of Harry's first wife that seeing her unexpectedly still took his breath away. For a moment he just looked at her then caught her in an embrace and found his tongue.

"Jennifer!" he said with genuine pleasure. "I thought you were in Jacksonville."

"I am," she said with a laugh. "The state sent me down here to help Harley with the Rhinelander case."

Still smiling, she hooked an arm through his and drew him toward her office. "You can't get over it, can you?" she asked, half dragging him along.

23

"You're more beautiful than ever," he said, dodging the question.

"Come on, Harry," she said, pushing him through the door. "You mixed me up with your first wife again, didn't you? Have a seat."

She had a spacious corner office, Florida paintings on the walls, a cool oriental carpet, and a large, gleaming black desk with chairs to match.

"For just a moment," he said, settling into one of the soft leather chairs.

The first time he had met Jennifer Fortunato, she was a new young lawyer in Harley Dillard's office. At that time, he had been close enough to his divorce from Katherine, and Jennifer looked so much like the Jennifer who had left him, that he had a great deal of trouble even being civil to her. However, he had frequent work with the DA's office, and Dillard, who had a dark sense of humor, always made Jennifer his contact person.

They gradually became friends and, for a short time before she was promoted as a new ADA and transferred to the northern part of the state, more than friends. He suddenly recalled that after making love the first time, Jennifer pinched his butt and asked, still a bit out of breath, "How was the foreign country?"

"What was that for?" he had gasped.

Rolling off him and lying sprawled on her back, she said, "Haven't you ever heard the saying, 'The past is a foreign country?' "

"Sure, but I still don't . . ."

"You said, 'Jennifer!' a few times."

Harry surfaced enough to make the connection.

"It was not Jennifer One I was thinking about!" he protested.

She rolled onto her elbows, grinned down at him, and said, "Prove it to Jennifer Two."

"Why are you sitting there with that silly smile on your face, Harry?" she asked now, leaning against the edge of her desk. He looked up at her and suppressed the thought that she was just about his daughter Sarah's age.

"The past is a foreign country," he said.

"Oh, God, Harry," she said springing up with a pained expression, "I'm getting married in November."

Harry counted a six month reprieve and noted that she was not wearing a ring. Then he felt very sorry for himself but pulled back from that precipice.

"I hope you'll be very happy," he said and meant it, trying to ignore the hearse parked where his heart was supposed to be.

"Thank you," she said, suddenly glowering down at him, her dark eyes snapping. "But why the hell didn't you call, e-mail me, drive to Jacksonville to see me? Harry, we could have worked out *something.*"

"No we couldn't," he said. "How old is the very lucky man?"

"About my age."

"There you are, a happy landing."

"Maybe."

She shook her head, paused, and gave a rueful laugh and said, "I hate it that I didn't even get a vote."

"You didn't call me either," Harry said with a smile, getting up to kiss her.

She wrapped her arms around his neck and, suspending thought, Harry got into it a little. When they eased back a bit, neither mentioned the obvious reluctance with which they were letting go of one another.

"Have you got time to talk to me about Lilly Rhinelander?" he asked when his cognitive processes found room to reassert themselves, and forced himself to stop thinking about how long it had been since he had held a woman in his arms.

"*She!*" Jennifer said with a shout of laughter, pulling a chair closer to Harry's and sitting down. "It was Lilly's death that brought me to Avola. Her murder has the state really freaked. Why are you interested in her?"

"Does the name Adrian Cooper mean anything to you?"

"Cooper?" she asked, shaking her head. "Never heard of him. Who is he?"

"A man who called me, claiming to be Lilly Rhinelander's son."

"Why call you?" Jennifer asked.

"He seems to think he may need my help."

"To do what?"

"He wasn't too clear, but I'm meeting him tomorrow," he said. "Is there anything you can tell me about Rhinelander's death that the media hasn't already reported—something that might help me to tell whether or not Cooper is lying about who he is?"

"Not really," Jennifer said, frowning, "but if you knew something about Rhinelander that he should know—if he really is her son—and doesn't, it might give you something to build on."

"Couldn't hurt," Harry replied.

She leaned back in her chair and tapped her chin with her finger. While she thought, he studied her face, thinking how remarkable the resemblance was between her and his ex-wife when she was this Jennifer's age. How old would that make her? A few years older than his daughter Sarah. He did not find that a profitable line of inquiry.

"Lilly Rhinelander's a riddle we haven't fully solved," Jennifer told him. "I don't think I'm breaking any rule of confidentiality by telling you that when she was first becoming known, she changed her name more often than a snake sheds its skin. How old is Cooper?"

"It's a guess, but judging by his voice, I'd say around forty."

Jennifer went back to her desk, sat down, and opened her laptop, and Harry listened a while to the soft clicking of the keys.

"Well, Cooper hasn't got a record. Now let's see . . . There it is," she said. "Rachel Comstock. For a while in the mid-sixties she was working in New York under that name."

"What was she doing?"

"She called it modeling," Jennifer said as she snapped shut her computer. "Her name began making the papers when she began appearing at high-end events on the arms of men whose enterprises would have put them in jail if they hadn't been connected."

"With the mob?" Harry asked in surprise.

"The mob, city hall, or Albany," Jennifer said with a wry smile.

"As one of the half-dozen richest women in the country, she had a modest beginning," Harry said, starting to find the woman interesting. "I haven't paid much attention, but I don't recall any mention of her being a prostitute."

"No," Jennifer said, "and for a while you won't. The family, if you can call those barracudas family, has closed ranks over the issue of Lilly's reputation."

The phone on Jennifer's desk jangled. She answered it and after a moment put her hand over the mouthpiece and said, "Harry, I've got to take this."

"Thanks for the help," he said, already on his feet. "It's been good seeing you."

"And you. Are you ever free for lunch?"

"I'll call you."

"Oh, sure."

3

Hammock, in the Indian language, meant "a cool place," and referred to small islands of land, a foot or so higher than the surrounding swamp, densely covered with trees, on which it is possible to live with dry feet, till the soil, and if you don't cut down too many trees, live ten degrees cooler than in the encompassing furnace. For Harry, Bartram's Hammock was his home and the place which had made life possible. Lately, however, it had begun to feel like the end of his trail. It wasn't a good feeling.

His talk with Jennifer Fortunato had led him into a Miltonic reverie in which he considered all the ways in which his light was spent and how dark and wide the world was. The reverie had stretched and proliferated lugubriously from Oyster Street to his turning onto the Hammock.

Meeting Jennifer and coming home to an empty house predictably led him to think of Katherine, his second wife. They had lived together on the Hammock for several years, and their divorce had created a tear in his life he had never properly mended. He and Katherine had eventually become occasional lovers again, but as she lived in Georgia, had refused to remarry him or to live with him, and didn't do weekends, he was left more or less twisting in the wind.

He had adopted Jesse and Minna, the two children she had from a catastrophic first marriage, and when he was willing to drive to the farm where Katherine and the children lived with

Katherine's sister, he could see them and Thornton, the child he and Katherine had together, whenever he wanted to, but it wasn't the same as sharing their lives.

His gloomy thoughts were interrupted by a very large blue-tick hound with a blue bandanna tied around his neck, which trotted purposefully around the Rover and, on seeing Harry, bared a full set of very impressive teeth. Instead of sprinting for the house, Harry greeted the dog with an immediate lift in spirits, knowing that the curled lips were Sanchez's way of smiling, and the smile was generally followed by a hearty boost in the crotch with his nose. For those not prepared for what was coming, the gesture produced an even more pronounced response than the bared teeth.

"Has Tucker sent me a note?" Harry asked, avoiding the boost by dropping to his knees and grasping the dog on both sides of his thick neck and giving his head a good shake, provoking an even wider grin, accompanied by a deep growl of pleasure.

Harry untied the bandanna and took out the note rolled in the cloth. As he read, he stood up and the bandanna slid off his knee onto the ground. Sanchez immediately picked it up, and with a muffled woof, pushed his nose into Harry's stomach, shoving him back a step.

"Oh, sorry," Harry said, stuck the note in his shirt pocket, and tied the bandanna around the dog's neck.

"Tucker's got something to show me," Harry told the dog when he had finished reading. "Come in the house. I'll write that I can't get there before this afternoon. While I do that, you can have a Milk-Bone and some water."

Harry had grown so used to talking to the dog that he no longer noticed the oddness of it. When Sanchez had finished his treat and slaked his thirst, Harry tied his note into the dog's bandanna, walked him out past the Rover, and saw him off on the white sand road. Then he went into the house and spent the next two hours on his computer, looking up material on Lilly Rhinelander. When he stopped, he had hardly scratched the surface of Rhinelander's recorded history, very little of which was edifying.

Tucker and Harry were sitting in a pair of ancient bentwood rockers, enjoying the deep, cool shade of Tucker's back stoop. At least Tucker was enjoying it. Harry was still too wrung out from his research to enjoy anything. The old farmer, a small, wiry man with a fringe of white hair above his ears that lifted like gossamer wings in every breeze, was dressed in faded overalls, work shoes, and a collarless white shirt. As he rocked, he sipped mahogany-colored tea from a white mug and stared out with apparent contentment at the soaring trunks supporting the dense green tangle of branches, trailing lianas, and pink and white flowering vines in the forest's upper story. Out of that beckoning shade came the rising and falling fiddle-music of cicadas, locusts, crickets, and a host of other stridulating creatures in pursuit of love's redemption.

Just then there was a crackling of brush at the edge of woods, and Sanchez struggled out of the tangle, panting, his tongue lolling. Behind him a very large, black mule, wearing a straw hat, strode easily through the thicket and paused to give himself a good shake. Both were soaked with sweat and splattered with mud.

Harry waved at the two animals before he caught himself.

Sanchez woofed in response, and the mule nodded his head before hurrying toward the stoop.

"They'll be thirsty," Tucker said.

Tucker set down his mug, but Harry was already on his feet.

"Let me," Harry said and disappeared into the kitchen, coming back with a bucket of water, which he set down on the front of the stoop, and patted Oh, Brother!'s neck while Sanchez drank.

The mule pressed his nose against Harry's chest and blew softly, an affectionate greeting the animal bestowed on very few people.

"All right," Tucker said when the animals had stopped drinking. "Down to the creek, and Sanchez, you stay in the shallows. Benjamin's down there somewhere, so keep your eyes peeled, Oh, Brother!"

"Have you seen him?" Harry asked as the dog and the mule trotted off. He had long since stopped doubting that the two would understand what Tucker said to them.

Harry was referring to the huge male alligator that came out of the Stickpen Preserve every spring to breed. His mating call sounded like the rolling of distant thunder, but he wasn't too busy breeding to eat some dog. As big as Sanchez was, Benjamin could have swallowed him in three or four bites.

"I thought he'd met his responsibilities for the year," Tucker replied, "but two days ago, I saw him courting that big female halfway between our places."

"Speaking of alligators," Harry said, "did you see the piece in the *Avola Banner* about that young house painter who was rinsing his brushes in the pond behind the house where he was working and got his left arm bitten off? If we don't find a way to curb their numbers, the hide hunters are going to demand the Fish and Game Department establish an open season on them."

"Yes, I saw it, and you may be right, but you and I know they're not nearly as fertile as they were a few years ago. If we keep on rinsing our paint brushes in their bath water, the problem may solve itself."

"Where's Jane Bunting?" Harry asked, noticing that Tucker's semi-feral calico cat was missing from his lap.

31

In the daylight hours if Tucker was sitting down, she was seldom anywhere else. The nights, however, belonged to her and the moon, in whose company she vanished into the woods for the hunt. Rabbits, mice, rats, and snakes were her specialties, although anything with hair and skin under the size of a raccoon was an object of interest. At first light she sheathed her claws, brought home something still living, and laid it at Tucker's feet for his breakfast, which, since she regarded snakes as a delicacy, and could open the screen door, had occasionally led to some liveliness in the kitchen.

Her absence reminded Harry that the first time he saw her he asked Tucker why she'd been named Jane Bunting and made the mistake of trying to pick her up.

"She's far too serious a cat to have just one name," Tucker had told him while dressing Harry's wounds after offering to buy him a new shirt to replace the one she had just shredded. "Anyway, it was Sanchez's idea."

"A one-man cat," Harry had remarked between gasps as Tucker had painted his wounds with iodine.

Tucker brought Harry back to the present by saying, "The lady's gone missing, and that brings us to the reason I sent you the note."

"Sanchez and Oh, Brother! were out there looking for her."

"That's it," Tucker said, shaking his head sadly, "and they didn't find her."

"If a cat doesn't want to be found . . . ," Harry said.

"True, and as a rule I wouldn't be concerned, and I wasn't until I saw the tracks."

The comment got Harry's full attention. Tucker was an old man alone, and Harry did not like the possibility that somebody had been sneaking around his place, probably at night.

"You recall that rain we had the other night?" Tucker asked.

Harry said he did.

"Well, the next morning I went out as usual to feed the hens; and in some of the soft ground around the run, I found two sets of coyote tracks."

Harry was both relieved and alarmed.

"If a breeding pair of coyotes has moved onto the Hammock," Harry said, "we can say goodbye to our gray foxes Bonnie and Clyde."

"And, more than likely," Tucker said grimly, "Jane Bunting as well."

Harry returned home to find a message on his answering machine. It was from an Evie Kronsky, asking Harry to call as soon as possible. It took him a minute to clear the cider fog. When he had, he realized it was Lilly Rhinelander's daughter Rita Evgenie. She had taken her middle name Evgenie and made a diminutive of it.

Because he had hoped to talk with her and her brothers, he made the call; but he made it with some hesitation, having no idea what to expect.

A woman with a strong Hispanic accent answered the phone, and Harry gave his name.

"Please wait," she said.

"This is Evie Kronsky, Mr. Brock. Thank you for calling."

The voice was strong, cold, and carefully modulated, carrying a tinge of New York and something else. Russian? Harry wasn't sure.

"I'm very sorry about your mother," he said.

"Thank you," she said, closing that subject. "I've taken the trouble to learn something about you," she continued. "I'm surprised to find you are, apparently, an intelligent, unusually gifted man in a profession largely populated with thugs."

Harry decided he had been condescended to enough.

"Why did you call me?" he asked, stepping on her next line.

"To tell you that if you and this Cooper person think you can drag my mother's name through the mud and, by doing that, blackmail us into giving you money to get rid of you, you are very much mistaken."

Her voice had risen considerably, and Harry, holding the phone away from his ear, had no trouble hearing her. When she finished speaking, Harry found the silence comforting and went on enjoying it until Kronsky asked sharply if he was still there.

"Only briefly," Harry said quietly and added just before hanging up, "When you have something sensible to say to me, I'll be glad to talk with you."

Harry and Adrian Cooper were seated across from one another in the Hollow Leg on Fifth Avenue, Harry's favorite bar in downtown Avola. Slow ceiling fans kept the cooled air moving without creating an ice buildup on the customers' heads. The sound from the TV over the bar was too low to be a distraction, the creaky old cherry booths gave the illusion of privacy, and best of all, the smoky, beery bar smell and low-watt illumination allowed the customers to think it was dark outside, a justification for drinking, even in the middle of the day. Since Katherine had left with Minna for Georgia, Harry had been spending a lot of time in the Hollow Leg.

"I'm surprised you agreed to see me," Cooper said, setting his beer mug down carefully on its coaster as if giving Harry time to think before he answered.

He was a large man and, Harry thought from the breadth and slope of his shoulders, a powerful one, someone comfortable with his size. Harry concluded he was financially comfortable as well. His conservative shirt and trousers had the look, and his sandals were high-end Volterras. He laughed easily, and if he was in any way stressed, Harry had found no evidence of it in his deep, slow voice or his broad, smooth, square-jawed face.

His hair, worn short, was sprinkled with gray although Harry did not think he could be much over forty, which meant, if Cooper was telling the truth, Lilly Rhinelander had given birth to him before she was twenty. It also made him the oldest of her children.

"I'm a little surprised myself," Harry responded. "But I don't get a call every day from someone who tells me he expects to be charged with murder and is an unacknowledged son of a woman who, when she was alive, was one of the richest in the country."

"Death attracts rascals as well as scavengers," Cooper said with a chuckle.

"Especially if the death is Lilly Rhinelander's," Harry said.

Cooper smiled. Harry registered the quiet response and pressed ahead.

"Before we get to the murder charge, let's assume you are Lilly Rhinelander's son. Do you have any idea how difficult it's going to be to persuade a court of that? I say in part because I've already spoken with Rita Evgenie Kronsky, your alleged half sister; and to say the family is going to fight you is way short of what you're going to run into."

"Their lawyer has said as much," Cooper responded with a dismissive wave of his thick hand. "Being imprisoned is one of the lesser threats, but if it comes to it, there's always DNA."

"Two things about that," Harry said. "First, before you reach the place where you can force such a test, you are going to have to penetrate a phalanx of Rhinelander lawyers. Second, cremation destroys DNA, and if Lilly Rhinelander is cremated, you're pickled before you begin."

"Although it varies from jurisdiction to jurisdiction, in murder cases the medical examiner collects a DNA sample from the victims; and in any case I have three half brothers and sisters," Cooper replied, apparently unruffled.

"Have you checked with anyone to find out if you can

establish a common mother in that way if none of the dead woman's DNA is available to you?"

There was that smile again.

"Yes, I have. A mother passes along to all her children her mitochondria, holding a set of genes which will be identical in each of the children."

Harry was impressed.

"Can these genes be identified without a sample of the mother's DNA?"

"Yes," Cooper said patiently as though he had fully prepared himself for this sort of grilling, "and a judge can require that the claimant and his alleged siblings in the suit submit a cheek swab sample to the court so that the mitochondria can be analyzed. There's quite an extensive body of legal precedent and procedure established regarding postmortem estate claims by individuals asserting a blood relationship with the deceased. The technology is also sufficiently developed to resolve relationship issues through DNA testing."

Harry nodded, thought a moment, and said, "Then your point is that if you're not her son, there would be no point in your saying you are because you can easily be proved not to be."

"Exactly."

Unless you're doing this not to try to share in Rhinelander's estate but for some other reason, Harry thought, reserving the possibility as he studied the calm, solid man looking back at him with that inscrutable smile.

"And the fact that you can be proved to be her son with her dead is one reason why you believe you will be charged with trying to kill her."

"You are a very quick study, Mr. Brock."

Harry decided to set aside for the moment the issue of Cooper's exposure to arrest.

"Not all that quick, Mr. Cooper. What have you got for evidence that will take you far enough into the court challenge to persuade the judge you're who you say you are?"

"I have three unsigned letters she has written to me over the years," Cooper said, leaning ahead slightly and displaying more animation than he had shown before.

"Does she say anything in them that would establish that she is your mother?"

"No, but the letters are written in longhand. I assume an expert could establish that all the letters were written by the same person and that, having compared the writing with an uncontested sample of her handwriting, conclude that the letters were written by her."

"Possibly," Harry said. "By the way, what was your mother's name when you were born?"

The smile returned.

"Rachel Comstock—at least that's the name on the birth certificate. That and no other."

Harry thought he saw a flicker of pain cross Cooper's face when he said, "That and no other," but it was too fleeting for Harry to be sure.

"One more question—do you know what this effort is going to cost you in money and general wear and tear?"

"Yes," Cooper said. "As a lawyer, I am probably more aware of it than even you."

He paused, regarding Harry with an expression that Harry could only call benign. It made him uneasy. He was not accustomed to being looked at like that and had no idea what it conveyed.

"Then why are you putting yourself through this?" Harry demanded, to deflect that look.

"I could be trying to get a slice of my mother's estate," he said, his eyes hardening, "but I'm not." He paused again as if trying to resolve some inner conflict. Then he said, "I want it established in law that I am who I say I am, the natural son of Lilly Rhinelander."

"All right," Harry said, "you've given me your answer. I don't want to go any farther with this until I've done some thinking and some more checking. Is that all right with you?"

"Of course," Cooper said. "I understand your hesitation, and if you want my fingerprints to run through the FBI files, I'll be happy to provide them."

"Fair enough," Harry said, hearing no sarcasm in Cooper's response. "Where can I reach you?"

"Unless you have strong objections, I'd prefer to call you."

The first bump in the road, Harry thought, keeping his reaction well buried.

"OK. Is there anything you want to ask me?"

"Only this, Mr. Brock: Why haven't you remarked on the fact that I'm a black man?"

4

Encountering Jennifer Fortunato so unexpectedly had destabilized Harry and set his mind digging into those years he would have preferred to leave undisturbed. Among the fragments his mind unearthed was one that made him smile. It was of him and Jennifer at Barefoot Beach with the sun rising through the palms on the back dune, the first cool breeze of the day ruffling the glassy surface of the sea with cat's-paws, and her naked body glistening with rosy light as she waded ashore, wringing out her long hair.

"All you lack is a clamshell," he told her.

Later, in bed with him, she asked, "Do I still need the clamshell?"

"You're perfect," he said, and at that moment he had meant it.

Meeting Jennifer and then talking with Adrian Cooper led Harry to the conclusion that he would quickly have to become familiar with Lilly Rhinelander's family and what was being done with her estate; and that conclusion led him just as quickly to decide he would have to talk again with Jennifer. After all, who could be of more help? Wanting to see her again, he assured himself, was only a coincidence.

Besides, he told himself, I really do owe her lunch, and as long as it's strictly business, which it will be, there's no harm in it.

"Harry, you old darling you, is this for real?" she responded with obvious delight to the invitation.

"Oppenheimer's is reserving a table for us even as I speak."

"Are there still doves in the trees?"

"There are and they do, but the management has put up umbrellas."

"What are you thinking about?" Jennifer asked him.

She had shed her dark suit jacket, and, seated safely under the rose-colored umbrella, Harry thought she looked very much at home and very lovely in her organdy blouse. A sea breeze was stirring the leaves of the enormous ficus trees shading Oppenheimer's outside dining area, and ring doves were burbling softly in the branches high above them.

"Having you back is better than a stick in the eye," he said.

"Thanks," she said. "I'm glad to be back."

Then the smile faded. "You know," she continued, "I don't think I ever fully left Avola, and when Harley Dillard decides to try for a judgeship, as he will before too long, if I can convince Alex to leave Jacksonville, I'm going to break my back trying to get his job."

"Your husband!" Harry said. "Good for you. Bad for me." And immediately regretted his words.

She blushed and reached for the menu.

"He's not my husband yet," she said in a voice Harry could not interpret.

A waitress arrived, and in a dull voice Jennifer ordered iced tea.

"It's dust and ashes," Jennifer complained, throwing down her menu, "but turning up at Harley's office with wine on my breath is a poor career move."

"Or, if you appear with your skirt on backwards."

"God, Harry," she said with a yelp of laughter, "don't remind me. It was a year before those jackals in the office stopped asking me what I'd had for lunch. Now tell me what you think of Adrian Cooper."

"He's very convincing. He said Rachel Comstock's name is on his birth certificate."

"Does it strike you as odd," Jennifer asked, "that, with her wealth, Rhinelander didn't make that birth certificate disappear?"

"From here it does," Harry agreed, "but forty years ago she *was* Rachel Comstock, not Lilly Rhinelander."

"True. Has he got anything else?"

"He claims to have three letters from Rhinelander, unsigned but written in longhand. And, finally, he claims that DNA or mitochondria, more specifically, will prove that he is a half brother to the three Rhinelander children. Is he right?"

"I'd say so. Of course, now that everyone has her own expert to cast doubt on the evidence, offer alternative readings, or flat-out deny the other side's expert is an expert and is wrong anyway, science doesn't always carry the day. Remember the Simpson trial, Harry. A jury not only has to see DNA evidence, it has to believe it."

"As I recall, it was a bloody footprint that decided the civil case against him, not the DNA."

"Right."

"If it's possible, I've got to talk with members of Lilly Rhinelander's family. Where do I begin?"

"I thought you were the expert," she said, as if surprised by the question.

"I suppose I am in the sense you mean, but what I don't have is a map of the castle or a list of its defenders."

Still serious, she regarded him with a slight frown, putting two lines between her dark eyebrows.

"I'll be skating close to the black ice to tell you anything," Jennifer said.

They paused to order, and then she said, "So, what I tell you isn't for attribution, and my name mustn't be used as a pry to force any doors. Agreed?"

"Agreed," Harry said.

"OK. First, there are no undefended points of access," she began and then said she was dropping the castle metaphor to talk about the Rhinelander operation. He told her what he had found on line. "It's a beginning," she said and opened her narration.

The food came, and, talking and eating while Harry ate and listened, Jennifer gave him a Cook's tour of the structure of the Rhinelander business empire.

"I'd totally forgotten just how great the Asian salad is in this place," she said twenty minutes later, sitting back in her chair with a sigh and tossing her napkin onto the table.

"You're a miracle," Harry said. "I gather you have a lot of business lunches."

"How did you know?" she asked.

"You can breathe and swallow at the same time."

"Flattery will get you everything. Oh, by the way, the sharks swimming in the moat belong to the law firm of Schlossberg, Pearson, O'Leary, and Gross. It's very heavy with litigators because Lilly sued first and often, and never, ever paid a bill unless she lost the countersuit—and not always then. Anyone who ever took her to court found himself waist deep in countersuits. 'Getting SHOGed' became a byword among those who had business with the castle."

While Harry waited for the check, he told Jennifer that he had another appointment with Cooper, carefully avoiding the issue of his expecting to be arrested.

"I can hardly wait," he said, only half joking. "The guy really interests me."

As they drove back to Jennifer's office, she took a page from

Jim's book and warned him that if he went to work for Cooper, he would be obliged to give her whatever had bearing on Rhinelander's murder. Then she passed him a slip of paper with a name.

"This is the Rhinelander's gatekeeper. Go to anyone in the family through him. By the way, where is Cooper staying, or does he live in Avola?"

Harry knew the question was not asked out of curiosity.

"Thanks for the name, and I don't know where he lives. He calls me."

"Odd," Jennifer said, but Harry translated that to mean *suspicious*.

"Fine way to end a romantic lunch," Harry complained, delivering her to her building.

She laughed, leaned over, and kissed him on the cheek.

"You'll survive," she said, grinning, and added, "Let's do this again and sooner rather than later."

Before he could respond, she unclipped her safety belt and put a hand on his arm and said in a voice stripped of humor, "And one other thing: watch yourself. You don't know what Cooper's up to, and the Rhinelanders are dangerous."

"How have I gotten along without you?" he asked as she got out of the Rover.

"I'd say not all that well. Call me."

Jennifer's cryptic response to his joking question about how he had gotten along without her had turned and bitten him as soon as she had slammed the door. Driving back to the Hammock through a short but sharp thunderstorm that first flooded the roads, then set them steaming, he asked himself what had prompted her remark. Turning onto the bridge, he seized on the thought that it might have come from residual anger over the way they separated after her promotion, but that flight of fancy crashed during takeoff, leaving him looking at himself.

"I'm not thinking about it," he told the box tortoise plodding across the sandy road in front of the Rover.

Even the tortoise didn't believe him.

Once in the house, he Googled Lilly Rhinelander and began focusing on her children. Her oldest was John Edward Kringle, thirty-seven, on his third marriage, managing director of Rhinelander's Baker's Dozen, a chain of bakeries with locations in all the major cities in New England, head offices in Boston. Beyond those facts, Harry found that Kringle was suspected by the state's attorney general of having underworld ties. His two divorces had been messy, and his third marriage was rumored to be going up in smoke. Another recurring rumor was that the business was being run into the ground.

The second child was a daughter, Rita Evgenie Kronsky, thirty-two, once married, divorced. Harry had no luck finding out any more about the woman except that she lived in New York and was the editor of *La Peinture,* an art magazine published by the gallery Espace, located on West Twenty-fifth Street, offering guidance in art and design for commercial and professional settings, so the advertising read. After a little more digging Harry discovered that Espace was owned by the Owen Shaw Company, a subsidiary of Wyman Basilevsky, Inc., art wholesalers. He smiled when he found that Wyman and Basilevsky was owned by Lilly Rhinelander.

At twenty-five Michael Joseph was the youngest and the only one of her children to bear the Rhinelander name. To Harry's surprise he found that Michael, unmarried, was a graduate student at Tufts University's Fletcher School, enrolled as a doctoral student in the law and diplomacy program. Harry gave a low whistle.

"It would have taken more than Momma's money to put you in there," Harry told the image of the fair-haired young man on the monitor.

Aside from a short account of his skills on the ski slopes and his impressive record as a mountain climber—he had been on most of the big ones—and having attended Phillips Exeter Academy, there was nothing further. Harry pushed back in his chair and turned to look out the window at the sun slanting through the live oaks and the shifting patterns of dappled light cast by their leaves on the sandy ground. Another part of his brain wondered what the odds were that one of the Rhinelander children had committed matricide.

He also wondered if Michael Joseph was as sharp edged as his sister.

The phone rang.

"I apologize for asking this," Cooper said as soon as Harry answered, "and it's terribly short notice, but could we move our meeting up to this afternoon?"

The man's voice was as deep and calm as ever, and Harry wondered what had prompted the request. He would also have liked to learn more about Rhinelander's family and her ex-husbands before talking with Cooper a second time, but he was extremely curious about the man.

"I could see you in forty-five minutes," he said.

"That would be fine. Do you want to meet in the Hollow Leg?"

Harry decided he wanted to see Cooper in another setting.

"Have you seen the fishing pier yet?" he asked.

"No. Is it in town?"

"Yes. I think you'll find it interesting. I'll tell you how to get there."

"That won't be necessary," Cooper answered. "I'll find it. Thank you for being so gracious."

Harry hung up the phone and glanced out the kitchen window

in time to see a silver Mercedes roadster with its top down wheel into his yard, trailing a tunnel of white dust. The bronzed man with a shaved head who got out of the car was dressed in a white short-sleeved shirt, white trousers, and white sandals. He looked around for a moment and then came toward the house with a long-legged stride.

"Got yourself turned around?" Harry asked, pushing open the screen door on the lanai.

His caller was wearing the kind of sunglasses that threw your own reflection back at you when you met the wearer's gaze. Harry did not like them. The man stopped with one foot on the granite step and took his time about answering.

"I doubt it," he said.

He spoke in a loud voice with a harsh and grating New York–Boston accent.

"Your name Brock?"

"That's right."

"I want to talk to you," he said and started to step onto the lanai and found himself pushed back off the step.

"Who are you and what do you want?" Harry asked.

The man was clearly offended at finding himself thwarted, and Harry could see from the way his jaw muscles were swelling that he might have a fight on his hands. It was not a prospect Harry found pleasing. He didn't like fighting, and the man in front of him outweighed him by at least thirty pounds, none of which appeared to be fat.

"John Kringle. The name mean anything to you?" he asked in a harsh bark.

"Yes," Harry said, watching him very closely, thinking perhaps Kringle's mother's death might have something to do with his anger and cutting him some slack. "I've talked with your sister. What do you want to talk to me about?"

"How stoned was she?" he asked, adding sourness to his aggression.

"You'll have to ask her," Harry said, wondering if he was going to have a role as camp counselor to the Rhinelander children.

"No point in it. I doubt if she remembers talking to you. You were one of the men who found my mother's body," Kringle said, turning down the volume on his voice, "and you're working for Adrian Cooper. I want to talk about both of those things."

Harry decided he wanted to hear what Kringle had to say and stepped back.

"Come in," he said and, pointing at the chairs, added, "have a seat."

Kringle wiped the seat of the chair and looked at his fingers before sitting down.

Harry let it pass without comment, having noted that Kringle's whites were spotless.

"What happened in that goddamned swamp?" Kringle demanded, having perched himself on the edge of the chair and resting his forearms on his knees.

Harry studied Kringle before answering and decided he was looking at someone who, for all his wealth, had a face that showed considerable wear. He didn't look like a happy man.

"Right now, only whoever killed your mother knows for sure. I wish I could tell you more."

"Don't you have any idea at all about how she got there? You saw the place. The goddamned police don't seem to know shit and everybody else asks more questions than they answer."

"This thing must have hit you hard," Harry said.

Kringle had seemed to grow quieter after he sat down, but Harry's comment about his mother's death set him off again.

"It's none of your business, Brock," Kringle fired back, "but I'll live. Now, how about answering my question?"

"Have you been told anything about the condition of your

mother's body when she was taken from the water?" Harry asked quietly.

"Somebody broke her neck. That's the medical examiner's report, which will stand unless the lab work turns up something else. Maybe then we'll get her body and do what has to be done."

Harry saw for a moment something that might have been grief twist Kringle's face. Then it was gone. By now Kringle was shifting around and flinging his hands through the air as if he was trying to get rid of them.

"I hope it's soon," Harry said quietly. "She had no obvious injuries at all. The small open area where she was lying is surrounded by large, heavily limbed cypress trees. That means she was not dropped from a plane or there would have been extensive damage to her and her clothes."

"Why not a boat?"

"The water is mostly too shallow to float a keeled boat," Harry told him, "and an outboard motor would be useless."

"An airboat?"

"That's a possibility, but the undergrowth is very thick. Also, it's unlikely that anyone not very familiar with the preserve could go in that far and come back to his starting point even with a compass."

"OK," Kringle said, in a calmer voice. "Now, what about this Cooper?"

"All I'm going to say about him is that he's a client."

"The asshole's going around claiming to be my half brother," he bellowed, fully charged again.

Harry found it hard to say whether Kringle was more infuriated or flabbergasted by Cooper's claim.

"Shouldn't your lawyer be dealing with that side of things?" Harry asked.

"Lawyers!" Kringle snorted. "With that bunch in control, it

will take months and months to get Lilly's estate settled. And that's without Cooper."

He jumped up, too agitated to stay seated.

"Now, unless someone shoots the son of a bitch, we may never see a nickel of that money."

Harry didn't miss the desperation that had crept into his voice.

"Take my advice," Harry said. "Make this the last time you say anything about Cooper getting shot."

"Why the hell should I listen . . ."

"Because if he has an accident," Harry said sharply, "you'll be the first person the police will call on, and they'll stick to you like paint."

5

Harry put the Rover in the municipal parking lot and walked down the short, palm-lined street leading to the pier, oddly amused to find that he was actually looking forward to seeing Cooper again.

"It was extremely good of you to accommodate me in this way," the big man said, shaking Harry's hand as if he was greeting an old friend.

"I'm glad it worked out," Harry said and suggested they walk out onto the pier.

In his high-end sandals and sunglasses, perfectly pressed tan shorts, immaculate white short-sleeved shirt, wide-brimmed, low-crowned, white panama hat, and Rolex watch, Cooper could pass as a visiting dignitary from the islands, thought Harry.

They had met on the raised walk leading up to the pier itself, which was built on heavy piles lifting the wooden structure over the beach and some twenty feet above the water.

"This pier is remarkable," Cooper said with a pleased smile as they passed the concession stand. "It's wide enough to drive a truck on. How long is it?"

"About a hundred yards," Harry said. "It was built in 1888, and in the early days carried a narrow gauge railway that transferred freight from the ships that docked here to load and unload their cargoes. Avola had a lot of water-borne commerce with Key West and Havana. It even had a post office until the fire in 1922 that destroyed most of the pier."

By now they were far enough out on the pier to begin encountering men, women, and children fishing, many of whom, especially the women, found a way to sneak a second look at Cooper, who seemed to be unaware of the attention.

Probably used to it, Harry thought with a mixture of amusement and envy.

"I would have thought that storms would have taken their toll out here," Cooper said, pausing to look over the railing at the blue-green water hissing and swirling around the thick log supports, encrusted below the waterline with oysters and trailing seaweed.

White laughing gulls with shiny black heads flew over and under the pier, bursting into a high-pitched din whenever someone threw a fish back into the water. Less frequently, porpoises, often with their babies beside them, surfaced, to roll their gleaming backs out of the waves and catch a breath before diving again, a sight that was, apparently, completely new to Cooper and set him laughing with delight.

"Where do you come from?" Harry asked.

"Oh, here and there," Cooper replied, and demanded an explanation when a large school of bait fish suddenly exploded out of the water, churning the surface into a white froth, which instantly brought a flock of screaming gulls that began diving into the frenzy to snatch fish out of the fray.

"There are big fish under the school driving them to the surface and attacking them from below," Harry replied, debating whether or not to repeat his question before deciding to try another tack. "Wherever it was, you haven't spent much time near the ocean."

"I suppose my questions reveal that fact," Cooper said easily.

They had resumed their walk along the pier and were approaching the roofed, forty-foot square, open-sided end of the pier, surrounded by a railing. The center of the square was equipped with heavy, raised cutting tables and hoses where a dozen people were cleaning fish they had caught.

Cooper looked around and wrinkled his nose.

"Fish," he said.

"There's a bench with a backrest along the front of this section," Harry said. "Let's sit down. There should be a breeze, and we can talk comfortably."

Cooper inspected the wooden bench very carefully before sitting down, but once seated he looked around at the water and the gaggle of sun-blackened, scantily clad men and women leaning over the rail fishing.

"Here and there isn't going to cut it," Harry said, breaking into his companion's sight-seeing. "If I'm going to work for you, I've got to know a lot more about you than I do."

Leaning back and settling into a comfortable position, Cooper took off his hat and placed it gingerly beside him on the bench. Then he lifted his face into the breeze, closed his eyes, and breathed deeply.

"I know nothing about the arrangements that took me to the place where I spent my childhood," he said after a moment's hesitation, which Harry noted. "I was raised by Everett and Dolly Cooper in Worcester, Massachusetts. They were black— or, as we were called then, Negroes. As I remember, most of our neighbors were colored, but our schools were integrated. After high school, I went to Northeastern University in Boston."

"Because of its co-op program?" Harry asked.

"That's right. The cooperative education program allowed me to pay for my own university education. Not everyone knows about the program."

"I lived in Boston for a while."

"N.U. does good work."

"Yes. Where do you live now?"

"In Albany, New York. I'm an attorney at the University of

New York at Albany and have a small law firm of my own. Most of my private work is mediation in large corporate cases." He chuckled. "We're the last stop before the grass begins to suffer."

"We?"

"Yes, I have four associates."

"Does the firm have a name?"

"Cooper, Perkins, Dalrymple, and Blue," Cooper said with his slow smile.

"I missed the significance of the grass," Harry said.

"You know the old saying, 'When great beasts do battle, the grass is the first to die.' "

"Good," Harry said and made a deliberate shift in focus. "What makes you think you're going to be charged with murder?"

This time, Cooper did not hesitate.

"Because I may have been the next to the last person to see my mother alive."

While they were talking, they were surrounded by a swirl of sound, the water sloshing around the pilings, the hiss of the waves rising and falling on their way to the beach, the voices of the people fishing, shouts of encouragement and excitement when someone hooked a fish. Suddenly the decibel level spiked. Several people to their right began crowding around and shouting advice to a burly, bearded man, struggling and grunting as his rod jumped and arced toward the water.

"Shark!" someone shouted. "Bring the net!"

A sturdy, bronzed woman in a red bikini came running with a coiled rope attached to a large flat net. Two men grabbed it from her, lifted it over the rail, and lowered it into the water.

"Shall we watch?" Cooper asked.

"Sure," Harry said, grinning at Cooper's enthusiasm. "But if it really is a shark, it may not be a good idea to get too close."

But Cooper was already hurrying toward the spectators,

crowding in for a better view. With a sigh, Harry followed. Without actually pushing anyone out of his way, Cooper cleared a path to the rail with ease. Harry traveled in the wake of his broad back.

They arrived in time to see the struggling fisherman regain enough line to bring a very large, violently-thrashing fish to the surface. Cheering broke out as two men eased the net under the fish and lifted it clear of the water.

"It is a shark," Harry told Cooper, "about five feet long."

"It's enormous!" Cooper shouted back over the din.

By now the two fishermen had jumped onto the railing, preparatory to heaving the bucking fish and net onto the deck.

"Stand clear," one of the men shouted. "On the count of three: ONE! TWO! THREE!"

Both men gave a grunting heave, hoisted the net with its flailing cargo over the rail, and dropped it with a heavy thud onto the deck. For a moment the gawkers closed ranks to stare at the shark, but an instant later they were falling over one another, the women screaming and the men swearing, and everyone yelling between screams and shouts, *"Look out!"*

Harry was hauling on Cooper's arm, trying to get him to fall back from the bucking fish.

"Back off!" Harry shouted. "Before you lose a leg!"

He might as well have been tugging on a post. Cooper was fascinated by the shark and appeared not to have heard Harry's warning or seen the danger. Once on the deck, the shark's thrashing had snapped the fishing line, and with nothing to restrain it, the dark-backed creature, with creamy white tips on its dorsal and wide lateral fins, began to buck and twist its thick but supple body and give every indication of wanting to sink its loudly snapping teeth into anything it could reach.

"Cooper!" Harry shouted again, seeing that the shark was slithering toward Cooper, having decided he was the closest chewable object. "Get away from that thing!"

This time he pulled Cooper off balance, forcing him to step back in order to keep from falling. And just in time to avoid the shark's lunge. Its formidable jaws slammed shut inches from Cooper's right knee.

"Whoa!" Cooper shouted and plowed backward, taking Harry with him.

At that moment a short, swarthy man in chopped-off dungarees, sandals, and a sleeveless undershirt, carrying what looked like a large old-fashioned billy club, jumped out of the crowd, danced around the shark, dodged a lunge, and brought the club down on its head, striking three times in quick succession. The shark stiffened, quivered, and died. The man straightened up and looked around until he saw the man who had hooked the fish.

"I will give you a hundred dollars for him," he said.

"Plus five steaks," the fisherman replied.

"Done," the man said, waving forward two younger and slightly less muscular versions of himself.

The three grasped the shark and, with some grunting, heaved it onto one of the cleaning stations. With remarkable dispatch, the older man drew a very serious knife with a thin ten-inch blade from his belt and gutted, definned, and deboned the fish, then sliced the meat into foot-long sections.

When he began work on the shark, the two younger men disappeared. Now they returned carrying two large plastic coolers, partially filled with ice, into which they began piling the meat. The older man grasped one of the sections and swiftly cut from it five thick steaks, tossing what was left into one of the coolers. Then, working quickly, he stacked the fins in cases, threw the head and the innards into the sea, washed the cleaning station with the hose that was placed there for that purpose, cleaned his knife and his hands, shoved the knife back into his belt, and pulled a hundred-dollar bill from a roll he took from a side pocket in his shorts, and gave it to the fisherman.

"*Gracias, amigo,*" he said with a flash of white teeth. "Eat in good health," he added, jerking his thumb at the shark steaks.

He hoisted one of the coolers onto his shoulder, barking an order to his assistants, and strode off down the pier, followed by his two helpers carrying the second cooler between them. With a final cheer, the crowd dispersed, leaving Harry and Cooper to their own resources.

"That was the most exciting twenty minutes I've spent in a long time," Cooper said, grinning with obvious delight.

"I'm glad you enjoyed it," Harry said. "What you watched was the commission of a crime, punishable by a stiff fine."

The smile vanished into a look of astonishment.

"You're not serious."

"Yes, I am. It's against the law to catch a shark from this pier. If you hook one, you're supposed to cut your line. White-tipped sharks are rapidly being hunted into extinction and ought not to be fished at all."

"No one seemed to be concerned," Cooper said, looking around at the people lining the rails again, fishing, laughing, and talking.

"They're not."

"What was the man who bought the fish going to do with all that meat?"

"Sell it to the top-end restaurants," Harry said. "The fins will turn up as soup in the oriental eateries. He and his sons will make a very tidy profit."

Cooper nodded.

"He was awesome with that knife."

Harry started to say the man had probably been cutting up fish since he was a child, but Cooper wasn't done talking.

"Are you going to accept me as a client?" he asked.

"Let's walk back," Harry said, a little disconcerted by the question.

"Fine, but as they say, 'Time's a' wasting.'"

Word of the shark catch had made its way the length of the pier, and a growing crowd of people, chiefly visitors, hoping for a replay, were pouring up the walkway, eager to reach the ocean end of the pier. Their eagerness made walking toward the shore difficult, and Harry took advantage of the difficulty to put together a response to Cooper's question.

When they stepped off the pier, Harry asked Cooper if he could drive him to his hotel. Cooper thanked him and accepted the offer.

"Here's where we are," Harry told him, turning into the downtown traffic. "First, I think you should be talking to your lawyer and the police, in that order, before the law finds out that you saw Lilly Rhinelander on the afternoon before she was killed."

"I have legal representation should I need it," Cooper said, and gave a name that Harry recognized as a very prestigious Miami firm.

"Where did you meet her?" Harry asked.

"In the bar at the Ritz-Carlton, at about two in the afternoon on the day before she was found in that swamp. You didn't ask what we were doing there, but I'll tell you. We had finished lunch, and Lilly suggested we go into the bar where we could talk with a little more privacy. That's what we did. She left about forty-five minutes later, and I went to my room."

"In the Ritz."

"That's right."

"OK," Harry said, his head swimming with all the ways in which this conversation could go.

He picked one.

"And this was the first time you had seen her?"

"Heavens, no!" Cooper said, his eyes widening. "I've been seeing her once or twice a year for as long as I can remember."

"Do the Coopers know who she is?"

"They were killed in an Amtrak passenger train wreck in Silver Spring, Maryland, on February 16, 1996."

"I'm sorry. Did they know who she was while they were alive?"

"No. They knew her only as Rachel Comstock."

"But you did?"

"Not until I was fifteen, I think it was. I finally saw her picture in *Time* magazine. The next time she visited me, I told her what I had discovered."

"You didn't tell the Coopers?"

"No."

"Why not?"

"First, I wasn't sure. Then, when she confirmed it, she also told me that if I breathed a word of this to anyone, I would never see her again, and the Coopers would never receive another penny from her. She insisted I go on calling her Mrs. Comstock."

"Not *Mother?*"

"Never, but she always brought me presents."

"Did they depend on the money?"

"For my needs, yes. We were poor."

Harry noted the *we* and recalled Cooper's saying he had put himself through college. The picture was emerging. It wasn't all that pretty.

"Had she asked you to come to Avola to talk with her?"

"Yes."

"About what?"

"I'm not at liberty to say."

Harry decided to let it go for the moment.

"Were you with anyone that afternoon and evening after leaving Rhinelander?" Harry asked.

"After going back to my room, I sat down for a while to rest and think about my conversation with my mother. It was nearly four when I next looked at my watch. I got up, changed, and went down to the beach. One of the attendants set up a beach chair for me and gave me a towel."

Harry put up his hand to stop the flow of words.

"Would you recognize him if you saw him again?"

"I'm not sure. I was still thinking about my recent meeting. I recall asking where I could get a drink later and was told one would be brought to me when I was ready. I thanked him, put my book and robe on the chair, and went for a walk along the beach."

"Did you talk with anyone?"

"Not that I recall. I became interested in the shells scattered on the sand where the waves had dropped them and began searching for the large spirally ones with orange lips."

"Fighting conchs."

Harry spelled the name of the shells.

"The word is pronounced *conks*. People who live in Key West call themselves conchs."

Cooper smiled politely.

"How long were you on the beach?"

"It was nearly seven when I returned back to my room. I ate dinner in the main dining room about eight."

"And aside from the beach attendant, you talked to no one who could say they had seen you."

Cooper shook his head and smiled.

"I told you I was going to be charged with killing her."

6

"When I first had her on the table, the rigor mortis hadn't lessened much," Kathleen Towers said apologetically. "That's why at first I missed the fact her neck was broken."

Harry was talking with Kathleen in her office in Building #3 of the Medical Examiner's compound. Like any bureaucrat, she spent more time at her desk writing reports and processing forms than she did in the autopsy wing where she labored to determine the cause of death of the careless, reckless, murderous, and just plain unlucky who were her clients.

"If you'd like," she said, starting to get up, "we could go over and take a look . . ."

"No, no!" Harry said quickly, pushing both hands toward her to emphasize his point. "I don't need to do that. As it is, you're giving me more time than you can spare."

Helen laughed, knowing about Harry's aversion to her workstation.

Harry grinned sheepishly and reflected that she was one of those rare people who looked attractive in a white lab coat. With her shoulder-length brown hair streaked a bit with gray, rimless glasses, and quick smile, she made him envy Jim Snyder.

"I'm not that rushed," she said, slipping back into her chair, beginning to look a little disappointed.

"That's OK," Harry said. "Any indication of how it happened?"

"Well," Kathleen said, leaning forward, reenergized by the

question, "because of the slight bruising along the right side of her jaw, I would say whoever killed her was probably standing behind her, reached over her left shoulder, grasped her jaw in his left hand, placed his right hand against the back of her head and twisted it hard."

"No signs of a struggle?"

"No. She lost a gold ear loop, which, judging by the look of the tear in her earlobe, was torn out after she was dead. No other marks on her body. She wouldn't have felt anything more than his hands on her and whatever surprise or fear accompanied that," she said with satisfaction.

"Could a woman have done it?"

"Ahh!" Kathleen said. "Good question. I'll tell you what I put in my report. It's possible, but, judging by the break, whoever did it had to be taller than Rhinelander and strong. I'm not saying a woman couldn't have done it, but it would be a stretch and not my first pick."

Harry thought of Cooper's size and undoubted strength but moved on.

"When was she killed?" he asked.

Kathleen got up, walked to the window that looked out over the pond. She pushed her hands into her jumper pockets and then strolled back to drop into a chair beside Harry.

"Her being in the water for several hours added some complications to the calculation," she said. "Tissue deterioration, infestations, and so on occur at different rates in the two mediums, but I'm reasonably confident that she was killed between four and seven P.M. and dumped in the Stickpen no more than eight hours later, probably sooner than that."

"And Toke Wylie found her the next morning about seven o'clock," Harry said.

Absorbed in calculating how Kathleen's times corresponded with Cooper's accounting for his activities during the same periods, Harry forgot to respond to Kathleen's assessments and sat staring at her without noticing what he was doing.

"I know I'm hot, Harry," Kathleen said in an ironic drawl, "but I didn't expect to render you speechless."

"Whoa, sorry," he told her, jumping up, feeling his face burn. "I got lost in my own head."

"That's a bummer. I thought I had you mesmerized."

"Believe me, you do," he said, "but Jim's my best friend and . . . you're not interested anyway. So, I'd better just leave."

She cocked her head and said, "You're not going to tell me, are you, why those numbers I gave you scrambled your brain for a minute?"

"Not yet, if that's all right with you."

"You sound just like Jim, but I understand. Just don't forget to tell me when you can."

"I promise." Her patient good temper was something he really liked about Kathleen. "Is there anything more, anything at all that you can tell me about this killing?"

She became serious again.

"Shortly before she was killed, Rhinelander had eaten a Caesar salad with chicken and drunk probably a couple of glasses of wine, and that's about it. In my report I gave her age as sixty."

"The papers have settled on fifty-seven," Harry said and asked, "How much longer are you going to hold the body?"

"Until Sheriff Fisher tells me to release it."

"John Kringle, Rhinelander's oldest son, told me the family wants it as soon as possible," Harry said.

"Call me cynical," Kathleen said, "but I wonder if getting to the distribution of the estate has anything to do with their restlessness?"

"I'm thinking about the bear and the woods," Harry replied. "By the way, I almost forgot to ask you. Is a DNA sample taken from the body of a murder victim in the course of an autopsy?"

"Always, if there's a suspicion of sexual assault, but practices vary in other situations. I always take several because you never know what complications are going to turn up as the case develops—and sometimes long after the trial if an arrest is made."

"So you have samples of Rhinelander's DNA?"

"Sure do, but this is off the record, right?"

"Absolutely. Thanks, Kathleen. I owe you."

"I hope it helps," she said, walking him to the door. "From what I've read, she was a nasty piece of work, but I don't think she deserved to have her neck broken."

"Somebody thought otherwise," Harry said.

Harry postponed his visit to Fillmore Wiggins until late in the afternoon, to be sure Wiggins would be home from his stroll in the swamp.

Wiggins was a thick-necked man with long, snarly hair, liberally streaked with gray, a square, sunburned face, rimless glasses, and a blue bandanna tied around his head. Dressed in ragged dungarees, a faded blue work shirt, and ancient sneakers, his outfit was less a statement of the fact he had come of age in the dawn of Aquarius, than a practical adaptation to his profession. Most mornings for the past twenty years, he had walked into the swamp in search of orchids just as the sun was setting fire to the eastern sky.

Wiggins made his living wandering alone through the swamps on the southwestern edge of the Everglades, a canvas sack slung over his shoulder, collecting orchids and whatever else people would buy. He had never stopped being astonished by what his customers were eager to take home. Orchids, he could understand. He had spent much of his life growing, studying, and collecting them himself; but what they saw in snails, frogs, salamanders, snakes of all kinds, and baby alligators—he'd as soon have an animated steel trap for a pet—remained a mystery. Nevertheless, he couldn't bring the critters out of the swamp fast enough to meet the demand.

Wiggins was content to be a poacher and offered no excuses for it. His brief exposure to the Vietnam War had left him with the unshakable conviction that governments were murderous and organized society insane. He had, however, made his peace with the knowledge a long time ago and withdrawn to the fringes of both. Wishing only to be left alone to pursue his passion for orchids, he had gradually persuaded himself that through his dissemination of orchids and critters he might even be contributing to the human stock of knowledge and awakening wonder in his customers at what nature created. He even allowed himself to hope, without much conviction, that contemplation of these wonders might make people less mad.

Unmarried, without close friends, without a dog or a cat or anything he might come to love and then lose, he was passionately interested in orchids the way some people were obsessed by horses, roses, or baroque music and had no intention of putting himself out of a job by over-harvesting. Having harvested an area, he did not return to it for five years, which he readily admitted was not much of a sacrifice, given the hundreds of square miles of swamp that grew orchids in Tequesta County, the part of southwestern Florida to which he had retreated when he was finally released from Fitzsimmons Army Hospital after his military service ended.

"You've been a stranger, Harry. What brings you way out here?" Wiggins said heartily, waving Harry onto his lanai. "You in the market for some orchids?"

"If I am, I've come to the right place," Harry said with a note of wonder in his voice as he turned around slowly, taking in as much of the screened lanai as he could see through the jungle of plants, hanging from the rafters and uprights of the long and deep structure.

"I believe that if it's native to the American subtropics, I've got it somewhere around here. Let's sit down. I was about to crack a beer. Will you have one?"

"Sounds good."

Harry settled into a cane rocker in a space free of plants at the front of the lanai with an unobstructed view of the swamp. The low, brown-shingled house was shaded by a pair of ancient live oaks whose combined spread of branches covered half an acre of ground and formed a kind of clearing in the tangle of trees and brush surrounding the house.

From the oaks' low branches Wiggins had hung a second forest of orchids that, like those on the lanai, ranged in the color of their blooms from vermillion to the purest white and from the size of a Johnny-jump-up to a huge staghorn fern as big as a small car, engulfing the low crotch of the massive tree on Harry's left.

"It's not for sale," Wiggins said with a grin as he passed Harry a sweating bottle of lager and sat down. "Do you remember that tangle we got into five or six years ago, smoking out of the Stickpen that quartet of Cuban alligator-hide hunters from the East Coast?"

"I remember thinking at the time that wading around waist deep in a swamp among cottonmouths and people who were trying to kill us was a damned poor way to make a living."

Wiggins laughed and said, "I never told you because I knew you'd be upset, but I kept a few of those hides, and that day you just mentioned was when I found the staghorn. It was so small I carried it home in my shirt pocket."

"I knew about the hides and thought it best not to mention your boosting them. What do you think the staghorn weighs now?" Harry asked, marveling at the huge, dark green epiphyte.

"A hundred pounds, probably more. It's not growing as fast as it once did, probably because a few months ago mealy bugs got into it and set it back. But it's all right now and should find its stride again soon."

"Glad to hear it," Harry said, judging he had met the demands of civility and could now turn to his reason for being there.

"Are you willing to talk with me about Lilly Rhinelander?" he asked.

"This must be a fishing expedition," Wiggins replied, "because you must know I never knew the lady."

"A fair assessment," Harry said. "Yes, I know that."

He did not want to lie to Wiggins. He had known him for a long time and considered him to be one of the best field biologists he had ever known. In addition to that, he liked him, despite the fact he was, in the eyes of the law, more than a little tarnished, and, Harry suspected, very dangerous if crossed.

"The thing is," Harry continued, "Rhinelander's will is going to be read as soon as the state releases her body. When that happens, I expect a war is going to break out among the heirs and whoever else thinks a piece of the estate belongs to them. I may be going to have a dog in that fight, and I'm trying to find out everything I can about her death."

"A client?"

"Maybe."

"Interesting. What do you want from me?"

"She was found," Harry began, "in a place about the same distance from here as it is from my place. I'm thinking that it's more likely than not Rhinelander's body was put into the swamp by a helicopter."

"And you want to know if I heard a helicopter pass over the night before Toke Wylie found her."

"I didn't hear one," Harry said, "and it's a fair guess that it came from the west because that's where the airports are on this coast."

"Sounds reasonable," Wiggins said. "I've been expecting a visit from Sheriff Fisher's people, but, so far, no one other than you has showed up."

"Well, unless you confess to a crime, what you tell me stays with me."

Wiggins nodded as though it was what he expected to hear.

"Helicopters are noisy things, but I didn't hear anything but thunder and rain on my roof that night. We had a sharp but short storm around two in the morning. It blew some, and I was a little worried about the orchids, but no harm was done."

"I didn't hear anything at all, and the sun came up on an empty sky," Harry said, not surprised by the answer.

"Well, this is Florida," Wiggins said. "It was all clear by daylight. Some of these storms ain't much bigger than a postage stamp."

Harry agreed.

The two men talked a bit longer about the development that was pressing in on all sides of the Stickpen and the way it was affecting the deer, bears, pigs, and panthers that were being crowded in a shrinking space. Then Wiggins asked after Tucker, and expressed relief to hear that he was doing well.

"He's the closest thing to an original I ever met," Wiggins said.

Harry agreed, finished his beer, and said, "It was good seeing you, Fillmore. Thanks for your help."

"I don't see that I told you anything you didn't already know."

"Well, it was worth the trip just to see that staghorn fern," Harry said, shaking Wiggins's hand.

7

"Do you think Fillmore was telling the truth?" Tucker asked, leading Harry into his vegetable garden, which was bursting with new growth.

"It's hard to tell with Fillmore," Harry gasped. "He's got a lot of reasons for not wanting the police in there."

He was pushing a very large wheelbarrow, heaped high with black compost, redolent with a rich combination of decomposed plants mixed with well-rotted hen and horse manure. Most of his gasping came from his efforts to push the wheelbarrow, talk, and not breathe.

Having supervised the loading of the wheelbarrow, Oh, Brother! and Sanchez found a patch of grassy shade under a black olive tree, and Sanchez flopped down and slept while Oh, Brother! grazed on the thick grass, looking up from time to time, to see how the work was progressing.

"You mean his orchid business," Tucker said, grinning over his shoulder.

"That and the rest," Harry replied.

"Let's put that load right here," Tucker said, stopping beside an opening in the garden, occupied by a triangle of three tall poles tied at the top and standing with their feet spread out on the cleared ground like the frame for a teepee. "Just dump as much as you can inside the poles. Pole beans are heavy feeders."

"But at least I didn't hear anything to make me change my

mind about how Rhinelander's body was put in there," Harry said, tipping the compost onto the ground under the poles.

"I take it you're ruling out Toke Wylie's johnboat," Tucker said, passing Harry a shovel.

"I suppose that has to be kept in," Harry said, "but I just can't see Toke as a killer."

"I was thinking more along the lines of an accessory," Tucker said and, not waiting for Harry to respond, added, "Let's dig this compost in. Later on I'll sow seeds around the base of the poles."

"You mean he poled the body in there, dumped it, then came and found me, to steer suspicion away from him," Harry said.

"Yes," Tucker said. "Money is powerful, and the Rhinelanders have a lot of it."

"Someone in the family then."

"Probably, although there's no reason to believe anything I've said here is true."

"Except for the power of money."

Tucker leaned on his shovel to catch his breath.

"Yes," he said. "Money and sex are wonderful servants and terrible masters."

"Can I quote you on that?"

"With proper attribution," Tucker said with a straight face.

Harry laughed and thought about Wiggins again.

"Fillmore did say that 'helicopters were noisy things.' Then he said there was a thunder shower around two that morning. It's interesting that the shower came along just about the time Kathleen Towers thinks Rhinelander was put in the water."

"Nothing is ever quite certain with Fillmore," Tucker said with an amused smile. "I group him with the rest of life's mysteries. I don't believe I know what the creator had in mind when he made Fillmore."

"Someone to take an interest in his orchids," Harry said,

pleased with his response.

Tucker laughed. "One could also say his swamps," he replied, "but both answers fail to do justice to the subject."

For a while both men dug in silence. As he worked, Harry marveled at the way Tucker wielded his shovel. A few years back the old farmer had been at death's door. Now he worked slowly but steadily with all of his old joy, and his garden was a thing of beauty where corn, beans, carrots, tomatoes, parsnips, lettuce, peppers, and herbs flourished in the rich soil that had never seen a spoonful of chemical fertilizer.

"Any sign of Jane Bunting?" Harry asked, not having seen the cat.

"Still missing," Tucker said.

Harry heard the pain in the old farmer's voice and dropped the subject.

"What are you going to do about Adrian Cooper?" Tucker asked when they were finished and were leaning on their shovels, admiring their work.

"I wanted to talk to you about that," Harry said.

"Then let's get out of this sun and see if I can find some cold cider to clear the dust out of our throats."

Oh, Brother! and Sanchez walked them to the back stoop then wandered off.

"Where are they going?" Harry asked.

"There's a female woodchuck in the citrus grove," Tucker said, "and they have been waiting to see the young ones. I'd be surprised, however, if she'll let Sanchez see them."

"Because?"

Tucker drank some cider, sighed with satisfaction, and said, "She's biased against the canine clan, having lost a lot of her relatives to them over time. What about Cooper?"

"I spent a lot of last night chasing vague objects through my dreams," Harry said, "and I think what I was looking for was a clear idea of what Cooper is up to. At the moment I don't know."

"Then you're going to turn him down."

"That's the way I was leaning when I came over this morning. Now I think I've changed my mind."

"Something in the cider?" Tucker asked with a chuckle.

"It probably came from breathing in the fumes from that compost, but whatever did it, I'm going to take him on."

"Does this mean you think he is Lilly Rhinelander's son?"

"I don't know."

"From what you tell me, he's not the spitting image of her."

"No," Harry said, grinning.

"Then you think that sooner rather than later, the police are going to talk with him; and when that happens, they'll arrest him?"

"He'll certainly become a subject of interest."

"Let's see, means, motive, and opportunity—isn't that the trinity to consult first in a situation like this one?"

"You're making fun of me, which in your lexicon means you think I'm making a mistake," Harry said.

"If I've been listening, Cooper may have motive and opportunity; but as for the means, unless he has an accomplice who knows the Stickpen Preserve like the back of his hand, there's no way, as you've already said, but by air or water that he could have gotten Rhinelander's body in there."

"So you think there's little or no chance the police would press charges against him," Harry said.

"That would be my thinking."

Harry nodded.

"As far as you've gone, I agree with you," Harry said, "and with the sheriff's department working on the case, I don't see where I've got much space to launch a second investigation into Rhinelander's murder."

"I hear a *but* coming," Tucker said, recharging their glasses.

Just then the quiet was disrupted by an outbreak of cackling and squawking from the direction of Tucker's henhouse.

"Something's got Longstreet and his ladies all worked up," Harry said, starting to get out of his rocker.

Longstreet was Tucker's Plymouth Rock rooster, and his *ladies* were a flock of a dozen hens.

"Nothing to worry about," Tucker said. "One of them probably caught a glimpse of either Bonnie or Clyde. Bonnie's got some pups about ready to come out of the den, and that means the parents are hard-pressed to put enough meat on the table. I saw Clyde the other day passing through the orchard. He's thin as a rail and run half ragged."

Harry laughed.

"To hear you talk about those gray foxes, it would be easy to think they were people."

"Well, Oh, Brother! says they're bright enough to talk, which coming from him is high praise. What about that *but?*"

"Cooper interests me on several levels," Harry said. "I haven't found out what brought him here and what his plans are now that Rhinelander's dead. I'm reasonably certain that in order to get the answers to those two questions, I'll have to let him hire me."

Tucker rocked in silence for a while, staring into the woods, obviously occupied with his own thoughts. Harry set aside his cider, which had begun to make his ears ring, and waited for his friend to return.

"I'm going to take advantage of your forbearance and say something if you'll let me," Tucker said, turning his rocker in order to look at Harry without having to turn his head.

"Say away," Harry told him, a little startled by Tucker's expression and tone of voice.

It was not like Tucker to be so formal.

"It's something about getting yourself involved with this

Cooper, and it troubles me that I can't say why it does as well as I want to. Shall I stop here?"

"No," Harry said quickly, curious now but also thinking he might not like what he was about to hear.

"All right, here it is. If you go to work for him and he stirs up the Rhinelanders the way I think he will, you are going to become as much the target of their resentment as he is."

Tucker faltered, then seemed to find his way and went on, speaking quickly.

"The Rhinelanders are not like you and me, Harry. They may look it, but they're not. All their lives they've reached out and taken what they wanted and brushed aside with impunity whatever got between them and something they wanted. If Mr. Cooper comes after their money, they will hit him with everything they've got. If you're with him, they will hit you just as hard."

"Thanks for the warning," Harry said, thinking Tucker was finished. Reaching over, he put his hand on Tucker's arm. "I'll be very careful."

"You're not taking me seriously, Harry," Tucker said, forcefully, clearly not wanting to be interrupted.

"Of course I am," Harry protested. "I always listen to you very carefully."

"When it suits you," Tucker said with a fleeting grin. "Don't confuse what comes next with flattery. It's not. You are one of those rare men who are nearly free from physical fear. Danger makes you feel more alive and never more so than when you've got a gun in your hand. Are you with me?"

"I suppose you're right," Harry said reluctantly.

He found it very uncomfortable to be told what he thought only he knew, but now he wanted to know where Tucker was going with his diagnosis, if that's what it was. Tucker nodded.

"What you're looking at in this Cooper/Rhinelander thing

will be different from anything you've ever before stumbled into. Do you remember those shootouts you had a while back with those human traffickers?"

"I'm not likely to forget," Harry complained. "They blew up one Rover then riddled another."

"That's right, and with some help from three remarkable women, you rid the world of most of them; but this time everything's going to be different. No cowboys and Indians stuff, no James Bond stuff, no Charlie's Angels. This time it will be a twenty-two caliber bullet in your brain case, ricocheting around, doing maximum damage, put there by someone you will never see coming."

"Am I your first customer?" Harry demanded.

"What?"

"You've taken up fortune telling."

"And you're angry with me."

"I was OK until we got to the part about the twenty-two slug."

"Good," Tucker said. "That's good. You got the point."

"Mr. Brock," a strong, assertive male voice said, "this is Randall Pearson. We need to talk."

"Why?" Harry asked, stalling for time while trying to place the caller.

Then he remembered it was Pearson's name Jennifer had scribbled on a piece of paper after their lunch. Pearson was the Rhinelander contact person at Schlossberg, Pearson, O'Leary, and Gross.

"Since meeting Adrian Cooper," Pearson continued, sounding like a man wasting time he couldn't spare, "we've completed a preliminary background check. It's time you and I talked. We could meet here, or somewhere more convenient for you. Your call."

Two days earlier, Harry had offered Cooper a contract, offering to do what he could to establish Cooper's innocence in the event that he was charged with killing Lilly Rhinelander but declining to search for her killer.

"With the sheriff's department working the case," he had told Cooper, "my interfering would raise hackles; but if I limit myself to protecting your interests, I might get some help from Jim Snyder."

Cooper had signed without comment.

"Do you know why Cooper hired me?" Harry asked Pearson.

"I know what he told me," Pearson said, a slight huffiness coming into his voice that implied he was the one asking the questions.

Harry waited, seeing no point in doing Pearson's work for him.

"It was an interesting conversation," Pearson bent enough to add.

"I don't doubt it. Why do you want to talk with me?"

"It would be in the interest of everyone involved for you and me to meet."

The ice had gone out of his voice, and Harry, overcoming a robust aversion to having anything more to do with Pearson, admitted that he had more to gain than lose by talking with him.

"This afternoon?" Harry asked.

Pearson suggested a time, and Harry said he would come to Pearson's office. As soon as he broke the connection, he called his old friend Rowena Farnham, rector and chaplain of St. Jude's Episcopal Church in Avola, and arranged to meet her an hour before his appointment with Randall Pearson.

"It's a pleasure to see you, Harry," Rowena said when she had Harry settled in a chair in her office with a cup of tea in his hand and hot, buttered scones on the small stand beside him.

Rowena Farnham was a large woman with a shining round face, sparkling blue eyes, a cap of white hair cut in a pageboy, and an endless fund of energy. Her church was one of the largest and most active and socially conscious in Avola. The fact that it was also the wealthiest in the county provided her and her people with the means to do a great deal of good. Haven House, their battered women's retreat and homeless rehabilitation center, was only one of their endeavors.

"Have you fallen on hard times and come for a handout?" she asked, peering at Harry over her teacup, her voice bubbling with laughter.

"I've got to see a lawyer by the name of Randall Pearson in about an hour," he told her when they had dispatched the scones and Rowena had poured them fresh tea.

"I know him. He makes an occasional appearance in the congregation—coming about as often as you."

"Christmas, Easter, that sort of thing?" Harry asked.

"That sort of thing," she replied dryly. "What do you want to know about him? St. Jude's has done some business with his firm, but I'm afraid there's not much . . ."

"No, it's something quite different." Harry put in.

He then told Rowena about Adrian Cooper, his claim to be the son of Lilly Rhinelander, and the uproar his claim was creating among the surviving members of her family.

"How much do you know about Mr. Cooper?" Rowena asked.

"I know he's who he says he is. Beyond that, not much, but there's something very appealing about him."

"Mmm," she said. "If I were you, I'd watch myself very carefully around him."

"You sound like Tucker," Harry said and hurried on. "I've been summoned to this meeting by Randall Pearson—I suppose he wants to grill me about Cooper."

"Why?" she asked, brushing some nonexistent crumbs off her

imposing front.

"There's something he doesn't know. Why else would he talk to me?"

Rowena put down her cup and saucer and sighed.

"I understand your point, but I wish I didn't."

"You're committed to shining light into dark places, Rowena. For good or ill, I occasionally have a professional need to create darkness to sneak around in," Harry said, only half joking. "You bring the truth. I have to go skulking after it."

Rowena laughed heartily.

When Rowena Farnham laughed, her entire body participated. Few people could keep from laughing with her. Harry was not one of those, even if it was his joke.

"Harry, I haven't heard such hogwash since I left the seminary," she said, wiping her eyes and blowing her nose.

"I thought you'd like that. Now for the serious part. Did you know Lilly Rhinelander?"

"No, although I do know several people in the congregation who had at least a talking acquaintance with her."

"Good," Harry said, mentally crossing his fingers. "Would you be willing to call them and ask them some questions?"

"Does this come under the heading of skulking after truth?" Rowena asked suspiciously.

"More like finding out things I can't discover in official documents."

"Gossip."

"Heaven forbid," Harry said with mock denial. "Finding out everything possible about her family from things she has told your informants or they have heard from reliable others who heard it secondhand. It's called research."

"Harry," Rowena said a bit brusquely, "of what possible use could such information be?"

"I think, first and foremost, I'd hope to hear some hint of

Rhinelander's having a child that she has never publically acknowledged—I don't know whether Cooper is telling the truth or that I just want to think he is. Failing that, anything that would tell me what the relationship was between her and her children."

"Harry," Rowena said in a rising voice rich with impatience, "go to the library! The woman and her family have been in the responsible and gutter media for the last four decades. Where have you been?"

She paused for a moment, then with an exaggerated seriousness said, "I think in referring to 'the responsible and the gutter media,' I drew a distinction without a difference."

"Cynicism becomes you. There's one other thing."

"What is it?"

"You can't tell anyone that you're doing it for me."

"I was already there, Harry," she said with a grim smile. "I will just be showing a ghoulish interest in the affair."

"Will you do it?"

"Do you think one of the children killed her?"

"Someone did."

"You didn't answer my question."

"It's called evasion, and I have no idea, but the chances are very good that whoever did it knew her and was probably close to her."

"A chilling thought supported by statistics," Rowena said. "As for your question—although it's way out of my job description, the answer is: Yes. I'll see what I can find out. When I've drained the septic system, I'll call you."

"Shine a little light," Harry said. "In this business you never know what you'll find—except that it is usually unpleasant."

"Speaking of the unpleasant," Rowena said, her voice dropping an octave, "have you talked with Soñadora lately?"

The question jolted Harry. He and Soñadora Asturias had

some history. They had worked together on a human trafficking case and, after a fashion, become friends. At least he thought they were friends. Sometimes, he suspected it was only their shared experience of having lived close to pain and violence that drew them to one another. At what he thought of as his weird moments, he wondered if he was in love with her. All he was certain of was that she was different from any other woman he had ever known.

In time she had come to trust him and had told him that her mother was a Mayan and her father, a white man she had never known, and that she had grown up in the northern mountains of Guatemala at a time when that country's government, with American aid, was combating a left wing insurgency by indiscriminately murdering rural population. Her mother was killed in one of the raids and Soñadora was brought up by a renegade Catholic priest, who had embraced liberation theology. When the Catholic Church withdrew their priests and nuns from the mountains, abandoning the Indians to the government death squads, he and others like him cast their lot with the Indians.

"She's still running Salvamento isn't she?" he asked, his stomach knotting at the thought something might have happened to her.

It was not a morbid fear. She and her co-workers rescued men and women caught in the net of human trafficking, providing them with safe houses, protecting them from the traffickers and the tender mercies of the Department of Immigration. The work exposed Soñadora to retaliation from the criminals involved in the trafficking and the Immigration officers, who regarded her work as assisting illegal immigrants.

"The answer is yes, but you're really asking how she is," Rowena said, giving him a steely look, "which means you haven't called her, probably not for some time."

Harry nodded. It was a sore spot with him. Having it prodded made him jump.

"We quarreled over her marrying Langston Pearson," Harry said. "I stopped seeing her. There didn't seem to be any point."

"That's what, a year and a half?"

"Almost two," Harry said.

"A fine way to treat a friend!" Rowena exploded in disgust. "Well, she's not married anymore."

"I heard there were problems," Harry said, stung into feeling both anger and shame by Rowena's criticism.

At the same time he experienced a tingle of pleasure at hearing that her marriage was over. It was a vindication he was ashamed to be happy about, but she should never have married Langston Pearson.

"You could say that," Rowena said, breaking into his thoughts. "The wretch left her without a penny or a roof over her head. She's been living in a room at the Salvamento for the last three months."

"Did he divorce her?"

"Yes, and I gather she didn't contest it," Rowena said with a sigh of resignation.

"Too proud," Harry said with a mixture of praise and criticism.

"I don't know the whole story because Soñadora, as you know, is a private person, one of the most private I have ever known."

"What were the grounds?" Harry asked.

Rowena paused, appeared to gather herself, and said, "She stopped sleeping with him. You're not going to ask why, but I'm going to tell you. From what she told me, he began having intercourse with other women a month after the wedding."

"Are you surprised?" Harry asked, anger beginning to burn its way through all his pretensions of indifference.

"No," Rowena said. "Harry, go and see her. You and I are the only friends she has."

"I doubt that she wants anything to do with me," he said, avoiding Rowena's request.

"That's not worthy of you," she told him, leaning forward and putting a hand on his shoulder. "Listen to me. It's going to sound like emotional blackmail, but it's not. You abandoned her once, and I can understand why. This time you have no excuse; and if you fail her again and something happens to her, you'll regret it the rest of your life."

8

The offices of Schlossberg, Pearson, O'Leary, and Gross were in one of the few new buildings the city had allowed to be built in that section of Old Avola in the last twenty years, but like its less elevated neighbors it was modestly clad in cream stucco and had been limited to five stories. Pearson's office was on the top floor, the remainder of the floor being occupied by the other members and minions of the firm.

Pearson came himself to greet Harry and escort him from the icy waiting room where the receptionist had placed him. As he slowly turned blue while thumbing through the pages of the current issue of *Forbes* magazine, he began to wonder if he'd been underestimating the advantages of having great wealth. Before he could decide whether or not to change professions, Pearson thrust himself into the room.

"Mr. Brock," he said, hand outstretched, "I'm Randall Pearson. Nice to meet you."

He was a tall, trim, sandy-haired man with pale blue eyes, a square jaw, and freckles showing through his tan. His dark suit fit him perfectly and his black shoes glistened.

"Come with me," he said and strode away down the corridor, dragging Harry in his wake.

"Have a seat," Pearson said, pointing Harry to a small, cherry conference table with six captain's chairs neatly tucked around it. "Take your pick," he added, gathering a legal pad and pen from his desk and planting himself across the table from Harry.

"Let's get right to it," Pearson said, elbows akimbo as he adjusted the pad and unscrewed the cap on his Mont Blanc fountain pen. "You're working for Adrian Cooper. Is that right?"

"Yes," Harry said.

Pearson leaned back in his chair and with a sarcastic grin asked, "What are you doing for the gentleman?"

"It's none of your business," Harry replied.

"Everything to do with the Rhinelander estate is my business, Brock," Pearson said, the voice shifting from sarcastic to condescending.

Harry got hold of his temper with both hands.

"I have nothing to do with the Rhinelander estate. Why am I here, Pearson?" he asked.

"What does Cooper want you to do for him?" Pearson demanded, ignoring Harry's question and for the first time showing stress.

"Ask Cooper. If he wants you to know, he'll tell you."

Before he finished speaking, Harry saw by the stiffening of Pearson's face that he had made a mistake. He would learn nothing from him; and if he stayed, they would quarrel. He didn't want that, because the chances were that if Cooper went where Harry thought he was going, both of them would need Pearson. He was halfway to his feet when Pearson leaned forward, throwing his weight onto his elbows.

"This is my fault, Brock. I apologize. You're quite right. You are not obliged to tell me anything. Do you still want to know why I called you?"

"Yes," Harry said, dropping back into his chair.

"Adrian Cooper's arrival here was absolutely unexpected. At this point, we think he's who he says he is, a credentialed member of the New York bar, and a solid citizen in his community, which makes the situation utterly bizarre and deeply troubling."

"There's an elephant in the room," Harry said.

"Yes, I've seen it," Pearson said with a sudden grin, and Harry instantly knew what the man had looked like as a boy.

"Then we agree that it's definitely an elephant?" Harry asked.

"Oh, yes, and I was desperately hoping that you were going to tell me what it's doing here."

"I only know what he's told me. He wants to prove that Lilly Rhinelander is his mother. More than that I don't know. I wish I did."

Both men stared at one another. There was a brief silence, broken by Pearson, who picked up his pen, glared at it as if it was an utterly disgusting object, threw it onto the yellow pad in front of him, and said, "Shit."

Harry thought that as a summary statement it was unimpeachable.

They shook hands, and Harry was at the door when Pearson said, "Wait, I've forgotten something."

Going to his desk, he took an unsealed envelope out of a folder and passed it to Harry.

"Open it, please," he said.

Harry unfolded the sheet of paper it contained and read the list of names printed on it: John Edward Kringle, Rita Evgenie Kronsky, Michael Joseph Rhinelander. Harry looked at Pearson, puzzled.

"It's a list of Lilly Rhinelander's children."

"That's right. I've advised them not to have any contact whatsoever with you and Cooper."

"Can they read?"

"Which means you've already seen them," Pearson said, wearing a crestfallen expression.

"Two of them called me."

"Let me guess, John and Evie."

"That's right. John drove out to see me, and Rita Evgenie called me."

"And?"

"You're going to earn your fee."

"All of them are here and have been since some time before Lilly's death," Jennifer Fortunato said.

"I know. A family conference?"

"We don't know yet. I don't think it was Mummy-love that brought them here."

They had been talking about Cooper and the case for the last half hour, and Harry was fed up with the subject. He was rapidly coming to the conclusion that working for Cooper was going to be heavy on negatives. Tucker's warning wormed its unwelcome way into his mind, but he quickly buried it.

He and Jennifer were walking on a boardwalk, leading from the parking lot to Barefoot Beach, through a sandy jungle of cabbage palms and saw palmettos. The sun was setting, and they paused to watch the final fraction of its flaming disc slip beneath the waves.

"No green flash tonight," Harry said, "too much haze."

"Have you ever seen it?" Jennifer asked skeptically.

"Hundreds of times," Harry said, picking up the cooler he had been carrying.

They resurrected an old argument over the question of whether or not the green flash existed. When they reached the beach, which was almost free of people, Harry said, "Don't take my word for it. Google it. You'll be very surprised. It's a simple refraction of light that causes it."

"Don't spoil my appetite," she said airily, looking around. "We'll have plenty of privacy if we go down there by that huge old stump."

With a bit of a shock, Harry recalled that it was very close to the spot where they had swum and made love before she left Avola.

"All it lacks is a seashell," he said, but she was already planning their evening swim; and if she heard him, she had either forgotten his comment or chosen to ignore it.

"Swim first, eat after?" he asked when they had spread out a pair of rainbow-hued beach towels.

There was a bit of awkwardness as they peeled down to their bathing suits. Harry was aware that he was carrying a few extra pounds, but on the Hammock he pretty much lived in shorts and sandals and was counting on being well tanned to make the spread less obvious.

"OK, Harry, face the music," Jennifer said in a determined voice, standing erect in her dark red bikini. "I haven't grown younger, but I have grown. So have you. You could lose some middle, and I've got thunder thighs."

"Turn around," Harry said, sounding serious.

"What?" she asked, coloring.

"Turn around, slowly."

"There'll be a certain amount of jiggling," she said, growing redder.

"No excuses."

Looking apprehensive, she edged around. As he studied her, Harry's pulse became quite a bit less sluggish. His memories of her had not done her justice. Top to toe, she was beautiful.

"You'll do," he said.

"Your turn." She told him, equally serious.

He was halfway around when she suddenly shouted, "Last one in is a wimp," and sprinted for the water.

Harry followed, less lightly than a running deer, and called after her, "Shuffle, Jennifer, shuffle!"

At the water's edge she skidded to a stop and went forward as if she was skiing, pushing her feet along the bottom. When she was thigh deep, she arched, gracefully as a seal, into a cresting swell. Harry followed, wondering why he didn't do this every evening.

When he surfaced, he was ashamed to find himself out of breath. Jennifer was bobbing and splashing beside him with a happy smile.

"I forgot about the stingrays," she said. "Isn't this gorgeous? The Atlantic is usually too rough to play in like this."

The temperature of the water was only a few degrees cooler than the air, the swells gentle, and the rosy afterglow of the sunset cast a flattering light over the water and the beach and the two frolicking swimmers.

"I'm starving," Harry said at last.

"Me too. Let's go in."

They swam toward the shore; and when they stood up, Jennifer sang out, "Florida shuffle," and plowed out of the water, roiling the sand, and chanting, "Stingray, stingray, swim away."

Harry watched her burst of high spirits with pleasure, and tried hard not to let it turn into something more. This woman was going to her own wedding in a few months.

"We'd better drag the blankets closer to the water," Harry said when they had dried themselves a little.

"I remember," Jennifer said. "Midges."

They rearranged themselves, and while Harry was opening the wine, Jennifer laid out shrimp salad, strawberries, blueberries, French bread and a packet of goat cheese. While they were talking and eating, a quarter moon climbed up through the palms on the back dune.

"It's lovely," Jennifer said with something in her voice that Harry couldn't interpret.

"Yes," was all he could manage.

They ate and talked but said very little about the Rhinelanders. Somehow the conversation kept coming back to one another and what had been happening in their lives. Eventually, the midges found them, and they reluctantly began clearing up the remains of their meal.

"Wait!" Harry said, rummaging in the cooler. "I almost forgot. Where's your glass?"

He interrupted his search to pour them more wine. Then he brought out a small box of French chocolates.

"Harry," she said with a cry of pleasure, "you remembered!"

"Yes. It's a miracle."

"My hands are covered with sand," she said. "You'll have to hold it for me."

They were on their knees, facing one another. He took a chocolate from the box and held it while she bit off half of it, closing her eyes as the chocolate melted in her mouth.

"Oh, my God," she breathed when she had swallowed. "Ambrosia."

"Second half," he said as she leaned toward him.

He started to put the chocolate in her mouth, but instead, all his defenses collapsing, he kissed her very gently. She returned the kiss, their hands on one another's arms. When they drew back, he pressed the remaining piece of chocolate against her lips; and she opened her mouth to receive it, their eyes never leaving one another.

"Now the wine," he said, breaking the spell by putting her glass into her hand and picking up his own.

"To a wonderful evening," he said, touching her glass with his.

"Not a perfect evening?" she asked.

"Not quite," he said quietly.

Harry did not sleep well that night, and he several times found himself keeping the moon company in its perambulations. His restlessness was due in part to his uncertainty about Adrian

Cooper and his having agreed to help him. Do what? was the question that kept coming up without evoking a satisfactory answer, followed closely by another regarding Cooper himself.

True, he had said he was in Avola at his mother's request, but what was holding him here was not clear. He's waiting to attend Rhinelander's memorial service, Harry told himself and heard cynical laughter. Cooper's assertion that he only wished to establish that Lilly Rhinelander was his biological mother seemed the first sentence in a much longer story. The fact he had arrived before Rhinelander was killed could not be ignored, and neither could the fact that she had died soon after that arrival.

As aggravating as those uncertainties were for Harry, they paled in comparison to the stress that thinking about Jennifer Fortunato was causing him. Actually, it would be more accurate to say that he enjoyed thinking about her, especially recalling what it was like kissing her. The internal uproar that was keeping him awake was being generated by having to admit how much he was attracted to her, how hard he must work not to act on those feelings, and how likely it was that he would fail.

Something else that had been hiding in a dark corner of his mind and now came out, dragging its chains, was Tucker's lecture on the risks he was running in taking on Cooper as a client and finding himself in a confrontational relationship with the Rhinelanders. Perhaps the most disturbing part of the warning was that it came from Tucker. Harry could not remember Tucker ever having commented on his actions with such vehemence.

Jennifer called him the next morning.

"Harry," she said, sounding bright and rested as though she had slept a full eight hours, "I need to talk with you about Adrian Cooper; but before I get to that, I want to tell you how much I enjoyed our evening. Let's do it again."

Without waiting for a response, she moved back to Cooper, leaving Harry gaping like a fish out of water.

"Here's the thing," she said. "Harley feels that we need to talk. We could see you about five this afternoon. Can you make it?"

"I'll be there," Harry said, "and before you hang up, what did you mean the other day by saying when I asked you how I ever got along without you, 'Not too well by the looks?' "

"It would take too long to tell you now," she answered hurriedly. "Harley is breathing down my neck and no, not that way. See you at five."

Harry turned away from the phone to see a fire-red Premium GT Mustang coupe turn into his yard with what looked to Harry like custom everything, including a muffler that had given him full notice that something was coming.

"Dust!" Harry muttered in disgust.

Whoever was in the car waited until the wind had blown most of airborne sand over the Puc Puggy before getting out of the car, giving Harry time to be waiting beside the car when the young man emerged. He was tall, muscular, somewhere in his twenties, with carefully tousled collar-length blond hair, sunglasses, designer jeans, spotless white T-shirt, and sandals.

"You're going to have to take it to the car wash," Harry said, carefully hiding his envy. Then, unable to resist commenting on what he saw as a desecration, "What ever persuaded you to put that rack on the car?"

Harry had always wanted and never allowed himself to buy the car of his dreams, which he was now staring at. He had once rented one for a while. When he drove it home, his eleven-year-old daughter looked from it to him and said, "Juvenile."

"I'm Mike Rhinelander," the man said, laughing. "I carry a

lot of shit around with me. The rack's a necessity."

"You're a mountain climber from what I've read."

He laughed again with a flash of teeth.

"That and kayaking are two ways I kill a lot of time," he said.

He pulled off his glasses, squinting around in the glare, and said, "Man, this is some place you've got here."

"Thanks," Harry said, deciding that Rhinelander's self-deprecating laughter was a parry he used to deflect questions. "I used to enjoy the privacy."

Rhinelander put on his glasses, giving his attention to Harry.

"Global positioning put an end to it," he said, suddenly serious. "There's no place on earth they can't find you."

Harry thought he spoke as if he had tried disappearing and failed. Then he wondered why a young man in his position would want to. Need to? He put out his hand and said his name. Rhinelander took it with a firm grip.

"Good to meet you, I've heard a lot about you. I understand you were a Maine warden at one time."

"That's right," Harry said, not wanting to talk about that, and had only to think of Pearson to answer how Rhinelander had known that detail about his life. "Let's get out of this sun. I take it you want to talk to me."

"I do."

"Are you thirsty?" Harry asked when they were on the lanai. "There's Coke, beer, bottled water, and my coffee, which I suggest you pass on."

"Bottled water," Rhinelander said, sitting down without testing to see if the chair was clean, winning points with Harry.

"I really like this place," he said when Harry returned with the water. "How did you ever find it?"

"The short answer is that I got lucky. The long answer is very long and not one I want to embark on."

That created a short period of silence which Rhinelander

Kinley Roby

spent studying the bottle he was holding.

"That came out harsher than I intended," Harry said. "What is it you want to ask me?"

"The family is facing a very odd situation."

"Oh?" Harry said, waiting to see where Rhinelander was going.

"Very odd."

He paused to twist the cap off his bottle and drink.

"Your client claims to be our half brother."

It was on the tip of Harry's tongue to say there was nothing new about that in your family and clamped down on the impulse.

Instead, he said, "He seems to be prepared to insist on it."

"So it appears. Can you tell me what he wants?"

"I'm surprised you haven't asked him," Harry said, wanting to let him down easily.

Rhinelander took another drink. Harry wondered why his generation drank so much water, and he amused himself by wondering if they took their water bottles with them to the toilet.

"Our lawyer has told us we can't have any contact with the man."

"That's too bad."

"Why?" Rhinelander asked, registering surprise.

"Because Cooper's a very interesting person. I think you'd like him. He's quiet, intelligent, and has a good sense of humor."

Rhinelander looked at Harry then quickly away as if he was hiding something. That, at least, was how Harry read the glance.

"Why are you people so afraid of him?"

Rhinelander gave a short bark of laughter, setting his bottle on the floor beside the chair.

"Experience has taught us that when there's a fin above the water, there's usually a shark under it."

"What harm do you think Cooper could do you?"

"I'd have to know what he wants before I could answer you."

Harry made a decision.

"I'll tell you what he told me. I suspect he told Pearson. He wants to be acknowledged as the natural son of your mother."

"That and what else?" Rhinelander burst out, springing to his feet and scowling down on Harry. "You might want to tell Mr. Cooper that I'll see him in hell first."

Rhinelander was pushing open the screen door when Harry, having followed him, said, "Mr. Rhinelander, I'm going to tell you what I told your half brother. If you're as smart as I think you are, you won't repeat to anyone else what you just said to me."

Rhinelander stepped off the lanai and turned to face Harry, who was holding open the door. He had apparently recovered his composure because he turned to Harry, ran a hand through his hair, and grinned.

"John told me what you said. I got a good laugh out of it. It's the first time I ever heard John quote anybody but himself. Goodbye, Mr. Brock. Thanks for the water."

9

Harry called the Ritz, gave his name, and asked to speak with Adrian Cooper.

A moment later a rich, pleasant voice said, "I've just come in from a swim. It's a beautiful morning, Harry. What are you doing with it?"

"Calling you and getting ready to talk with Harley Dillard, the state attorney, and a deputy state attorney who's been sent from the East Coast to beef up the staff."

"And the reason for this conference?" Cooper asked in an amused voice.

"You. And before I see them, I want to talk to you."

"What time is your meeting?"

Harry told him.

"Will two o'clock work for you?"

"I'll pick you up," Harry said.

Cooper was waiting for Harry in the lobby, very well turned out in tan shorts, a dark red short-sleeved shirt, and pair of brown, woven leather loafers. Harry noticed with some amusement that most of the guests trooping through the lobby made Harry look like a well-dressed man. Cooper was so well dressed that he was probably being mistaken for a member of the hotel's administrative staff.

"Where are you taking me?" Cooper asked after shaking Harry's hand and picking up his hat from the chair beside him.

"Not far, but I think you'll find it interesting," Harry said as they walked to the parking lot.

"I hope it's as exciting as the pier," Cooper said.

"It's a nature walk," Harry replied, turning onto the street, "but don't worry, it's all on a boardwalk raised above the ground."

Half an hour later Harry turned the Rover onto a narrow road, leading deeper into the flat, heavily wooded area through which they had been driving.

"We're going to an Audubon preserve that is one of the best of its kind," Harry said. "Have you ever been to one?"

"I can't say that I have," Cooper answered with no enthusiasm.

Harry had noticed that Cooper had grown increasingly silent as the houses diminished in number.

"Have you spent much time in the country?" Harry asked.

Cooper shook his head. Harry let it go and turned into the parking area, bordered by slash pines and pin oaks.

"It's called the Corkscrew Swamp Sanctuary," Harry said as they walked toward the reception center. "It covers about eleven thousand acres of cypress swamp, pine flatwoods, and wet prairie, all of which we can get a look at from the boardwalk."

"Sounds interesting," Cooper answered without a flicker of conviction.

But the sight of the large, sprawling, brown building with glass and sloping roofs seemed to restore his confidence, and he even paused to look at some of the nature exhibits beside the path. Harry did what he could to expand a little on what Cooper had seen and read; and, by the time they were through the visitor center and following the twisting dry sand and gravel trail taking them to the boardwalk, Cooper was even beginning to take an interest in the open pine woods through which they were passing and the birds that were flitting among the trees and singing lustily.

"If we could go back a hundred years, these woods would look much as they do today," Harry told him.

"Why don't they fill up with brush?" Cooper asked.

"In the past these dry, wooded areas burned over about every year, limiting the growth of just about all the trees except for the pines and the saw palmettos, which are low growing because most of their trunks are under the ground. Fire only burns the tops, which quickly grow back. Today the caretakers set controlled burns to do the work."

The snowbirds had gone back north, and Harry and Cooper had the place to themselves. By keeping Cooper's attention occupied, Harry got him onto the boardwalk and several hundred yards into the wet prairie, to a roofed observation platform off to the side of the main trail. A wooden bench was built into the shelter's back wall; and Cooper was glad to sit down and, with his hat off, enjoy the breeze blowing through the open structure.

"Harry, why are we out here?" Cooper asked when he had finished dabbing his face with a monogrammed handkerchief.

"Several reasons," Harry told him, watching a doe with two fawns moving slowly through new grass and stopper bushes, feeding as they went. "I wanted to show you some animals. Do you see that doe with her two fawns?"

With slow movements he pointed them out to Cooper, but Harry gathered from Cooper's lack of response that the five-foot black rat snake that slithered across the boardwalk almost running over Cooper's right foot had maxed him out on nature.

"I told you that I was meeting the state attorney later," Harry said. "He's going to want to talk about you. I don't know what he's going to ask me, but I can guess, and I want to answer his questions without sounding like an idiot or a liar. Harley Dillard could be a big help to us or a severe liability, depending on how we respond to his concerns."

"I still don't see what we're doing in this steaming wilderness," Cooper said, dabbing his face again.

"That's easy. I wanted to show you a part of Florida you might miss on your own, and I wanted us to talk where we wouldn't be overheard or disturbed."

"Except by snakes, deer, and raccoons."

Harry laughed, despite trying not to. A big coon had clambered up one of the boardwalk posts and waddled along with them for a short way until the trail took him to where he was going, at which point he clambered over the railing and slid down a post like a very fat fireman and began foraging among the cypress knees and twisted roots for frogs, salamanders, and other delicacies. Cooper had not enjoyed the animal's company, doing his best to keep Harry between him and the masked bandit.

"So let's get to it, Adrian," Harry said. "I gather you told Randall Pearson why you're in Avola."

"That's right," Cooper said, assuming the bland expression he had so far always worn when talking with Harry about his personal affairs.

Harry did not know what to make of that calm voice and contemplative smile. Perhaps because he couldn't penetrate it, it had begun to irritate him.

"You did tell him Lilly Rhinelander was your mother."

"Of course. That was the purpose of my call."

"And that you wanted to establish that you are her natural son."

"Yes."

"But you didn't say you expected to be charged with her murder."

"That's right."

"Did you tell him you had talked to her?"

"Yes."

"What did he say?"

"He asked me what we talked about; and I refused to tell him."

"How did he respond to that?"

"He was rather angry and asked me why I had waited until now to make my alleged relationship with Mrs. Rhinelander public. Without waiting for an answer, he demanded to know 'what the hell I was doing in Avola.' I was puzzled by his attitude and somewhat surprised to find a man in his position becoming so emotional. Naturally, having answered the question once, I ignored it. I did tell him I was at the Ritz and would be there at least until after the funeral. Then I left."

As far as Harry could tell, Cooper was not at all distressed by Pearson's demands and threatening manner.

"Adrian," Harry asked, trying to make the question sound as innocuous as he could, "did you come to Avola to tell your mother that you were going to make the relationship public?"

For several minutes Cooper stared out over the sundrenched expanse of reeds and grass and scattered clumps of dwarf willows in silence. A pair of swallow-tailed kites was giving life to the scene by hovering and swooping over the watery prairie. Harry doubted that Cooper even noticed the birds. Waiting with as much patience as he could muster, Harry watched the kites, knowing that he had about the same chance of forcing an answer from his companion as he did of moving Mount Rushmore.

"I find," Cooper said at last, a bit stiffly, shifting on the bench to look at Harry, "that I'm disinclined to answer your question and wonder why you would ask it."

Ridiculous and disingenuous as the statement sounded to Harry initially, after a moment's reflection, he was persuaded that the question had hurt Cooper's feelings.

"I'm sorry," Harry said, "although I can't imagine that you wouldn't expect both Pearson and me to ask it. You said yourself that you expected to be charged with killing your mother. If you really believe that, you must also believe the police think you had a motive for committing the crime. Following that thought a little further, we come to the place where it would be reasonable to suppose that you came here to kill her, which leads to my question: 'Aside from the one you've given me, do you have any other reason for being here?' "

"Do you think I killed her, Harry?"

It was Harry's turn to reflect in silence for a moment before answering. He was not sure what Cooper expected him to say, but he decided on the truth.

"I don't know whether you killed Lilly Rhinelander or not," he said. "That said, I'm going to ask you again, Will you answer the question?"

"No."

"For God's sake, Adrian! Why not?"

"Isn't it obvious? My mother asked me not to."

10

"Thanks for coming in, Harry," Harley Dillard said, shaking Harry's hand and leading him into Jennifer's office.

Dillard was a short, powerfully built man, balding, with an air of bustle and competence that Harry liked. Dillard was an effective and popular state attorney, who would be making a move into politics soon, Harry thought, if the Feds didn't steal him for the bench.

"Jennifer tells me you've stuck your head in the lion's mouth again," Dillard said with a pleasant chuckle. "You live what the Chinese would call an interesting life."

"I'm not altogether happy with my present situation; but in this instance you're right about the interesting part if you call driving toward a cliff interesting."

"I guess it depends on whose hands are on the steering wheel," Dillard said, urging him into a chair. "I'm sorry I can't sit in on this with you and Jennifer, but one of the governor's aides is waiting for my call. It's a call I can't postpone. How about coffee, soda, tea?"

"No thanks," Harry said.

"OK, Alice," Dillard said to a nervous paralegal, hovering at the door, "let's find out how wrung out the state's chief administrative officer is. Harry, watch your back."

Before Harry could decide whether Dillard had been serious or making one of his black jokes, Jennifer walked in, burdened with her briefcase and a stack of manila files. Harry stood up and smiled, but all he got was a distracted nod before she dumped her briefcase and files onto her desk.

"Harley can't be with us," she said, scowling. "The governor has him. First things first."

She did not sound pleased.

"He told me," Harry said. "What happened to the happy, smiling woman who called me this morning?"

"Did he tell you why you're here?" Jennifer asked, ignoring his question.

"No, but I assume you and he want to talk about Adrian Cooper."

She still hadn't really looked at him and slumped into a chair beside him still scowling at something Harry couldn't see.

"Why didn't you tell us Cooper talked to Randall Pearson?" she demanded.

"I only found out yesterday. I thought it could wait."

She finally managed to break connection with whatever she had been glowering at and faced him. At close range, Harry saw that she looked either ill or severely stressed.

"You have a cell phone."

Her voice was cold.

Several responses occurred to Harry, none of which would have increased the civility of the exchange.

"Jennifer," he said quietly, "what's going on?"

"Let's skip the personal stuff and stick to the subject."

The outburst was so harsh that Harry just looked at her.

"What?" she demanded.

"Stingray, stingray, swim away," he sang, seriously off-key.

"No fair!" she said, blushing. "And that dinner by the sea got me into a lot of trouble."

Harry started to speak, but she thrust her hands out at him. "Stop!" she said. "I'm not talking about it. Understood?"

"Understood," Harry said, assuming that she had made the

mistake of telling her fiancé about their evening swim and was paying the price.

"What's so important about Cooper's talking to Pearson?"

"What did they talk about?" she asked. "Pearson was as helpful on that score as a clam."

"I'm willing to tell you some things but not others," Harry told her, glad to see her relaxing a little. "There are certain things which at least for now I can hang onto. Agreed?"

She nodded.

"First, he refused to answer most of Pearson's questions, just as he refused to answer those same questions when I asked them."

"What are they?"

"What brought him to Avola? What demands, if any, is he going to make on the Rhinelander estate?"

Harry kept back all references to Cooper's having talked with his mother on the afternoon preceding her death, betting that Pearson had done the same.

"Sounds right," she said as if she never again expected to hear good news.

"Are you going to question him?" Harry asked.

"Officially, you mean?"

Harry thought she sounded a little less hostile.

"I know it sounds weird, coming from me, but I think you should talk to him."

"Why?" Jennifer asked, sounding interested.

"For his protection."

"From what?"

"Himself."

"Harry," she said, actually smiling at him, "stop trying to be mysterious."

"I'm not. Do you know what he said to me when I asked him why he wouldn't answer my questions?"

"He didn't want to?"

She was grinning.

"He said, 'My mother asked me not to.' "

When she stopped laughing, she said, "Maybe we should take him into protective custody."

"From what people have been saying about the Rhinelanders," Harry said only half joking, "it may not be a bad idea."

"Are you hoping he'd tell us what he won't tell you and Pearson?"

By this time they were standing companionably together, talking easily. Jennifer's mood had brightened, and Harry hoped he had helped her to feel better.

"I'm not sure what I want. I can't figure the man out," Harry replied. "There may be no more to him than what I see, but I can't shake my conviction that he's far more complex in every way than he appears to be."

"OK," she said with a friendly grin, "we'll take a look at him, but it will be fairly informal. Harley says we don't know enough about him and his relationship with Lilly Rhinelander to regard him as a subject, much less a target." She hesitated and then said, "Harley thought you might tell us what we needed to know." She gave a short laugh, "I told him you wouldn't. I suppose I should thank you for making me right."

"Well, I've talked with all three of Rhinelander's children," Harry said. "They all either were mad or got mad before we finished talking. Pearson has warned them not to have any contact with Cooper. I guess talking to me was their best alternative."

"And?"

"They're all very angry about his claim to be their half brother. This is only my take, but for some reason I think they're all very afraid of him. I asked Michael why but got no response."

They went on talking amiably for a few minutes until she

said, "I really must get on with things," tilting her head at her desk and the files piled on it.

"Thanks for agreeing to talk with Cooper," he said.

They said goodbye, and just as Harry was starting to open the door, Jennifer said in a rush, "Wait. Harry, why did you kiss me last night?"

She looked and sounded as if she expected to be hurt by his answer. He closed the door and turned to face her, trying to find an answer that would take some of the stress off her and keep them off the rocks.

"I wanted to," he said.

"I'm glad you wanted to because I wanted you to," she said in a slightly defiant voice, "but I'm not supposed to, and you must feel uncomfortable, to say the least. If you want to stop seeing me outside the office, I'll understand; and I won't . . ."

At her abrupt halt, Harry made a show of looking down, pausing, and frowning over her question. Actually he was thinking as quickly as he could about what he did want and what she was trying to tell him. He got as far as deciding what he wanted and abandoned the rest.

"It's a tough call," he told her with a straight face, "but I think I'd like to go on seeing you jiggle, thunder thighs and all."

She gave a yelp of laughter, blushing and suddenly looking years younger.

"You have no idea how badly I'm going to punish you," she cried as he ducked out the door.

11

Harry knew that the hour of Rowena Farnham's call, in which she would tell him what she had learned about the Rhinelander family, was fast approaching. That would be the good part. The bad part would be when she asked if he'd seen Soñadora yet. He hadn't. When he got home from talking with Jennifer, he checked his watch, and, seeing it was nearly seven o'clock, he called her Salvamento number, hoping that she had left and he could leave a message.

On the second ring a woman with a strong, cool voice said, "Salvamento."

Harry hesitated so long that the woman said, "Can you hear me?"

"I can hear you," Harry said, "but I'm too scared to talk."

"I thought you were dead," Soñadora replied.

She did not sound amused.

"Thought or wished?" Harry asked in a cowardly gesture.

"You are not important enough for me to wish you dead."

"It's that bad."

"Worse."

"Have you eaten yet?"

Harry heard a muffled, choked sound that might have been the beginning of a laugh or someone starting to throw up.

"No," she said, having regained her composure.

That she had answered his question was for Harry the sight

of a tiny cloud of hope no bigger than a hand on his mental horizon.

"Neither have I," he said. "Let's go somewhere and eat boiled chicken feet."

It was an old joke, involving the fact that she usually refused to eat in anything remotely resembling an upscale restaurant, and he hoped it would weaken her resistance, forgetting she had never thought it was funny.

"Pathetic!" she said, and then more loudly, "Pathetic!"

Harry picked her up half an hour later. Salvamento was located in a dark corner of East Avola in an area given over, for the most part, to substance abuse, mom-and-pop chop shops, body shops, thirdhand car lots, vacant lots, and general dereliction.

The rescue mission itself, however, was a neat, cream-colored, one-story stucco building in a fenced square of carefully tended land, planted with cacti, dwarf palms, oleander, hibiscus, plumbago and other flowering bushes. Some years ago the mission had been bombed and burned to the ground; but with the help of Rowena Farnham's congregation and the Hispanic community of East Avola, it had been restored. Over the years bedrooms, bathrooms, and a kitchen had been added, to absorb the overflow from the organization's safe houses.

Soñadora came out the door as soon as Harry drove into the yard. She was tall and slender with long, black hair, which she usually wore in a braid. This evening she had wrapped the braid in a tight coil around her head. She was dressed in a deep blue blouse and red, calf-length skirt, and sandals. Harry had walked around the Rover and opened the rider's door for her. Watching her come towards him in the rose twilight, he saw that she was thinner and her face more worn than when he last saw her. And he wondered how anyone so beautiful and brave and dedicated could also be so certain that she could not be loved.

She stopped beside him and spoke rapidly in a language he could not understand. Then she gave him a brief, fake but dazzling smile before clambering, poker-faced, into the Rover. He stood holding the door and watching her while she put on her safety belt.

"Well?" she said.

"You've forgotten, I don't speak Quiche."

"I have forgotten nothing, and I was using language to describe you that I cannot duplicate in either Spanish or English."

"Primitive Mayan talk," he said.

"Idiot," she said, her black eyes the only part of her face expressing any amusement.

Harry backed out of the driveway feeling like a kid on his first date.

"I'm very sorry things didn't work out for you," he said when they were seated in the restaurant she had chosen for them.

It was small, with wooden chairs and a dozen tables spread with orange cotton tablecloths. There was no air-conditioning, but fans in the corners were keeping the room comfortable. The kitchen was a lean-to attached to the rear wall with two doors opening into the eating area. As the two waitresses in white blouses and brightly colored skirts hurried in and out of the kitchen, they brought with them the rich smells of the cooking.

"Do you want to tell me you were right, that I should never have married him?" she demanded, her face stiff with pain.

She was sitting with her hands folded, her forearms resting on the table, staring straight at him as if she was bracing herself to be hurt. The table was small, and Harry had to reach forward only a little to place his hands on top of hers. She started to pull away from him.

"Don't," he said.

It was more an entreaty than a command. He felt the tension

go out of her hands. She dropped her eyes.

"What I want to tell you," he said, feeling as if the virtue had all gone out of him, "is that I am more ashamed of myself than you can imagine for having avoided you all this time. It was very selfish of me."

Her eyes instantly found his. Harry could not tell whether she was angry or not, but he was astounded by what he had just said. He had no idea he was going to carry on like that, and he thought he had probably behaved like the idiot she accused him of being. He started to apologize for the apology, but she interrupted.

"Was what I did so terrible that you could not bear to be near me?" she asked.

"Yes. No. No. I couldn't understand why you had done it. I went off and sulked. I'm really sorry."

Her eyes instantly filled with tears. She snatched her hands back, pulled a tissue out of her skirt pocket, stemmed the flow, and blew her nose.

"This is all your fault," she said, loudly enough to attract the attention of several people at nearby tables. "I have not cried since the last time I was with you," she continued fiercely but more quietly, dabbing at her eyes. "You do this on purpose. I hate you."

"You are the only woman I have ever known," he said, "who is beautiful crying."

The tears started again, but she was also laughing.

"You are twisted," she said, "and you are *idiota.*"

The waitress arrived, and Soñadora ordered for them in Quiche. Harry felt as if he had just run up a very steep hill strewn with large rocks. But it was worth it. When she wanted to call him idiotic, which was chiefly when he paid her a compliment, she did it in Spanish. It was the closest thing to a thank you she ever gave him.

"How is the work going?" he asked, trying to steer the conversation onto safer ground.

"Much as always," she said without the enthusiasm he was used to hearing in her voice when she talked about the Salvamento.

"Jim Snyder's been telling me that the trafficking has been reduced. Do you agree?"

"No," she said. "It is just more hidden. The captain and his people have been trying very hard to stop it, but they don't have the money, the officers, or the training to do more than scratch at the edges of this thing."

She paused, frowning, before going on.

"The most . . . how do you say *irónico?*"

"Ironical."

"The most ironical thing about all of this Department of Immigration effort to keep illegals out and deport those who are already here is that it is increasing the demand for people, and many who would have hired illegals are just as glad to have them as slaves. The traffickers cannot begin to meet the demand."

"Very discouraging," Harry agreed. "Is Immigration still harassing you?"

"All the time. The way it was, I could hire illegals, train them, keep them with me until they learned English and could find better paying jobs, become a part of the community, and make good citizens. It is much more difficult now."

Their food came; and, to Harry's delight, Soñadora ate with gusto. Chicken, beans, corn, tomatoes, zucchinis and chilies. She usually refused to eat in Anglo restaurants, especially the pricey kind, because she considered it immoral when so many people were hungry. While Harry was thinking about this and enjoying himself watching her eat, he bit into a small, red chili pepper.

He made an indescribable sound of extreme suffering. Soñadora looked up.

"What is the matter?" she demanded with a stricken look, dropping her fork in her plate and reaching for him. "Harry, why are you crying?"

"Chilies," he croaked.

She passed him a tortilla and said, smiling, "Eat it with some of the beans."

"Did you always eat in these places when you were with Pearson?" he asked when he could manage a full sentence.

"No, and why must you mention him?"

"Because you married him."

"Yes. Fortunately, he divorced me. Can we leave it?"

Harry thought for a moment and said, "I can, but can you?"

"Of course I can," she said sharply, picking up her fork.

"It's not what Rowena Farnham told me. She said things were not going at all well for you."

"Rowena should not have told you that," she replied, beginning to eat again.

"Is it true?"

She shrugged and avoided his gaze.

"It's all right," he said.

"What is?"

"Finish your dinner. Then you can tell me what's wrong."

She did, but it did not come easily. When they left the restaurant, Harry drove to one of Avola's public access points to the beach and parked where they could look through the palms at the cool silver glow of moonlight on the still water and listen to the wind in the palms.

"Would you like to walk?" he asked.

"No," she told him. "I want to look at that beautiful water and tell you what has happened to me."

"Good," Harry said.

"Not good. Do you remember that I told you I never knew my father?"

"Yes," he said quietly, "and that your mother was killed when you were seven. You also said a Catholic priest brought you up."

"His name is Paulus Jogues. Before becoming a priest, he had been a medical doctor, and as far as I know, he never stopped treating people although I doubt that his faith survived his break with Rome."

She drifted away for a moment, sighed as if she was struggling with something, and said, "I have just learned that he is my father."

"That's heavy news," Harry said. "Did you have any idea that he might be?"

"No. He says he should have told me years ago. He hopes I will forgive him."

She gave a sudden bitter laugh.

"It is not clear whether I am to forgive him for fathering me or for not telling me he is my father sooner."

Harry thought of several things to say and rejected all of them. It was not the time to say something about giving the conscience a quick polish before making the big jump.

"Why tell you now?"

"He thinks he will not live much longer."

"Was he good to you?" Harry asked, trying to find a silver lining.

"He saved my life, and, yes, he was kind and caring. He fed me and clothed me, and sent me to school, but he was a very busy man, fighting to stay alive as was everyone then."

"Liberation theology," Harry said.

She looked puzzled.

"Many nuns and priests who were living among the Indians in that part of the world defied the Church and began taking the side of the people against their governments," Harry said.

"Many of them were killed by the death squads. The press said they were practicing liberation theology."

"Yes, that happened," Soñadora said. "And I was expected to take care of myself and help him in the clinic as much as I could. By that time he was more a doctor than a priest, although he still said Mass, always in Quiche. Then, later, when he sent me to be educated by the sisters at St. Anne's in Mexico City and urged me to make a new life in this country, I thought he was finished with me, that he had done all he was prepared to do."

"How old were you then?"

"Fifteen."

Harry started to ask her why her mother had kept it a secret and then saw that the reason was obvious. He was a priest. The consequences might have been severe for all of them.

"How did you feel?"

"Very alone and unwanted."

"And you have had no contact since?"

"Very, very little. For years it was not safe. Remember, by the early eighties your Administration was aiding the Guatemalan army, funding the death squads. Rios Montt was destroying whole villages, killing everyone. My father feared for my safety."

"And that they might trace him through you?"

"Perhaps."

"Now he wants to see you," he said.

"Yes."

"Would it be safe to go? Do you want to go?"

She smiled grimly.

"I would not have to go. He wants to come here."

"How did he find you?"

"Through his Guatemalan contacts. He congratulated me on the work I was doing with Salvamento."

"He has probably kept track of you all these years," Harry said.

"Don't defend him!" she snapped.

"Just thinking out loud," he said, holding up his hands in mock defense.

"Don't," she snapped. "It is not your lengthy suit."

"Long suit," he said.

"Whatever."

"Where did you learn to say that?" he demanded.

She made a dismissive sound and fell silent, staring at her fists.

Then she said, the words tumbling over one another, sounding more to Harry like a cry of pain than an outburst of anger, "I am furious, Harry, absolutely furious, and I don't know why."

Her voice fell, and Harry had to strain to hear her as she went on speaking, more and more softly.

"And all of the old pain from that early time that I thought was behind me has come flooding back. What am I to do, Harry? What?"

"What do you want to do?" he asked.

"Get him here and kill him before he escapes," she said.

12

Harry was startled by her outburst, but he did not tell her she didn't mean what she had just said, although that's what he believed. She was certainly angry with Jogues, and probably had every right to be. Nevertheless, it seemed more probable that her anger with Harry had pried loose some old, suppressed anger, the source of which she could not yet confront, and she had transferred it to her father. At the same time he wondered if Cooper harbored any anger against Lilly Rhinelander for refusing to acknowledge publically that he was her child.

He left that question and gave his attention to Soñadora, asking her about her father. She answered him jerkily and almost hostilely at first, demanding to know why he wanted to know, and what business was it of his, still obviously distraught. Gradually, however, she grew calmer, and they talked about those parts of her life Harry had not heard her mention before. Then she said she was very tired and asked him to take her home.

When they reached Salvamento, Harry told her he would call her soon.

"I apologize for losing my temper," she said. "It was unpleasant for you."

"I never lose my temper," Harry said.

He expected her to respond as she usually did when he made ridiculous statements; but instead of insulting him, she sat staring out the window, looking sad and distracted. He reached over and took one of her hands in his.

"It's going to be all right," he said. "You'll work it out; and if you'll let me, I'll give you all the help I can."

She sighed, sat up a bit straighter, and retrieved her hand.

"Harry," she said, "I do not want to be a burden to you or an object of pity. I am responsible for my own life. Thank you for dinner. I hope you liked the chicken feet."

"They were delicious," Harry said, moved by her pride and stung that she could think that his offer of support was prompted by pity. "How long have we known one another?" he asked a bit sharply.

She looked at him with a frown.

"For a little more than three years," she said. "Why do you ask?"

"How much pity have you had from me in that time?"

"None," she said with no hesitation. "I . . ."

"That's how much you're getting in the future. Can you live with it?"

"It won't be easy under any circumstances," she shot back.

He walked her to the door.

"I'll call," he said again.

"It will be on your own head," she said and let herself in the door.

Harry walked away very pleased with himself.

The next morning Harry called Randall Pearson.

"Why didn't you tell Harley Dillard that Cooper talked with Lilly Rhinelander the day before she was killed?"

"I gather you didn't tell him either. By the way, I saw Fortunato in the state attorney's office when I was there. I think I remember that you used to know her."

"I did," Harry said, pretending he hadn't heard what Pearson had really said. "She was working for Harley then as an ADA."

"Very attractive woman, Harry."

"Yes. Now, about Cooper, if you're done having fun . . ."

Pearson laughed.

"I was stalling, actually, because I'm not entirely sure why I withheld that information, but I suspect it was for the same reason you did."

"I don't see how our motives could be the same here. I didn't want him arrested, but I did try to talk Jennifer into calling him in for an interview. Harley nixed it."

"Cash flow problem?"

"So I was told. Have you been in Jim Snyder's office lately? It looks as if it has been furnished by things Goodwill had thrown away."

"It's the same all over the county," Pearson said. "Property values dropping, tax revenue shrinking."

"Right. What's your reason?"

"The same as yours. I don't want him arrested because they'll only have to let him go. They're putting their bucket down a dry well with him. There's no way he could have put her out in that swamp. Besides, she was his golden goose."

"Very colorful," Harry said. "You didn't want him to get the publicity that his being interviewed as a suspect in Rhinelander's murder would bring him."

"The duck just came down from the ceiling."

"You're too young to remember that Groucho Marx show."

"Reruns," Pearson said.

"You didn't tell them you talked with Rhinelander just before she was killed?" Harry asked incredulously.

He and Cooper were wandering through the outdoor section of the Avola Botanical Gardens, Harry having decided that Cooper felt safer in a controlled environment. Cooper had just told him with no show of interest that he had responded to a call from the state attorney's office that morning and had a pleasant "chat" with attorneys Dillard and Fortunato.

"Did you tell them you had talked with Rhinelander just before she was killed?" Harry repeated, holding his breath.

"No, why?" Cooper asked, his voice expressing surprise.

It took Harry a moment to adjust to the news; and he forgot Cooper's question as soon as it was asked, crowded out of his mind by Cooper's answer. He glanced at his watch. It was a little after two.

"Adrian," he said, trying to remain calm, "you and I are going to see Harley Dillard right now, and I want you to tell him about that meeting."

"No," Cooper replied with a firm shake of his head, "it would, in my opinion, interfere with the progress of my claim by possibly creating a major distraction."

"You're missing the point," Harry insisted.

Cooper had surprised Harry by being very interested in the plants they were encountering. Now he bent over to examine closely the thrusting rod of white blossoms on a Spanish sword.

"What point?" Cooper asked, straightening up.

"That you have just withheld information from the very people whose sworn duty it is to investigate your mother's death," Harry burst out, cursing himself for having asked Jennifer to persuade Harley to bring Cooper in.

"I thought you didn't want me to tell Dillard about the meeting," Cooper said, still admiring the Spanish sword.

"That was before you were asked to talk with him," Harry said, his impatience showing. "And why didn't you call me, to say where you were going?"

"It seemed a minor thing," Cooper said calmly, moving toward a red Rose of Sharon bush.

"Adrian," Harry said, trying to get the big man's attention. "Listen to me."

When he was satisfied Cooper was paying attention, he said,

"You're forgetting that Randall Pearson knows you talked to her."

"No, I'm not," Cooper said, frowning.

"The only reason he did not give that information to Dillard during their first interview is that he didn't think you were a credible suspect in Rhinelander's murder, and he doesn't want you becoming generally known before he and his people can quash your attempt to get your case into court."

"My attorneys have already taken the initial steps to do that. Pearson's firm will have the filings within one or two days," Cooper replied.

"Jesus, Adrian," Harry said in alarm. "Why am I just hearing about the filing? No, don't answer that. Just listen," Harry told him. "I now think that you are going to have a terrible time with the Rhinelander family. They will force Pearson to use every bit of influence he can find to thwart you."

"That's not news, Harry," Cooper said, turning toward the flowering bush again.

"Stay with me."

Cooped paused, frowning, and turned back.

"When Pearson decides the time is right," Harry said, speaking rapidly, "which means when he thinks he can do you the most harm, he will go to Dillard and tell him that you were with Rhinelander shortly before she was killed.

"He will say that he delayed turning over the information because he was sure you would come forward yourself. Seeing that, surprisingly, he had been wrong, he was hurrying to correct his error."

Cooper continued to frown, but he remained silent.

"If Pearson doesn't already know that you've talked with Dillard, he will before the day is out," Harry told him. "The moment he knows it, he will find out what you told Dillard; and when he does he will make the call to Dillard."

While Harry paused to let what he had said sink in, he watched Cooper closely, to see the effect of his words.

"Well," Cooper said, smiling, "you are concerned about my welfare. I'm touched by that. Have you said everything you want to say?"

"No," Harry replied, "Dillard has the governor calling him, the family pressing him, and his already crowded docket exerting pressure on him to get results in this investigation. When he learns that you have been withholding information, he is going to be very angry. You're a lawyer. Why do I have to explain this to you?"

"The information you withheld during the interview is, as you must surely know, crucial to the investigation. Dillard's assumption is going to be that you deliberately withheld it because you knew it was incriminating."

He paused for a response; but Cooper, ignoring the question, only waited, watching Harry with a bland expression as though nothing that was being said had very much to do with him.

"Harry," he said at last as if he was humoring a demanding child, "if you feel this strongly about it, I'm willing to accompany you to Attorney Dillard's office." He paused long enough to drop a heavy hand on Harry's shoulder and said, "But, you do know, don't you, that I didn't kill her?"

"No, Mr. Dillard," Cooper said, wearing his most benign smile, "I'm not going to tell you what we discussed."

Harry didn't slap his forehead with his hand, but he wanted to. He knew what was coming. So did Jennifer, and she was already grinning at Harry.

Dillard, too focused on Cooper to notice, said with a rising voice, "Why not?"

"My mother asked me not to," Cooper replied.

"Not good enough!" Dillard said in a still louder voice.

"You're a lawyer, Mr. Cooper. You know it's not good enough. If I have to, I'll put you under oath."

"If you are, you are planning to charge me in my mother's death," Cooper said calmly. "I will want to consult with my attorneys."

"Who are?" Dillard demanded, having modulated his voice.

Cooper gave him the name of the firm, and Dillard actually smiled.

"The best team of criminal lawyers in the state," he said admiringly. "This is getting interesting. Did you hire them after our conversation this morning?"

"Harley," Jennifer said, "I think Mr. Cooper hired them after learning of Rhinelander's death."

"That's right, Harley," Harry said.

"Just before I phoned Mr. Brock," Cooper said. "It seemed the prudent thing to do."

"You figured you were going to be arrested and charged with killing Rhinelander?" Dillard asked.

"It seemed a distinct possibility, given my intentions to force her family to recognize me as Lilly Rhinelander's natural child."

"Is that why you came to Avola?" Jennifer asked.

"I do not wish to answer that question, Ms. Fortunato," Cooper said, cushioning his refusal with a smile.

Harry saw in Cooper's face and heard in his voice a warmer, more personal response to Jennifer than either he or Dillard had elicited.

"You will appreciate," Cooper continued, "that my endeavor is going to be met with significant resistance."

"I think that's an understatement," Jennifer said, rallying him a little.

"Yes," Cooper replied, his smile holding. "That being so, I must keep to myself as far as possible all information regarding my motives and intentions, not because they are in any way criminous but because if I don't, they will be twisted and bent into a weapon to be used against me. You see that, don't you?"

"Yes, I suppose I do," she conceded.

"Are we finished here?" Harry asked, having noted that Cooper's appeal appeared to shift Jennifer's interest in Cooper as a potential suspect to interest in him as a man.

He was irritated to find a trickle of jealousy burning a thin line across his mind.

"Yes," Dillard said, standing up. "Mr. Cooper, you're free to go, but I'm going to ask you to keep yourself available."

"I expect to be in Avola for some time, Mr. Dillard."

Harry watched them shaking hands and thought for the first time that it was very possible that Cooper would be charged with Lilly Rhinelander's murder.

Three mornings later Harry woke, showered, went downstairs, and turned on his coffeemaker. The night before, Cooper had called to say with no obvious excitement that Pearson was in contact with the Miami attorneys. Harry recalled thinking that Cooper was now within range of the Rhinelander family guns and saw no way of protecting him. Prior to the call, he had not had much time to think about Cooper, having spent the past two days in court, testifying in an insurance fraud case that had required his presence but had been more boring than watching grass grow.

Waiting for his coffee, from the kitchen window he watched a thin, silver mist swirling over the creek, stirred by the dawn wind. It was a familiar sight but one that never wearied him. The kettle whistled; and as he turned away from the window, he thought he heard someone cough. He turned off the unit under the kettle and went to the door, opened it, and stepped onto the lanai. On the granite step was a small huddled figure.

"You're an early riser," he said to the rounded shoulders and bent head.

"I'm Franklin, Toke Wylie's son," the boy said quietly, getting to his feet and turning to face Harry.

"You couldn't be anyone else," Harry said, noting the boy was wet to his waist and trying not to shiver. "Come in," he said, opening the screen door.

"I'm going to get your floor wet," Franklin said, still standing on the ground.

"It will dry. Come in here and get out of those dungarees. You can wear something of mine until yours are dry."

Harry didn't ask why the boy was here. Franklin would tell him when he was ready. Neither did he ask if the boy was hungry. Once he had put his dungarees and sneakers into the drier and had the boy in a pair of his chinos and a flannel shirt and slippers, he began frying bacon and scrambling eggs. Franklin sat at the kitchen table, warming his hands around a mug of Harry's coffee. He had taken a couple of sips and given up on it.

"Want me to heat that up for you?" Harry asked, placing a plate of scrambled eggs, bacon, and buttered toast in front of him.

"I'm not much for coffee," Franklin said, grasping his fork eagerly.

"That's a whopper, but we'll let it go," Harry said in a resigned voice, pouring the boy some orange juice.

Nobody liked his coffee, and over time he had become somewhat reconciled to his limitations in the coffee-making department. Franklin ate without speaking. Finally, he sat back from his plate and refused Harry's offer to fill it again.

"I can't find my father," he said, staring at the table.

Harry waited.

Franklin put his elbows on the table and leaned his head into his hands.

"I've been looking two days."

Harry decided it was time for him to help Franklin say what the youngster was having trouble saying.

"How long has he been gone?" he asked.

"Four days."

"Has he stayed away before?"

Franklin shook his head.

"When he left, did he say where he was going?" Harry asked.

"No."

"Did he leave with anybody?"

"I don't know."

The boy suddenly covered his face with his hands, and his shoulders shook, but there was no sound. Harry waited. After a moment or two, Franklin rubbed his face hard and sat up.

"Who's at home?" Harry asked when he was sure the boy had recovered himself.

"Nobody. I took Martha and Abe to stay with our grandmother until I can find him," he answered a little shakily.

Harry knew that Wylie's wife had died of cancer a year or so ago. Now he knew he had been taking care of himself and the three children on his own.

"What made you think he was in the Stickpen?" Harry asked.

"His boat was gone."

"Whose boat are you using?" Harry asked.

"My uncle's."

"Do he and your grandmother know your father's missing?"

"Nobody knows but me. I told the young ones he's guiding some fishermen so that they wouldn't worry."

"And he's never done anything like this before?"

"No."

"I'm glad you're here, but what brought you to me?"

"My father told me that day we found the woman in the water that if I ever needed help, I should come to you."

The boy's face was etched with weariness and pain.

"All right," Harry said, sitting down beside Franklin and trying to sound confident. "You did the right thing in coming here. I know you're worried. I would be worried if it was me, but it's too soon to think that something bad has happened to your father. But you need some help in looking for him."

Franklin nodded. Harry could imagine that it was pride that had kept him from telling any of his people that Toke was missing. Probably ever since his mother had died, Toke, with Franklin's help, had been doing what he could to keep the family together; and Harry could imagine that some of his relatives wanted to separate them and put the children into relatives' families.

"Also," Harry said, "for the sake of making sure we get all the help we can, I think we should tell the police."

Franklin shook his head.

"My father wouldn't like that. I was hoping you could help me find him."

"If he took his boat and went into the Stickpen, it would take the two of us a year to make even a dent in searching all the places he could be."

He paused to see how Franklin would respond.

"He wouldn't want the police," the boy said flatly.

"Then we had better talk to your uncle," Harry told him quietly. "It wouldn't be fair to Toke not to."

"I will go home and do it," the boy said, his disappointment written on his face.

"What's your uncle's name?"

"Henry David. Mostly, people call him H.D."

"Do you know his phone number?"

The boy gave it to Harry, who dialed it. When a man's voice

answered, Harry held out the phone to Franklin, who after some hesitation told his uncle what had happened and where he was. Then he listened, and then he passed Harry the phone and went outside. Harry heard the lanai door slam.

"Thank you for calling me," Wylie said. "Franklin will come home. I'm sorry he bothered you."

"He was no bother," Harry said. "Something you said upset him. Do you know what it was?"

"I told him I was going to call the police," Wylie said. "Do you have any idea what's happened to Toke?"

"No. Do you know that he found Lilly Rhinelander's body and came to get me?" Harry asked. "Franklin was with him that day. That's probably when he told the boy to come to me if he needed help. Maybe he thought there might be some trouble connected with what he'd found."

"All I know about it is what I read in the paper," Wylie said.

"Why would Toke object to having the police help to find him?"

"Toke's independent," Wylie said. "Send the boy home, and thanks for calling me."

Harry found Franklin sitting under the big live oak, head on his knees and his arms wrapped around his legs, looking the very picture of misery.

"Your uncle says for you to come home," Harry told him. "If you'd rather stay here, I'll call him back and tell him that."

Franklin scrambled to his feet, his face wet with tears, but he was composed now.

"I'd better go back," he said.

"Do you want me to go out to the boat with you?"

The youngster shook his head.

"I can get there," he said, showing a little edge.

"I know you can," Harry said quickly. "I was just offering you some company."

"Thanks. I'll be all right."

"Sure you will," Harry said.

A few minutes later Franklin left, wearing a new Eagle Pride T-shirt that Harry was never going to put on.

"It will be all right," Harry said, walking him to the road.

Franklin nodded and walked off as if he didn't believe a word of it.

Neither did Harry.

13

Harry went back into the house and made himself some breakfast. While he was doing that, he found he couldn't stop wondering if Toke's disappearance had anything to do with Rhinelander's death. By the time he had the kitchen cleaned and the dishes put away, he was satisfied that the only way there could be a connection was if Toke was somehow involved in her killing.

He called Jim Snyder and asked if he'd had a call from Henry David Wylie.

"Yes," Jim said impatiently. "I don't want to be stereotyping anybody here, but when someone tells me a Hierba Alto who has spent his entire life in the Everglades is missing, I have all I can do not to say, 'Give it a week and then call me.' "

"The boy is really worried," Harry said after telling Jim about Franklin's visit. "I'm wondering if there could be some connection between Toke's disappearance and Rhinelander's body being dumped in the Stickpen."

"Harry, you're letting your imagination run away with you," Jim said.

"You're probably right. What are you going to do about Toke?"

"We're stretched tighter than a drum head. Fisher says give it forty-eight hours. If he doesn't show up, we'll put together some kind of search."

"This will be the fourth day since anyone's seen him," Harry said, thinking of Franklin.

"It's the best I can do."

"You're thinking Toke does know something he doesn't want to tell you. Isn't that so?" Harry said. "You're thinking that he didn't wait for your people to come, and now he's gone to the saw grass."

"It crossed my mind. Frank just came in with some more bad news. That's all he ever brings me. I'll talk to you later."

Henry David Wylie met Harry outside the tribal office building. He was a large, heavyset man with close-cropped black hair. Dressed in dark trousers and a white dress shirt with a western string tie and large silver belt buckle, he was a strong contrast in appearance to his brother Toke.

"Come in," he said after shaking Harry's hand.

The building was a sprawling single story, pink stucco structure that did not prepare Harry for the luxury of the office into which Wylie led him. A large gray, rose, and white storm pattern Navaho rug dominated the room. On stands against two of the inside walls were a pair of modern Hopi pots. The art on the walls was not, Harry guessed, anything you'd see being offered along the road. Two black leather chairs faced a gleaming black metal desk.

Harry stood for a moment, taking in the room, adjusting to the fact he would have to work about a year to buy the rug.

"Very impressive," he said.

"Thank you," Wylie said, taking one of the leather chairs. "Sit down. Do you like Indian art?"

"I like yours," Harry replied, thinking that Wylie's people had come a long way in fifty years.

"How much trouble do you think Toke is in?" he asked after thanking Harry.

"Do you mean the Rhinelander murder?" Harry answered.

"Yes."

"Do you have any reason for thinking he might somehow be involved?"

"No, but my brother and I are not close now."

"But you were once?"

"Yes. You've known him for some time?"

"Nearly five years. He would stop by the house now and then. He took the loss of his wife pretty hard, but he seemed to recover. You'd probably know better than I whether or not he had serious problems."

Henry David sighed and leaned back in his chair, a frown darkening his face.

"I wish I could say yes to that, but I can't. Toke and I began going separate ways many years ago," he answered. He hesitated, then said, "If you could tolerate it, I'd like to tell you something about Toke and me. It might help us to talk to some purpose."

"I'll be glad to listen," Harry told him and meant it.

"I'm a couple of years older than Toke. Our father died when I was ten, leaving my mother with no money. She went to work as a waitress in Avola. Not everybody would hire an Indian back then, and she didn't get the best jobs. Fortunately for us, our mother was a smart woman, and she found ways to make ends meet. She also leaned hard on us to be serious about school."

He interrupted himself to ask Harry if he would like some coffee. Harry said he would; and a few minutes later two middle-aged women in black skirts and white blouses came in with a chrome trolley. From it they took out folding trays, mugs, and a black thermos. Without fuss they opened the trays, laid out the mugs, spoons, cream, and sugar and poured the coffee.

When they were gone, Henry David said, "There are four of them. They formed a business and sold us the idea of hiring them to do all our catering. We have a lot of meetings and have to entertain a lot of people. It's the best business decision we've made since building the casino."

Harry grinned. The coffee was delicious.

"Who, exactly, is us?" he asked.

"The tribal government."

"And you're part of that?"

"That's right. I take care of the financial end of things."

"I see," Harry said, thinking but not saying that Henry David was managing a several-million-dollar budget.

"I'm almost finished with this story," Henry David said. "Are you bearing up all right?"

Harry said he was.

"I was speaking about my mother's insistence that Toke and I work at our studies. It took with me, but when he was about twelve, Toke rebelled."

Wylie looked out the window at the expanse of sky and golden grass, moving gracefully in the wind, and seemed to be lost in his own thoughts. Just as Harry decided he should interrupt the reverie, Wylie turned back to him.

"For many young Indian males living in an environment that suggests a choice," Wylie said, "there's a time in their lives when they feel faced with a choice between some degree of cultural integration with the white world and a rejection of that path in favor of fully embracing the traditional Indian way. Toke chose the traditional way."

"You didn't," Harry said.

"No, and it has become a barrier between us. He has been drawing Franklin in that direction."

"I'm not sure I understand . . ." Harry began, but Wylie stopped him.

"No, of course you don't," Wylie said. "You can live on the edge of the Stickpen without feeling you have to live in it and pretend all the rest of the life going on around you doesn't exist."

Wylie's voice had deepened with bitterness and a thinly veiled anger.

"The problem is that Toke's choice has kept him living below the poverty line for years. His wife worked and kept the family going. When she died, Toke was forced to face the reality of what he was doing."

"Are you suggesting that when he had to admit he couldn't support his family by guiding fishermen and hunting and trapping, he bridged the gap by doing things he ought not to be doing?"

Harry thought he might have crossed a line of his own in laying out what he was thinking that flatly, but it seemed time to say it.

"I'm afraid so, yes."

"I'm thinking alligator hides, feathers, orchids, that sort of thing," Harry said, suppressing for the time being the question of drug smuggling.

Wylie nodded.

"That and, possibly, more. Do you know if there was more?" he asked.

"No," Harry replied. "Do you know any way in which he might have been involved with Rhinelander's death?"

"Until you called, it had not occurred to me that such a thing was possible," Wylie said sadly. "Now I find myself asking what Toke was doing in the Stickpen? Why was Franklin with him when the boy should have been in school? Why did he involve himself by coming to tell you what he had found? It was not like Toke to involve himself. By the way, Franklin and his brother and sister are staying with my wife and me and are back in school."

"I'm relieved," Harry said, then, hoping to ease Wylie's mind and also avoid addressing his other questions, questions that only now began to acquire significance, he added, "Toke said the thought of her in the water made him feel bad."

Wylie nodded but did not seem very impressed.

"Some of our people are looking for him," he said. "Some of them know the places he frequented. I have called the Village to ask if anyone has seen him. I suppose it is possible he has business there."

Harry knew the Village was a larger Hierba Alto settlement further to the south.

"Maybe later today he will come home and clear up the mystery," Harry said, preparing to leave and having no reason to believe his hope was grounded on any reality.

"It does not seem likely," Wylie said, "but hope is good if it can be sustained."

"The county will bring in its help soon, according to Jim Snyder," Harry said as they walked out to the Rover, broiling in the sun. "I hope your people find him first and that he's all right."

"The captain is a good man," Wylie said, shaking Harry's hand. "If it's possible, I would like a warning if the investigation of Rhinelander's death swings toward us."

"I'll do what I can. It was good meeting you. I'm sorry it had to be under these circumstances."

Driving back to the Hammock, Harry began to wonder what Franklin knew about Rhinelander's death and if he was in any danger.

By dark, Harry had heard nothing from Henry David and put in a call to Fillmore Wiggins.

"I've got a favor to ask you," Harry said. "Is your old airboat still in use?"

Wiggins said it was.

"What would it take to hire you and your boat tomorrow, to look for a missing man?"

"Who?"

"Toke Wylie. His oldest son came to see me. He said his father had been gone four days, and his boat was missing."

Wiggins swore colorfully and said, "A hundred and a five-gallon can of gas. Toke was a good man, and finding his body would help nail the son of a bitch who killed him."

"Whoa," Harry said. "I don't know that he's dead."

"If Toke Wylie went into the Stickpen and didn't come out, it's safe to say he's dead. The man's been traveling the saw grass and the cypress swamps since he was a kid. Be here at daylight."

As much as Harry hated the idea, he had to admit that Wiggins was probably right.

Wiggins had moved his boat to the floating wharf and was pouring gasoline into the tank when Harry arrived the next day.

"I hate carrying gasoline in the Rover or any other car or truck," Harry said as he set down the gas can and the rest of his gear.

"You'd be safer transporting dynamite," Wiggins said with a grin.

The sun had not yet come up, but, when the boat's tank was full, they packed food, water, and Harry's can of gasoline in the large wooden box bolted to the boat's ten-foot, flat-bottomed hull.

"You've got some new carbon-fiber propellers," Harry said approvingly, studying the propellers, housed in a heavy wire cage over the engine, when they were ready to cast off.

"And I've doubled the mufflers on the engine, but she's still loud," Wiggins said with a grin as he passed Harry a pair of thickly padded ear mufflers. "The good news is that with two of us she'll fly on about four inches of water. That means in the Stickpen we can go about anywhere we want to go."

In the next five minutes they decided on a plan for making their search as effective as possible. The swamp was vast, but it was not featureless. Water moved from roughly north to south through all of it, but there were areas where islands of semidry land created obstacles and forced the water to flow more rapidly, scouring channels deep enough for bass, alligators, gar, suckers, crabs, and a host of smaller species to make life interesting for wading birds, raccoons, mink, otters, and alligators. It was those areas that Harry and Wiggins had decided to explore.

"If Toke was hide and meat hunting," Wiggins said, "that's where he'd be."

Harry agreed, and he and Wiggins clambered onto the high seats in front of the propeller, which had been elevated, to allow the driver and the rider to see over the tall grass and reeds, through and over which they would be traveling.

After a few minutes of fairly swift travel through the edge of the cypress swamp, Wiggins slowed down and inched the boat through thirty or forty yards of much thicker growth and then, cutting back on the throttle, let the boat drift into an area that Harry thought he recognized.

"Is this where Toke found Rhinelander?" Wiggins asked.

"It looks right," Harry said. "How did you know?"

"From what you told me when you were at the house, I figured it was somewhere here."

Wiggins advanced the throttle, putting an end to their conversation. Riding an airboat doesn't encourage conversation; but once back on more open water—Wiggins had maneuvered them at a fairly breakneck pace through the shallows and thickets to an extensive stretch of deeper water—he cut back on the throttle and began steering them up a twisting channel, staying close to the brushy shore, giving them a chance to talk.

"There's been a lot of deer and raccoons moving through here," Harry said after a few minutes of watching the shoreline on his side of the boat.

"A while back, I saw where pigs have been rooting and generally raising hell with things," Wiggins said with a laugh, then killed the engine and pulled off his ear covers.

"What is it?" Harry asked.

"Listen. Tell me if you hear anything."

After a few moments of hearing nothing but the sound of the moving water and bird calls, Harry caught a dull thunk that was repeated.

"Hear that?" he asked Wiggins.

Wiggins nodded. The sound was recurring at short, irregular intervals.

"What does it sound like to you?" he asked.

"Somebody poling a boat and hitting the gunwale every now and then," Harry said.

"Well, let's check our hardware," Wiggins said, sliding a twelve gauge pump out of its greased leather holster strapped to his seat and, jacking a shell into the chamber and pushing on the safety, laying the gun across his lap.

Harry did not need to check his CZ. He had done that before leaving the house.

"We're good to go," Wiggins said, gripping the upright steering column to the left of his seat and advancing the throttle.

A few minutes later they swept around a tight bend in the main channel they had been following and came upon four johnboats; the first three boats each had a man sitting in the bow and a second standing, propelling the boat with a long pole. The fourth boat, tied to the third, was empty except for something lying between the seats and covered by a piece of canvas. Wiggins instantly cut back on the throttle and let the airboat wallow towards the boats at a crawl.

"That fourth boat has something under a canvas," Harry said to Wiggins.

"Could be supplies, but I doubt it," Wiggins said. "Hold it, I think I know the man seated in the first boat."

"Hello, Mark," Wiggins said, addressing the man in the front of the first boat when they were within speaking distance. "You looking for Toke Wylie?"

"Found him," the man replied.

The second boat slid up beside the first. The third followed. Wiggins dropped his shotgun back into its sleeve.

"For those of you who don't know him, this here is Harry Brock. He lives on Bartram's Hammock. He and Toke were friends. Toke's boy Franklin came to see him yesterday morning, looking for help in finding his father."

Mark and the other men nodded in silence, and that ended the introductions.

"We heard about that," Mark said. "We been out since yesterday. We found him about an hour ago."

"Is he under the tarp?" Harry asked.

Mark nodded.

"What happened to him?" Wiggins asked.

"Somebody shot him in the back of the head," Mark said.

The news slammed into Harry, his own sorrow quickly buried by concern for Franklin, who had lost his mother and now his father. Anger quickly roiled with the rest of his feelings, but he forced it aside in order to deal with the situation facing him and Wiggins.

"Anybody called the police?" he asked.

"Too late," Mark said. "He was dead."

"Was he in the boat?" Harry asked.

"Yes," Mark said, turning to look at the boat. "We left him just as we found him."

"Any tracks around the boat?" Harry asked.

"No," Mark said. "It looked like the boat had floated down to there and got caught in the grass."

"No sign of anybody having been there?" Harry asked.

Mark shook his head.

Everyone sat and listened to the wind in the grass for a while. Then Harry said, "I'd better call the sheriff."

No one made any response to that, so Harry turned to Wiggins and asked if the airboat could tow the boats to Toke's village.

"Sure," Wiggins said. Then, turning to Mark, he asked, "You all want a tow home?"

Mark looked at his companions; and, when they nodded, he said, "Yes."

While Wiggins dug a coil of rope out of the locker behind the seats and attached it to an iron ring in the boat's transom, Harry called Jim Snyder's office and left word with the dispatcher that Toke Wylie had been found, and the men who had found him were taking him to Toke's village.

"How long will it take us to get to the village?" Harry asked Wiggins.

"An hour and a quarter, maybe," Wiggins said.

Harry passed the information to the dispatcher and told her that if possible the ME should be there to meet them with her crew because the scene of the crime was a boat and they were bringing it with them.

When the rope had been passed to each of the men in the front of the boats, Wiggins eased the airboat around and carefully pulled the rope taut. Then he slowly advanced the throttle until all the boats were sliding along behind the airboat comfortably. Once, Harry felt his cell vibrate but left it unanswered. The propeller was making it impossible to hear anything else.

While they slipped along, Harry thought about Toke Wylie's death and the fact that Toke probably knew whoever killed him. If he was killed in the boat, he almost certainly knew him. Why would anyone want to kill him? Was his murder connected with Rhinelander's death or was he killed for some entirely different reason?

By the time they reached the village, Harry had given up thinking about the cause of his death; and the anger flooded back, along with the bitter knowledge that a young man had been killed and Franklin and his brother and sister were left with no father and no mother.

14

"It would make my job a lot easier if you'd go out there with me." Frank Hodges said, trying to make his round face look worried. "You know some of them people, which is more than I do."

"I knew Toke a little, and I've met his brother," Harry said, waving Hodges onto the lanai. "I was just going to have some lunch. Want to join me?"

"Is it a salad?" Hodges asked.

"It can be."

"God, no," Hodges said, stamping into Harry's kitchen. "My wife's fed me so many greens in the past month my nose has taken to twitching, and I'm starting to hop."

Harry laughed.

"How about a beef sandwich?"

"That will do it."

"All right. I'll make some fresh coffee. Have a seat."

"You don't have to make the coffee on my account," he said quickly.

"No trouble," Harry said. "Are you making any progress with the Rhinelander case?"

Hodges sighed and sat down, dropping his hat on the chair beside him.

"The sheriff has released the body to the family," he said without enthusiasm. "We're picking at the edges of things. The immediate family's all been questioned about whereabouts and so on at the time of the disappearance. We got nothing there."

He blew out his cheeks.

"When you come down to it," he complained, "what have we got?" He began ticking items off on his fingers: "A swamp for a crime scene, no slugs for forensics to evaluate, no prints, no blood but Rhinelander's, no known witnesses. It's a desert."

"And everybody closely connected with Rhinelander has, apparently, an equally strong motive for killing her."

Harry put the sandwiches on the table.

"What's the greenery?" Hodges asked, staring at his sandwich suspiciously.

"Arugula," Harry said with a grin. "Try it. It's peppery, and here's some horseradish if you really like heat."

Hodges waved away the horseradish and bit into his sandwich.

"Mmm," he said, chewing and talking at the same time. "Now that's what I call a sandwich."

They ate for a while, Hodges carefully avoiding the coffee.

"Has Jim got any thoughts on Toke's killing?" Harry asked when they were done eating.

"He's worried about the fact he was shot in the back of the head," Hodges said, falling back from his plate with a groan of pleasure. "Kathleen Towers's guess is that she's going to find a twenty-two caliber slug in his head, probably fired at point-blank range."

"That pretty well eliminates suicide," Harry said, clearing the table.

"I think it's the possibility of its being a professional job that has the captain worried," Hodges replied, picking up his hat when Harry took his own down from its peg beside the door.

"What would a professional killer be doing with Toke in a johnboat on the eastern edge of the Stickpen?" Harry asked as they left the house but got no answer.

★ ★ ★ ★ ★

"I appreciate your coming out here with me," Hodges said as he parked the cruiser in front of the tribal administration building.

Harry had seldom seen Hodges so uneasy and assured him he was glad to do it because he had a personal interest in Toke's death. A very serious Henry David Wylie met them at the door.

"Hello, Harry," Wylie said, extending his hand.

"It's good to see you in a bad time," Harry said shaking his hand. "This is Sergeant Frank Hodges."

The two men shook hands.

"I've got Mark Crowley in my office," Wylie said, leading them into a waiting room and closing the door. "But before we get to him, and if it's all right with you, Sergeant, there's a few things I want to say."

"Let's hear them," Hodges told him after glancing at Harry, who gave Hodges an encouraging nod.

"There's two parts. The first part is that I'm doing this instead of Chief Thomas Black Wing, the Head of the Tribal Council. Because Toke is my brother, I have been asked to deal with the interviews and other contacts. The second part is, I recognize that the Tequesta County Sheriff's Department has law enforcement jurisdiction on the reservation, and I will do all I can to cooperate with your investigation."

Wylie paused and surprised Harry by seeming to be stymied as to how to go ahead. Hodges just waited, equally at a loss.

"I think there's a *but* coming," Harry said quickly with a smile. "Don't worry. Frank's heard a lot of *buts* in his career."

"All right," Wylie said. "The thing is, the reservation is in almost all other regards, excluding the law enforcement area, an independent nation. Some of our people resent the intrusion of government representatives from outside coming into our space without being invited."

"You saying I'm not welcome here?" Hodges asked, bristling.

"Henry David," Harry said, trading heavily on his earlier meeting. "Speaking as a person with no official connection with the sheriff's department, I've known Sergeant Hodges and Captain Jim Snyder for many years, please believe me when I tell you neither of them nor any of their staff will be anything but respectful of your prerogatives."

Turning to Hodges, Harry said, "Would you agree with me, Frank?"

"Yes," Hodges said to Wylie with no trace of hostility, obviously welcoming Harry's remarks, "and just so everyone understands that our job here is to find out who killed your brother if we can."

"Good," Wylie said, his voice growing a bit lighter. "What I want to get you ready for is the possibility that Mark Crowley and the rest of those men who found Toke may not be as cooperative as you would like when you start questioning them."

"That won't be nothing new," Hodges said, managing a laugh.

Wylie nodded, still poker-faced.

"I suppose that's true," he said. "What I'm leading up to is a request," he continued, speaking more quickly and with more assurance now, "I think things would go a lot better if I could be present while you're questioning them."

"I don't know if that would be possible," Hodges said.

"Would you feel better asking Captain Snyder?" Harry asked.

"I guess I would. I'm not sure I could go ahead here on my own."

Harry already had his cell out and was punching in a number. When it rang, he passed the phone to Hodges. It took a few minutes to get him on the line, but once he heard what Hodges had to say, he gave his permission at once.

"We can do it," Hodges said to Wylie with relief. "And he wants Harry sitting in as well if that's all right with you."

"Good," Wylie said. "Now, let's go to my office and get started."

On the way, Harry asked Wylie about Franklin and where he was staying, fearing that the boy had insisted on staying in his house.

"He and his brother and sister are with me and my wife. It wasn't easy, but we finally managed to convince him by saying it would be what his father wanted."

"That's the best news I've heard so far," Harry said, much relieved.

Mark Crowley, dressed in dungarees, a blue work shirt, and beaded moccasins, stood up when Wylie strode into the office, followed by Hodges and Harry. He was a big man, taller than the other three with long, black hair pulled back from his lean face in a ponytail, but it was his hazel eyes, deeply flecked with gold, that caught Harry's attention. Set off by his dark face and black hair, they seemed to burn with an inner light and gave his stare a startling intensity.

Wylie introduced him to Hodges and Harry, but Crowley did not offer to shake hands with them. If he recognized Harry, he gave no indication that he did. Harry was not surprised. Of the six men in the boats only Crowley had spoken, and he had said very little. At the time Harry recalled thinking that it was indifference rather than hostility that characterized their response to the two white men, but perhaps he had been mistaken.

"If you're willing, Mr. Crowley," Hodges said in a business-like manner, taking a small sound recorder out of his pocket, "I'm going to ask you some questions concerning your finding Tocqueville Wylie, and I'm going to record it."

Then he paused to give Crowley a chance to respond. The man nodded.

"I'll need a small stand or something to put this recorder on," he told Wylie, who placed one of his Hopi pots on the desk

143

and placed its stand in the center of the circle made by the four men.

"Let's pull up the chairs and sit," Wylie said.

When they were settled, Hodges turned on the recorder, placed it on the stand and gave his name and rank, the date and location, the name of the person being interviewed, and the names of the other men in the room.

"Mr. Crowley," Hodges said, "please state your full name and address."

Crowley did in a heavy, sullen voice.

Hodges then asked Crowley to describe the events that led up to him and his companions finding Wylie's body. Crowley answered briefly and clearly. Harry began to relax, and he noticed that Henry David was beginning to lean back in his chair when Hodges hit a wall.

"Did you and Toke have any connections beyond knowing one another?"

Crowley didn't reply, and Hodges tried again.

"Did you and Tocqueville Wylie have any business dealings or any other activities in which you and he were involved together?"

Crowley sat silent and stonefaced. After a few moments Henry David said quietly, "It would be a good thing, Mark, to answer Sergeant Hodges's question."

Crowley only shook his head.

Harry held his breath because he was sure that Hodges was going to tell Crowley he could either answer the question here or at police headquarters, but instead, to Harry's surprise, he leaned forward and said he was interrupting the recording briefly and turned off the recorder. Then he sat back and waited.

"Mark," Henry David said in the same quiet voice. "I want someone's killer found. Do you?"

Crowley nodded.

"I think it would help to answer the sergeant's question,"

Henry David said.

Crowley made no response. The room fell silent except for the beeping of a delivery truck backing up somewhere near the building.

"Mr. Crowley," Hodges asked suddenly, "are you concerned that answering that question might put you in some kind of jeopardy?"

"Maybe," Crowley said after looking at Henry David and receiving a nod.

"The recorder's off for now. We could talk about what it is that's bothering you."

"No," Crowley said.

"Could I say something?" Harry asked, including both Henry David and Hodges in the question, and got an affirmative response from both men.

"I suggest that the sergeant ask Mr. Crowley if he knows of any activities that Toke Wylie was engaged in that might have led to his being murdered without asking if Mr. Crowley was in any way involved."

Hodges picked up the recorder, switched it on, and talked his way through the formalities of reopening the interrogation. Then, addressing Crowley, he converted what Harry had said into a question. Crowley turned to Henry David and waited.

"I think you should tell what you know," Henry David told him.

"Crowley just says, 'someone,' and never mentions Toke Wylie's name," Jim said in disgust when the tape was finished.

Harry and Hodges were in Jim's office after returning from the interview. Harry had tried to beg off, but Hodges said he needed Harry, to get him over the rough places.

"I know it's weird, but you can tell who he's talking about from my questions," Hodges said defensively.

"I don't think Dillard is going to buy that," Jim retorted, his ears getting red.

"The reason Crowley wouldn't mention Toke Wylie's name," Harry put in, "is that Crowley is what Henry David calls a traditional. Crowley follows the belief system of the pre-conquest people, and in some of those systems it was and is considered not only bad manners but extremely dangerous to name a dead person. Naming a dead person might invoke the spirit, which could do you great harm."

"I suppose if we needed him, Wylie would testify to that, which might do it," Jim responded, partially mollified.

"The point here is that if Crowley was telling the truth, Toke was messing with some bad shit."

To Harry's disgust, their discussion was derailed again by Jim's telling Hodges that he knew better than to use that kind of language in the office and not to do it again or he'd be slapped with a demerit.

"Alligator hides, probably drugs, and what is likely to be much more important to you," Harry said, addressing Jim, "he had been doing something for some white man that involved trips into the Stickpen."

"But Crowley couldn't or wouldn't tell us anything about the man," Hodges said, "or what the trips involved."

"He said he'd never seen him," Harry said, "which might be true because I thought Henry David helped Hodges pump Crowley pretty dry."

"You're thinking that man Crowley mentioned had something to do with Lilly Rhinelander's death," Jim said.

"It's a possibility," Harry said.

"I'm living among dreamers and people who believe in ghosts," Jim said, throwing up his hands.

"Do the best you can with what you've got where you are," Harry said solemnly, making Jim's ears light up.

Then he asked, "Where's Toke's johnboat?"

"The Evidence Section's got it. Why?" Jim said a little testily.

"I'm not sure. It just came into my mind."

"It's like having an itch I can't scratch," Harry told Tucker, gathering up their tools.

He and the old farmer had just finished putting split bamboo frames around a dozen young tomato plants and were making their way to the barn by way of the bee hives, which were Harry's least popular part of Tucker's farm.

"And all you know is that it has something to do with Toke and his boat," Tucker said, moving confidently toward the six white hives, set in the partial shade of a small gathering of pink oleander bushes, just coming into bloom.

Harry hung well back and tried to ignore with little success the bees zipping around him on their way to and from the busy hives.

"That's about it," he told Tucker, who had left the unused bundle of bamboo with Harry and was lifting the tops off the hives, indifferent to the buzzing cloud of bees rising around him.

"They look healthy," he told Harry glumly, returning to gather up the stakes, "but so did all the other hives I've lost, until their bees began disappearing."

"Is there a chance that the colony collapse disorder is winding down?"

"It's too soon to know. All we're sure of is that there's a group of insecticides and miticides commonly used in fruit orchards that are proving deadly to bees. So probably there's a bunch of manmade chemicals contributing to the problem. These six hives are all that's left of the thirty I was tending five years ago."

"What's kept these safe?" Harry asked.

"I think it's because these bees gather pollen almost entirely from my orchard," Tucker replied, "which I don't spray, and from the wildflowers on the Puc Puggy's floodplain that must be at least ninety percent free of those poisons."

They stored in the barn the leftover stakes, twine, and hammers they had used to put up the frames and walked toward the house.

"How is Cooper getting along with the Rhinelanders?" Tucker asked.

Harry wasn't surprised by Tucker's swift change of subject. He knew the old farmer, stoical as he was, could not talk long about the loss of his bees because the possibility that anything as altogether marvelous as bees should be placed in danger of extinction from human actions caused him profound pain.

"It's hard to say. Judge Rankin has been assigned the task of sorting through the complications of Cooper's filings and will eventually rule on them."

"What are the odds that she will find in his favor?"

Their walk took them past the henhouse where Longstreet and his hens were busily scratching in their run. At their appearance the big gray and white bird raced to the fence and greeted them with a lusty crow, which brought all the hens to instant attention.

"He gets bigger every time I see him," Harry said.

"He fluffs himself up a little when company comes," Tucker said, digging into a pocket and tossing half a handful of dried corn through the fence.

Longstreet instantly called his hens and strutted around in a lordly manner as they crowded in to gobble the corn.

"I'm not sure this fence is up to keeping those coyotes away from Longstreet and his hens," Tucker said in a worried voice.

As he and Harry walked on, he added with a chuckle, "I'm not sure the contents of Fort Knox would be safe from their predations if they happened on it and smelled hens inside. Now, what about the judge?"

"I think Rankin will allow him to go ahead," Harry said. "How could anyone resist saying yes to the request, knowing what was going to follow?"

"You're particularly playful this morning."

"It's all a false front," Harry said. "I'm really all wound up trying to find some way of determining whether or not Toke Wylie was mixed up with the Rhinelander killing."

"I've thought a little about it," Tucker said, "and what I've thought of won't make you feel any better. Of course, you may have thought the same thing."

"Which is?"

"Franklin," Tucker said, pausing to let a glistening black rat snake cross the path and slip into the ferns.

"I've been trying not to think of him," Harry said, "but you've seen that there's a good chance he knows something, if not all or even most, of what his father's been up to. How could he not? Henry David told me Toke frequently kept the boy out of school to be with him."

"Does Henry David know what a bad spot that puts the boy in?"

They had stopped beside the back stoop to talk.

"I'm not sure what he knows, but it was clear to Hodges and me that Mark Crowley and probably the rest of the men who had been with him on the morning they found Toke knew more about Toke than Crowley told us in Henry David's office."

"Are you going to try to talk with the boy?" Tucker asked.

Harry made an unhappy face.

"Not right away. I don't know enough, and Henry David will not allow me or anyone else to question Franklin until he's convinced he can't stop it from happening."

"Come in and have some coffee. I think there might be some

149

of that carrot cake left that Doreen brought me the last time she was here."

Harry laughed. "You know, you must have done something outstanding in your previous life. There isn't a woman who knows you who wouldn't walk naked through a raspberry patch if you needed her to, and no," he added reluctantly, "I can't stay even for Doreen's carrot cake. My time's not my own. By the way, has Jane Bunting come back?"

"Not yet."

"Well, cats are supposed to have nine lives," Harry said, trying for a light tone that collapsed during the delivery.

Tucker nodded, then said, "Just remember, you've got only one."

15

Harry met Cooper at the Ritz Grill for lunch.

"I'm not as hungry as I thought I was," Harry said, putting down the menu.

Cooper, looking buffed and cheerful in his white shorts and dark orange short-sleeved silk shirt, laughed and said, "Not to worry, Harry, you're my guest. Eat anything you want."

"My appetite is restored," Harry said, retrieving the menu. "Actually, if you hadn't picked up the bill, I was going to stick you for it anyway."

Cooper found the comeback amusing, which led Harry to mentally shake his head and admit that he was no closer to understanding his client than he had been on the day they met.

"When do you expect to hear from Judge Rankin?" he asked after they had ordered.

"Possibly today," Cooper said.

"I'm surprised," Harry said. "Things are about to get a lot more interesting."

"Yes," Cooper replied calmly and with a ready smile, "and that leads me to ask how the investigation into my mother's murder is developing."

It was a question that Harry knew he was going to have to begin answering with increasing circumspection and decided now was the time to say so. He felt uncomfortable doing it because no matter how he framed the statement, buried in it would be the implication that Cooper was himself a suspect. On

151

the other hand, if he wasn't straightforward with the man across the table from him, a man he was coming to like and one who could, under different circumstances, easily become a friend, he would be dishonest, something he was determined not to be, not with this man.

"I can't answer you fully, Adrian," he said, keeping his voice as light as he could, "because at least some of what I know is privileged; and I came by it while working with the sheriff's department."

"I see," Cooper said, losing his smile.

"Here's what I can tell you," Harry continued, not wishing to become apologetic. "The man who found Rhinelander has been killed. He was a Hierba Alto Indian by the name of Toke Wylie. So far, the police have no suspects. Also, and this you may already know, Rhinelander's body has been released to her family."

"Yes, I do know that," Cooper said, still somewhat somber. "I have not been invited to whatever services and ceremonies the family has planned."

"Did you expect to be?"

"She is my mother. I have as much right to attend the final formalities as the rest of her family."

Cooper sounded both hurt and offended, but Harry saw no way to commiserate with him and even found Cooper's statement annoying. How could the man have expected the family to acknowledge him as her son?

"You do know, don't you, Adrian," Harry said, "that the family is going to fight your claim tooth and nail?"

"I'm quite prepared for that," Cooper replied as though the question had nothing to do with his earlier comments.

"Good. Have you heard anything further from the state attorney's office?"

'No," Cooper said, showing no interest.

You will, Harry told himself and prepared to the give the waiter his order.

Harry's copy of the *Avola Banner,* which Tucker had once called, "the local mullet wrapper," came with his mail. Midmorning the next day, taking a break from his report writing, he walked out to the road and paused to lean on the bridge railings and glance through the paper. Tucked discreetly away from anything of general interest was a small notice, announcing that a memorial service for Lilly Rhinelander would be held in St. Jude's Episcopal Church the following day. No mention of the internment was included.

When he reached home, he called Cooper and told him about the service and where to find St. Jude's.

"If there's to be a committal service, it's not mentioned. Will you go to the church service?"

"Certainly," Cooper replied, "and I'm sure someone at the funeral service will tell me where she's being buried."

"It is almost a certainty that she will be cremated," Harry said.

"No matter," Cooper responded. "I'll be there."

But he wasn't. As Harry learned from Jennifer Fortunato about an hour after it happened, Cooper was summoned to the state attorney's office the following morning, and transferred from there by two sheriff's deputies to police headquarters where a rigorous interrogation was begun.

"I'm not going to say much, Harry," Jennifer told him. "Harley made the decision very quickly."

"Who got to him?"

"I assume his decision was based on sound police procedure," she began, but Harry interrupted her.

"Jennifer," he said, "you're talking to me. Nothing you tell me is going anywhere unless you say otherwise."

There was a pause, a short sigh, and then she spoke again.

"OK, I think it was the governor who made the biggest stink, but he had a lot of help from Pearson and company. I had no idea how much clout the Rhinelander family carries. Its tentacles are everywhere."

"No surprises there," Harry said. "Has he had an opportunity to call his attorneys?"

"The CID people doing the interrogating have been told to postpone that as long as possible."

"Because once a lawyer steps into that room, he's going to stop what's happening."

"You're right, but if we make a breakthrough, it will be worth bending things a bit."

She sounded a little defiant, and Harry understood why.

"Harley and you may find yourselves being wrung out over this," he told her. "There isn't a smidgen of real evidence against Adrian Cooper. This charade is being put on to get the political pressure off your backs."

"In part," she countered, "no, mostly, but there's always the chance we might get lucky."

"Don't say I didn't tell you," Harry said, preparing to hang up.

"Harry, wait," Jennifer said in a softer tone of voice. "For the rest of this week, I'm totally fogged in with work; but then I'm carving out time for myself. Let me take you to dinner."

"Lucky me," he said. "What works for you?"

"Tuesday night?"

"Done. It's really very generous of you. I'll look forward to it."

"So will I."

Before calling Cooper's attorneys, Harry wondered what he was letting himself in for by fostering this relationship with someone already engaged to another man. More to the point, why was she encouraging it? What did he want from it, aside from the pleasure of a desirable woman's company? What did she want? He found it less uncomfortable to puzzle over the last question than to make an honest effort to answer the one before it because to do that, he would have to confront his own loneliness.

An hour later Cooper called Harry and asked to see him. He was at the Ritz.

"I want to thank you for coming to my aid," Cooper said.

They were in the lounge bar, and Cooper had finished his single malt in one go and was signaling urgently for a refill. Harry had never seen him so ruffled. His speech had lost most of its rotundities, and he was restless and out of sorts, shifting around on his chair and unable to find a comfortable place for his hands. He ordered another drink as soon as his second arrived.

"It was mostly politics," Harry said, both concerned and amused.

It occurred to him that being put in a cruiser and left to stew in the interrogation room for some period of time, denied access to a phone, not given any clear explanation of why he was being questioned, and hectored by a team of unsympathetic, plainclothes CID officers had stripped Cooper of his sense of control.

"I'm considering taking legal action against the county," Cooper said gruffly.

"I think you would be wasting your time and money," Harry said.

"They had no right . . . ," Cooper began but Harry interrupted him.

"Wait," Harry said. "Were you handcuffed?"

Cooper's face darkened into a scowl, which cleared with his answer.

"No, that was one indignity to which I was not subjected."

"Did you ever ask if you were going to be charged with any crime?"

"No."

"Too bad. Were you charged with anything and read your rights?"

"No."

"Then you could have left any time you wanted to. No one would have tried to stop you."

Cooper smiled at Harry.

"My God, Harry," he said, "don't you see why I couldn't do that? As far as I know, I haven't committed a crime. I certainly didn't kill my mother. Walking away would have suggested I had something to hide."

"Let's not argue. Instead, let's get some good out of what happened to you, aside from this whiskey," Harry said raising his glass, "which is way above my pay grade."

"Have another," Cooper said, waving in a waiter.

For the next half hour Harry grilled Cooper about the questions he had been asked and the answers he had given. When Harry was satisfied he had heard it all, Cooper said, "You're worse than those police officers when it comes to asking questions. What did you learn?"

"That the police have no idea who killed Lilly Rhinelander, but they are now assuming that it was done by someone close to her." Harry hesitated, looking for the best and least alarming way to say it. "They have nothing to link you to the crime, but you are definitely a person of interest."

Cooper had been nursing his third drink. Now he emptied

his glass and set it gently back on the table.

"I didn't kill her, Harry," he said quietly.

"Harry, you can't just take her out, buy her corn, beans, and chicken, dump her on the steps of Salvamento, and then ride off to the Hammock," Rowena Farnham said, her face growing pink with suppressed impatience. "Couldn't you see how wasted she is?"

Harry and Rowena were seated in Rowena's office. He had not heard from her about Rhinelander and had come to ask about her survey of the congregation. Instead, he was defending himself against charges of neglecting Soñadora and ruffled by the charges.

"What am I supposed to do with her, Rowena?" Harry protested, striving for an injured tone. "The woman will hardly talk to me. Getting her away from Salvamento is harder than pulling teeth. And when I do manage to take her out, she insists on eating subsistence-level food in places so strapped there's not even any air-conditioning."

"Are you finished?" Rowena asked when Harry paused for breath.

"Finished what?"

"Feeling sorry for yourself and giving lame excuses for neglecting that poor girl."

"That's not fair. She's no longer a girl, and I can't help it if she doesn't want anything to do with me."

"Good Lord, Harry," Rowena said, shifting irritably in her chair. "The woman's in love with you and has been for a long time."

"Oh yes!" Harry fired back, "and so is Queen Elizabeth."

"I can't speak for Her Highness," Rowena said, exploding in laughter.

"Did Soñadora tell you she was in love with me?" Harry

asked, not believing Rowena but still intrigued.

"Of course not. She hasn't even told herself yet and won't unless you break through that wall she's built around her heart."

"I see. She loves me and that's why she married Langston Pearson."

"I doubt it's that simple because I've already told you she doesn't know she loves you, or, at least, won't admit it."

"Then why did she marry Pearson?"

"She didn't love him, which made him safe; and you didn't offer to make an honest woman of her."

Harry suddenly felt gloom gathering around him like a cold fog.

"She didn't need me to make her an honest woman."

Rowena's expression changed to one of profound astonishment.

"Are you telling me . . . ?"

"Yes, and I don't want to talk about it."

"Well, you *idiots*," Rowena said, shaking her head and giving Harry an angry look. "No wonder she married that sociopath Pearson. What on earth is wrong with you?"

"It's probably congenital but not communicable," Harry said, becoming angry for reasons he refused to try to identify. "Can we talk about Lilly Rhinelander?"

"Of course," Rowena said, leaning over and patting Harry's knee, a gesture he interpreted as expressing pity and affection for someone a couple of bricks short of a full step.

For the next several minutes Rowena gave a précis of what she had learned. It added up, Harry thought, to a minimalist portrait of a woman consumed by selfishness, greed, arrogance, and chilling vindictiveness.

"Pretty," he said when Rowena stopped speaking.

"The term *bitch* came up frequently," Rowena said with a straight face. "I must say, by the time I had made my last call, I was deeply saddened."

Harry nodded, but he had been listening with only half his mind to the account. With the rest, he had been thinking about what Rowena had said about Soñadora.

"Maybe someone in your congregation killed her," he said.

"I retain my Christian charity with difficulty."

"Rowena, what did you mean by calling Soñadora and me idiots for not having slept together?"

Rowena sat for a few moments studying her hands, folded in her spacious lap.

"I'm sorry," she said at last, looking up with a sad expression. "I overstepped myself. I hope you'll forgive me."

"I will if you'll answer my question."

"All right. Perhaps I owe you that although I should change hats before going on."

"Feel free," Harry said.

Rowena smiled, and Harry saw both warmth and mischief in her glance.

"You know," she said a bit more seriously, "you are like a pair of waifs who have been knocking around the world alone too long."

"That doesn't help," he said.

"I know," she said with a sigh. "You've both lost the capacity for trust."

"What does trust have to do with having sex?"

"I'll forgive you that bit of stupidity, which was, I *trust,* spoken in haste. But let me answer you. Unless you are either a cretin or a moral degenerate, you would not willingly enter into a sexual relationship with someone without trusting both yourself and the other person."

"What does that say about Soñadora?"

"And Pearson?"

"Yes."

"Simple. She didn't love him and made the terrible mistake of trusting him before she really knew him."

"A sexual attraction," he said coldly.

"I doubt it. Men and women in about equal numbers make deals with the devil and don't find out until it's too late that only one of them was acting in good faith. And that's all I'm going to say on the subject. If you want to go into it further, I can recommend a good therapist, not that I think it's a suggestion either of you is likely to follow up on."

Harry wasn't sure he fully understood what Rowena had just said, but he was certain that for now it was all the clarity he wanted. Her suggestion that he see a therapist scarcely registered.

16

Randall Pearson had called while Harry had been talking to Rowena, and once back in the Rover, Harry returned the call. Pearson went straight to the point.

"Against my best judgment, Harry, the three principal heirs want a meeting with Cooper as soon as possible," he said in a strained voice. "I know it's irregular, and you're free to refuse, but they want you to attend. Are you willing to do that?"

Harry was very surprised by Pearson's agreeing to such a meeting.

"If you think it's a bad idea, Randall, why not refuse to convene it?" Harry asked, suspicious without being sure why.

"I was outvoted by my partners," Pearson answered with poorly suppressed bitterness.

"Never kill the golden goose," Harry said. "Why do you want me there?"

"To keep an eye on Cooper. His attorneys will look out for his legal interests, but my guess is that they don't know him, not nearly as well as you do."

Harry was puzzled.

"I still don't see . . ."

"Well, I haven't said what I really want to say," Pearson admitted, "and it's this: I think it's somewhere between possible and probable that he murdered Lilly Rhinelander. Putting him in a room with John Kringle, Evie Kronsky, and Michael Rhinelander could be like tossing a lighted match into a can of gasoline."

"*Pace* the bit about his being a murderer, Randall. I think your desk is more likely to break up your meeting than Adrian Cooper. I'll come; but being serious for a minute, I think John Kringle is much closer to exploding than Cooper. When I last talked to him, Kringle was strung tighter than a bowstring."

Sounding offended, Pearson quickly gave Harry the date and time of the meeting, thanked him brusquely, and hung up.

"Lawyers," Harry said, still smiling and thinking he wouldn't miss that meeting for a case of the scotch he and Cooper had been drinking at the Ritz.

As amused as Harry was by Pearson's concern, it didn't keep him from thinking about his talk with Rowena; and he gave that conversation some serious attention. By the time he drove over the hump-backed bridge onto the Hammock, he had persuaded himself that Rowena was wrong in thinking Soñadora was in love with him and equally wrong in suggesting that he was overly defended against emotional involvement with women. In fact, he thought himself far too susceptible.

As for the charge that not having had sex with Soñadora was a proof of his having unresolved emotional limitations where she was concerned, he rejected it completely, although he thought that much of what Rowena had said was true of Soñadora.

With most of the afternoon still before him after he had put away the groceries he had bought on the way home, Harry decided it was time he took a look at the north section of the Hammock, to see if the coyotes, whose tracks Tucker had seen around his henhouse, had been just passing through or had moved onto the Hammock. But even as he went about getting his gear together, he kept on thinking about what Rowena had said about Soñadora's looking ill and unhappy and decided he would have to do something to help. He was surprised by the jump his spirits took at the thought of seeing her again.

Unfortunately, before he could call her, a police cruiser eased into his yard.

"I was out this way and took a chance on finding you home," Jim Snyder called, unfolding his long frame from the driver's seat and striding toward Harry, who was holding open the lanai door.

"You hungry or thirsty?" Harry asked, when Jim stepped onto the lanai.

"No, and I can't stay, but there's something I want to talk about with you."

"Is it about you and Kathleen?" Harry asked, instantly concerned.

"No, and I wish you'd stop saying things like that. You'll be having me worried next."

"Fair enough," Harry said. "What is on your mind?"

"It's Franklin Wylie," Jim said, folding himself into one of the white cedar lounge chairs.

"Has anything happened to him?"

"Not that I know of, but I can't help thinking the boy might be able to help me to find out what Toke was doing in that part of the Stickpen on the morning he showed up at your place to report finding Rhinelander's body."

Harry savored his relief for a moment before speaking.

"Fillmore Wiggins wondered to me if there was any chance Toke had put the body there," he said, not wanting it to be true, "and then reported on it to throw off suspicion."

"In which case, Franklin would have to know what had happened," Jim said.

"Maybe," Harry replied, "but either I don't believe Toke had anything to do with her death or I don't want to so much I

163

can't believe it. I think Fillmore's suggestion is too convoluted. What would Toke have gained? Who besides his son could have known he was even in the Stickpen? Even his brother didn't know where he was most of the time."

"Maybe especially his brother," Jim said, shoving his long legs out in front of him.

Harry was surprised by the comment. Jim was seldom cynical.

"But my people have questioned administrators in every airport in the county," Jim continued. "None of them reports any helicopter traffic in or out of their airports on the night of Rhinelander's death. No deputy on night patrol anywhere in the vicinity of the Stickpen can recall hearing a helicopter anywhere around the swamp."

Frowning out at the sun-drenched yard, he stopped speaking and waited for Harry's response.

"Which means you don't believe Rhinelander was dumped in the Stickpen from a helicopter," Harry said, hating what was coming next.

Jim nodded.

"That leaves us with airboats and johnboats, and we've talked with every person in the area who owns an airboat and come up dry."

"Have you tried the reservation?" Harry asked. "There must be half a dozen at least out there."

"I haven't mastered the bureaucratic structure of their government, but the airboats are all in the hands of the two outfits that offer airboat rides. Frank Hodges says they have twenty-four-hour security on the boats."

"It's at least possible that someone was bribed," Harry said.

"We'll have to look into that, of course, but what brings me out here, disturbing your tranquility, is a request."

"Let me guess," Harry said with a sinking heart. "You want

me to go to Henry David Wylie and persuade him to let you talk to Franklin."

"That's it," Jim said, springing to his feet. "I want to talk to the boy. I want you and his uncle present, but at least until this mess is cleaned up and whoever killed her is found, I don't want anyone outside of you, me, Wiley, and Franklin to know the conversation took place."

"I'm thinking Franklin and his uncle are a lot more interested in finding out who killed Toke than in solving Rhinelander's murder," Harry said.

"That's true," Jim answered.

They were silent for a moment.

"However," Harry said as if there had been no pause, "if Toke was involved in Rhinelander's death, finding who killed her will tell us who killed him."

"That's my thought," Jim said. "Will you do it?"

"He may not let me near Franklin," Harry said. "If I was in his place, I don't think I would."

"But you'll try?" Jim asked.

"Yes," Harry said, "because if our speculations are true, the boy is in grave danger, and I want Henry David to know it."

As soon as Jim left, Harry forced himself to stop thinking about Franklin Wylie and called Soñadora, determined to find out if she really was as unhappy as Rowena thought, and if she was, why he hadn't seen it when they were last together.

"It's me," he said when she answered.

"And who is *me?*" she asked in an icy voice.

"Father Christmas," he said, stung as always by her harshness.

"Idiot," she said.

Harry immediately felt better.

"I want you to do something for me," he said.

"Is this one of your childish jokes?"

"In the next twenty minutes," he told her, ignoring her question, "I want you put on some clothes you won't mind getting dirty. Then I'll pick you up and drive you back here where we will take a walk and see a bunch of interesting things."

"Do you think I can just stop working at a moment's notice to take a walk?"

That question was not so encouraging, but Harry did not intend to lose this one.

"Yes, and it is not at a moment's notice. You have twenty minutes. Check your watch. You're wasting time. I'll be there in twenty minutes."

"What do you want me to do?"

"I'll tell you once we're here."

He hung up. It was a gamble, but one he thought she'd let him win. Before he left the house, he took two ham steaks out of the freezer and stood for a while, staring into the refrigerator. He made a stop at a Publix on his way to pick her up.

His gamble succeeded. When he entered the Salvamento driveway, she was sitting on the steps, dressed in dark slacks and a white, sleeveless blouse. Her hair was braided and coiled around her head.

In a burst of gallantry, Hodges had once said she looked like an Indian queen. Harry thought, watching her walk toward the Rover, that Hodges had gotten it just about right. She was beautiful, but with his eyes sharpened by Rowena's criticisms of him, he had to admit that she was thin. And good bones or not, her face was pale and drawn. Although she walked with a regal stride and straight back, no one would have mistaken her for a happy woman.

"Well, you've got me," she said, breaking the silence as they were leaving Salvamento. "What are you going to do with me?"

He reached into his shirt pocket and gave her two root beer

barrels, wrapped in cellophane.

"First, we're going to have one of these," he said.

"I don't . . ." she began.

"One of the things I want you to do for me is to suck on a root beer barrel while we drive, unwrap one for me so that we can both have one, and then talk to me."

"That's three things," she said but was unwrapping the beer barrels as she spoke.

"Thank you," he said, popping the candy into his mouth. "Now tell me something about your day that pleased you."

"It's almost over," she said, resting her head against the back of the seat.

Harry chanced a look at her. Usually, when he did that while he was driving, she would tell him to keep his eyes on the road, that she didn't want to die in something as ridiculous as a silver Range Rover. This time he escaped censure because she was sitting with her eyes closed, the candy making a bulge in her cheek.

She looked worn out, but looking at her still made him smile.

Now, if the rest of this afternoon goes right . . . , he thought.

"Stop staring at me and look where you're going," she said, glancing at him from under her long, black eyelashes and shutting her eyes again.

When judging Soñadora's state of mind, Harry attended more to how she said things than to what she said. The comment scored *Encouraging* on his mood meter.

"Have I ever told you about Jane Bunting?" he asked.

"Who's she?" she demanded coldly, opening her eyes.

"She's very interesting," Harry said, "and if you like the type, very beautiful."

"What type is that, and is she someone you've just met?" Soñadora demanded.

"I'd say fiercely independent. I met her several months ago."

"Where?"

"At Tucker's place."

"I don't really care, and it's none of my business, but why am I just hearing about her?"

By this time Soñadora was sitting upright and turned toward Harry.

"I thought I'd mentioned her. It's odd I haven't told you about her."

"Is this a serious relationship?" she asked sharply.

"It's an on-and-off thing. She's been missing for a couple of weeks. Tucker's worried about her."

"Aren't you?" Soñadora demanded, her eyes wide.

"No," Harry said, shaking his head, "cats come and go."

"Cats!" Soñadora burst out. "Is Jane Bunting a cat?"

"Yes, a Maine coon cat. Gorgeous animal, but fierce."

"You wretch!" Soñadora exclaimed, taking her root beer barrel out of her mouth. "You did that on purpose. You deliberately misled me."

At that moment she abandoned English for Quiche and burned Harry's ears for a while. He had no trouble understanding the gist of what she was saying. When she was finished, she popped the candy back into her mouth and, turning away, refused to speak to him until they were crossing the bridge onto the Hammock. At that moment one of the small swamp deer trotted across the road in front of them, followed by two tiny fawns, still in their spotted coats. Harry stopped to let them pass.

"Oh, Harry," Soñadora said in a wondering voice, leaning forward, "they are exquisite."

The three animals paused briefly to study the strange creature on the bridge, then disappeared into the tall ferns beside the road.

"I did not know that deer were so small," Soñadora said when they were gone, "or so beautiful."

"They're Virginia white-tail deer," Harry said. "In the states north of us, they're much larger."

"Why?" she asked.

Harry gave himself a point for awakening her interest.

"Mammals like deer and bears tend to be larger in the coldest parts of their range and smallest in the warmest. It's more efficient to be large if you're living where it's cold, and the other way around here in the subtropics."

She made no response but went on staring after the deer. Between the bridge and Harry's house, Harry stopped for a gopher tortoise and a six-foot indigo snake to cross the road. Soñadora had seen gopher tortoises on the Salvamento grounds, but the shining dark indigo snake both fascinated and frightened her.

"It is huge," she said, a little uneasily. "Is it poisonous?"

"No," Harry told her. "They're a treasure because aside from being beautiful they help to control the rodent population."

While he was talking, the snake, apparently liking the sunny heat of the sand, lowered its head and prepared for a nap.

"I'll just chase him out of the road so that we can pass," Harry told her, freeing himself from his seatbelt and pushing open the door.

"Don't shoot it!" she said, her voice rising in alarm.

"Come out with me," he said, motioning her toward him. "You will be glad you did. Come on."

With considerable hesitation, Soñadora joined Harry in front of the Rover and walked slowly with him toward the snake.

"What will he do?" she asked in a whisper.

"Probably nothing," Harry said, "and you don't have to whisper. Snakes are deaf."

"I know that," she said.

"Then why were you whispering?" he asked her.

By now they were standing about five feet from the snake

that was paying them no attention.

"Because I think one should speak softly around anything this big and this beautiful," she said. "I didn't know such a creature existed."

He started to say, *Leaving out the size factor, I could say the same about you,* then suppressed the impulse.

"I'm sorry, snake," he said, "but we have to pass."

Stepping forward, he stirred the snake with the toe of his sandal. The snake raised his head about level with Harry's thigh and turned to examine whatever it was that was annoying him, the sun flashing off his deep blue scales and its tongue flickering in and out of its mouth.

"Can you see its eyes?" Harry asked, resting his hands on his knees to study the snake more closely.

Soñadora came to stand beside him.

"I don't like them," she said, "but they are as strange as the rest of him."

Harry said, "Very few people do. What do you feel, meeting that gaze?"

"A chill," she said.

"Yes," Harry agreed. "I think it's because a snake's eyes convey no warmth, express no recognition, look at us from another world."

With that, Harry gave the snake's thick body a gentle but significant push.

"Get going." This time the snake responded with a convulsive ripple of its muscles that sent it slithering away so suddenly it made Soñadora gasp and jump back.

Ten minutes later Harry emerged from a downstairs closet and passed Soñadora a pair of white women's tennis shoes.

"Try these," he said. "They belong to Minna, but she won't mind your wearing them. By now she will have outgrown them."

"I could just wear my sandals," Soñadora protested.

"Not where we're going," Harry said.

"When I was a girl . . ." she began, but Harry stopped her.

"You've been off that mountain a long time."

Still complaining, she sat down on the floor and pulled them on.

"They fit," she said in surprise.

Walking, pausing, looking, surrounded by the myriad sounds of insect choirs and fiddling legions, Soñadora looked and listened with more and more intensity the deeper they penetrated into the forest. Harry let her set their pace, answering questions when she asked them, except when there was something he did not want her to miss, such as the female opossum giving three of her babies a piggyback while she quietly hunted for grubs between the roots of a huge ficus.

After a while they came to the edge of a shallow, bowl-shaped clearing that was dry now and covered with grass and vines but which would be a small pond as the wet season advanced.

"Let's sit down here for a few minutes," he said.

"I'm not tired," she told him.

"Good," he said, having noticed that what little wind there was blew across the opening towards them, "but let's rest a bit anyway."

"If you'd like to," she said.

The spot he had chosen in the thick shade gave them a good view of the opening, which was filled with the late, slanting sunlight.

"It is beautiful," she said very quietly and with a sigh after they had been sitting for while in a companionable silence. "I almost wish I could stay here forever."

"Almost?" Harry asked, also quietly.

He was gratified to see that some of the worry lines had been smoothed from her face and relieved to hear her speaking softly and calmly, even though there was a tinge of sadness in her voice.

"There is so much that I must do," she replied.

"Later," he said gently. "For now you can look and listen and let your mind rest."

She surprised him by smiling and saying, "All right."

A moment later, Harry saw two animals, resembling dogs, with yellowish brown backs shot through with streaks of darker rust step into the clearing almost directly in front of him and Soñadora. It happened so suddenly and silently that the two creatures with large, pointed ears and long, narrow snouts might have materialized out of the sunlight glinting on their coats.

Soñadora, Harry realized, had not yet seen them. He turned his head very slowly and whispered close to her ear, "Don't move or make a sound, but directly in front of you are two coyotes."

He had just finished speaking when the animals separated and, ears cocked, eyes on the grass, began a stealthy search for mice in the grass, stopping every few steps to listen for a tell-tale rustle. A moment later a vagary in the fitful wind carried the scent of the two humans into the bowl. The coyotes' heads shot up. For an instant they froze, sniffing the wind, and then they were gone as swiftly and silently as they had arrived.

Soñadora grasped her face in both hands and, eyes wide, turned to Harry with a look of wonder. Harry grinned with pleasure. Suddenly, she threw her arms around his neck and hugged him, saying over and over, "Thank you, thank you, thank you."

"You were wearing your lucky sneakers today," Harry said, hugging her back and laughing.

When she released him, she was blushing, but her face was still lit by a smile.

"They were wonderful," she said, obviously delighted by what she had seen.

"You've got a friend somewhere," Harry said, getting to his feet and holding out a hand to her. "There are hunters who have spent years in the woods without seeing one."

She took his hand—another first, Harry thought—and rose gracefully.

"Have you seen them before?" she asked.

"No. They've just moved onto the Hammock. The other day Tucker saw their tracks around his henhouse for the first time."

"Do they eat chickens?" she asked as she and Harry began retracing their steps.

"They will eat almost anything. It makes them difficult neighbors," Harry said. "Tucker's afraid they may have killed Jane Bunting."

"A little earlier," Soñadora said with an embarrassed laugh, "I would have liked to kill her. Is she actually in any danger?"

"Not if she's near a tree when they find her," he said. "If she's not, they will kill her."

"It is sad that anything that lovely are killers," she said.

Harry said something about all animals having to eat. She made no response, and they went on in silence with the shadows growing longer as the sun slid toward the horizon.

They were nearly home when she asked, "Why did you tell me that story about Jane Bunting?"

Harry turned and let her overtake him and went on beside her.

"If I hurt your feelings, I'm sorry," he said. "I wanted to make you laugh."

"Bad joke," she said and slapped her arm. "Mosquitoes. Are we nearly there?"

"Yes, are you hungry?"

"A little. I'm afraid you are going to have a late dinner. You still have to drive me home."

"Not until you've eaten the dinner I have planned."

"Harry," she said sharply, "you know I don't like . . ."

"We're dining in. There'll be just you, me, and Jane Bunting if she drops by."

He braced himself for an argument, but instead she asked, "Why are you doing this?"

"Because I want to," he said, "and because it will give me a great deal of pleasure."

They stepped out of the woods into the cleared area behind Harry's house. She took his hand just long enough to say, "If you burn anything, you will be very sorry," then hurried on ahead.

17

Dinner went well, except for the coffee, which had to be made twice, Soñadora supervising the second brewing. Harry found it very disconcerting to have her in the kitchen with him. She, to his surprise, seemed quite at ease, insisting on helping him prepare the dinner but allowing him to choose the things for her to do.

At one point, lifting plates down from the cupboard, she happened to look out the window and saw the moon coming up over the Puc Puggy, spreading its silver light over the front yard.

"The last time I was here, there was a beautiful moon like that," she said.

"Yes," Harry said, "and while we were walking toward the house, you were shot." He suppressed a shudder. "And all because I helped the police free some women from a gang of human traffickers."

"Yes," she said, still looking out the window, "but I prefer to remember how lovely the trees were with the moon in their branches."

"You saved my life," Harry said, pausing to look at her. "That bullet was meant for me."

"I'm glad I was there," she said and went to the table with the plates.

"Should I say, 'So am I.' or should I say, 'I wish you hadn't been'?"

She laughed.

"Since we are both still here, although there were times when I thought we might not be, you might as well say, 'So am I.' "

"When you slumped against me," Harry said, "I was terrified that I had lost you."

"You couldn't lose me, Harry," she said. "I couldn't even sit up, much less wander away."

Harry found himself floundering for a moment, the implication of his words breaking in on him.

"I meant I was afraid you had been killed."

It was her turn to be confused.

"An idiom?" she asked.

"Yes," he said quickly, "an idiom."

"As if something treasured might have been taken away?" she asked, coloring slightly.

"Yes," he said, "it could mean that."

The timer rang.

"Everything's ready," he said gratefully.

When they sat down, they talked of other things.

At ten the next morning, Harry drove to Avola to attend the meeting Randall Pearson had called against his better judgment. Ever since taking Soñadora home the night before, Harry had been in low spirits, despite the fact the evening had gone much better than he expected. They had talked freely and even laughed occasionally. At her insistence they had cleaned up after dinner, working together comfortably. When they left, she became quiet; but, he reminded himself, she was often quiet.

Harry was particularly dissatisfied with how they said goodnight. They got to the door of Salvamento and seemed to stick, unable to either stay or go. They kept saying they had enjoyed the evening and stood like a couple of tongue-tied kids. Soñadora finally broke the impasse by grasping his hands, kissing him quickly on the cheek, saying, "Goodnight," and slipping through the door.

He drove home feeling like the Ancient Mariner, alone on a wide, wide sea of self-loathing and recrimination. But why? Had she given him any indication she wanted more from him? Had he offered her more? He had wanted to but couldn't. She was not to be trifled with. She was much too fragile, much too easily hurt.

Somewhere, however, Rowena's voice was whispering, "Idiot, idiot," and that was the cause of his dissatisfaction; but he clung grimly to his story, all the while feeling a fool.

The meeting was held in a large conference room with framed and lighted paintings of yachts and schooners, aslant in the wind, sails bellied, and spray flying. Reminders, Harry thought, that while the pain of divorces, paternity suits, falling stock prices, and testamentary disappointments was fleeting, the sea and its pleasures were eternal. All that was missing was a copy of *A Little Boat* on the gleaming cherry table.

"I think we're all here," Pearson said, shuffling some papers in front of him and trying to smile.

No one else made the effort, and Harry noticed that no one was looking at anyone else, except for Cooper, who was watching him with an amused expression. But Harry left Cooper with a nod and moved on to Felix Cochran, Cooper's attorney, a large, baggy, bald man with rimless glasses, who was bulging out of a tan suit so rumpled it might have been slept in, and who was sitting beside him.

"Cutting to the chase," Pearson began with an attempt at jocularity even more feeble than his smile, "the purpose of this meeting, called at the request of John, Evie, and Mike, is to seek a solution to Adrian's astonishing claim to be the natural son of the recently deceased Mrs. Lilly Rhinelander."

Cooper's attorney interrupted at that point to say in a harsh New York accent, "Counselor, I request that you address each of us by our last names preceded by Mr., Ms., Mrs., or whatever other forms of address are appropriate."

"Why?" demanded Rita Evgenie Kronsky before Pearson could respond.

Without being obvious about it, Harry had been studying her and trying to match the elegantly turned out, pale-haired, somewhat Slavic looking woman with cold blue eyes to the voice that had attacked him over the phone and, hearing the voice again, saw the connection.

"Your client, I think, Counselor," Cochran replied with a beefy laugh.

"Put a sock in it, Evie," John, her older brother snapped.

He and Michael were seated on each side of their sister, and Harry thought it likely that she needed at least two minders.

"It's an interesting question, Jack," Michael said with a sarcastic grin. "Let Randall answer it if Cochran can't."

"Won't, Mr. Rhinelander," Cochran responded.

Harry was wondering how far this would go when Pearson got himself together and, addressing the three acknowledged legatees, said, "Mr. Cochran's request is reasonable. Professional intercourse on the East Coast tends to be more formal than it is over here. I suggest we grant his request and move on."

Rita Evgenie went on looking like a wolf that wanted blood, but her brothers merely shrugged. Harry thought Pearson had handled the situation very well and leaned back in his chair, prepared for further fireworks. But he heard instead a quick summary by Pearson of why the meeting had been called and what he thought were the principal topics his clients wanted covered.

"The first," Pearson said, "goes to the heart of the matter. Put simply, why should Mr. Cooper's claim to being the natural child of the late Lilly Rhinelander be taken seriously? The second, so closely linked to the first that it will be difficult to address them separately, is what is it that Mr. Cooper wants, aside from being legally declared the son of Lilly Rhinelander?"

Pearson stopped speaking and the room fell silent until Cochran cleared his throat, pulled a handkerchief out of his jacket pocket and polished his glasses before wiping his forehead.

"Counselor, have you read the filing addressing the first issue that is before Judge Pauline Rankin in the Twenty-second District?"

Pearson said he had.

"Then you know she will either allow my client's claim to go forward or she won't. That's all we have to say on the subject."

"It's not enough," Rita Evgenie protested, her voice climbing. "This . . . this *person* appears out of nowhere and claims to be my mother's son, and it's all for the money. Even being the bitch that she was, you have only to look at him to know—"

"Whoa!" John shouted, rounding on his sister. "Lighten up! The world is full of scum bags. It's not personal."

"I'd say it was," Michael put in. "Nothing that woman did would surprise me, right down to fucking a—"

Pearson and Cochran were now both on their feet, shouting themselves. Rita Evgenie was talking at the top of her voice, and if Michael finished the sentence, Harry didn't hear it over the competing voices. But John and Michael must have begun to quarrel because in a momentary lull, Harry heard John, now also on his feet and pointing an accusing finger at Michael, say, "If you did anything but shag women on mountains and, when you're here, spend most of your days in that damned kayak, you might . . ."

Harry lost the rest because the exchange between Cochran and Pearson drowned it. Cooper, Harry noticed, was sitting calmly with that Buddha smile on his face watching the verbal fracas as if it had been staged for his amusement.

Kinley Roby

Harry was so disgusted that he had half risen from his chair. With a groan, Harry sank back in his chair. Cooper wanted him to stay. He would stay.

Once out of the meeting and in the Rover, Harry, feeling as though he had just left a practice session for living in hell, phoned Henry David Wylie.

"I've got something to ask you," he said when his call had been put through, "and I don't want to do it over the phone. Is there a time today you could see me?"

"An hour from now I will be free for a while," Wylie said.

"I'll be there."

Harry arrived a few minutes early and wandered out of the parking lot on a bleached crushed shell path that led into a small stand of Canary Island palms. Harry stepped out of the palms onto sand and saw stretching away to the horizon a vast expanse of saw grass and water, silent under a blazing sun. The sight never failed to awaken in Harry a sudden and overwhelming sense of having stepped into the presence of an enormous, sentient creature. For a moment he held his own breath, trying to hear its breathing.

"I come out here when I have been thinking too much."

Harry turned to find Wylie standing beside him. Harry thought he looked more worn and burdened than the first time they met and supposed Toke's death had been weighing on him.

"Imagine a few people, living on hammocks in chiki huts, in the midst of this vast space," Harry said.

"And no mosquito control except smoke from their fires," Wylie said with a dry chuckle.

The two men walked back through the palms and into the administration building.

"What do you have to ask me?" Wylie said when he and Harry were seated in his office.

Wylie took a deep breath and braced himself.

"This is difficult," Harry said. "I think I or someone from Jim Snyder's department has to talk with Franklin."

"Why?" Wylie asked, his expression hardening.

"Because if his father was involved in Lilly Rhinelander's death, it looks as though Franklin would have to know about it."

Harry then gave Wylie a limited look at how Jim had concluded that the body was taken into the Stickpen by boat.

"The captain's conclusions are all based on suppositions," Wylie said.

"Yes," Harry said, pushing his feet out and leaning back in his chair, "he knows that. It troubles him."

"What is Franklin supposed to have seen?"

"He was with Toke the morning Toke told me about finding Rhinelander's body. I think they had spent the night in the swamp, probably in the boat. If he saw anything, he might have seen Rhinelander's body being put into the water."

"From Toke's johnboat."

"Yes."

"Is it the captain's thinking, that Rhinelander was killed in another place and then brought here or somewhere near here and taken by Toke into the Stickpen?" Wylie asked, fiddling with a pen on his desk.

"Not necessarily," Harry said. "The body might have been picked up somewhere else."

"Where?"

Harry thought of saying Fillmore Wiggins's wharf and changed his mind.

"I don't know."

Wylie swung around in his chair to look out the window.

"Franklin is taking his father's death very hard," he said. "If it is not true, to ask him questions implying that his father was involved in that woman's death will do him a lot of harm."

"I'm afraid it might," Harry agreed. "But if he does know, it must be causing him a lot of pain and doing him a lot of damage. Telling someone about it might begin the healing process."

Harry was now where he least wanted to be, but he had to do what needed to be done.

"Henry David," Harry asked, "have you faced the fact that if Toke was involved in Lilly Rhinelander's death, and if he was killed to silence him, Franklin is now in grave danger?"

Wylie swung back to face Harry.

"Yes," he answered grimly, "I have thought of that; and it's keeping me awake at night; but before I give you an answer, I must talk with some people."

"Call me soon," Harry said. "Time is not our friend here, and the sheriff is pressuring Jim to show some progress with the case."

"I understand," Wylie said, rising with Harry to shake hands across the desk.

"I'm sorry about this, Henry David," Harry said as he was leaving. "I wish Franklin could have been spared."

Wylie, who accompanied Harry to the door, said, "Yes, so do I, and I am afraid for him."

As Harry drove away, he thought Wylie had reason to be afraid.

On his way home, Harry stopped to see Jim Snyder. He wanted to make his report in person rather than over the phone because he wanted Jim to give Wylie whatever time he needed to make up his mind.

"He's that boy's guardian or whatever they call it in the tribe," Jim said impatiently.

He was not happy with Harry and was not trying to hide it.

"How do we know he's not just putting us off?" he burst out

just as Harry was starting to speak.

"I'll be surprised if that boy doesn't vanish into the family of some member of the tribe who's living in Montana," Hodges added.

Harry grinned. Whenever Hodges wanted to evoke some remote place, he always named Montana. The sergeant had spent a winter there while he was in the army and the cold, the wind, and the emptiness had come to represent for him the grim and utter outer edge of the habitable world.

"I don't think Wylie's trying to put you off, Jim," Harry said seriously, "and I would bet the farm he wouldn't let that boy leave him for any reason," he added, glancing at Hodges. "It's one or two or three of the oldest, most respected members of the tribe that he wants to talk to. He wants Toke's killer found even more than we do."

"But we want to talk to the kid about Rhinelander's murder," Hodges put in, frowning his concern.

"That's right," Harry said, "but if he has to cooperate in catching her killer, to find who killed his brother, he'll do it."

"You seem very sure," Jim said, getting up to take a walk across his office and back, regarding Harry with a scowl.

"I suppose I am," Harry said. "I like Wylie. He's a good man. The only crack in my certainty comes from my knowing how much he wants to protect Franklin from any more pain. If he refuses to allow him to be questioned, it will be because he's concluded Franklin has nothing of use to tell us."

"What about the tribal elders?" Jim asked, dropping back into his chair.

Harry shook his head.

"He'll do what's expected of him—go to his base, so to speak—but in the end, he'll do what he thinks best."

"I'll give him three days. If I don't hear from him by then, I'll talk with Harley Dillard and start proceedings to have the boy made available."

"OK," Harry said, knowing when arguing with Jim was useless. "What else is happening?"

"We're trying to establish the place and time when every single person in the Rhinelander's house last saw her alive," Jim said. "It's been like pulling teeth."

"The staff is still so scared of her, dead or not," Hodges said, "they're afraid of saying anything. And aside from guests and family members, there are about a dozen full- and part-time people working in and around that house," Hodges complained.

"She must have had someone who took care of her social affairs," Harry said.

"That would be Doris Whitcombe," Jim said. "She's been a lot of help. In fact, we gave up talking to anyone on the staff without having her present."

"They're about as scared of her as they are of Rhinelander," Hodges said with a wide grin. "It also turns out there are big holes in Whitcombe's calendar," he added. "On the day Rhinelander disappeared, Whitcombe doesn't have anything recorded for her between about noon and seven o'clock."

"Only for that day?" Harry asked.

"No," Jim said, rubbing his head, an action Harry knew was a sure sign of stress. "According to Whitcombe, Rhinelander was secretive. So much so, that she often made appointments without telling Whitcombe and then criticizing her when she missed one."

"And she made a habit of disappearing for hours at a time without telling Whitcombe she was going," Hodges added. "The captain had to tell her about her meeting Cooper for lunch at the Ritz. I think her brain was a little fried."

"Did Lilly Rhinelander go home after talking with Cooper?" Harry asked.

Jim shook his head.

"Are the whereabouts of any other members of the family unaccounted for that afternoon and evening?" Harry asked.

"Michael was off kayaking," Hodges said. "At least that's his story."

"Ms. Kronsky was shopping and visiting galleries and making a point of not being recognized. She doesn't remember the names of the galleries. No one in those we've checked recognized her by her picture," Jim said, "and Mr. Kringle was in the Avola branch office of his broker and in his room working the phone and computer, dealing with Baker's Dozen business most of the afternoon and early evening."

"The broker confirmed his visit?" Harry put in.

"Yes," Hodges said, "but nobody on the staff remembers seeing him after lunch."

"Which isn't as bad as it sounds," Jim said, "because that house is big as a hotel, and each of the three has a suite and a private entrance. The grounds crew doesn't know anybody in the family."

18

"Evie, John, and Michael are all, at least theoretically, in play," Harry said.

"And none of them ate at home that night," Jennifer added, "and no one in any of the places where they ate can make an ID of them from their pictures. It's a mess."

The paused to think their own thoughts for a moment.

They were sitting at a linen-covered deck table in Waterside, a restaurant on the tidal end of the Seminole River. Harry turned to take in the candlelight glinting on their china and silverware and on the settings at the surrounding tables. Beyond the railing the black water, ruffled by the warm breeze, was making soft, wet sounds against the pilings and breaking the moonlight on the water into glittering flakes.

"Do you like it?" Jennifer asked, startling Harry, who had become lost in the dance of moon and water.

"Very much," he told her. "It's one of my favorite places in Avola. You really laid yourself out, Jennifer."

"Once in a while I get it right," she said, her smile slipping a little.

Harry caught the change and looked more closely at her. She was dressed in a black V-neck stretch satin dress that looked to Harry as if it had been designed for her. When he picked her up at her apartment, he had complimented her on it; and she had blushed like a schoolgirl, to Harry's delighted amusement.

"Don't laugh," she had protested. "It's nice to be told you're beautiful even if it isn't true."

"Cinderella at the ball didn't look half as good to the prince as you do to me," Harry replied.

"That's what I want to hear, Harry," she said as he handed her into the Rover.

"Did I just hear a note of bitterness in that comment?" Harry asked in response to what she had said about occasionally getting it right.

"Nothing serious," she said.

"Is Harley giving you grief?" he asked, guessing that Harley had nothing to do with it.

"Not really," she said. "It's just that I don't get told a lot that what I do pleases."

"Shame on them."

The wine came with a certain amount of flourish and panache that interrupted their conversation and gave Harry time to consider whether or not he wanted to pursue the subject. It might, he thought, be wiser, even kinder, not to; but he wanted to know why she was showing this much interest in him. Any information might help him to answer the question as well as help him to see where this thing of theirs was going.

"What shall we drink to?" she asked when they were left with their charged glasses.

"To you," Harry said without hesitation and raised his glass.

"No fair!" she said with a little cry of protest, then countered, "To us!"

They drank to that; and when he put his glass down, Harry said, "What exactly, Jennifer, is *us?*"

She didn't answer right away, but looked hard at him, frowning slightly, as if she was trying to read something written on his forehead—at least that was Harry's uneasy impression. She had lovely, large brown eyes, flecked with gold, made for candlelight;

but at the moment her stare was so intense, Harry found them disturbing.

"What do you want it to be, Harry?" she asked.

"The game begins," Harry said, waiting a moment to see if it caught.

It didn't. Her expression remained frozen.

"If you're getting married in a few months, Jennifer, what difference does it make what I want?"

He tried to keep the irritation he was feeling out of the question, but he apparently failed because she shoved back her chair and said, "Excuse me," and hurried away.

"Congratulations," Harry said aloud to his water glass. "Good work. Well done."

A waiter had been hovering a short distance from the table, and at the sound of Harry's voice hurried over and asked if there was something he wanted. Harry did not tell him, "To be born in a simpler time," but managed to send him away just as Jennifer came striding back, looking grim.

Harry stood up.

Seeing, despite her repairs, that she had been crying, he said as she sat down, "I'm sorry, I probably could have given a better answer."

The waiter appeared. Before he could ask if they wanted to order, Jennifer thrust her hand toward his face, without taking her eyes off Harry, her fingers spread in an unmistakable five.

"Certainly, Madame," he said, taking a step back. "There's no hurry. No hurry at all."

"Forget it," she said to Harry. "I had it coming, and these days I cry at weather reports."

Harry started to speak, but she cut him off.

"Another question: If I wasn't getting married, and we were where we are, and I asked you the same question, what would you say?"

Cat in the cellar with a no-hole mouse, Harry thought.

"As a rule," he said, determined to lighten the mood, "I don't answer hypothetical questions."

"Make this an exception," she said.

The waiter was hovering again.

"Let's order," Harry said. "It's either that or we'll have to ask him to join us."

"Coward," she said, picking up her menu.

That part of the ritual completed, Harry said, "Some history first. We have a little. I haven't forgotten any of it. It was pretty much all good. That said, with you in Jacksonville and me in Avola, how could anything be different?"

She shrugged.

"Work places are fungible."

"Not mine."

That was rough; but Harry thought that for her sake as well as his, this game, whatever it was, had better be ended before someone was hurt.

"Yours may not be, but mine is," she said, unfazed. "I said I wanted to move back here."

Harry tried another approach.

"Jennifer," he said more gently, "I want you as much as I did when we were together. You're behaving toward me as though you want me, even though you're engaged to be married in November to another man. It's making me crazy."

"My wanting you, or my marrying another man?"

A glimmer of mischief and something else had softened her eyes as well as her voice.

"Both," Harry said.

Their food came, and they ate and talked briefly about the Rhinelander case and then about Toke Wylie's murder, which Jennifer knew almost nothing about. Harry filled her in and found he wanted to talk about Franklin and Henry David. He thought often about the boy. Jennifer listened with interest and asked a lot of questions.

"A hermetic world," she remarked at one point.

"Especially for the traditionalists," he said; "but when I listen to Henry David, I sometimes get a glimpse of something spacious, like the sky they live under."

"Take me out there," she said. "I'd like to see it. Although I've driven across the Alley enough times on Harley's business to do it with my eyes closed, you make me think I've missed something."

"If Henry David decides we can talk to Franklin, maybe he'll let you participate," Harry said.

The dinner was excellent to the end, and Harry admitted that he had enjoyed it and Jennifer's company. The admission, he found, made him a little sad. Before he had time think about that, they were finished, and she had dealt with the check. They stood up.

"I liked that," she said to him with a smile.

"So did I," he replied.

"Good," she said, taking his arm. "My place is closer than yours."

The next morning, driving back to the Hammock, Harry diminished his self-esteem by trying to find an excuse for what he had just done several times, most recently in a green decision to shower together, which made Jennifer even later leaving for work than she was before they saved all that water. However, the brush with his conscience ended with a complacent smile as stirring images of Jennifer and their companionable night dispelled the boredom of his drive to the Hammock.

He had an appointment later in the morning with Cooper, but the day was so beautiful that rather than working on his reports, he chose the soft option of walking to Tucker's, to tell him about the coyotes.

"I suppose you've already eaten," Tucker said to Harry after shaking hands and receiving the formal greetings of a chest bump from Oh, Brother! and a grin from Sanchez.

"No, I haven't," Harry said. "I spent the night with Jennifer, and time ran out for her before we got to breakfast."

"You reek of boastfulness and smugness, not to mention indiscretion," Tucker said sternly, driving the garden fork he had been wielding into the ground and pointing Harry toward the house.

Once there, Harry was given a mug of steaming coffee and told to exercise the rocker while Tucker unlimbered the frying pan.

"I took Soñadora out to the north end of the Hammock the day before yesterday," he said, as Tucker put eggs and bacon on the stove and began mixing a batch of pancakes, "and while we were sitting down, we saw a pair of coyotes."

"Then they're here to stay," Tucker responded, checking the eggs and bacon and dropping pancake batter into a frying pan.

"They're youngsters, and my guess is that they are just setting up housekeeping," Harry responded. "Whatever their shortcomings as neighbors, they are handsome animals."

"You've got to admire them," Tucker admitted. "I lived for a while in northern New Mexico—that was many years ago—and guns, traps, poison, bounties, and the federal government's deadly force weren't enough to rid the country of them. I guess we'll find out what it's like to share the Hammock with this new family. You're not planning to shoot them are you?"

"I wouldn't think of it. There's nothing in my contract with the state that says I have to shoot coyotes."

"Now," Tucker said, "tell me how you came to allow yourself to start sleeping with an engaged woman."

If Tucker wasn't going to mention Jane Bunting, Harry

decided he wouldn't. He didn't want to address Tucker's question but saw no civil way to avoid it. Part of the challenge would be to answer the question to his own satisfaction, which up until now he had not even attempted.

"Attraction, deprivation, desperation, she wanted me to, the devil made me do it," he said, feeling moderately stupid as well as irritated.

"In other words," Tucker said, flipping a pancake, "you switched off that part of your brain that usually tells you to step out from under a falling tree."

"That's possible, but Jennifer and I go back a ways, Tucker," Harry said. "Being with her again feels, in some strange way, as if we never split up."

"Are you in love with her?" Tucker asked, bringing two loaded plates to the table.

Harry waited until they had both begun eating before answering because he had needed some time to think before answering.

"I could be," he said finally. "I think I was before she left Avola."

Tucker nodded and paused to drink some coffee.

"She's getting married in November?" he asked, setting down his mug.

Harry laughed, feeling no mirth.

"That's what she says."

"She's wearing a ring?"

"No, she's not."

"Interesting. Have you asked why not?"

"No, I haven't."

Harry could feel the gates closing.

"It might be a good place to start," Tucker said.

Harry found Cooper in his beach chair under a dark blue

192

umbrella, sharing his shade with a perfectly tanned woman with long, heavily streaked blonde hair. She was wearing designer sunglasses, a gold bracelet, a significant sapphire ring, lip gloss, and that was about it. Cooper was reading *The New York Times* and she, the *Wall Street Journal.* From the looks of the small tables beside them, they had just finished brunch.

"Are you homesick yet?" Harry asked Cooper.

Cooper looked up from his paper and took in the figure standing at his elbow, dressed in naturally faded denim shorts, sandals, a Tommy Bahama shirt of many colors, and his Tilley hat. A slow, comfortable smile spread across Cooper's face.

"Harry," he said in a welcoming voice, folding his paper, "are you aware that there are whole reaches of you that never left Maine?"

"Good shot," Harry said as Cooper came out of his chair with remarkable ease for a man of his size.

"Persephone," Cooper said turning to the woman, "I want you to meet Harry Brock. Harry this is Persephone Aristides."

She leaned out of her chair, pushed her glasses onto her head, revealing dark blue eyes and a flashing smile as well some lines at the outer corners of her eyes that told Harry that she was probably about Cooper's age, and thrust out her hand.

"Great hat, Harry," she said with apparent admiration. "Call me Sophie. It helps me to forget that I have to spend half the year in Hades."

Harry leaned across Cooper's chair and shook her hand. She had a strong grip.

"Thanks. I see you've been up long enough to get a great tan."

"The little bit you can't see is the same shade," she said, still smiling.

"I'm sure it looks just as good as the rest of you," he said, thoroughly enjoying himself.

It wasn't often he found someone who shared his sense of humor.

"Time!" Cooper said, making a T with his hands.

"Spoilsport," Sophie complained, getting to her feet. "I suppose you'll want to talk." She wrapped a Ritz beach towel around her waist and said to Harry with a straight face, "No thongs in the lobby."

"Their loss," Harry said.

"Sophie," Cooper said, raising his hand to stifle her response, "you stay. Harry and I will go inside, talk for a few minutes, and I'll come back."

"Bring Harry with you," she said, dropping back into her chair and picking up her paper.

"I want a cup of coffee," Cooper said, pulling on a blue silk robe as they walked up the ramp to the boardwalk. "Can I interest you in one?"

"Sure," Harry said.

Cooper led them into the circular beach restaurant and to a table beside an open window. The wall of the entire structure was constructed of windows, most of which were open. Large ceiling fans and the breeze off the Gulf were gently stirring the air, and the AC was holding the heat baking the roof at bay.

"She's an investment banker," Cooper said. "I met her about a week ago."

"Where's she from?"

"Chicago."

"Which accounts for the *Wall Street Journal*," Harry said.

Cooper nodded.

"How much have you told her?" Harry asked.

The waiter came and Cooper ordered their coffee.

"That I am the son of Lilly Rhinelander, and that I intend to establish my claim in law."

"Has she asked you a lot of questions?"

"Ah, I see. No, nothing beyond what one would expect someone interested in you would ask, given that information. You have a suspicious nature."

"Worse than that."

Their coffee came. While Cooper signed the chit, Harry looked around and saw that no one was seated close to them and that the general conversation and the noisy coming and going of the guests, drifting in and out from the beach, made it safe to talk.

"I advise you to be very, very careful with Sophie," he said, "until you've established beyond a doubt that she is who she says she is."

"Who else could she be?"

Cooper's smile was slightly sarcastic. Harry assumed he was approaching a line.

"Someone the Rhinelander tribe has hired to find out what it is you're up to."

Cooper laughed easily.

"I haven't exactly made it a secret."

"No one but you and, possibly, me believes your claim to be Lilly Rhinelander's son is anything but a stalking horse."

"I see, and you are not altogether sure you know what I want."

"Right, but I'm willing to give you the benefit of the doubt. They're not."

"Warnings and reservations noted. Is there anything else?"

"It's not the time for me to explain why I'm asking you this, Adrian," Harry said, "but can you recall from your last conversation with your mother whether or not she told you where she was going when you parted?"

Cooper thought for a while, sipped his coffee, looked out the window at the water, and finally said, "To the best of my recollection, she did not."

"Did you make any plans to meet again?"

Cooper shook his head.

"She always made those plans without consulting me."

Harry heard the resentment, not entirely masked by his calm response, in Cooper's answer.

"Am I the first person to ask these two questions?"

"I think so, but I was asked so many questions when I was interrogated, I could have forgotten."

"Listen to me, Adrian. Harley Dillard and the sheriff's people are running out of time," Harry said with some urgency. "They need to charge someone with Rhinelander's murder. As far as I can tell, they are becoming increasingly convinced that you were, as you originally suggested, the last person to talk with your mother before whatever was said between her and her killer; and your refusing to answer all of their questions makes you an increasingly attractive target."

"I'm not surprised, but what do you expect me to do about that?"

"Stop pretending that you can pick and choose what questions you'll answer and which you won't without incurring some very nasty consequences. For example, have you told your attorneys what you and your mother talked about over lunch?"

"No. Their task is to compel the legal system to recognize me as Lilly Rhinelander's natural child. I didn't kill her, and I refuse to be bullied or harassed by anyone into abandoning my goal."

He finished his coffee and stood up.

"Harry, I must return to Persephone. We have plans for the day. Thank you for your concern. Please go on working with Jennifer Fortunato and Jim Snyder on my behalf. I'm confident that if you don't give up, you will help them to discover who killed my mother."

With that he walked off.

"Is this man real?" Harry asked himself.

19

Henry David called Harry that afternoon.

"I've decided," he said, "that if Franklin tells the police what his father did on the day Rhinelander's body was found, it will help him to heal, make him feel that he has done all he can to find his father's killer."

"How is Franklin?" Harry asked.

"Not too good. He thinks he failed his father."

"By not being traditional enough?"

"That and not being there when his father needed him," Wylie said. "I guess Toke asked him if he wanted to go with him, and Franklin said he had school work and didn't want to miss school the next day."

"Well," Harry said, "it's a good thing he didn't go or he'd be dead too. I also think you've made the right decision even though you don't sound too happy with it."

"I'm not. For Franklin it may be what needs to be done. For the rest of us, it may not be."

"Why not?"

"Well, without trying to sound mysterious, when you throw a rock into the water, you do not know how far the ripples will travel."

"Are you concerned about what Franklin might say?"

There was a pause, and then Wylie said, "Let's talk about arrangements. How many people will Captain Snyder bring with him?"

"Possibly Sergeant Hodges, attorney Jennifer Fortunato from the state attorney's office, and me," Harry said at once.

"I do not want a lot of people questioning Franklin."

Harry was making some of this up as he went along, but he felt sure Jim would be happy with the arrangements.

"Unless you object, Jim will ask the questions. If anyone else has a question, it can be written down and given to Jim. I hope you plan to have your attorney present."

"Yes," Wylie said. "He will protect Franklin and the tribe's interests. I don't want Franklin questioned on matters that aren't connected with Toke's death."

"No fear," Harry said, knowing that the last thing Jim wanted was to be sidetracked from the murders he had on his hands.

"Good. Will you talk to Captain Snyder, Harry, and have one of his people get back to me with some possible dates and times?"

"I will, and I'm glad this is happening."

"Let's hope it helps Franklin."

Jim was pleased with Harry's report on his talk with Wylie, and they quickly settled on a time.

"We'll do this as soon as we can," Jim said. "I don't want him changing his mind."

"There's one more thing, Jim," Harry said. "Jennifer Fortunato wants to be there. She told me she wanted a glimpse of the place and the people, but I'm guessing she would like to hear what Franklin has to say."

"And Wylie knows about this?"

"He only said that he didn't want a lot of people questioning the boy. When I said you would do the questioning, he was satisfied. He even agreed to let us give you questions in writing."

"I suppose I could call Harley and make a fuss about having

Jennifer present, but I think I'd rather keep the peace than break it. No point in having the state attorney mad at me, but it's not like Harley to poke in this way."

Harry agreed but didn't say that he doubted that at this point Harley knew anything about it.

"By the way," Jim said with a grin, "there's a rumor around that you and Jennifer were at the Waterside the other night. Were you?"

"We were," Harry said as if it was the most natural thing in the world. "Have you and Kathleen eaten there? The food is excellent."

"Yes, we've been there a couple of times. The prices are way above where the buzzards circle."

"True," Harry said, congratulating himself for having avoided being cross-examined about Jennifer, but he had jumped from one hot spot to another.

"Kathleen and I were talking about you the other night," Jim went on, leaning back in his chair and lifting his feet onto the corner of his desk.

"That must have been a boring conversation," Harry said with an inward groan and abandoned all hope of a quick escape.

"Nope, in fact it was very interesting. It turns out we both thought that after Soñadora's divorce you and she would get back together, but it doesn't seem to have happened. What went wrong?"

"She and I were never together in the first place," Harry protested, surprised and shaken by Jim's remarks. "How in the world did you two ever get the idea we were?"

First Rowena Farnham and now Jim and Kathleen! He felt as if he'd had his cover blown when there wasn't anything to cover up. He was even beginning to feel offended by such a suggestion. Its coming from Jim only made it worse.

Jim appeared not to notice Harry's discomfort.

"Well," Jim said, "we both agreed you would make a really classy couple."

Then he seemed to lose interest in the subject because he dropped his feet back onto the floor and stood up, put his hands in his pockets, and said, looking down at Harry with a concerned expression, "Oh, I just remembered, Kathleen was in Tallahassee a couple of days ago at a meeting and was talking with a medical examiner from Jacksonville, a man she's known since they were graduate students at Florida State together; and he said that six months ago Jennifer Fortunato broke up with a man she'd been living with for some time and that three months later she had become engaged to somebody in the Florida Department of Business. He didn't have any more details. Kathleen wanted me to ask you if she'd said anything to you about it?"

"Not a word," Harry said, desperately wanting to escape. "Look, I've got to be going. I guess we're all going to drive ourselves to the reservation. I'll see you there."

The moment Harry reached the safety of the Rover and got his heart rate down to a moderate level and stopped wanting to throttle Jim, he dialed Jennifer's number.

"Hi," he said. "Are you where you can talk?"

"I can talk anywhere . . . well, as you know, sometimes and in certain situations I become a little incoherent and tend to repeat myself and call on God for support and succor and say 'Yes, yes, yes.' "

She laughed conspiratorially and said after a pause, "You're supposed to laugh. Why aren't you laughing?"

"I don't feel like laughing. Jim Snyder just told me that Kathleen Towers told him that in the past year you and someone you had been living with for some time broke up and that three months later you announced your engagement to someone working in the Florida Business Department. A month later you transferred down here and very recently you and I spent the night together."

The words had come pouring out of him, and he cut them off.

Silence. Then the click of her phone disconnecting. Harry began swearing and banged his head against the steering wheel, all the time calling himself all the names denoting stupidity, insensitivity, and reckless abandonment of sanity that he could muster under the stress of the moment.

That done, he called Jennifer back. When she did not answer, he left a message.

"Jennifer, I would like to take you out to dinner tonight. Please carry a gun. At a moment of your choosing when you are sick of watching me grovel, shoot me. It's the only decent thing to do. No jury in Tequesta County would convict you."

A few moments later, she returned his call, saying only in a graveyard voice, "Six-thirty. I'm cooking. I'm furious. Your wretched life hangs by a thread."

As one does while living under a sword, Harry passed the rest of the day, as Eliot describes the process, by taking in the milk and paying the rent.

It was not his best afternoon. Feeling as he did, he decided he might as well write insurance surveillance reports, reasoning that doing them could not possibly make him feel any worse. He was wrong. Not only did he feel bad for what he had said to Jennifer, he was also savagely bored as well. Nevertheless, he bent to the mind-crunching labor and then walked along the Puc Puggy, trying to decide what he was going to say to Jennifer.

Despite his dread of what would follow, he arrived at her door on time.

"Come in," she said, and immediately walked toward the

kitchen, leaving him to follow under his own recognizance.

Oddly, being in her presence calmed him; and, walking down the hall behind her, watching the aggressive swing of her hips, it came to him that he had wasted an afternoon wandering in abstractions. Thinking about Jennifer, he had not thought of this woman in front of him but of Jennifer The Insulted, who must be mollified, and of himself as The Offender, burdened with the task of making amends. Also, all that ratiocination had driven everything else from his mind. It was remarkable how badly the mind could behave.

Once in the kitchen, she turned and said, "You'll be lucky if you ever eat another meal, but this one will be outstanding."

The kitchen was small, but Harry liked kitchens, and this one was clean, bright, and smelled of home cooking.

"Good," he said, "I'm starved."

She was standing across the table from him, her hand resting on the back of her chair, and Harry thought that in her pale orange dress she looked very lovely and said so.

He had upgraded to trousers, tan, short-sleeved shirt, and loafers for the occasion.

"Where's your hat?" she asked, dimming his hopes for an early rapprochement.

"It was rocking on the lanai when I left," he said.

"Let's get this over with," she said, pulling out her chair. "Sit down."

They stared at each other across the table. It was very quiet.

"Jennifer," he said.

"Me first," she told him.

The cover on one of the pots on the stove began to rattle a little.

"Everything all right over there?" he asked, failing to quell his conviction that pots unwatched always boiled over, and her back was towards the stove.

"Yes," she said, her eyes remaining fixed on his. "Now listen up. I should have told you what happened to me, but even giving you that, you were really scummy when you called."

"Granted," Harry said. "Where's your engagement ring? Tucker said I should ask you that."

"Have you been talking to Tucker about me?"

"I didn't mention that thing with the pillows," he said.

She suddenly laughed and blushed.

"You're not still angry?"

"No."

He thought of saying, "It's none of my business," but, fortunately, thought better of it.

"It's in its box in a drawer in my bureau. Satisfied?"

He shook his head.

"You're thinking, *'Why?'* "

"Yes."

She got up, went to the refrigerator and came back with two glasses and a bottle of white wine and set them in front of him.

"You pour," she said. "If I'm going to answer that question, I'll need a drink."

"I'll probably join you," he said, picking up the bottle.

"When this one's gone, there's another," she told him.

For the next fifteen minutes, Jennifer talked, telling Harry, among other things, that she had not seen the breakup coming, had been crushed when she learned that he had been sleeping with another woman for months, and instead of being furious with him, had fallen into a paroxysm of guilt and self-loathing, blaming herself for what had happened—gaining weight, letting her grooming slip, working too many nights and weekends, the usual self-immolation. In a desperate attempt to regain some self-respect and save herself from complete collapse, she had gone looking for another man and found Alex Goodweather.

"Jesus," Harry said. "What a tangle."

"You could say that and worse," she said. "Now I'm waiting for two questions."

"Let me guess," Harry said. "Do you love him and what do want from me?"

"Ouch," she said making a face. "Right. Are you still hungry?"

Harry said he was; and as they ate, Jennifer tried to answer the first question, but Harry didn't think he knew much more when she had finished than when she began.

"Is there a *yes* or a *no* in there somewhere?" he asked.

She put down her fork and stared at her plate. Harry thought she was genuinely stuck.

"Here's what I think," he said, recharging their glasses. "Unless you're sleeping with me in order to get even with somebody for being screwed over the way you were, I don't think you love him."

"Could I possibly be that bad?" she asked, looking up, wide-eyed with shock at the thought.

"Just the opposite," he told her. "You're not getting even with anybody."

"Then why am I sleeping with you?"

"Because you like me? Because I make you feel wanted and attractive? Because I'm safe? Any port in a storm?"

She laughed, the anxiety falling away from her.

"Try this," she said. "I never stopped loving you, and when I came back to Avola and met you again, I came running home."

"To heal," he said, lifting his glass toward her. "Here's to healing."

They drank to it. Harry helped her clean up and put the dishes in the dishwasher. As they worked, they talked a little about the Rhinelander and the Wylie cases. Jennifer was pleased that she was going to sit in on Franklin's interrogation.

"I want you to do something for me," he said a little later.

"Do I have to take off my clothes?"

"Not yet."

He told her about Persephone Aristides and asked her to see if she could establish her identity.

When they had finished working, Jennifer reached out for Harry and kissed him.

"Is it time yet?" she asked.

Harry was slow and looked puzzled.

"To take my clothes off. God, Harry, what does a . . ."

Everything after that they did together.

On the morning that had been chosen for talking with Franklin Wylie, Harry picked Jennifer up at her office.

"A break from the routine," she said happily as she got into the Rover. "Is it all right to be happy?"

"Yes," he told her, pleased by her good cheer.

"Good," she said, "but I've got some news that may not be so good. I can't find this Persephone Aristides anywhere. You said she worked for an investment bank in Chicago, right?"

"That's what Cooper told me," Harry said experiencing a flare of concern. "She's staying at the Ritz, which means she's probably not flying coach."

"I didn't run her name through the flight records of people flying over the past three weeks from Chicago to Fort Myers. I'll do that, when I get back to the office."

"How many investment banks can there be in Chicago?" Harry asked.

"Around twenty," Jennifer replied with a little frown. "Her name doesn't show up on any of their personnel rosters. I don't suppose that has to be sinister. She may have her own reasons for not telling him where she lives or works or even what her real name is. She could be having a fling and doesn't want any follow-up."

"Is she registered at the hotel as Aristides?"

"Yes, she is," Jennifer said. "Her credit card checks out."

"That's something," Harry said, trying to bring the issue into a rational perspective. "Actually, I kind of like her. She has a quick mind and a bawdy sense of humor."

"That would do it," Jennifer said, showing a little edge.

"Or, she could be an assassin," Harry added, ignoring Jennifer's gambit.

"Harry," Jennifer protested, "you don't have any reason for thinking that."

"I suppose not," he replied, forcing his mind away from the subject of Aristides by turning to the work at hand. "I hope Franklin isn't too upset by this interrogation."

"Is he an especially sensitive child?"

"I don't think so, but he's being pulled at least three ways."

Jennifer had been watching the snow-white thunder heads piling up in front of them on the eastern horizon, but Harry's comment pulled her attention back into the car.

"Is he being harassed?" she asked, surprised.

"Not the way you mean," Harry said, "but he's somewhere between the Indian and the white worlds; and also between two kinds of Indian life."

"You've got to do better than that," she complained.

"Most of the people on the reservation have opted to partially integrate with the non-Indian world surrounding them. Each one does it in his own way and to the limits of his own tolerance, taking what he wants and rejecting the rest."

"Those who do that are being smart," Jennifer said, sounding to Harry a little dismissive.

"Perhaps it's not so simple as you're suggesting, but not all the Indians want that compromise—and there is some cultural compromise involved. Some want to live entirely separate from the rest of us or as near to that ideal as possible."

"They can't do it unless they've learned how to go back

several hundred years," Jennifer insisted, her face coloring a little from her feelings. "They are deceiving themselves if they think otherwise."

"Maybe. For Franklin it's probably more a matter of personal loyalty. Toke hadn't gone all the way back, which Mark Crowley has done."

"Didn't Sergeant Hodges interview Mark?"

"Yes, he was a friend of Toke's and a full traditionalist. Franklin knows him and, growing up, may have seen a lot of him."

"What about this Henry David?"

"Toke's brother, very integrated, wears his hair short, college educated, good administrator, very white collar. I gather there was considerable tension between him and Toke. He made it clear to me that he disapproved of Toke's keeping Franklin out of school."

"To do what?"

"That's what we hope Franklin will tell us."

Harry parked near the shell path, then walked with Jennifer through the palms and let her look out over the expanse of water and saw grass. For a few moments there were no sounds but those made by the wind in the palms and the swaying grass.

"It looks different from here," Jennifer said, turning away from the scene to look at Harry. "Driving, it's like a picture, but here . . ." She gave a little shiver. "You can almost believe it's breathing."

"Toke and Franklin used to spend whole days out there," Harry said, nodding toward the water. "Imagine how it felt to them."

"Scary and not for me," Jennifer said firmly, looking at her watch. "Come on, it's time."

A young woman in a black suit and white blouse greeted them when they entered the administration building.

"I'm Doris," she said. "You are Ms. Fortunato and Mr. Brock?"

Once that was confirmed, she said the others were in the conference room and led them down a long corridor to a large, bright room with tinted glass and decorated with Indian paintings, pottery, and a Navaho rug under a polished table of what Harry judged to be South American hardwood dense as granite.

Wylie shook hands with them and turned to the short, broad shouldered man beside him with his hair in a thick braid, dressed in light gray trousers and a blue blazer.

"This is our attorney Sam Birch," Wylie said.

He shook hands without smiling, and Jennifer gave Harry a 'what's his problem' glance.

"I knew Toke for years and never saw him smile. It's not unfriendliness," Harry told her quietly as they moved to their places at the table.

Before sitting down, Harry stopped to say hello to Franklin. The boy had had his hair trimmed and was dressed in shorts and blue shirt under a dark red windbreaker. Harry thought the boy's change in dress style was probably not voluntary.

"You doing all right?" Harry asked, shaking the boy's hand.

Franklin nodded after making fleeting eye contact. He's frightened, Harry thought, feeling guilty for being part of the reason the boy was being put through this grilling.

"You'll do fine," Harry said, giving Franklin's shoulder a light squeeze before moving on.

"Franklin," Wylie said, "we're going to start now. Captain Snyder is going to ask you some questions. If Mr. Birch doesn't tell you not to answer, it's all right to answer. Is that clear?"

Franklin nodded again.

"Good," Wylie said. "If you're ready, Captain."

Jim placed a recorder on the table halfway between himself and Franklin, who was seated across from him, and gave the date, time, and place where the interrogation was taking place and the names of those present.

"I want to begin by saying, Franklin," Jim began, "that every person in this room is your friend, and the questions I am going to ask you are being asked in the hope that your answers will help us to find the person who killed your father. Is it all right if I begin?"

Franklin nodded.

"Franklin," Wylie said quickly, "you have to say yes or no for the recorder."

"Yes," Franklin said.

"What is your full name?"

Franklin gave it.

"And Tocqueville Wylie was your father."

"He is my father," Franklin said with some spirit.

"Yes, of course he is," Jim said and then moved on to simple questions about the day he and his father found the body of Lilly Rhinelander. That all went smoothly, and Franklin, Harry noticed, began to speak more freely. Then Jim asked him what he and his father were doing in the Stickpen Preserve.

Franklin didn't answer. Instead, he found a spot on the wall behind Jim and made it his.

"Let's leave that for now," Jim said calmly and asked if he and his father had slept at home the night before they found Rhinelander's body.

Franklin shook his head.

"Franklin," Wylie said. "You have to say yes or no."

"No," the boy said.

"Where did you sleep?"

"In the boat."

"Did you often stay out all night with your father?"

"Now and then."

Harry thought he saw where this was going.

"What did you do the nights you were out?"

"Slept."

"Did you and your father meet anyone else the night before you found the body?"

Harry saw Wylie and Birch exchange glances, and Birch nodded.

"It's all right for you to answer the question, Franklin," Wylie said.

"No it's not!" the boy shouted, glaring at his uncle.

Jim said nothing and sat back, watching Wylie. Jennifer leaned over and whispered to Harry, "Five will get you ten that they did meet somebody, and his father told the boy not say anything about it."

Harry thought it was very likely. He tore a page from the small notebook in front of him, scribbled a note on it, and pushed it in front of Jim.

Jim glanced at the note and said to Franklin, "Did your father tell you not to say anything about what you did that night?"

"Yes," Franklin replied, shifting his attention to Jim.

Birch, who had seemed to Harry to be half asleep, stirred in his chair and said, "Captain, could you suspend these proceedings long enough for me to confer with my clients?"

Jim nodded, picked up the recorder, spoke into it briefly, and shut it off.

"Mr. Wylie, Franklin, and I," Birch said, rising, "we'll step outside for a few minutes if that's permissible."

"Yes," Jim said.

"I'd rather we didn't talk about what we've heard so far," Jim said once the three had left.

"It's all right with me, but I've got a question," Jennifer said. "Is there any other person Toke Wylie was close to out here besides his son?"

"Yes, his name is Mark Crowley," Harry responded. "As I

mentioned to you, he's a deep traditional. He spoke for the six men who found Toke, dead in his boat, the morning Fillmore Wiggins and I were out looking for Toke."

"I recall the name," Jennifer replied.

Just then Birch, Wylie, and Franklin came into the room.

"If we can stay off the record for a minute more, Captain," Birch said, "I'd like to clarify something."

"Go ahead," Jim said.

Birch nodded.

"I've learned from Mr. Wylie that in his and Mr. Brock's presence, Sergeant Hodges from your department questioned Mark Crowley, a tribal member, about his and some other unnamed male members of the tribe's having found Tocqueville Wylie's body."

"That's right," Jim replied, "but I don't see how that bears on this interrogation."

Harry saw Franklin flinch at the mention of his father's body and asked, "Does Franklin have to hear this?"

"I'm almost finished," Birch said. "I believe that in his responses, Mr. Crowley says that Tocqueville made trips into the Stickpen Preserve either with or on behalf of a white man. Mr. Crowley also alleged that Franklin's father had been engaged in unlawful activities involving the sale of alligator hides and drugs. Is that correct?"

By now Franklin was sitting leaned over the table, resting on his elbows, his hands over his ears, his nose nearly touching the table.

"I don't think it's right to put the boy through this," Harry protested, his anger rising.

Birch turned to Harry and said coldly, "I don't know what your role is here, Mr. Brock; but one thing I am sure of is that you're not here to tell me how to protect the interests of my clients."

"Henry David?" Harry asked.

"It's all right, Harry. I understand your concern, but Franklin has to know these things and has to learn to live with them. He can't be spared. He is bound to find out. I'd rather he learned them here among people who have his welfare in mind."

"All right," Harry replied, not thinking it was all right but knowing he had gone as far as he could.

"Could we get on with this, Mr. Birch?" Jim asked.

"Yes. I think you already have the information you need. I recommend that the interrogation be ended."

Jim turned to Wylie.

"I strongly disagree with your attorney's recommendation," Jim said. "Franklin may have more to say; and, at the very least, he may be able to confirm or deny what Mr. Crowley has said. If you instruct Franklin to refuse to answer any more of my questions, I will recommend to Deputy State Attorney Fortunato that her office seek remedy through the court to secure Franklin's testimony. In my view it would be far better for Franklin if he gave it here."

Wylie sat stone-faced for several moments. Then he said to Birch, "I want Franklin done with this part of the investigation into his father's death as soon as possible. If it's possible, I want it done here."

Birch looked like a thundercloud, but he said nothing and sat back in his chair, his arms folded.

Wylie turned to Jim.

"Captain," he said, "continue. Franklin, please sit up and answer the captain's questions as well as you can. It has to be done. The pain has to be borne. Are you ready to go on?"

The boy had pulled himself together and said, "Yes," in a strong voice.

In the next few minutes in response to Jim's questions, Franklin said that his father had gone into the Stickpen several times to meet someone. Franklin had asked once who he was, and his father said no one of importance. Franklin took that to mean that he was not an Indian. His father had not said what he did for the man, which was unusual because his father usually talked to him about what he was doing.

"Why didn't you ask him?" Jim asked.

"I saw that he did not want to talk about it."

"And he always went to see the man in his boat?"

"Yes."

"He left late in the afternoon when he went to see the man and came home after dark?"

"Yes."

"Is there anything else you want to tell me?"

"No."

Jim gave the time, said the interrogation was complete, and shut off the recorder.

"Well done, Franklin," Jennifer said to him, giving him a warm smile.

"Thank you," the boy said but he looked sad and very tired.

Jim thanked him and Wylie for their cooperation. Harry shook the boy's hand, congratulated him, and shook hands with Wylie.

Birch left without speaking to anyone.

Jim left soon after Birch, but Harry and Jennifer remained briefly to say a few words to Franklin and to his uncle.

"I hope he will be kept away from the rest of this investigation," Jennifer told Wylie.

"That we can agree on," Wylie replied, seeing her and Harry out the door.

"Walk with me down to water, Harry," she said when they reached the shell path. "There are times when I find my job very unpleasant. This was one of them."

They stood for a while without speaking, looking out over the great ocean of saw grass and water, the tall golden grass rippling gently in the breeze.

"Was it worth doing?" Jennifer asked at last, turning back toward the path.

"I don't know," Harry said. "Crowley claims never to have seen the person, and his calling him a white man is probably an assumption."

20

The phone dragged Harry out of a deep sleep. It was Jim Snyder.

"Harry, are you awake? Harry, it's Jim. Wake up!"

"The New York accent confused me," Harry said, struggling into a sitting position.

"Very funny. What comes next is not so funny. Adrian Cooper has been shot."

"Is he dead?"

"Not as of ten minutes ago, but from what I've been able to get out of the staff outside the operating room, he's critical."

"The lady from Hell!" Harry said, swearing colorfully.

"What?" Jim demanded.

"I'll explain later. Are you at the hospital?"

"Yes."

"I'm on my way."

When Harry reached the hospital, Cooper was still in the operating room. The two senior brain surgeons had been called in along with their assistants. That was all the duty nurse could tell him.

"He was apparently shot in the head," Harry told Jim when he found him in the waiting area. "Whether he was shot anywhere else, I can't find out."

"I sent Frank Hodges to interview the medical team that responded to the 911," Jim said, rubbing his hand over his face.

"You look fairly wasted," Harry said. "Are you sick?"

"Of not getting any sleep," Jim grumbled. "This is the third night this week that I've been rousted out of bed."

"Couldn't you pass this ambulance chasing off to someone else?" Harry asked.

"Don't go there! You sound like Kathleen. Now, tell me what you meant with that 'Lady from Hell' remark."

"Her name, or more probably one of her aliases, is Persephone Aristides. Cooper met her at the Ritz. From what Cooper told me, they have been seeing a lot of each other recently."

"What do you know about her?" Jim asked.

"Not very much. I persuaded Jennifer to do a background on her. Cooper told me she was an investment bank executive, living and working in Chicago."

Harry paused in his story to burst out, "I told him to watch himself. She's somewhere in her upper thirties, blonde, really attractive, stunning body, and a great sense of humor. I'm ashamed to say that, thanks to her sense of humor, I liked her right away."

"What did Jennifer find out?" Jim asked.

"None of her sources could turn up a Persephone Aristides on the Chicago investment bank payrolls."

"Didn't that do it for you?" Jim asked in obvious surprise.

"It should have, but Jennifer said Aristides was probably putting some icing on her holiday cake with Cooper and didn't want any follow-up. I told Cooper what I'd found or hadn't found, but he only laughed. I guess they were having too much fun for him to spend any time worrying."

"I hear you," Jim said ruefully. "It's just what Kathleen would have said and added that I was just being a worry wart. And, to be realistic, what could you have done?"

"Found out at once what name she was registered under at the hotel. Jennifer's checked on that, and she is registered under that name and her credit card is legitimate."

"What about the 'Lady from Hell' thing?" Jim asked.

"Don't you remember the Greek story of Demeter and her daughter Persephone?" Harry asked and, when Jim looked puzzled, went on to tell him the story of Hades, king of the underworld, carrying Persephone away to his dark kingdom to become his bride; Ceres, grief-stricken, stopped caring for the earth, letting it wither into its first winter, forcing the gods to intervene and make a deal with Hades, allowing Persephone to return to her mother, bringing spring with her, but after six months having to return to Hades for the other half of the year, leaving Ceres to mourn and the earth to wither again until her daughter's return.

"And, by God, that's the way it's been ever since," Hodges said solemnly, slapping his knee with his hand as the story ended.

"That's right," Harry said, "and if she shot Cooper, the bit about her spending half the year in the underworld is hair-raisingly appropriate."

There were several days when it was not clear whether Cooper would live or die or if he lived, whether or not he would regain consciousness. None of the doctors attending him held out much hope that even if he did regain consciousness he would be even remotely the man he had been. Harry visited him every day, sharing the room with a series of deputies which the sheriff had ordered to guard Cooper against a second assassination attempt; but after ten days Fisher ended the watch.

"Sheriff Fisher will tell you it's no longer needed," Jim said to Harry in response to Harry's call when he visited Cooper and found no deputy sitting outside his door, "but the real reason is the shortage of men and money."

Harry wanted to protest, but saw that it would be a waste of time. He had been looking in on Cooper every day and sitting a while with him. Twice, Harry found Jennifer sitting beside the silent figure in the bed.

"She was registered at the Ritz as Persephone Aristides," Jennifer said the first day they met. "But from there it's a dry well. Her credit card was issued by a bank in California, which has her address as a *poste restante* in Juarez, which is paid for by cash that is mailed in once a year. No mail, aside from her credit card bills, which the post office has been instructed to discard, has ever come for her. Her credit card is used for only a week or two, three to five times a year. Charges are paid by cashier's check."

"Sounds right," Harry said. "A professional."

"If he lives," Jennifer said, tilting her head at Cooper, "which looks more probable every day, Persephone is going to be in trouble, and we may get another crack at her."

Harry shook his head.

"She won't risk coming back here. She'll hire someone else to finish the job."

"Do you think she's checking to see if he's still alive?" Jennifer asked.

"Probably."

"She has a contact then?"

"Not necessarily," Harry said, seeing the futility of trying to locate her through phone calls, all undoubtedly made from call boxes and never from the same one twice.

Jennifer shrugged.

"It doesn't matter anyway," she told Harry dismissively. "There's no pressure to come up with the money and people it would take to try to chase her down. She left nothing in either her room or Cooper's, no prints, no DNA, nothing. She vanished."

"By the time she left Avola," Harry said, "I'll bet the farm she looked nothing like the woman I met on the Ritz beach."

"Safe bet. And anyway, I'm more interested in knowing who called for the execution."

"Unless there's something dire in Cooper's back story which has been overlooked, the one who made the call is probably in Avola," Harry said.

"And, unfortunately," Jennifer added glumly, "not necessarily the same person who killed Lilly."

Before she left, Jennifer told Harry she'd been called back to Jacksonville for a week or so, a case she had worked on was going to trial, and she was needed.

"Don't forget who I am while I'm away," she said, giving him a quick kiss on the way out the door.

Although he tried not to, he found himself wondering if he'd been lied to about why she was going back to Jacksonville. He also wondered if it mattered. Would she be seeing her fiancé? Would they sleep together? Would it be better not to park your antique roadster under a crow's nest?

While Harry waited for news of Cooper, he caught up on work he had been neglecting and, with his client comatose, found himself wondering how Soñadora was getting along.

"This has nothing to do with Jennifer's being gone," he told the barred owl that was hooting at the moon from one of the live oaks outside his bedroom window on another wakeful night.

It was the second or third time he had asked himself the same question that day; and now that he had come wide awake at three A.M., he had the thought again, this time accompanied by a bite from his conscience. The next morning he made up his mind to stop dithering and go and see her. So after having had breakfast with Tucker, shortly after sunrise, he drove into Avola.

"Have you been up all night?" she asked him after opening the Salvamento door in answer to his knock.

It was much too early for the organization to be open for business, but Harry knew she was an early riser.

"Go ahead," he said. "There must be more you want to say."

"Did you mistake this place for a soup kitchen, and if you did, we don't serve breakfast."

"How about coffee?"

"We can manage that. Come in."

"Who's *we?*" he asked with an unwelcome jolt of jealousy.

He throttled the feeling and stepped past her into Salvamento's work space, a large room with two walls lined with file cabinets and the center of the room occupied by a dozen work stations, each with computers and telephones.

"Who's *we?*" he forced himself to ask a second time.

"Me, myself, and I," she said, leading him across the room into a combination kitchen and rest area with a table and six chairs.

Scattered around the remaining space was a sofa, some overstuffed chairs, and a coffee table piled with Spanish language magazines. While she dealt with the coffeemaker, Harry had time to study her. Although she had obviously dressed with care in a long, blue, flaring skirt and freshly ironed white blouse, she looked tired. The smudges under her eyes, Harry thought, had become permanent, and her expression was somber. The thought of her living alone in this barn of a place saddened Harry and at the same time made him angry.

"Can't you find a place of your own to live in?" he asked as she brought him coffee in a bone china cup with a gold band around the rim and a matching saucer.

"This is my place," she told him.

"Do you sleep on the floor?"

The coffee was delicious, even better than his, he thought, and told her so.

She sat down opposite him at the table and, for the first time since he had arrived, smiled.

"Bread should be soaked in your coffee and placed in corners, to kill cockroaches," she said.

"What do you hear from your father?" he asked, no longer wanting to play the avoidance game with her.

"His housekeeper has written to say that his health has grown worse, and he cannot travel," she told him in a tight voice, avoiding his gaze.

She was sitting with folded hands resting on the edge of the table. The sun had reached the corner of one of the windows facing her, and a few of its rays were shining on her face, increasing its paleness. She looked so vulnerable in the harsh light that without thinking, he leaned across the table and squeezed her hands.

"I'm sorry," he said.

Then remembering what had happened the last time he held her hands, he snatched his hand away.

"What's wrong?" she demanded.

"I don't want to make you feel worse. What are you going to do?"

"Well, I'm not going to cry, if that's what you're thinking," she said angrily. "Or perhaps it's that you find it unpleasant to touch me."

"That's it!" Harry said loudly, pushing back from the table and jumping to his feet.

He marched around the table and, reaching her, said, "Stand up."

"Harry!" she said, staring at him in some alarm.

But she got up, leaving the chair between them. He snatched the chair aside, and, striding forward, said, "Put up your arms like this."

His held his arms out toward her as if he was going to embrace a barrel. She did.

"Good," he said, and instantly walked right between them and embraced her.

"Now, you do what I'm doing," he said.

"What are you doing?" she demanded, sounding puzzled and a little afraid, but she tightened arms around him.

Harry didn't answer her but held her against him. After a moment, she relaxed against him, at the same time tightening her grip on him.

"Are you going to tell me what you're doing?" she asked, looking up at him.

"Waiting for you to apologize, and you may as well know that I'm ready to do this all morning."

"Well, I'm not," she snapped. "Let me go."

"Do I really have to?" he asked.

She stopped struggling.

"Whatever the silly thing is you're doing, my neck is getting stiff," she said and leaned her head against his shoulder.

Harry found holding her very pleasant and something more. She might be thin, he thought, but she's not thin everywhere. As soon as he thought that, he realized that he couldn't go on doing this long, no matter what he'd told her.

"Do you still think I can't bear to touch you?" he asked her, pressing his face against her head.

"No," she said in a whisper, and for an instant, pressed herself against him before loosening her hold.

He let her go and stepped back.

"Now look what you've done," she said, trying to glare at him and failing.

Tears were running down her cheeks.

"Your shirt is all wet, and it serves you right."

"I'll never wash it again," Harry said.

"Idiot!" she said, running to pull a tissue out of a box on the sideboard.

When she had wiped her eyes and blown her nose, she came back to the table and said, "Your coffee's cold."

"I know," he said. "What are you going to do about your father?"

She emptied their cups and refilled them.

"I don't know. Sit down. There is something Ernesto Piedra wanted me to tell you."

Piedra was a longtime friend of Harry's and in his eyes a kind of Hispanic Robin Hood. He was also a cat burglar by trade, visiting the homes of the wealthy by night and working at part-time jobs during the days. He was a strikingly handsome man with a thick shock of curly black hair and soulful brown eyes.

He did not get much sleep. Women adored him, and he adored them with the result that he was the father of many children with many mothers. He referred to the children as his *responsibilidads,* and to their mothers more solemnly as *las Madres.* He contributed heavily to the support of all of them, called on them frequently to ask how they were, with the result that his *responsibilidads* increased.

"How is he?" Harry asked with a grin.

Soñadora colored slightly. "Tired," she said, trying to smother a laugh. "But what he told me is not so amusing. He told me that he had heard that the woman who shot Adrian Cooper was a hired killer and that another such person, a man, had come into Avola sometime in the past three days."

"Did he know anything more about this second hit man?" Harry asked.

"No," Soñadora replied, "but I remembered your saying that the murder of an Indian on the reservation might be connected to the Rhinelander woman's death. Two days ago an undocumented Hispanic woman from the reservation came into Salvamento with a four-year-old daughter, asking for shelter. She is the wife of an Indian. She had recently overheard him talking to another man about a murder. When her husband discovered she had overheard the conversation, he threatened to cut her up and feed her to the alligators if she said anything to anyone about it, including her priest."

"What's her name?" Harry asked.

"Harry, you know better than to ask me that."

"I know you protect their identities, but people are being killed. I'm trying to stop it, and I need every scrap of information I can cobble together."

"Carla Rodriguez," she said after a pause, "but she would not tell me her husband's name or say anything about him except that he was a traditional and very harsh and that she was terrified of him and decided to leave."

"Did you know that Tocqueville Wylie, the man who found Lilly Rhinelander, was an Indian?" Harry asked.

"Yes. He was killed, isn't that so?"

"That's right, and his body was found by Mark Crowley and five other Indians. Crowley is a traditional. Is the woman still with you?"

"No, she's in a safe house. A traditional is one who follows the old ways?"

"Yes. Could you find out if her husband's name is Crowley?"

Soñadora shook her head and said firmly, "No. It is our policy not to ask those who come to us any questions about their background beyond what they are willing to tell us, especially those who are at risk in the way she considers herself to be."

"Sounds right to me," Harry said, thinking that he could find out from Henry David if Crowley's wife had left him.

The front door opened, and the voices of women interrupted his thoughts.

"Your working day begins," he said, getting to his feet. "Thanks for the coffee."

When they came out of the kitchen together, there was a flurry of racy comments from the women, mostly in Spanish; and a chorus of ribald laughter accompanied them to the door where they did a worse job of saying goodbye than they had the last time and ended up shaking hands, which embarrassed both of them. Harry did manage to say that if she wanted to talk about her father, to call him. She said that was unlikely, and he left with his face burning as if he'd been bent over a hot stove.

Harry called Jim and got Frank Hodges.

"You want some roast pig?" Hodges asked as soon as he heard Harry's voice. "Last week my brother, the one who lives down in Glades, went on a pig hunt and came back with a young boar that dressed out at close to eighty pounds. Well, he and Sheila, that's his wife, decided to have a pig roast and invited the whole town. Even so, he had a lot of meat left over, and he gave me about twenty pounds to take home. I spitted the thing for him and roasted it over hardwood coals, and I think I must've eaten five pounds of cracklings before it was even off the fire."

Hodges was shouting by now and laughing and had to stop to cough and catch his breath. Harry leaned back, grinning, and waited for him to finish.

"Well," Hodges said when he had recovered, "somebody had gotten hold of a couple of gallons of white lightning, you know, bootlegged corn whiskey, and between drinks and eating, he went round filling everybody's glass as soon as there was room to pour more in."

Hodges choked himself laughing again.

"Anyway," he concluded, "before that pig was well et, the ground around the pit was littered with men and women sprawled on the ground, 'til it looked like Jonestown, some singing, some praying, some laughing, some speaking in tongues, others crying. Two were trying to fight, but every time one of them swung at the other, he would fall down. By the time he could back onto his feet, the other one had fallen down and gone to sleep. Another fella was lying flat on his stomach, all spread-eagled and holding onto the grass as hard as he could.

"I watched him for a while. Then I went over and said, 'Why are you clinging to that grass so hard?' and he said in a kind of desperate voice, 'I'm trying not to fall off.' "

That set Hodges off again. When he had recovered, he asked Harry again if he wanted some of that roasted pork. Harry thanked him for the offer but said he didn't and asked him when Jim was expected back.

"He's just coming in the door," Hodges told him.

"Did Frank try to give you some of his pig meat?" Jim asked when he came on the line.

"Yes, and he told me about the barbeque at which, I gathered, there was the sound of revelry by day and night."

"Well, drinking that mountain dew will do it. I've known otherwise rational men to jump down a well with enough of it in them. I proposed to the school teacher once after drinking a jar of corn liquor. I was nineteen and she was forty-five."

"I guess she turned you down," Harry said laughing.

"She did worse than that. She hit me in the side of the head with a song book she was carrying and knocked me right off my feet. While I was trying to get up, she kicked me in the seat of my pants and flattened me again. Then she walked up the length of me, stepped off, and said, 'When you're sober, James Yellen Snyder, you can apologize for insulting me.' "

"Did you?"

"It took me almost a week to scrape together enough courage to do it, but I did. It cured me of drinking corn liquor. I've always wondered why the hippies never took to the stuff. For a real hallucinatory experience, it would be hard to beat."

The thought of Jim Snyder nineteen years old and drunk was

almost more than Harry could get his mind around. It belonged in the category of a dog walking on its hind legs. He also found it hilariously funny, and when he stopped laughing, Jim said, "I haven't thought about that for years, but it seems from where we are now much longer ago than the years alone suggest."

"Well, there's nothing funny about what I've got to say," Harry said, "and I guess what you're referring to is a paradigm shift."

"I'm not saying I'd want to go back," Jim said quickly, "but I'm not too happy about going forward either. Tell me your good news."

"I've learned from moderately reliable sources that there's a contract killer in town. This one's a man, and he came in shortly after Aristides left. I don't have anything more than that, but I think it's safe to assume he's going to try to finish off Cooper."

"If you're right," Jim said, "he's probably becoming familiar with the hospital, and when he's done that and planned his entrance and escape, he'll make his move."

"It's likely to be sooner rather than later."

"Yes," Jim agreed. "I'll put the deputies back outside Cooper's room today, but Sheriff Fisher won't let me keep them there long. In fact, he'll probably ream me for doing it at all, especially given Cooper's condition."

"There's something else," Harry said. "I've learned that the wife of a man on the reservation has left him after overhearing him say in a conversation with some unidentified man something about someone being killed."

"It could have been anybody," Jim said dismissively.

"Yes, but when he found out she'd heard the conversation, he threatened to feed her to the alligators if she mentioned a word of what he'd said to anyone, including her priest. It turns out she's Hispanic and an observant Catholic. She was frightened enough by his threat to take their daughter and run away."

"Well, I'd better send someone to tape her," Jim said, showing more interest.

"No such luck. Wherever she is, we can't reach her."

"You don't know where she is?"

"No."

"Whoever told you knows."

"Probably, but I can't give you a name."

"Salvamento or Haven House," Jim said sourly. "That would be Soñadora and Rowena Farnham."

"No comment."

"None needed. I wouldn't get squat from either one of them; so there's no point in trying. What's to be done? We need that man's name, at the very least."

"I was thinking I might have a talk with Henry David. He either knows or knows how to find out which man out there has lost his wife recently."

"I could probably lean pretty hard on him," Jim responded, "but I'd rather not have to, considering his cooperation over Franklin and all. By the way, how is the boy?"

"I don't know," Harry said, "and I've been meaning to ask. It's time I found out."

"Let me know when you've talked to Wylie. It's probably nothing, but we might get lucky."

Jim hung up, not sounding as if he thought it likely.

21

Wylie greeted Harry as courteously as always, but his natural graveness had deepened.

"You're not going to ask to question Franklin again, I hope," he said when they were seated in his office.

"No," Harry said with a deliberate finality. "How is the boy?"

"It's hard to say," he answered with a frankness that surprised Harry. "He goes to school, performs the tasks I've given him at home without complaint, but I would be lying to say I thought he took any pleasure in anything."

"Misses his father, I suppose."

"Yes, but there's something more," Wylie said. "I think it has to do with what he heard about his father the day he was questioned by Captain Snyder. It has bitten deep."

"Someone said, 'The eye altering, alters all.' "

"William Blake," Wylie said. "I think Franklin has lost more than his father, he has lost the world that he had when his father was alive and still above reproach. It's very sad to face disillusionment at his age."

"It is," Harry said and waited patiently while Wylie looked out the window and thought that, judging from the expression etched in the man's face, Henry David may also have lost something more than a brother.

After a lengthy silence, Wylie shifted in his chair and pulled his eyes away from the window, forced his voice into a less somber timbre and said, "What did you want to ask me?"

"Do you know whether or not Mark Crowley's wife and daughter are missing?"

"How did you know Mark has a wife and daughter?"

"I didn't until you spoke. I gather he does."

"Yes."

Harry nodded.

"This is the hard part," he said. "I can't answer your question. All I can say is that if they've gone missing in the past few days, their going probably has a bearing on the death of either Lilly Rhinelander or Toke."

"Are you being deliberately mysterious?" Wylie asked a bit more sharply. "Has something happened to them?"

"They're well and safe. That's all I can tell you."

"And you think they are the wife and child of Mark Crowley."

"If you tell me his wife and child are missing," Harry said, "and no other woman with a young child has gone missing from the reservation in the past few days and if his wife is Hispanic, I think it's safe to say that they are Crowley's wife and child."

Again, Wylie sat in a stone-faced silence. Harry waited.

"He is married to Carla Rodriguez," Wylie said finally. "She kept her maiden name. They have a four- or five-year-old girl, but I haven't heard anything about their being missing."

"That's the name," Harry said.

"And that's all you're going to tell me."

"I'm also going to ask you to confirm for me that they are missing."

"You're certain that they're all right?"

"Yes, but that's all I can tell you."

"Are they in police custody?"

"No," Harry said.

"Harry," Wylie said, pushing back from the desk and standing up, wearing a worried look, "this could get very sticky."

Harry was there before Wylie but decided to listen to him before saying anything.

"Why?" he asked, giving him space.

"I'm sure Birch would tell me that the child is a member of the tribe and is too young to have given her consent to be taken off the reservation."

"I expected you to say something like that," Harry replied calmly. "I'm surprised you haven't included the mother in your comments."

"That's more complicated," Wylie replied. "Her affiliation with the tribe is by marriage. Besides, she's an adult; and Hierba Alto or not, she can go where she wishes."

"Henry David," Harry said as sympathetically as he could, "I understand your interest and your concern, but could you set them aside for the present? I'm sure you're already satisfied that you know, in a general way, where Rodriguez and the child are and that they're safe and being well looked after."

"Granted," Wylie said, coming around the desk to lean against it with his arms folded, "but I don't know why she's there."

"And you've long since decided she's not there because she and Mark Crowley had a fight."

"That's true. Why is she there?"

Harry blew out his cheeks in frustration and said, "I can't tell you yet."

"But it does have something to do with the murders of Toke and Rhinelander."

"That's probable. I'm also going to ask you not to tell Crowley that you and I have had this conversation."

"The man's pretty worked up."

"I can believe it. So was his wife. I've got to go. As soon as I can, I'll tell you what's going on."

Wylie gave a mirthless laugh.

"You've put me in a pickle and no mistake," he said, shaking Harry's hand.

"That's what comes of associating with white eyes," Harry said as he was going out the door.

As soon as Harry was back in the Rover, he called Jim's office and told him that Wylie had confirmed that Mark Crowley was Rodriguez's husband.

"Does he know why she went to ground?"

"No," Harry said, "and in addition he agreed not to tell Crowley he and I talked. My guess is he's not going to say anything to Sam Birch either, which is likely to come back to bite him. When this is all over, Sheriff Fisher should throw him a recognition dinner."

"When a cow climbs a tree," Jim said with bitter emphasis.

"You're getting cynical," Harry said, driving out of the administrative complex.

"It comes from working in law enforcement and trying to get Frank to eat less."

Harry grinned to himself and said, "I asked about Franklin. The news is not good. He took what he heard about his father at the interrogation pretty hard. Henry David says he's been withdrawn and depressed ever since. I blame it on that hard-assed Birch for pushing the way he did."

"I'm sorry to hear it, but it's possible that Wylie was right in saying the boy would have to hear it sometime."

"Cold comfort," Harry said. "What are you going to do about Crowley?"

"Think about it. Discuss it with Harley Dillard. Say, I heard Jennifer was called back to Jacksonville to testify in a case and wasn't expected back for a week. What are you doing with your nights?"

"Hope for a brighter tomorrow," Harry said and hung up.

That afternoon Harry visited Cooper and found his room door open and nurses and an occasional doctor entering and leaving with pleased expressions.

"He woke up," the gray-haired deputy sitting outside the door told Harry. "There hasn't been a quiet moment since."

"I haven't been able to read a word," he complained, holding up a boating magazine.

Harry started to go in and was promptly ejected by a nurse who didn't look as old as his daughter Minna, a freshman in high school. He retreated to the desk where the duty nurse presided and asked her how long Cooper had been conscious and what was his condition. Fortunately, the woman recognized him as a regular visitor. She was a slim woman with short gray hair, rimless glasses, and a quick smile.

"He woke about ten o'clock," she told Harry with a pleased smile. "Fortunately, a candy striper was in the room and heard him trying to speak. Then he went to sleep and has been awake for short periods, then sleeping ever since."

"Can he speak?" Harry asked.

"Well," the nurse said, showing some impatience, "that's not how it works when coming out of a trauma-induced head injury as serious as Mr. Cooper's."

"Does he know who he is, where he is?" Harry persisted.

"Of course he doesn't, Mr. Brock," she replied as if he'd asked if pigs could fly. "At this point there's no way of knowing if he will ever reach that level of awareness."

Harry risked another question.

"If he is going to recover, how long will it take?"

"Weeks, months . . . if ever. Be happy he's come back this far."

"My last question," Harry said, holding up his hands. "When can I see him?"

"Come back tomorrow," she told him, "or, better still, call, but don't expect miracles because there won't be any."

Harry left, remembering his seventh grade teacher had enjoyed saying things like that.

That night, Harry had just finished cleaning away his dinner dishes and was looking out the window over the sink, admiring the last of the reflected pink sunset glow on the thunderheads towering over the Puc Puggy Creek, when the phone rang.

"I hear Cooper's come to," Jennifer said as soon as he answered. "Have you seen him?"

"Who's asking?"

"Harry!" she said, stretching out the name and placing heavy emphasis on the last two letters.

"Oh," he said, "I remember. Is this the person who left town on short notice?"

Harry hadn't known until he heard her voice that he had any complaint about her leaving. Now that he knew, he was allowing himself to sound aggrieved, although somewhere in his head a voice was telling him to stop behaving like an adolescent.

"Jesus, Harry," she said, "you can be a major . . . never mind. How much longer is this going to go on?"

"That depends on you."

"There's no snow up here. Otherwise, I would offer to go outside and crawl around in it bare-assed. How would that work?"

Sanity restored, Harry had a lot of trouble smothering his laughter. When he could without laughing, he said, "You're just trying to excite me."

"Give me a challenge," she replied.

"How are you, and what have you been doing?" he asked.

"Not great. This trial is killing me."

"When are you coming back?"

"It's taking as long to answer that question as it's taking to get this creep convicted. What's going on with Cooper?"

Harry decided he was not going to get a straight answer and settled for a quarter of a loaf.

"He's waking and sleeping," he said. "He can't talk. I don't know whether he knows who he is or not. One of his doctors is going to talk with me tomorrow. I don't expect the news to be good."

"Harley was going to bring him in again; and if he wasn't more forthcoming, Harley was going to charge him and try to persuade the judge to deny bail on the grounds of his being a flight risk."

"Did Harley tell you there are rumors of another contract killer having come in after Aristides left?"

"To finish her job?"

"I think so."

She was quiet for a moment.

"You watch yourself, Harry," she said. "I don't want you getting popped."

It was not a topic he wanted to explore.

"According to Wylie, Franklin's not doing too well. He reacted badly to what he had to hear about his father trading in alligator hides and other contraband."

"I'm sorry to hear it. He's a nice kid."

"Whether his being questioned is connected to it or not, I don't know; but Mark Crowley was overheard by his wife discussing someone's being killed out there. It was reported to Jim Snyder. I haven't heard what if anything Jim's going to do."

"If Harley knows about it, he hasn't told me."

"Then we're both traveling in the dark."

"Isn't that the truth," Jennifer answered, and Harry knew she meant more than Mark Crowley's indiscretions.

The next morning Harry met briefly in a sparsely furnished

waiting room in the IC unit with Cooper's head surgeon Dr. Bruce Crane, a dark-haired, saturnine man, dressed in a white coat, worn open over a gray suit, dark gray shirt and red tie.

"I'm only talking to you because our lawyers have given me the go-ahead," Crane said, immediately after entering the room and sitting down beside Harry, looking at Harry as if there was a bad smell in the room, "presumably because the hospital has been unable to locate any relatives and Cooper's lawyer vouches for you, which means, I guess, the hospital and I won't find ourselves being sued."

"I'm glad to hear it," Harry said.

"I am going to be quick about this, Mr. Brock," he said, ignoring the comment, "because if I gave you the long version, we'd be here all day; and I haven't got an hour, never mind all day. You're probably not going to be satisfied with what you're going to hear, but I can't help that. Mr. Cooper's brain has been knocked around very badly. The bullet entered his skull at an angle, which probably saved his life; and for reasons only a forensics expert could account for, instead of ricocheting back and forth through the brain, as I suspect it was intended to do, it pretty much confined itself to traveling around and around inside the skull like a motorcycle in one of those Circle-of-Death carnival shows."

He paused to ask Harry if he understood the metaphor.

"When I was a kid, I used to watch them at the county fair until I ran out of quarters," Harry said.

"Good. To finish up, the banging his brain took from being slammed around inside the skull by the bullet's path and the damage done to the brain tissue itself account for Mr. Cooper's present condition. We also had a certain amount of difficulty removing the slug, which didn't help."

Except for the short pause to glance up at Harry, to ask if he understood the reference to the Circle-of-Death, Crane had given his account leaning forward with his elbows on his knees, staring at the floor. Now he looked up.

"Questions."

"Is he going to live?" Harry asked.

"Probably."

"How badly will he be impaired?"

"At this point the degree of impairment can't be predicted."

"When will we know?"

"We will *begin* to know something as soon as he starts speaking, if he does."

"Recovery?"

"Assuming he lives, it could be weeks or years or not at all. We'll do what we can for him, Mr. Brock," Crane said getting to his feet, and extending his hand, which Harry shook, still sitting down, and watched Crane stride out the door, his coat floating behind him like a musketeer's cloak.

Crane had been right. Harry was disappointed with the account; but, assuming Crane had been honest, and Harry thought he had, there was no cause for complaint.

Immediately after leaving the hospital—he had left Cooper sleeping—Harry called Cooper's attorneys again and spoke with Felix Cochran. He had come to like Cochran, finding him a concerned, almost courtly man, a strong contrast to the ruffian he had appeared to be in the Pearson meeting.

"What's going to happen with his filing with Judge Rankin?" Harry asked as soon as he had given Cochran an update on Cooper's condition.

"It would have taken an army to look after Cooper," Cochran said with a rueful sigh. "I hope you're not blaming yourself for this."

"Well, hindsight's twenty-twenty, but I do think I could have been more suspicious."

"Cooper is a very presentable man," Cochran said. "Today, his color is not an issue among the people who party at the Ritz. It's more likely than not that most women would find him attractive. Has it occurred to you that Aristides probably did and thoroughly enjoyed the time she spent with him, setting up the hit?"

"A chilling thought," Harry said with an inner shiver. "What about the filing?"

"It's a nasty irony, but Judge Rankin is sending out signals that in light of what's happened to him, she is going to rule in Cooper's behalf."

"Is this good or bad?"

Cochran laughed.

"It sounds like a crazy question to ask a man's lawyer," he said, "but I take your point. That said, I think that if Cooper isn't scamming us, he's got a very good chance of winning his point."

"In court."

"In court. My guess we'll come to a point where the Rhinelanders will fold."

Harry thought a moment and said, "One, if Cooper lives, two, if he can get past Pearson and actually have a DNA test made."

"We will prevail," Cochran said with a chuckle.

Harry enjoyed the reference but wondered how Cochran could find anything about Cooper's situation funny. Lawyers, he thought.

When Harry next went to see Cooper, he was still asleep; but Harry sat down anyway and, while settling himself beside the bed, noticed an envelope addressed to Cooper propped up against a box of tissues. Just then a red-haired nurse came in to check on one of the machines to which the patient was attached.

"It smells heavenly," she said in a strong Australian accent. "I'm dying to know who sent it."

She made a note on a form on her clipboard, looked up and, giving her hair a bit of a flip, said, "It looks like our mate was something of a larrikin," winked at Harry, and swung out of the room.

Harry laughed. If he remembered correctly, a *larrikin* was a fast young man. The idea of Cooper being fast was funny. Then he remembered Aristides. He saw her as she had looked getting up from her beach chair. For a moment Harry wondered if, perhaps, she might have been worth being shot for.

Harry picked up the envelope and brought it up to his nose. Red was right. It did smell heavenly. Without asking himself if this ought to be given to Cochran, he turned it over. There was no return address. He slid a thumb under the partially sealed flap. It opened without tearing the envelope. Then he stopped.

This is, he reminded himself, potentially evidence. Holding the envelope behind his back, he went to the door. The red-haired nurse was at the nurse station. He walked quickly to her and said, "Could you get me a pair of tweezers? I've picked up a splinter."

"Right," she said, "you and my Aunt Susan," but she hurried off and returned with the tweezers.

"Need any help?" she asked.

"No thanks," he said and went back into the room, keeping the envelope out of her sight.

Reaching inside the envelope with the tweezers, Harry extracted the folded note and stood it up like a little tent on Cooper's bedside table. Then he grasped one of the sides of the tent with the tweezers and lifted it, turning the folded edge down. Taking a pen from his shirt pocket, he glanced down, to be certain the ball point was retracted. Then he pressed open the fold and read the message.

"Adrian, it was supposed to have been quick, painless, and permanent. Sorry."

It was signed, "Sophie."

"Jesus, loving Christ!" Harry whispered, his heart pounding.

Harry laid the plastic sandwich bag on Jim's desk. He had already called Harley Dillard and Cochran.

"Here it is," he said.

"OK," Jim said. "Frank, get this on its way to the labs, but make sure it's signed into the Evidence Section first. Then make sure it's sent on. Don't leave until you see it in the mail bag."

Before Frank was out the door, Jim turned to Harry and said, "If your opening that envelope interferes with any significant evidence connected with that note, you are in tall trouble."

"You're right, I shouldn't have opened it," Harry said cheerfully, "but look on the bright side, Jim; I didn't touch the note with anything but the tweezers and the point of a BIC pen. And you know as well as I do that there will be no traces of saliva on the flap or hair, bone, or fingerprints, beside mine and the postman's, anywhere."

Jim dropped into his chair and shook his head.

"How do you explain her doing that?" he asked. "I thought I'd seen about everything this law business had to reveal, but a would-be-killer writing her victim a note, apologizing for not killing him outright as she had intended, beats everything I've ever seen."

"Looks to me," Harry said, still not sure whether he ought to be more amused than appalled or the other way around, "as if Adrian scored pretty high on the lady's satisfaction scale."

"But then to shoot him!" Jim protested.

"It does sound like over-compartmentalizing," Harry agreed. Harley Dillard must have burned tails over the letter because

Jim had a response in three days instead of two weeks. After he'd called Dillard's office, he called Harry.

"They've done everything but boil it in oil," Jim said in disgust, "and come up empty. She must have written the note wearing latex gloves and wet the stamp and flap under a faucet."

"No surprise there," Harry said.

"Anything new on Cooper's condition?"

"He's awake a little more each day, but he's still sealed away as far as communicating goes. It doesn't look good."

"Then we'll wait. Can you come in? I want to talk about Mark Crowley."

"Will around three be OK?"

"Yes."

He had thought about telling Jim that he was having lunch with Soñadora but quickly rejected the idea, not wanting to encourage speculation between Jim and Kathleen over his and Soñadora's relationship.

"Ridiculous idea," he told the mockingbird watching him as he crossed the lawn to the Rover.

22

"Do you like grouper sandwiches?" he asked her when he picked her up at the Salvamento building.

A cold front had pushed down the Florida peninsula, dropping the temperature in Avola into the low eighties, winter weather; and Soñadora was wearing an orange and gold silk shawl over her shoulders and a robin's egg blue dress. Harry thought she looked beautiful, except for the weariness or sadness that robbed her face of its natural vitality.

"I thought we were going to . . ." she began as he was backing out of the driveway, but he interrupted her.

"Not today," he said. "Today, we're eating with the gringos."

"But I'm not dressed for . . ."

"You will be the best-dressed woman in the place as well as the most beautiful. We're going to the Lagoon in North Avola, just off 41. Do you know where it is?"

"What business have I in North Avola? Stop! I'm getting out!"

Harry pulled off the street in front of an abandoned liquor store, the sudden stop kicking up a cloud of dust around the Rover.

"You and Jane Bunting have a lot in common," he said in a conversational voice, as he watched her struggling with her seat belt.

"What?" she said, stopping to look at him, her eyes like molten onyx.

"I said you and Jane Bunting have a lot in common."

"Jane Bunting is a cat. I do not appreciate being compared to a cat. Did you come to see me to insult me?"

She went back to yanking and jabbing the release mechanism on the seat belt. Harry reached across her and released the buckle.

"No," he said, "I came to take you to lunch and share with you the best grouper sandwiches made in Tequesta County. Once you have eaten one of them, you will never eat them anywhere else."

A smile was twitching the corners of her mouth although she held it in check.

"Why did you make comparison between me and Jane Bunting, whom I have never seen and who is an animal?"

"Because you are both more than half wild and live among the rest of us reluctantly with grave reservations, always fierce, slipping away every chance you get, to wander in the forest. There is one difference between you, however," he said, keeping his own face straight. "Jane Bunting hunts in the real forest while you wander in jungles of your own making."

Harry had remained bent toward her, and she was looking down slightly at him as he was speaking.

"And you are *demente*," she said more softly. Then, pushing him upright, "I thought you were taking me to lunch."

"How do you like it?" he asked after she had taken her first bite of the sandwich, which was large and running with juice and butter and lemon dressing.

The restaurant, two small rooms, was crowded with people, who all seemed to be talking.

"Are gringos always this noisy?" she asked when she was able to speak.

She did not wait for him to answer but immediately took

243

another bite, staring reverently at the sandwich as she chewed. Harry sat watching her, smiling like the Cheshire cat.

"Stop staring at me like an idiot," she said peremptorily but not very clearly. "Eat while it is still hot."

When she had finished, she fell back from the ravaged remains of lettuce, chips, and coleslaw on her plate, wiped her mouth, groaned, and tossed the napkin onto the table. No trace of the sandwich remained.

"I guess you won't want to come here again," he said as they left the restaurant.

"Not before tomorrow," she said, looking longingly out her side window as they drove away. "But if I ate that way very often, I would roll along the road like a ball."

"I think I might like you better fat," Harry told her as if he meant it.

"It's not going to happen," she said with some edge.

"We need a little fresh air and exercise," he told her, turning south on a palm-lined street that quickly took them closer to the water and eventually to a park running along the Seminole River.

The white, shelled-covered paths twisted through a deeply mottled shade of palms, oleanders, Dahoon holly trees, and hibiscus bushes. Harry was surprised that she hadn't protested taking more time away from work. He was less surprised to find her so apparently lost in her own thoughts.

"You're worrying about something," he said as they started along a path, startling into flight a small gathering of black and white butterflies that rose and fluttered around them. "Is it your father?"

She lifted a hand, extending it toward the butterflies, palm upward in what looked to Harry like a supplication. To or for what, he wondered.

"Yes, but it cannot interest you," she said. "You have a friend lying near death in the hospital. You are working with the police to find murderers. Of what interest can an aged man in Guatemala be?"

"Coming from anyone but you," Harry said calmly, when he would have liked to jump around and swear with frustration, "I would be offended; but I am going to assume that you are not deliberately trying to insult me. Or am I wrong about that?"

"I am being serious, Harry," she said, turning to him in protest.

"Then tell me why you are worried. Even if I can't do more than listen to you, I would like to do that and more if I can."

"Have I hurt your feelings?" she asked.

"Yes, no, never mind that. Just tell me why you are worrying and not that I'm too busy to care about your problems."

"I am not trying to insult you, Harry," she said, starting to walk again and staring at the path as she spoke. "I am not feeling sorry for myself," she said with emphasis on the *not,* "and I do not want you to pity me."

"I understand," Harry said, giving her plenty of room.

"No you don't, but I have had to be responsible for myself for so long that is very difficult to share my troubles with anyone."

She paused for three steps and added, "I have a horror of appearing . . . *patético.*"

"Pathetic," Harry said, shaking his head. "You are never pathetic."

He gambled.

"How could Jane Bunting ever be pathetic?"

"Are you ever serious?" she demanded sharply.

"Do you have any idea who you are?"

"What?"

"Please! Never mind! Tell me about your father. I want you to tell me. Seriously."

"I am all twisted up in a knot inside," she said, turning away from him and shaking her fists at everything in front of her.

"I am angry with him and ashamed of myself for my anger. And I have these feelings for him as well that I have always had even before he was my father!"

The words poured out of her. Then she stopped speaking and appeared to Harry to be in the grip of emotions she could not find words for. She had begun to tremble. Harry stepped closer to her; and although he knew he might regret it, he put his arm around her shoulders and pulled her against him.

"We can just stand here, or we can walk. Take all the time you need; and when you're ready, tell me the whole thing."

Gradually, her body relaxed against his.

"If he had told me all those years ago that he was my father, that he loved me, if he did, and I think he did, then I would have been free to let myself love him, which I wanted to do and which I think I did."

She turned out of his embrace in order to face him, and she stood looking intently into his eyes as if she was searching for something there.

"I wanted so much to know him, you see, but he was a priest; I was so confused and frustrated that I kept it all locked up inside me."

She gave a brief, humorless laugh.

"It still is," she said.

To say that last bit, she had grasped his hands, pulled them up between hers, and pressed them against her chest.

"Perhaps it's not too late for you to tell him what you have just told me," Harry said.

"It is impossible," she said.

"No," he said, "it isn't. If there is a problem with money, I will take care of that part of it. Everything that needs to be done can be done. Believe me."

When he finished speaking, she glanced down at her hands and blushed and stepped back, pressing his hands away from her.

"I am so sorry, Harry," she said, the color rising and falling in her cheeks. "I didn't realize, please forgive me."

"No," he said, "there's nothing to forgive. Do you understand? Nothing."

While he was speaking, he had grasped her hands, and he held them while he finished saying what he wanted and needed to say to her.

"Soñadora, it is a good thing to do what you did." He gave her hands a little shake. "I'm going to let you go," he said, "and when I do, I want us to talk about the possibility of your going to see your father."

He released her, not with a calm heart because their exchange had left him somewhat shaken and invaded by feelings he could not account for, given his view of their relationship. They went on walking and talking about Harry's idea that she should go to Guatemala, but nothing was decided.

"Are you taking any special precautions?" Tucker asked.

He and Harry were sitting on the bench Tucker had built into the bank in the northern quarter acre of his citrus grove. He called it with amused wryness the locus of his contemplative life. At this time of year with the spring glory over, the bench under the lemon and the orange trees was a cool, green oasis, flecked by sunlight and cooled by the breeze rustling the leaves.

"If there really is a contract killer in town, I'm reasonably certain he's focused on Adrian Cooper. Who would benefit from having me dead?"

"You're likely to know the answer to that better than I," Tucker said. "But keep in mind that you and Jim are still looking for whoever killed Lilly Rhinelander and Toke Wylie. I would also give you odds that the same person who killed Rhinelander tried to kill your client."

Harry's attention was caught by Oh, Brother! and Sanchez who were picking their way between the trees at the south end of the orchard, Sanchez in front, moving in a half crouch.

"What are those two doing?" he asked.

"Trying to sneak up on the woodchuck," Tucker said with a grin. "She's got two young ones out of the den. Last winter I sowed clover just beyond the end of the lemon trees. She's been taking the cubs out there for a while every day, introducing them to the wonders of grass, clover, and other delicacies."

"Such as beans, carrot tops, lettuce, and whatever else your garden has to offer," Harry said.

"I plant extra, to compensate," Tucker said comfortably, "but it will be a while before she ventures that far with them."

"What do the two naturalists think of them?"

"Oh, Brother! would give half a bag of oats to be able to make friends," Tucker said, nodding approvingly. "Sanchez is less frank about his intentions. I expect he's conflicted. He has a weak spot for young things, but his genes are whispering how much fun it would be to chase all three of them."

"Any chance the hunter will win the argument?" Harry asked, half seriously.

"Doesn't matter," Tucker said. "The cubs' mother won't let him get between them and the den. So if he tries anything funny, which is unlikely, they will be down their hole before he gets near them."

They sat for a moment watching the two. Then Harry said, "Fillmore Wiggins keeps intruding on my thoughts. Do you know any more about him than I do?"

"As I recall, he moved out there beside the Stickpen in the late seventies, not long before Reagan was elected president. What's got you thinking about him?"

"You've already said it. He lives close to the Stickpen," Harry answered. "The Hammock and Fillmore's place are the only access points by road to the Stickpen anywhere close to where Rhinelander was found. Do you agree that nobody drove in here the night she was killed?"

"I don't see how they could have done it without leaving tracks, without one of us waking, or without Sanchez raising a ruckus."

"That's what I think," Harry agreed. "And the night before last when I should have been sleeping, I remembered something I'd forgotten. When Fillmore and I went looking for Toke and before we had gone very far, he cut the motor and let us drift into the place where Toke took me to see Rhinelander's body."

"How did he know where to go?" Tucker asked at once.

"I asked him the same question, and he said that from what I'd told him this would be the place. Then he cranked up the motor and put an end to any more questions. Shortly after that we came on Mark Crowley and the other men, towing Toke's boat with him in it. Until the night before last, that incident put out of my mind Fillmore's driving without hesitation to the spot where Rhinelander was found."

"Had you described the place to Fillmore?"

"Only that it was about halfway between his place and mine."

"What are you going to do about it?" Tucker asked.

"I guess I'm going to have another talk with him but I don't think he's going to be very interested. I'm not even sure I am."

"Is it in your mind," Tucker asked, "that Wiggins had something to do with Rhinelander's murder?"

"That's too specific, but I do think he may know something he hasn't told me or Jim's people."

Tucker nodded.

"One thing is certain," Tucker added. "Few people know that swamp the way Wiggins does. It's probable that your saying it was about halfway between your places was all the clue he needed."

"Yes, but I'm still uneasy."

"So you'll talk with him. Are you sure you want to?"

"I'll sleep on that. Right now I've got to decide what I want to do about Mark Crowley."

"What you want to do," Tucker said, "is to be very careful. Just remember, he doesn't like white people; and that's only for openers."

"I haven't seen any signs of hostility in my dealings with him," Harry said with a chuckle. "He just ignores me."

They got up and watched Sanchez and Oh, Brother! hurrying back through the orchard.

"By the way," Harry said, "have you seen Jane Bunting?"

"No," Tucker said, "I'm beginning to think we've lost her."

"Sad news," Harry said, surprised to find he really was sorry.

Oh, Brother! and Sanchez hurried up to Harry to greet him.

Harry reached up and straightened Oh, Brother!'s hat while he patted his neck, and the mule picked Harry's Tilley off his head and dropped it on the ground. Sanchez woofed and grinned, then sneezed and shook his head. Blood sprayed off the end of his nose.

"What's this?" Harry asked the dog while picking up his hat.

"He's cut his nose," Tucker said, holding the dog's head. "What have you been up to?"

Oh, Brother! nudged Harry with his nose then pushed it against his chest.

"Oh, that's it," Tucker said, having watched the mule.

Sanchez whined and tried to pull away from Tucker. Tucker held onto him, and looked at him sternly.

"I told you to leave her alone," he told the dog. "You got just what you deserve."

Oh, Brother! crowded up closer to Harry and leaned on him,

waggling his ears at Tucker and the dog.

"Yes," Tucker said to the mule, "but he's a slow learner. It's the dog in him."

"Is one of you going to tell me what's going on here?" Harry asked, dusting off his hat and staggering a little under the mule's weight. "I like you too," he told Oh, Brother! and with a grunt of effort stepped away from him, "but holding up half a ton of mule is above my lift grade."

"What happened," Tucker said, "was that Sanchez succumbed to the temptation to see if he could outrun Mrs. Woodchuck to her den door. Well, he got there just after the cubs dodged down the hole. When he put on his brakes to let her dodge down the hole after the cubs, she jumped right into his face and bit his nose."

Sanchez whined again.

"No good deed goes unpunished," Harry said with a laugh.

"That's right," Tucker said, releasing the dog, "but he doesn't deserve any sympathy. He probably scared the tar out of those cubs. But Oh, Brother! says there's a bright side to it. If those coyotes come around while the cubs are out of the den, they'll dive for cover without waiting for the coyotes to declare their intentions."

"And Oh, Brother! told you all that," Harry said as they turned back toward the house.

"Of course," Tucker said in a surprised voice. "You heard him. You were standing right there."

23

Harry was at a loss as to whether he should talk with Crowley before the police got to him or whether he should talk to Wiggins first with the chance of learning something that would help him with the Crowley interview—if Crowley agreed to talk with him, a large *if*. Something else that had been lurking at the edge of his mind was the fact that Ernesto Piedra had been the one who got word to him about a second shooter.

He had intended to call Ernesto but had kept putting it off. Whatever had been blocking him, he decided to deal with it, glanced at his watch, and picked up the kitchen phone.

"I thought you'd be up by now," Harry said in a pretense of surprise.

"As you see, I am now awake," Ernesto grumbled. "Why are you calling at such an hour?"

"It's almost noon, Ernesto. I've been up six hours."

"You are a crazy *blanco*. What do you want?"

"I need your help."

"I hear that all the time, and you are not even one of my *responsibilidads*."

"You called Soñadora and asked her to tell me that there was a second shooter in town. Why didn't you call me?"

"I was at Salvamento on business. It saved me a call."

"Thanks anyway. Now, here's what I want to ask you. Do you think it would be possible to find this person?"

Ernesto groaned with such conviction that Harry was afraid

he we was ill.

"I would be ill for a little while, if I started asking questions about that person. Then I would be dead."

"Stop being dramatic. Whoever it is, that person is not interested in you. Now, put on your thinking cap."

A querulous female voice broke into their conversation in rapid-fire Spanish.

"The cleaning lady?" Harry asked.

"Marta cleans her plate, her teeth, and my wallet. Otherwise, *nada*."

The volume of the voice rose.

"I take it that she speaks English."

"Yes. Ouch, that hurts."

Laughter.

"Ernesto!" Harry said loudly. "Not now."

"Just a little squeeze, to keep the peace. What was I saying?"

"You were going to tell me how we are going to find the shooter."

"Very risky, Harry. I must think about this and make some calls. I will call you."

The call ended in a variety of expostulations from Marta that suggested to Harry as he hung up that Ernesto might be about to increase his *responsibilidads*.

In the end, Harry decided to tackle Fillmore Wiggins first. Then he did something that he seldom did. He called Jim and told him what he was going to do and when.

"You're getting smarter in your old age," Jim said.

"How do you mean?"

"Don't turn your back on him."

"That's pretty rich," Harry said, "suggesting Fillmore of being dangerous."

"If you didn't think he has some connection to Lilly Rhinelander's death," Jim asked, "would you be going out there to question him?"

"Probably not," Harry admitted.

"And remember, you're not immortal."

Harry wanted to be resentful of the reminder, but as it came from Jim, thought better of it.

Before he could get out of the house, however, he had a visitor.

"Your boy has really crapped on us this time," John Edward Kringle said without preamble, striding across the lawn from his Mercedes.

Harry noticed he'd put the top up as most people did by the end of May or risk frying their brains, if they had any, in the summer sun. Harry wasn't sure whether Kringle had any or not. He did know he did not want to have to talk to him. Harry stepped off the lanai to meet the man, advancing at speed and dressed in white shorts, a red T-shirt, black socks, and tennis shoes. He shoved his sunglasses up onto his head and glowered at Harry.

"He hasn't done much of anything for while," Harry answered, not offering to shake hands.

Neither did Kringle.

"He got himself shot, and I'll be a son of a bitch if that goddamned judge hasn't allowed Cooper's suit to go ahead. Now the fucking will can't be probated until it's decided whether or not Cooper's Lilly's son."

"Does it bother you at all that someone tried to kill him?" Harry asked.

"Hell, no! I'm just sorry she bungled the job."

"Even though he may be your half brother?"

"Are you trying to piss me off?"

"I don't care whether I do or not, but I've heard all I want to hear from you. Just turn around, get back in your silver miracle, and get out of here."

Kringle's shoulders slumped and he blew out his cheeks in a gesture of frustration and exhaustion.

"You got anything to drink?" he asked.

"Beer?" Harry asked.

The truth was, there was something so outrageous and pathetic about the man, Harry couldn't stay angry with him.

"Yeah."

"Come in out of the sun," Harry said, waving him toward the lanai, thinking his head was scrambled badly enough without further cooking.

Sprawled in a lounge chair with a cold beer in his hand, Kringle began to recover some of his edge.

"This is a hell of a mess, Brock," he declared loudly, scowling at Harry.

"You speaking in general or thinking about something in particular?"

He gave a bark of harsh laughter.

"That's rich. Do you know what I do?"

"You manage Baker's Dozen, a string of your mother's bakeries," Harry answered.

Kringle's dark face grew darker.

"Yeah, some fucking job," he complained. "I was hoping Lilly's dying would cut me loose. The damned business has always been on the edge of failing, and she would never let me make any changes in how the operation was run. My total support is a percentage of the profits, and those profits have been shrinking, and there's not a damned thing I can do about it."

He drank some of his beer and sat brooding and watching two young raccoons run across the yard, squealing and knocking one another over and rolling in the thin grass.

"You live in a goddamned zoo, Brock," Kringle said, beginning to chuckle at the antics of the young animals.

Their mother made a sudden appearance, cuffed them soundly, and followed them back into the bushes.

"Just like Lilly," Kringle growled. "Just when I was having some fun, she'd come along and belt me up the side of my head."

"You'll miss her," Harry said.

Kringle made an ambiguous sound.

"She was a tough old bitch and sadistic, but I gotta say that nobody fucked with her and kept their hair."

"Do you know why the mother raccoon smacked the two young ones and ran them back into the woods?"

"You tell me."

"A pair of coyotes have moved onto the Hammock; and if they'd come on those cubs playing like that and not paying attention to what was going on around them, the coyotes would have snapped their necks before you could snap your fingers, which is a high price to pay for a little fun."

Kringle grinned at Harry, looking suddenly boyish. "Just what Lilly used to tell me, 'John, you're going to pay a high price for your fun.' "

"I'm sure you didn't drive out here to tell me that," Harry said in a friendly voice.

"I'm not sure why I did come out here, Brock," Kringle said, pausing to drain his beer before continuing, "unless it was to tell you that things have gotten really nasty."

Rather than ask Kringle to elaborate, Harry jumped the conversation to another subject.

"Is Cooper going to live?" he asked.

Kringle gave him a half startled look, then said gruffly, "I'm the wrong one to ask," and levered himself out of his chair.

"Who should I ask?"

"The doctor, maybe."

"That's not much help."

"I know it isn't, but it's all I can tell you, except that if I was putting money on it, I'd say the odds are against his coming out of the hospital alive."

Harry was surprised by Kringle's response. They walked to Kringle's car without speaking, but when Kringle pulled open the door, Harry asked, "Can you tell me anything about Cooper's being shot?"

"Yes, I didn't have a piece of it."

"Do you know who does?"

Kringle pulled his glasses down over his eyes.

"Thanks for the beer, Brock. Keep your eye on the two coyotes."

That evening Harry went to talk with Fillmore Wiggins. When he turned down the narrow track from the county road leading to Wiggins's house, the sun, which had sunk almost to the horizon, was a brilliant vermillion and looked as big as a burning barn. Harry didn't particularly like sunsets—they reminded him of all the things he hadn't done—but this one was a beauty. He stepped out of the Rover to find Wiggins's house, the water in front of it, and all the woods soaked in its flaming light. He also noticed stacks of new lumber and dimension stock piled in back of the house.

"Did you order this just for me?" Harry asked, swinging an arm to take in the whole bright scene.

Wiggins said, "Sure," but didn't sound amused. "How about a drink?"

"I'll pass on that," Harry said. "I think sinister forces are working to make all my shorts too small."

"Well, come in anyway. At least we'll be out of the mosquitoes."

Wiggins not being in the mood for small, arthritic jokes, Harry sat down beside his host and said, "I'm back to talk again about Rhinelander's murder, and we can now add Toke Wylie's to the list."

"Why not throw in Cooper's near miss while you're at it," Wiggins said, leaving Harry uncertain as to whether he was being sarcastic or not.

"All right," Harry said. "Here's where the investigation is at the moment. There seems to be agreement that Rhinelander was not dropped into the Stickpen from a helicopter or a plane. What that means is that she had to have been transported to the spot where she was dumped by either a johnboat or an airboat."

Harry stopped to see how Wiggins would respond to what he'd said so far.

"I can see why you'd take out the option of her being dropped from a plane," Wiggins responded, "but why couldn't she have been dropped from a helicopter? It seems to me the likeliest way of getting her in there."

"Jim Snyder's people have decided to their satisfaction," Harry said, "that there was no helicopter in the air near where the body was found on the night she was killed."

"How could they be sure of that?" Wiggins scoffed. "It would have been flying under the radar from the Southwest Regional Airport. Who was here but you, me, and Tucker to hear it, us and any poachers working out there with jack lights? There's none of them going to say anything."

"Good point," Harry said, "and I've gotten that far, but I'm betting that the sheriff's people can demonstrate beyond a reasonable doubt that the body wasn't transported by helicopter."

Wiggins shrugged.

"I don't see how," he said dismissively.

"All right, but if they're right, where does that leave us?"

"What are you expecting me to say, Harry?" Wiggins

demanded in a hard voice. "I'm getting the feeling that you're fishing again; and if you are, you've come to the wrong place."

"Let me be clearer," Harry replied. "I've got a client in the hospital. As you know, he was shot in the head, probably by a hired killer, but the thing went wrong; and he didn't die."

"I learned all that from a checker in Publix soon after it happened. What's your point?"

"The Rhinelander killing, Toke Wylie's death, and Cooper's being shot are all connected."

"How do you know that?"

"Can't tell you, but I'm back to my original question. If she wasn't put in there by plane or helicopter, where did the killer put the body into a johnboat or an airboat?"

Although the light was fading, Harry could still see Wiggins's face harden at the question.

"There are only two roads, yours and mine," Harry added, "that lead to the Stickpen and are close enough to where the body was found to have been used for whoever put it there."

"It could have come from the Hierba Alto Reservation," Wiggins said flatly, but Harry could hear the anger that he had seen a moment before in Wiggins's face.

"To have come that distance," Harry said quietly, "it would have had to come by airboat. The reservation security says no one used one of their concession's boats or trailered one in that night."

"That leaves you and me," Wiggins said.

"That's right," Harry said, getting to his feet. "How long do you think it's going to be before we're going to be looked at hard?"

"Well," Wiggins's said, stepping past Harry who was holding the screen door open for him, "let them look. They're not going to find anything."

"I see you're building something," Harry said as they approached the Rover. "Are you adding some rooms?"

"I'm building a space for more orchids. It's going to have a workshop, a potting shed, a nursery, some variable shade and wind protection. It's going to be big. I've waited a long time for it," Wiggins said with obvious satisfaction. "I'm thinking that in a couple of years I'll be able to open an on-line order business."

"Expensive," Harry said.

"Yes it is," Wiggins said with a grin.

"Thanks for your time, Fillmore," Harry said, climbing into the Rover. "Take care of yourself."

"You do the same," Wiggins said, "and I'd say your ass is out in the wind farther than mine."

Driving home, Harry thought over what Wiggins might have meant by saying Harry was carrying more risk than he was and decided the comment could have meant Harry was more exposed by being more visibly involved with Cooper, who was already a suspect. A more sinister reading was that by being actively engaged in the investigation of the murder, Harry had become a target from another quarter. That might mean that Wiggins might know that Rhinelander's killer had begun watching him.

The next morning Harry worked at home, and just before noon he had a call from Hodges.

"This has got to be quick," Hodges said in his booming voice, which always surfaced when he was worked up. "You know that Indian, Mark Crowley? Well, the poor bastard got himself shot. We don't have any details, but the captain wanted me to call you. So I've done it. Come in when you can. It's beginning to look like a massacre."

Harry had no sooner put down the phone than it rang again.

"Harry, it's Henry David. I've got two pieces of bad news. The first is that Mark Crowley's dead. He was shot some time yesterday and left drifting in his boat where he bled out. One of the airboat guides found him this morning. He towed Crowley and his boat back to the landing. He had some pretty upset people. It had rained in the night, and the boat was awash with blood. We gave them all back their money, of course, but we had to call in one of our doctors to deal with three of the women."

"Anybody see anything?" Harry asked.

"Not so far as I know. Our security people are doing what they can."

"I suppose there have been a lot of people climbing in and out of that boat."

"I'm afraid so. Is there any way you can reach Carla Rodriguez? I don't want her to learn her husband's dead by seeing it on television."

"I'll do what I can. Anything else you want to tell me?"

"Yes, Franklin's disappeared. The day before yesterday, he took one of my johnboats and said he was going fishing. He didn't come home. I wasn't too worried. He's slept out with his father many times. In fact, I thought it might have been a good thing; but when he didn't come home last night, I became worried. Since daylight, we've had three teams out in airboats looking for him, but so far they have not found him."

"I don't think anyone would want to harm the boy," Harry said, feeling his nose grow.

"Let's hope not," Wylie said, "but I think we both know that whoever killed his father might feel better if Franklin was dead."

"Yes," Harry agreed, impressed with Wylie's clarity and courage.

"Have the sheriff's people been out yet?"

"A CID team is here. So is the medical examiner."

"Kathleen Towers," Harry said. "She's good. Give her all the help you can."

"It's being done. When you can, I'd like to talk with you."
"As soon as I can," Harry said.

24

"I'm a messenger with a request," Harry said when Soñadora came to the phone. "Mark Crowley has been killed. Can you get word to Carla Rodriguez, hopefully before she sees it on the local news station? It would be best if you can arrange for someone to be with her when she hears what you have to say."

"Yes, Harry," Soñadora replied in her God-give-me-strength voice. "Perhaps you have forgotten, I have to convey tragic news of some kind to someone at least once a week, but thank you for caring. What can you tell me about his death?"

Harry, swearing silently at his blunder, ran through what Wylie had told him and added, "Franklin Wylie is missing. I'm very afraid the killer has found him, but I'm hoping the boy is just trying to come to terms with his father's death."

"Is there room to hope?" Soñadora asked.

"I think so."

She hesitated. "Are you fond of the boy?"

"Yes."

"I hope he is safe. I will make the call."

Harry spent the rest of the afternoon with Jim and Hodges, working with Henry David Wylie, fighting off Birch's efforts to interfere with the CID people's getting Crowley's boat transferred to the department's evidence division, and trying to contact all the men who might be able to shed some light on what Crowley was doing when he was killed.

As they were winding up their work, Harry took Jim aside

and said, "I've had another visit from John Kringle. I'm not certain why he came to see me at all. He's such a weird mixture of aggression and neediness that he's hard to read."

"Was he in search of information?" Jim asked.

"Possibly, but he didn't ask many questions."

"Did you learn anything you didn't already know?"

"That's what I want to talk to you about. Not expecting to hear anything useful, I asked him if he knew anything about the shooting. His answer surprised me."

"Harry, the sun is already low."

"OK, he said, 'Yes, I didn't have a piece of it.' "

"Why did that surprise you? It's not likely he would have said he planned it."

"I think he was telling me something; so I asked him if he knew who did, and his answer was, 'Keep your eyes on those two coyotes.' "

Jim scowled and said, "Harry, this is not the time to tell me an animal story."

"How many brothers and sisters does Kringle have, not counting Cooper?"

"Two," Jim said, looking interested again.

"Right. Earlier, I told Kringle that two coyotes had moved onto the Hammock and were posing a threat to some of the animals already living there. 'Keep your eyes on those two coyotes' is, I think, an answer to my question."

"His brother and sister."

"That's what I think."

Jim shook his head.

"Consider this: Kringle is thinking we might be getting ready to jump him. What would be better for him than getting us to shift our focus to his brother and sister?"

"I thought about that, and you could be right. Also, he might have been making a wise-ass remark."

"More than likely. I don't think you've got anything."

Harry thought he did have something, but at the moment he did not know what to do with it. Thinking about it as he drove home did little to help beyond giving him time to reflect further on what Kringle had said and to strengthen his conviction that Kringle had not been trying to sidetrack him. At the same time, Harry kept in mind that with Cooper, his brother, and his sister out of the way, his mother's estate would descend on him.

It was nearly dark when Harry drove under the big oak and killed his lights. He sat for a moment, letting his eyes adjust to the dusk and feeling the peace of the place begin to sink into him. That was scattered when he caught a movement in front of the lanai and, looking more closely, saw that it was the figure of someone getting to his feet from the granite step in front of the lanai door.

Harry slipped his CZ out of its holster and eased himself out of the Rover, keeping the door between himself and whoever was waiting for him, but there was something wrong. The dark figure wasn't tall enough to be a man or even a grown woman.

"Harry?"

"Yes," he said, quickly getting his gun out of sight.

It was Franklin.

"Are you hurt?" Harry asked, hurrying toward the boy.

Harry got him into the house as quickly as he could and turned on some lights.

"Let's have a look at you," he said.

"I'm all right," Franklin said in a voice that didn't carry much conviction.

"When did you eat last?" Harry asked, taking note of the wet dungarees, the stained T-shirt, and his tangled hair, still carrying leaves and twigs from the boy's walking out of the swamp.

"This morning," Franklin said. "I'm more thirsty than any-thing."

Harry pulled a can of Sprite out of the refrigerator, popped it, and passed it to him.

"Work on that while I make a call. Then we'll do something about dinner."

"You can tell him I'm not going back, and if they make me, I'll just run away again," he said in a suddenly belligerent voice.

"You want to stay here with me for a while?" Harry asked.

"I'd do that," Franklin said, losing the hostility.

"Good," Harry said. "Now, I've got to tell your uncle that you're here and that it's all right with me if you hang your hat here for as long as you want to. OK?"

"If he doesn't want to come get me, that Birch will. He'll want me back on the res. He never wants anybody to leave. You should have heard him shouting about Mr. Crowley's wife and kid running off."

"I can imagine," Harry said, "but your uncle's not like that. He's been good to you hasn't he?"

"I suppose."

"Then it's all right if I make the call?"

Franklin managed a nod, and Harry picked up the phone before the boy could change his mind.

"Is he there with you now?" Wylie asked after expressing his relief at hearing Franklin was safe.

Harry said he was.

"Then we really can't talk, and that can wait. Are you sure it's all right if he stays with you for a few days?"

"As long as he wants," Harry said, giving Franklin a wink that produced no response from the boy.

"All right, Harry. Call me when you're alone."

"I will."

"He didn't want me back, did he?" Franklin asked when

Harry hung up.

"Of course he wants you back. He said he'd come right now to get you. That's when I said you wanted to stay with me for a while."

Harry thought something needed saying and he said it.

"He's a good man, Franklin. He and your aunt have been really worried. I'd be surprised if they slept much last night. A lot of people who care about you have been looking for you and will be really glad to know you're safe."

"If you want me to feel bad about running away, I'm not going to," Franklin responded.

"Then let's not hear any more about his not wanting you back," Harry said. "Now, there's a shower off the bedroom at the top of the stairs. There's a towel on the rail right by the shower door. While you're tending to that, I'll round up some clothes for you. I'll pile them on the bed and get supper started. All right?"

"Yes, thank you."

Harry rubbed his hand over the boy's head.

"Come on," he said, getting him up and starting for the stairs. "You came in with half of the Stickpen hanging off you."

His son Jesse, who was now studying marine biology at Berkeley, had over the years left a scattering of clothes at what had once been his home. Harry had kept them all in a chest of drawers in a back bedroom. Rummaging through the collection, he found a pair of dungarees, underwear, socks, and a short-sleeved shirt that looked as if they might fit Franklin and left them on the bed.

Jesse's clothes brought back a flood of memories, many pleasant; but all the pleasure was washed away by the painful reminders of his and Katherine's separation. They had been driven apart by his refusal to find another line of work and her inability to go on living in fear of his being killed. During their years together, he had been shot, run off the road, and beaten with an iron pipe, among other adventures. He never denied that Katherine had reasons for worrying.

Franklin came downstairs, washed and dressed in dry clothes, to a kitchen smelling of hamburgers and onions frying in an iron skillet.

"How's the fit?" Harry asked, checking the potatoes.

"All right," Franklin said.

"There's plates in that cupboard and glasses and mugs in the one beside it," Harry said, noting the boy's gloom had not lifted but determined to leave it alone at least until he had eaten. "Knives and forks in the drawer beside the sink. Set the table. We're going to be eating here in a few minutes. If you want to munch on something, there are pretzels in the bread box. Oh, put those plates in the oven to warm."

As they worked, Harry kept the lurking silence at bay by telling Franklin about the coyotes and about Tucker's farm and Sanchez and Oh, Brother! Franklin occasionally asked a question but did not seem to be able to sustain his interest in anything for very long. Harry decided that aside from being nearly worn out the boy was overburdened by his father's death and something more. It was the something more that Harry hoped to penetrate, guessing that it was what the boy was running from.

"That should do it," Harry said when he had two plates filled with mashed potatoes, carrots, onions, and hamburgers. "The gravy's coming. You get ketchup and the pickle relish out of the refrigerator; and there's steak sauce, if you want it."

He had managed to keep Franklin's mind off his problems by giving him tasks and talking to him; but once they were sitting down with their food in front of them, Harry hoped the boy would just eat. And for several minutes he did until, apparently, the edge had gone off his hunger. Then, Harry saw that between bites he increasingly stared at the table, his food forgotten.

Deciding now was the time to ask some questions, Harry began with the obvious ones.

"If you're finished with the meat and potatoes, how about some ice cream and chocolate cookies?"

"I guess so," Franklin said as if he had not really heard Harry's question.

Harry cleared their dinner plates away and came back with the ice cream and the cookies.

"Do you like chocolate swirl ice cream?" he asked, passing Franklin a spoon and putting one down beside his own dish.

"It's the kind my little sister likes best," he replied. "I like straight chocolate best. My little brother, he'll eat anything except vegetables."

That was the most the boy had said in one go since his arrival. Harry began to have hopes.

"When my son was your age, his favorite flavor was pistachio. His little sister thought he was crazy."

"So do I."

Harry laughed. "So did his mother. I like it all right."

Franklin was nibbling at a cookie and began staring away again.

"What's on your mind?" Harry asked as if he was asking him to pass the salt.

"Uncle Henry is ashamed of my father."

"Oh? Did he say that?"

"He doesn't have to. I can tell by the way he looks when my father's name is mentioned."

"I thought it wasn't polite to speak the name of people no longer with us."

"Some of us say *someone,* but my uncle doesn't allow that in his house. We have to give the person's name."

"How did your father feel about that sort of thing?"

Franklin looked surprised.

"I don't know."

"Didn't you or he ever speak of your mother?"

"He always just said, 'Your mother.' "

Harry nodded. Now he would try to move closer to what he wanted to get at.

"Your uncle told me that when he was talking to people like Mark Crowley, he never mentioned the dead by name."

"He was a traditional," Franklin said quietly.

"Did you know him well?"

The boy nodded. "He and my father were friends."

"I would like to know why he was killed," Harry said.

Franklin ate some more ice cream, and Harry thought his question had shut him down. But then he put down his spoon and, looking at Harry, said, "I think he and my father were both killed by the same man."

"Oh?" Harry said without much emphasis and reached for another cookie, which he didn't want. "What makes you think that?"

"I've heard my uncle say some things to Aunt Susan about my father and Mr. Crowley associating with bad people."

"Do you think it's true?"

"I didn't at first, but then I began to remember things like our staying out over night for no reason I could see. My father used to say he was teaching me how to live in our land and find my way and find things to eat and to get to love it like he did."

"Did you learn a lot from him on those trips?" Harry asked.

"I guess so, but then Mr. Crowley started appearing, and they would go off in Mr. Crowley's boat and stay away for a long time. When they came back, my father would never tell me what they had been doing."

"Did they always go away in Mr. Crowley's boat?" Harry asked.

"No. Sometimes they went in our boat, and I would have to stay in Mr. Crowley's boat."

Harry mentally crossed his fingers.

"Did they do that the night before the morning when you found Mrs. Rhinelander's body in the Stickpen?"

"Yes," Franklin said. "I remember because Mr. Crowley was angry when he saw that my father had me with him."

"Why didn't they use Mr. Crowley's boat?"

Franklin looked away, hesitated, then, turning back, with what Harry thought was a look of relief, said, "I guess it can't do any harm now to say. Mr. Crowley's boat had some alligator hides in it. I didn't want to get into the boat because they smelled so bad, but my father said they wouldn't be gone long, but they were."

"How did you happen to find Mrs. Rhinelander the next morning?"

"When my father and Mr. Crowley came back, I got back into our boat, and Mr. Crowley got into his," Franklin said, speaking in a way that told Harry that the incidents of that night were still fresh in the boy's memory because, without hesitating, he told everything as if he were watching it unfold again.

" 'Lie down and go to sleep,' my father said as soon as Mr. Crowley poled away. I asked him what had taken them so long, but he only said, 'Go to sleep.' And I did. At the first light, my father shook my foot and said, 'We are going. Get up. Make your breakfast.' I don't think he had slept at all because the first thing he always did after waking was piss over the back of the boat. This morning he just stood up and began poling. He would not eat any of the cold biscuits and cooked deer meat he always packed for our trips. I ate alone. He didn't stop poling until we got to where the body was."

Franklin stopped speaking and sat, staring past Harry but,

Harry was sure, seeing nothing but what was in his head. Harry sat and waited.

"I saw it first," he said finally.

"What?" Harry asked.

"What you saw," he said. "The red shoe. At first it was all I saw. Then I saw the leg and shouted at my father to stop."

" 'Be quiet,' he said. 'Think before you call attention to yourself. Sit down.' I did and found that I was shaking although it wasn't cold. 'Look away,' he said. And I did. By then he had turned the boat, and when I could make myself look back, the trees had hidden the shoe."

"Then your father told you he was going to get me," Harry said.

"Yes. I wanted to go with him, but my father told me I had nothing to fear, that he would come back, we would go home, and not speak of it again."

"Did it rain the night you waited for your father and Mr. Crowley to come back?"

"There was a shower, but it was mostly wind up in the cypress tops. I spread the tarp over me and the boat for a while." He paused and was lost in his thoughts. Then he said, "It got hot again. I rolled it up. This is the first time I've talked about that night from then to now."

25

Harry did not go to bed until Franklin was asleep. While waiting, he sat as he often did in a chair by the west-facing window in his bedroom thinking and watching the moonlight in the live oaks and listening to the onshore breeze stirring their branches; but the scene brought him no comfort.

Franklin's account confirmed what Harry had suspected. Toke Wylie and Mark Crowley had played a role in Lilly Rhinelander's death, and now both were dead. Whoever killed them was eradicating all possibility that he could be betrayed or blackmailed, which accounted for Harry's uneasiness. It seemed more than likely to him that it was only a question of time before the killer got to Franklin. He was probably also searching for Crowley's wife in order to silence her.

Before Franklin woke, Harry started breakfast. At seven he called Soñadora.

"At least you didn't show up here asking for something to eat," she said.

"I'm making breakfast for myself and my houseguest. Can't you smell the bacon?"

"Who is with you?" she demanded sharply, and instantly retracted the question. "No, don't tell me. It is not my business. Why are you calling me?"

"Franklin Wylie," Harry said, wanting to tease her but repressing the impulse. "He turned up on my doorstep last night, very wet and very tired. He'd been missing from his uncle's house for two days. I was relieved to see him. With his uncle's consent, I'm keeping him for a few days. Has anyone been seen hanging around your safe house in the past week?"

"Wait! Wait!" Soñadora burst out. "First tell me about the boy. Is he all right? Is he very upset? No coffee for his breakfast. Make him some cooked cereal with warm milk. Fruit juice if he will drink it."

"Actually, I was planning to fry a piece of steak for him, and there are some crullers that aren't too old . . ."

"Did you know that you are not a serious person?" she said.

"Back to the question. Do you know or can you find out?"

"Why are you asking?"

"I don't want to frighten you, and I may be wrong; but I think someone is looking for Carla Rodriguez."

"Why?"

Harry did not think it would be fair to lie to her.

"To kill her," he said.

"Is this connected with Mark Crowley's murder?" she asked.

"The short answer is, if I'm right, yes."

"The long answer?"

"I'll have to tell you that later."

"Promise?"

"Yes."

"No one has been seen. Our people are trained to watch for such things. This must not go beyond you, but Carla does not wish to leave. She has said that she does not feel ready, but no more."

"Good," Harry said. "The longer she stays with you, the safer she will be."

"Harry," she said, "be careful with him. Even if it is not showing, there is pain there. Watch for it."

"I will. Have you been thinking about going to see your father?"

"I have been very busy. Is Mr. Cooper still in the hospital?"

"Yes," Harry answered, not wanting to press her. "He's only partly conscious, but the doctors are satisfied with his progress. I can't see the improvement, but I'm hoping it's there. Did I tell you that Judge Rankin officially approved his filing? His lawyers are going to present the Rhinelanders' attorneys with a request for recognition of Cooper as a natural child of Lilly Rhinelander. If Adrian's lawyers don't get it, they will enter into a lawsuit."

"It is stranger than strange," she said. Then she asked in a rush, "Are you in any danger from this person who is looking for Carla?"

"No," Harry said in a flat-out lie. "I doubt he even knows I exist."

Franklin came down to breakfast ready to eat, and Harry filled his plate with scrambled eggs, bacon, and a fried banana, drizzled with honey.

"There's somebody I want you to meet," Harry told him when they had finished cleaning up. "Are you up for a walk?"

"I guess so," Franklin answered, sounding a little doubtful.

"No wading in swamps this morning," Harry said, dropping his arm over the boy's shoulder.

As they walked along the sandy road, Harry kept his companion naming plants and trees and pausing over new plants, to examine them and talk about their characteristics. Franklin proved to be very knowledgeable about his swamp world and was especially quick with birds. For Harry, the walk was a mixture of pleasure and pain. It was very pleasing to him to see Franklin taking such an interest in the natural world and a bit painful to be so strongly reminded of Jesse and the hours he and his sister Minna spent with him wandering over the Hammock, studying and reveling in its bounty.

"Oh, oh," Franklin said in a low voice, coming to a stop.

Hurrying toward them were a very large hound, showing his teeth, and a big, black mule without a halter but wearing a straw hat.

"They won't hurt you," Harry said. "They're just eager to meet you."

"What about those teeth?" Franklin demanded, starting to back away from the rapidly approaching animals.

"He's smiling," Harry said. "You'll get used to it. It scared me half to death the first time he did it to me. Just don't make any comments about the mule's hat," Harry added in a lower voice.

Harry made the introductions. Sanchez gave Franklin the ritual boost of initiation with his nose, and Oh, Brother! pushed his nose into the boy's chest so eagerly that he almost upended him, much to Sanchez's amusement, which set him grinning and barking. Once the introductions were over, Harry made a stirrup with his hand and heaved the boy onto the mule's back, and they all went along the road and up Tucker's driveway in a cheerful group.

"You look as if you could eat a piece of apple pie," Tucker said to Franklin after shaking his hand. "I've got one just out of the oven."

"I ate quite a big breakfast," the boy said, glancing worriedly at Harry.

"Excellent," Tucker said, putting an arm around Franklin's shoulders, "a piece of pie will just settle that breakfast and get your day off to a good start. Then, if you're up to it, there are some things I'd like to show you. How does that sound?"

Sanchez and Oh, Brother! led the three to the back stoop and went off on their own business once Franklin was seated at the kitchen table with a slice of pie in front of him, and Tucker and Harry, also seated, were nursing mugs of steaming tea.

"Have you ever seen a working farm?" Tucker was asking

Franklin, who with his mouth full could only shake his head.

"That's what I thought," Tucker said. "When you finish with that pie—don't hurry—we'll remedy that; and, perhaps, you'll help me with some work on one of the bee hives."

Harry, satisfied that the boy was at ease with Tucker and obviously interested by the old farmer, got up and said, "Franklin, I've got some errands to run. Are you going to be all right here with Tucker until I get back?"

"Yes," Franklin said, laying down his fork with a contented sigh, "but I don't know much about bees, except that they sting."

"Oh, mine are trained not to," Tucker said, picking up the plate and carrying it to the sink, "but, you know, it's an odd thing, I can't get Sanchez and Oh, Brother! to believe it. Oh, Brother! says, 'Bees can't be trained.' Franklin, give me a hand here."

Franklin hurried over and took the dish towel Tucker held out to him.

"Then I'll be going," Harry said.

The two raised their hands in farewell gestures; and Harry went out the door just as Tucker was saying, "It's been my experience that mules tend to be dogmatic," and then paused to explain what *dogmatic* meant.

Harry was just turning onto the county road beyond the bridge when his cell vibrated.

"I have been wondering," Soñadora said without preamble, "why Carla Rodriguez doesn't want to go home. Her husband is dead and can no longer hurt her, but she is still afraid. Does she know someone is trying to harm her?"

"Either that or she is afraid of being questioned by the police. She said she married Crowley within a year of coming here from Mexico. She probably fears the police. Can you ask her?"

"No, I can't. She may also be an illegal; and while thinking about her and what she may be afraid of, it occurred to me that if it is a person, that person may be a threat to the boy."

Harry wanted to tell her what Franklin had told him, which would have only confirmed her fears; but he thought telling anyone other than Jim Snyder would be a mistake. Until now, it had not occurred to him that the killer might be on the reservation. Even now, he thought it very unlikely, but her concern about Franklin's safety had increased his own.

"I think something else," she said. "Franklin would be much safer in our shelter than he is with you or his uncle."

"No one but Henry David and his wife know he's with me."

"I think you do not know much about life in a village," Soñadora said sharply.

"When I was a game warden, I lived in a lot of villages," Harry told her, "but I suppose it's possible that Henry David or his wife told someone, who told someone . . ."

"And now everyone knows," she said for him. "The boy would be safer with us. It would not even be necessary to use his real name."

"Thanks for the offer. Let me think about it."

"Don't take too long, and you be careful."

Harry found Jim and Hodges in Jim's office, wrestling with their perennial problem of covering more miles of county roads than the department's deputies could reasonably cover. They greeted Harry with relief, glad to be diverted.

"Last night," Harry said, "Franklin Wylie turned up at my door. He had walked in from his uncle's johnboat and was soaked to the waist and looking like a half-drowned rat. I got him washed up, dressed in some dry clothes, and fed. He had been sleeping in the boat, keeping away from all the men from the reservation that were out there looking for him."

"Where is he now?" Hodges asked.

"With Tucker."

"And he doesn't want to go back to Henry David's family," Jim said.

"No."

Jim and Hodges listened intently to Harry's account of his call to Wylie and his talk with Franklin. When he finished, Hodges gave an astonished whistle.

"Why under God's blue sky did Toke ever take that boy out there with him?" he demanded.

Harry only shook his head.

After saying how glad he was the boy was safe, Jim asked with equal force, "As for that, why did Toke go near that body the next morning?"

"I think I know the answer to that," Harry replied. "Just before Toke whistled in Franklin with the johnboat and before I called your office, he told me that finding the body gave him a bad feeling."

"Which tells me he didn't much like what he had done the night before," Hodges put in.

"And he didn't want her body left to the alligators," Jim added, "but he and the boy never talked about the incident again."

"That's Franklin's story," Harry said firmly.

"Then your reading of what Franklin told you," Jim said, leaning forward, forearms on his desk, "is that Crowley and Toke had something to do with putting Rhinelander's body into the water."

"I think they must have."

"Where did they get it?" Hodges asked.

"Good question," Jim said.

He and Hodges stared at Harry and waited.

"Well," Harry said, finding himself where he was not comfortable being, "I can't prove it, but since Franklin said his father was gone a long time but back before daylight, I think they picked up the body from Fillmore Wiggins's wharf, ferried it out to where I saw it, and dumped it in the water."

"Then Fillmore knows who killed her," Jim said, closing his eyes as if talking hurt him.

"How do you get there from what's been said?" Hodges demanded.

"Frank," Jim protested, "think! How else could the killer get that body onto his wharf?"

"Maybe Fillmore wasn't to home," Hodges replied.

"Good thinking, Frank," Harry said. "Did anyone ask Fillmore if he was away from home at all that night? He told me there was a thunder shower sometime in the night but that it didn't last long."

"I don't remember," Jim said, "but it will be easy enough to find out."

"Franklin said there had been some rain," Harry said, "and he had spread a tarp over himself."

"We're going to have to talk to that boy again," Jim said, "and I expect trouble from Birch over that, especially if Henry David objects."

Harry nodded, already feeling like a traitor.

"If we can find out when that shower passed over the Stickpen, we'll know when Crowley and Toke were planting the body, in a manner of speaking," Hodges said.

"I'm guessing," Harry said, "but I'll bet if he's asked, Fillmore will say that he was out part of the evening, although he didn't mention it when we discussed not hearing a helicopter that night."

"And he'll have witnesses to prove it," Hodges said sourly.

"So that if it comes to it, he can say the body must have been put in there and taken away while he was out," Jim said, expressing more disgust and throwing his long frame back in his chair and hoisting his boots onto his desk.

"Lord! Lord!" he exploded. "Is man a piece of work or what?"

"How do we prove all this heady speculation?" Hodges asked.

"Have you still got Toke's boat in the evidence section?" Harry asked.

"Along with Crowley's," Jim said.

"We now know Toke's boat was used the night Rhinelander's body was put in the water. I suggest you take that boat apart board by board, to see if anything was overlooked in the first screening."

"You mean that literally," Jim said.

"Yes. Rhinelander lost an earring that night. According to Kathleen, she was dead when she lost it."

Jim brought his feet to the floor with a solid thud.

"Frank, give the order, tell them what they're looking for, but don't tell them they should have found it the first time."

Hodges left, complaining that Jim deprived him of a lot of pleasure.

"Next," Jim said, unfolding himself to his full height, "we talk to Fillmore, and if we don't like the answers he gives us, he's going to hear his rights and find himself a guest of the county, charged with aiding and abetting in the death of Lilly Rhinelander."

"Before you leave here in hot pursuit," Harry said, "I've got something else to tell you."

Jim lowered himself onto the edge of his desk, prepared to listen.

"On my way here, Soñadora called to say that after learning that her husband was dead, Carla Rodriguez had refused to leave the safe house."

"Well, there, you could have told me where she was in the first place," Jim complained.

"Probably, but it wouldn't have done any good."

Harry paused to collect his thoughts.

"Soñadora thinks, and I believe with good reason, that Rodriguez knows something she's keeping to herself," he said, "and we agree it has to do with Toke and Crowley's murders. I think it's safe to assume she's afraid of being killed. Soñadora thinks she's afraid of being questioned by the police, which may also be true. That led Soñadora to say that if Carla's at risk, so is Franklin and that he'd be better off in the safe house than with me because by now the whole reservation probably knows where he is. It made some sense to me, but I'm reluctant to let go of him. Henry David will probably not let him go to the safe house unless you put him there under police protection."

"I'm going to have to talk with Harley Dillard about that," Jim said. "The Hierba Alto are good neighbors, but they're sticklers over their prerogatives. We have to be very careful how we move their people around. Birch is already raising a stink over Mark Crowley's daughter. How worried are you about the boy?"

"Not very, but perhaps I ought to be. What do you think?"

"I think he's better off with you and Tucker for the time being. Let's see what Harley says. What's the best time to find Fillmore at home?"

"Just about sundown. He comes out of the swamp about then."

"I hate it that Fillmore is mixed up in this thing," Jim said with a sigh. "I thought he had more sense."

"He doesn't have a high opinion of the rest of the world," Harry said.

"I like to think most people are doing the best they can with what they've got," Jim said.

"I know," Harry said going to the door, "and there's a good side to it. You're not likely to run out of disappointments."

After leaving Jim's office, Harry stopped at the hospital to visit Cooper. A very bored deputy, tall and wide with a wind-burned face and close-cropped blonde hair, was lounging against the nurses' station. He greeted Harry like a long-lost friend.

"I'm Corporal Austen T. Brickman," he said, crushing Harry's hand in the warmth of his greeting, "and you're Private Investigator Harry Brock. I've seen you at the station a few times. Sergeant Frank Hodges says you're one of the best investigators in the whole state of Florida, and that's high praise, coming from Sergeant Frank Hodges. Sergeant Hodges is not all that fond, in general, of private investigators; but Sergeant Hodges surely likes you."

"I'm pleased to meet you Corporal," Harry said, breaking into the flood of smiling words. He had to bite his tongue to stop himself from saying Corporal Austen T. Brickman. "What does the T. stand for?" he added, the Devil making him do it.

"Thank you for asking. That would be Thaddeus," Brickman said very seriously. "Thaddeus Warren Turnbull was my grandfather's name on my mother's side. Austen was my father's mother's maiden name. They were the Tampa Austens. You may have heard of Judge Atwood Collingsworth Austen. He served for many years on the Florida Supreme Court. The Ocala Austens are a connection but somewhat distant."

Harry, eyes glazing, listened to the deeply accented voice rolling on and thought, *You have only yourself to blame.* Rallying, he broke away and escaped into Cooper's room. Cooper's eyes were open and appeared to be focusing. Sandbags, braced against both sides of his head, kept Cooper from moving; but his eyes followed Harry.

"Do you know who I am?" Harry asked, leaning slightly over the bed to give Cooper a better view of his face.

"Are you a total idiot?" Cooper asked.

"Almost," Harry said. "Was it my face that gave it away?"

No answer.

"I'm Harry," he said. "Who are you?"

"Abraham Lincoln, and, by the way, kiss my ass."

"I'd like to, but my religion forbids it."

A nurse had been standing in the door for a few moments, listening, and now broke down laughing and came into the room.

It was the redhead with the Australian accent.

"It's a phase," she said and looked at Cooper's chart and then at his monitors.

"Does he know who he is?" Harry asked, looking at Cooper in some alarm.

"You're conscious, aren't you, mate?" she said.

"You're not the one with the big tits," Cooper said querulously.

"No, dearie, that's Angelina."

Harry was waiting for an explosion, but none came.

"He doesn't know the difference between appropriate and inappropriate statements and questions," she said to Harry, making some notes on the chart.

"Are you hungry or thirsty, darling?" she said to Cooper, putting her hand on that part of his forehead that was not covered with the bandages.

"No, but I'd like to know what I'm doing in here. Where the hell am I anyway?"

"You're in the hospital and getting better. I'm going now and taking this boomer with me," she said in her on-camera voice. "You get some rest."

"All right," he said and closed his eyes.

When she turned toward him, Harry was standing close enough to read her name tag.

"Alice," he said, "I'm Harry Brock."

"Alice Saunders," she said. "You a blue heeler?"

"What?" he said.

"Sorry, keep forgetting. Copper."

"No, a private detective. I work for Cooper—at least, I did."

"Whoops."

"You could say that."

"What happened?"

"The perp was sleeping with Cooper and she was beautiful."

"The note with the high-end perfume?"

"Yes."

"Deadset."

"What's his situation?"

"Iffy. He has no short-term memory to speak of, although Angelina's boobs seemed to have stuck," she added with a rakish grin. "No memory at all of the event itself which put him here. He has nearly total amnesia. However, where he is now is good news. If he continues to heal, the scattered and suppressed parts of his mind will continue to recombine and revive. He may come all the way back, and he may not."

"I hope he does, but someone still wants him dead."

"If I'm really lucky, I won't be in the room when the chariot arrives."

"That's why Austen T. Brickman is here."

"I feel better already."

They looked at one another straight-faced.

"It's not really funny is it?" she asked.

"I wish it was."

26

Harry wanted to be home in time to make dinner for Franklin, although he suspected Tucker might insist they eat with him, in which case, Harry admitted, Franklin would fare better than with his own frying pan cooking. He also wanted to talk with Henry David Wylie; and once outside the hospital, he glanced at the sun and decided he had enough time to do it.

Henry David was waiting for him outside the administration building.

"Let's walk down to the water," Henry David said. "I've been inside all day."

"I can talk outside as well as in," Harry replied, thinking that Henry David looked as if he had aged ten years.

Lines of weariness and strain had scored his face, and there was no bounce in his step.

"Tell me about Franklin," Henry David said as they went down the shell path. "I am feeling very bad about the boy. There were twenty-four hours when I thought we had lost him."

"He arrived tired, wet, and hungry, and, I guess, angry," Harry responded, "but none of that's your fault. I think it's really between him and his father."

As they walked out of the striped shade of the palms onto the strip of white sand and into a blaze of light, Harry decided this was not the time to tell Henry David that Franklin thought he was ashamed of Toke. In front of them the great clarity of sky, water, and saw grass vanished into the horizon.

"I am afraid that he has become very protective of his father while at the same time being deeply hurt by what his father has done."

"I'm fairly sure he doesn't know exactly what he's done, but he knows it's something bad."

Henry David stood facing the water and grass, hands pushed deep into his trouser pockets, shoulders bowed.

"What has he done, Harry?"

"I don't think he's killed anybody," Harry said, avoiding the question.

"Whatever it is, he's been killed for it, and so has Mark Crowley."

"Probably," Harry agreed, "and that brings us back to Franklin."

"Yes. It would have to."

"I think he's in some danger," Harry said, steeling himself for what he was going to say. "I can't go into this very much, but whoever killed Rhinelander probably had contacts with Toke and Crowley. How much, I don't know, but enough to want them dead after he was done with them."

"Does Franklin know what his father did for the killer?"

"I don't think so, but he's a smart boy; and if he keeps on thinking about it, he will know he did something."

"Do you know?"

"Perhaps, and that's all I'm going to say right now on the subject."

"Was Franklin out there with his father the night Rhinelander was put into the Stickpen?"

Here comes the hard part, Harry thought.

"I'm not going to answer that because knowing it leads to knowing what Toke and Crowley did out there. Knowing that has gotten the two of them killed."

"And Franklin?"

"I think it would be irresponsible not to assume he's in a great deal of danger."

"Is he safe with you?"

"I desperately want to say yes; but it is almost impossible to protect a person if someone wants to kill him and you don't know who that someone is."

"He wouldn't be safe here," Henry David said grimly. "Toke and Crowley may have been the only two of my people involved, but I don't know that, and I won't bet Franklin's life on my being right."

"The greatest risk comes from the killer's knowing where Franklin is," Harry said in a rush. "And I think there's a good chance he knows the boy's with me. The chance is good that you or your wife or one of the children has told someone outside the family where Franklin is."

"You may be right. What's to be done?"

"I think I have a solution."

"Let's hear it."

Harry quickly told Henry David about Soñadora and Salvamento and the safe house. He also reminded Henry David that Franklin's being a minor and a reservation Indian made it impossible for Jim to move officially to put the boy into Salvamento's safe house. Even if he could do it, news of where the boy was would be generally known.

"But there's something that can be done," Harry said. "With your permission I can arrange for Soñadora to pick up Franklin in such a way that the transfer could not be anticipated and for her to put the boy into the safe house under an assumed name. He would vanish."

Henry David looked up, squinting at the sky.

"This sun is hot," he said. "Shall we move into the shade?"

Harry followed him into the palm grove. Henry David stopped by a bench and looked at Harry.

Harry nodded, and they sat down.

"Toke lost his way," Henry David said after a lengthy silence. "His wife's death broke something in his mind. His thinking was not right."

"What about Franklin?"

"Put him in the safe house, but he may not stay there. His father is still doing bad things."

Harry found Tucker and Franklin sitting on the back stoop, snapping green bush beans.

"There's a lesson in this, Franklin," Tucker said, pausing to grin at the boy, who looked to Harry as if he was actually enjoying himself, and studiously ignored Harry's arrival with Sanchez and Oh, Brother! as an honor guard. "Some people like you and me do useful work. Others drive silver, gas-guzzling sports utility vehicles and then appear around supper time expecting to be fed."

" 'They also serve who only stand and wait,' " Harry said as piously as he could.

"Do you know what he's going on about?" Tucker asked Franklin, who was now grinning ear to ear.

"I think it's a quotation," he said.

"That's right," Tucker said. "It's from John Milton's poem 'On His Blindness,' a work your friend should take a lesson from."

"Franklin," Harry said. "One thing you'll learn about Tucker is that you never can call on him, not even for a five minute talk, without finding yourself with a shovel, hoe, rake, or pitchfork in your hands and an hour's heavy lifting ahead of you."

"I've had a really good time," Franklin said. "My father knew a lot about things, but being with Mr. LaBeau is like going to school and finding it interesting. Did you know that the queen bee in a hive goes around and kills all the grubs that would grow up to be a queen if she didn't? But when the hive gets big enough to divide, she lets one grow up and leave to start a new hive, taking some of the worker bees with her to make enough honey to get them through the first winter?"

"I do know it because he told me. He's a good teacher," Harry said, coming onto the stoop and placing a hand on Tucker's shoulder. "I never come here without learning something that makes life more interesting."

"Thank you, Harry," Tucker said, getting to his feet. "Franklin, although flattery always has an unworthy object, in this case a growling stomach, we've snapped enough beans here to feed three people. Shall we ask him to stay?"

"Probably we should," the boy said.

When the meal was over and the dishes cleared away, Franklin hung up the dishcloth he had been using and sat down at the table again, leaning on one hand to listen to Harry telling Tucker about Cooper's situation. Because of Franklin, Harry edited the account heavily but managed to convey the oddity of Cooper's present mental state.

"He doesn't know his own name and can't remember much of anything from one sentence to the next, but the staff seems to think that where he is shows progress and possibility."

"It looks as if you've lost part of your audience," Tucker said with a laugh.

Harry turned and saw Franklin fast asleep, his head resting on the collapsed arm that had been holding up his head.

"Bedtime," Harry said. "What do think of him, Tucker?"

"A good boy, more burdened than a child should be. Have you figured out what to do with him?"

"I don't want to part with him, but he's not safe with me," Harry said, feeling a sharp wrench in his innards.

"It's not safe for him here either, although he'd be more than welcome," Tucker said, regret sharpening his voice.

Because he was still struggling with the question, Harry did not mention Soñadora's offer, possibly because he did not want Tucker to know where the boy was going. Harry drove a very sleepy boy home through the last of the sunset and was turning lights on in the house when the phone rang. It was Jim.

"Brace yourself, Harry," he said. "Fillmore's dead. Shot in the back of the head, just like Toke and Crowley. Is Franklin with you?"

"Yes."

"He's too exposed where you are. Something has to be done."

"Yes. I'll see to it."

"Good. Call when you can talk, and for the Lord's sake, watch yourself."

"Sure."

Franklin had been watching Harry's face.

"What is it?" he asked in a worried voice as soon as Harry hung up the phone.

Harry went to the boy and said, "We've got a problem. Whoever shot your father and Mark Crowley has just killed someone else who was with them on the night we talked about. I've got to get you away from here because your uncle and I and Captain Snyder agree it's no longer safe. Too many people know you're here."

"If it's not safe for me, it's not safe for you," Franklin said.

"He doesn't care about me," Harry lied.

"I don't want to leave you. You can protect me," the boy said. "You've got a gun."

What Harry had feared was happening. Franklin, he guessed, had just begun to feel safe, to feel that there might be something worth getting up for in the morning. Now he saw it being taken away from him, a loss which might harm him more than not having helped him at all.

"I can't because if someone wants to harm you, he can do it from anywhere. We would not see him. I'm asking you to be brave about this. You've got to leave here. It won't be for long, and you will be among people who care about you."

"My father said I could trust you," Franklin burst out, anger and pain making his voice harsh.

"Franklin," Harry said, "you can trust me. I've spent the last thirty years learning how to deal with people who hurt other people. When you want to protect a person, the first thing you do if you can is to take them out of harm's way."

"I don't see how sending me away can help," Franklin said, almost shouting now. "You just said that if a person wants to hurt someone he can."

"I said that the person has to know where you are," Harry told him, speaking slowly and quietly. "I think he knows that. That's why I want you to go somewhere for a while where he can't find you."

"Where would I have to go?" Franklin asked.

Judging by the tone of his voice, Harry thought he had begun to listen with less fear.

"There is someone in Avola who can protect you. She is a good person, one of the best I've ever known. She and others who work with her operate what is called a safe house."

"Mrs. Rodriguez and Maria are in one of those," Franklin said without enthusiasm.

"That's right," Harry said, not telling him that it was all that was keeping her alive.

"I thought it was a place only for women," the boy said with renewed alarm.

"Some of them are, but the safe houses Soñadora Asturias operates are for men too. Much of her work is done with people who have been kept prisoners by human traffickers and made to work without pay."

"Have you known this person long?" Franklin asked, still sounding suspicious.

"Yes. It was Soñadora who suggested to me that she take you in and care for you until whoever is doing this stuff is caught."

"That might be never," Franklin said despondently.

"It will happen soon," Harry said, trying to sound more confident than he felt. "No one can do what he is doing and get away with it for long."

"When do I have to go?" Franklin asked.

"As soon as I can arrange it."

"All right then."

"There's one more thing," Harry said, taking the boy very gently by the shoulders. "You have to promise not to run away because if you do, none of us will be able to protect you."

"OK," he said.

For an instant, Harry saw Toke in the child's strained face. Harry bent over and hugged him.

"It's going to be all right. You'll see," he said.

Harry called Soñadora and told her what had happened.

"How are you going to get him to me?" she asked.

"Here's what I think will work. Can you can get someone from the safe house to pick you up in the next half hour and drive you to Carrabba's Italian Grill on 41?"

"Yes, I can do that."

"Here's what we'll do."

When he had finished explaining, she said, "When I have the person with the car here, I will call you. You and Franklin will leave, and we will leave fifteen minutes later."

"Right," Harry said and hung up.

Then he and Franklin went upstairs to put together some things for Franklin to take with him.

The call came, and Harry and Franklin left. As they were

getting into the Rover, Harry, who was not given to prayer, said one anyway. Giving Franklin into the care of someone else was proving harder than he had expected.

Carrabba's Grill was one of the noisiest eateries in Avola and the most crowded. Patrons began lining up at four in the afternoon; and although by eight or nine the crowd had thinned slightly, it was still crowded and twice as noisy, which was why Harry had chosen it.

"Are you ready?" Harry asked Franklin as he parked and turned off the engine.

"I guess," he said in an uncertain voice, "but I really don't like the wig and dress part."

"I know it's tough," Harry said as seriously as he could. "The good part is you can take them off as soon as you're in the car and whoever is driving says you can."

"OK, but it still sucks."

Harry had to look away to hide his grin. Here was a boy more concerned about putting on a dress than getting shot. As they entered the grill through its brass-fitted double doors, Harry tried to imagine being ten again and failed.

Once inside, they were met by a roar of voices. Harry had to bend over and speak into Franklin's ear to avoid shouting.

"Here we go," he said and began moving Franklin through the tangle of waiters, waitresses, and customers, making their way to and from the bar. "Remember, Soñadora will pass us. She won't look at me, but I'll say, 'Go,' and you'll follow her very closely."

Franklin managed a nod. He was carrying a sack with a leather strap slung over his right shoulder, and most of his attention was taken up trying not to get stepped on or having the bag knocked off his shoulder. Harry had managed to walk him halfway down the crowded aisle between the booths and the bar before Soñadora was beside them.

"Go," Harry said to Franklin and propelled him forward.

He looked over his shoulder at Harry and tried to say something, but Soñadora reached down deftly and, grasping his left hand, pulled him away without a word. It happened very quickly. In another five seconds, she and the boy had vanished in the crowd. Harry put his back against the rear of the booth to his right and waited, not knowing whether to be relieved or more worried. A very few minutes later, Soñadora reappeared.

"There's been a change of plans," she said, smiling at him as if she was greeting him. "Franklin will stay with me at Salvamento for a few days instead of the safe house where we were going to keep him."

Harry was startled and angry, but before he could protest, she said, "I must go with them. I will call you."

And she was gone. Harry forced himself not to follow her but, instead, pushed his way to the bar and ordered a beer. Standing in the raucous crowd sipping his beer, he managed to quiet his racing thoughts and think about what Soñadora had told him. And once his anxiety and anger, brought on by the sudden shift in plans subsided, he was able to see that nothing serious had occurred.

Salvamento had a wing with five bedrooms, in addition to Soñadora's, that served to absorb the overflow from the group's safe houses. The only disadvantage that he could see to the new plan was that he could not go to Salvamento to see Soñadora as long as Franklin was there. He was surprised to find he was troubled by that development but would not allow himself to ask why he was feeling so deprived.

The next morning Harry had a call from Dillard's office, asking him to come to an eleven o'clock meeting. He was there a little early; but when the receptionist led him to the meeting room, he found Jennifer already seated at the head of the table, working on her laptop.

"Hello, Harry," she said without looking up. "I guess the phone lines are down between here and Jacksonville."

"The paper blames it on a tornado, but I think there's been a native uprising just north of Lake Okeechobee."

He thought it was a weak comeback but the best he could do at such short notice.

"Very funny."

She suddenly slammed her chair back, jumped up, and strode down the length of the table towards him. Harry had to get a grip on himself not to back up as the distance narrowed between them. She walked right into him and threw her arms around his neck and kissed him hard on the mouth. She was a substantial woman, and Harry had to embrace her or go over backwards. As it was, the impact of her body against his knocked him back a full step.

The kiss lasted a while, and Harry grew steadily more interested in it. Then she pulled her head back, somewhat out of breath, and gasped, "Could we do it right here on the table?"

"We could," he answered hoarsely, "but it might be the last thing we did together in public for some time."

"Shit," she said and backed off, tucking her blouse into the waistband of her skirt and then doing something rapidly with her hands in her hair. "You're looking a little seedy, Harry," she said in a concerned voice. "Have you been sick?"

Harry had a moment when he thought either he or she might have gone round the corner, but it gradually became clear that it was just him and Jennifer getting reacquainted.

"No, but a lot of people are dying around here, and I think it's taken away some of my jollity and buoyant high spirits."

"That's what I hear," she said, folding her hands in front of her, prim as a school teacher.

There was a stretch-moment when they stood looking at one

another, neither moving nor speaking.

"Hi," she said very softly.

"Hello, Jennifer," he replied.

Jim Snyder strode into the room, breaking up their séance.

"Is this a Quaker meeting?" he demanded, going forward to shake Jennifer's hand. "Welcome back, Counselor. You've come into a sorry mess. Hi, Harry."

"Sit down, sit down," she said. "Harry and I were just discussing how to make the world a better place."

"Any breakthroughs?"

"Not yet, but we're expecting a visitation from a higher power any moment," Jennifer replied, marshalling some of the papers in front of her. "Harley wants us to start without him. He may drop in later, but don't hold your breaths."

"What needs doing?" Jim asked.

"Mostly, I, we, need filling in on where you think we are. To summarize the situation, we have four murders, one attempted murder, three more people whose lives are in serious danger from this killer, and no suspect in sight. What have I left out?"

"A very small bright spot," Jim said. "It may actually be possible that Lilly Rhinelander was put into the Stickpen the way we say she was."

"You mean Toke's johnboat?" Harry asked.

"That's it," Jim said, managing a smile. "You were right, Harry. We took that boat apart board by board and found the earring jammed between the end of the center seat and the side of the boat. If we hadn't taken the seat out, it would never have been found, and it's a match."

"Good work," Harry said, his spirits rising.

"I'm farther behind than I knew," Jennifer said. "Explain."

Harry did.

"Brilliant!" Jennifer said when he was finished. "Now, this is where we can do some good. For all of this to have happened, a lot of money must have been passed around. My guess is that it either went into bank deposits or some significant spending has occurred."

"The addition," Harry said, a light going on. "Fillmore has started a construction project that is going to cost at least ten thousand dollars. I didn't make the connection."

"It will be fairly easy to locate Wiggins's money," Jim said, "but what about Toke and Crowley?"

"We'll have to go through the tribal legal team to pursue their accounts," Jennifer said, making a face.

"Talk to Henry David," Harry said. "I think he will run interference for you. He really wants his brother's killer found."

"Where's Franklin?" Jim asked.

"In a safe house."

"I didn't hear that," Jennifer said.

"Me either," Jim said, "but thanks to him, Harry became convinced he was right about how Rhinelander's body got to the Stickpen."

"I've got another suggestion," Harry said to Jim. "I thought of it last night just after you called. Then getting Franklin relocated pushed it out of my mind. It would be a good idea to take mud samples from John Kringle and Michael Rhinelander's cars' tires."

"And match it with the mud in Fillmore's driveway?"

"Yes. That muck is made up almost entirely of decomposed plant matter, shot through with sand. When it dries, it's like cement. If one of them drove in there in the last few days, there's a good chance some of it will still be in the treads."

"What evidence do we have that either of them has anything to do with these murders?" Jim demanded.

"None, but as suspicious as Fillmore was of people, whoever killed him must have been someone he knew and trusted," Harry replied.

"I'd like to look at their bank accounts," Jennifer said in a musing tone, "but it would be worth my life to try it and get caught."

"Then there's Cooper," Jim said. "I don't know why an attempt hasn't been made on his life."

"What's this?" Jennifer asked, her voice rising.

"We got word through one of Harry's disreputable acquaintances," Jim grumbled, "that a second hired gun had arrived in town, a man this time. I put a twenty-four-seven deputy on duty outside his hospital room. Since then there hasn't been anything."

"Don't sound so disappointed, Jim," Harry said. "It gives the public the wrong idea."

"I'm thinking of the budget," Jim complained.

"Aren't we all?" Jennifer said.

"Are you going to check those tires?" Harry asked.

"I'll see what Sheriff Fisher says," Jim replied.

The meeting ended with Jennifer saying over her shoulder to Harry as they filed out of the room, "Do you need a note to remind you to call?"

Jim turned and grinned at Harry, who felt his face burn.

"Do you need more information?" he asked, hoping to regain ground.

"You know what I want," she said, striding away from them.

"That's not what you think," Harry said hurriedly to Jim.

"Of course not," Jim said, beaming down at Harry. "It never crossed my mind."

27

By the time Harry reached the hospital, the excitement had died down, but people were still milling outside Cooper's door.

"What's the word on Brickman?" Harry asked Hodges, who was watching the Crime Scene people finishing their work.

A hospital clean-up crew stood patiently waiting, to swab the blood off the floor, all talking excitedly in Spanish.

"Austen T. Brickman is fast asleep as we speak," Hodges said with an affected seriousness, "having at least three twenty-two slugs picked out of him, none of which will do him any permanent harm."

"The hired gun got away?"

"He may be carrying some lead," he replied. "You got time to listen to a story?"

Harry could tell that Hodges was bursting with it.

"Sure," he said.

Hodges got hold of Harry's arm and led him away from the crowd.

"Good," he said, "because it's a doozer. There's a redheaded nurse up here." He looked around without seeing her.

"Alice Saunders," Harry said, hoping to hurry him on. "Australian accent."

Hodges grinned.

"That's right. Leave it to you," he said. "Well, it was about eleven forty-five. Half the staff on their way to the cafeteria, the rest taking a break, visitors gone home for lunch. She was coming along the corridor from down there."

He pointed past the nurses' station.

"She was carrying a loaded bedpan with a hand towel thrown over it. Except for Corporal Austen T. Brickman who was sitting on his folding chair, which she said made him look like a red roo on a toadstool, with his chin sunk on his chest, the hallway was deserted. She thought he was asleep and was going to whistle at him. She showed me. She can whistle through her teeth loud enough to be heard in Fort Meyers."

Harry saw this was going to take the rest of the day if he didn't get Hodges back on track.

"Then what?" he asked.

"Well, she never got to whistle because just then an orderly wearing a green O.R. hat came out of that fire escape door, carrying a tray with something on it covered by one of them tin covers that keeps food on a plate warm. I got to say, she's a sharp little ticket. Right off, she saw something was wrong, when he stepped easy past Austen T., to turn into Cooper's room.

"She shouted, 'Hey!' and jumped Austen T., who no sooner got his eyes open than he reached for his gun, twisting toward the green hat, who knocked the cover off what Alice saw was a revolver. Austen T. was drawing his gun when the chair buckled under him and dumped him on the floor. Alice began screaming. The shooter by now had his gun in his hand and fired three times into Austen T. as he went down.

"Alice made a run at the man and threw the bedpan at his head. He ducked a little too late, and the bedpan hit him on the shoulder, and what was in it splattered over his face. She said he began swearing right up there with the best of them. That gave Austen T. time to roll over, raise his gun, and fire. The shot clipped him, and he gave a yell; but still trying to wipe his face, he turned to take a pop at Cooper. Before he could, Austen T., still scrambling around on the floor, shot him again. He gave another yell, and, whipping around, raced for the fire exit like a man with his pants on fire.

"Right then, Austen T. gained his feet, bleeding like a stuck pig, but lifted his gun to let fly when Alice, finding herself looking into the barrel of that forty-five, shouted, 'Austen T., don't shoot! It's me!'

"Austen T., who had been grazed on his forehead by one of the bullets and half blinded by the blood running down his face, lowered his gun and, weaving like a tree about to fall, said, 'Nurse Alice Marie Saunders, is that you?'

"Before she could answer, he fainted dead away and crashed into the floor like a falling tree, scaring her real bad because she thought he was a goner. But he wasn't. In addition to being shot, he had banged his head when the chair gave way, and it was the crack on the head that did him in. Anyway, he's going to be all right."

Hodges was about out of breath, but he managed to say, "If Alice hadn't banged the shooter with that bedpan, I figure she, Cooper, and Austen T. would be signing up for the heavenly choir even as we speak."

"Where is she?" Harry asked.

"When they carried off Austen T., she was sticking closer to him than a burr on a dog."

"We have prints, blood samples, and maybe some hair," Kathleen said, arriving between Harry and Hodges in a blue jumpsuit and latex gloves. "It's a rich dig," she added, smiling with satisfaction. "I think we can make this one. It's very gratifying."

"Wasn't he wearing gloves?" Harry demanded in disbelief.

"He shed them and his greens on the first landing below us and was so rattled he held onto his gun for another floor before dropping it."

"Did you check the men's rooms on that floor and the next one down?" Harry asked.

"Why?" she asked, puzzled.

"You're forgetting the bedpan," he said.

"Oh, my God!" she shouted in delight and ran off, calling for her team to follow her.

"One man's poison," Harry observed, going to take a look at Cooper, who was out of the O.R., asleep, and looking completely peaceful.

"You've seen the last of him," Harley Dillard observed glumly, giving himself a spin in his swivel chair. "Brickman nicked him a couple of times, but the miracle is that all that shooting didn't fill that corridor with corpses."

"Thanks to Corporal Austen T. Brickman and the bedpan lady," Harry said.

"Are we missing something?" Jennifer asked, looking from Jim to Harry.

"You and Harley should visit Brickman," Harry said. "He would appreciate it, and you would have a unique experience. But before you go, brush up on your genealogies."

That proved too much for Jim, who burst out laughing.

"You two are having fun at our expense," Harley said with a pretense of disapproval. "Let's get back to work. Jennifer, give them the news."

"Right. I had a talk with Wylie; and he overruled Birch, who was threatening all kinds of trouble. Toke Wylie and Mark Crowley's savings accounts in the East Coast Savings and Loan have had several cash deposits of five thousand dollars each over the last eight weeks, totaling about twenty thousand dollars for each man. Wiggins banked with the Avola Trust Company. His savings account showed the same pattern of deposits, followed by a couple of large withdrawals."

"Broken up in small segments, hoping not to trigger a Currency Transaction Report to the IRS by the bank," Harry said.

"What about the withdrawals?" Harley asked.

"Wiggins was having a major addition put on his place," Harry said. "I assume they were down payments on building contracts."

"May as well check it out," Harley said to Jennifer.

"That's only in his savings account," she said. "All told, counting his investment portfolio, and his money market accounts, he was worth about three quarters of a million dollars."

"Black market orchids go for a high price," Jim said.

"So does providing a landing stage for contraband alligator hides and whatever else Crowley was shipping out of the swamp," Harry added.

"Drugs?" Harley asked.

"I don't think a lot of it," Jim answered, "but there's a certain amount of undocumented plane traffic in and out of the reservation back country."

"Anything else we need to know?" Dillard asked.

"There's one thing," Jim said. "Yesterday, we took soil samples from the tires of both John Kringle and Michael Rhinelander's automobile tires. The detectives sent to take the samples did Rita Evgenie Kronsky's car as well. Although Rita Kronsky's samples won't show anything, we've sent them all along, including soil samples from Wiggins's road, to the labs, asking for comparisons. We'll get them back sometime. Only the Lord knows when."

"Give us the identification data," Jennifer said, "and we'll do some leaning."

"Do Kronsky and Rhinelander know they were taken?" Harry asked.

"I would think so," Jim said. "My people didn't talk to them, but their groundskeeper took us to the vehicles and watched the samples being taken."

The conversation continued for another fifteen minutes, devoted mostly to the issues of Jim's not having secured a search warrant and whether or not the evidence could ever be used in court. Harry scarcely listened.

Just before they broke up, Harry said, "There is at least a chance that the killer we are looking for learned yesterday that dirt samples were collected from the tires of his car. What is he going to do?"

Harley Dillard, who had no taste for speculation, slapped his folder shut and said, "Mind-reading isn't in my job description."

"If I were him," Jennifer answered, "I would conclude that I had become a serious object of interest; and I would begin to study my options very actively."

"I'm interested in what those options are," Harry said.

Despite his earlier statement, Harley began to look interested.

"I would make sure my connections to the crimes had been erased and my escape routes cleared," Jim said with brisk authority.

"He's been doing that pretty effectively already," Harley said with a bitter laugh.

No other options or suggestions surfaced, and Harry got up to leave with the others. Jennifer went out with him.

"Can I have some more of your time?" she asked lightly when they reached the hallway, and set off at a brisk pace, not waiting for an answer.

Harry followed, hardly aware that he was following. His mind was thoroughly occupied with Jim's response to his question. By the time he reached Jennifer's office, Harry had concluded that there were only two, possibly three people left, counting himself—Franklin and Carla Rodriguez.

"Tell me if I'm wrong," she said, closing the door behind

him, catching one of his hands in hers, and leading him to the two chairs in front of her desk. "But last night, even when we were making love, you seemed to be only marginally with me. I noticed it again this morning. Is something wrong?"

Harry was ruffled by the question. He thought he had concealed his worries while he was with her, and now he found he had not. It made him slightly angry with her for having penetrated his disguise.

"No," he said, "I had a very good time last night. I thought you did as well."

She had pulled her chair around so that they were facing one another. She leaned back in her chair, hands loose in her lap with her legs thrust out, apparently thoroughly relaxed, wearing a slightly puzzled smile as she regarded him.

"I did," she said, leaning forward in a quick movement to touch his arm, "but you're not a good liar, Harry, never were. You're one of those people who should always tell the truth."

"Are you telling me I didn't have a good time?" he demanded, trying to be offended without much success.

"Come on," she said, "out with it. What's gnawing on your liver? Is it us? Have I worn out my welcome?"

"It's not us. It's not you," Harry said, dumping the resistance. "It's Franklin Wylie and Soñadora Asturias and another woman named Carla Rodriguez."

"Two mystery women from south of the border," she said, her smile slipping a little. "Are their husbands hunting you? And how does Franklin figure in here, aside from probably being one of the people I would get rid of if I were Rhinelander's killer?"

"He is almost certainly working very hard to find out where Franklin and Rodriguez are," Harry said. "And with the money he has, it is only a matter of time before he buys the information he's looking for."

"You know where they are, don't you?" she asked.

"Yes."

"Who is the Asturias woman? How is she connected to this affair?"

"I shouldn't have mentioned her at all," Harry said.

"Why are you concerned about her? Are you in love with her?"

"No!"

His answer, almost a shout, made him feel as bad as if he had said it to Soñadora.

"Look," he said, forcing himself to lower the volume, "she's at risk of becoming collateral damage. Just talking to people about her will endanger all of their lives."

"You're very worried about them, aren't you?" Jennifer asked, trying to smile.

"You could say so," Harry admitted.

"Has it occurred to you, my dear," she asked quietly, tightening her grip on his arm, "that one of the killer's ways to them is through you?"

28

The more Harry thought about what Jennifer had said and what had been said in the meeting with Harley Dillard, the more worried he became about Franklin and Soñadora's safety. He reasoned that, although the killer could not know exactly what Franklin and Rodriguez knew, he had to know that one or both of them might have enough information to link him to Toke, Mark, and Wiggins. His next logical next step, Harry assumed, would be to kill both of them.

"My problem," Harry said, "is that by trying to protect them, I may have increased their exposure."

"How does that work?" Rowena asked.

Late that afternoon, Harry had gone to talk to Rowena Farnham with an idea that only she could implement.

"Well, it's possible that the killer is keeping track of my comings and goings in hopes that I will lead him to whoever's harboring Franklin and Carla Rodriguez."

"How would that be possible?"

"By planting a tracking device on the Rover would be one simple way."

"Haven't you looked?" Rowena asked in surprise.

Harry laughed.

"Oh, yes, every few days, and I've never found anything," he said, "but the devices are small and easily hidden. Whether I'm being tailed or not, my going to Salvamento attracts attention. I'm assuming that the killer knows of my connection with his victims and with Franklin."

"I expect a lot of people know about it," Rowena conceded, pouring Harry more tea and passing him the dish of lemon tarts, which he had already sampled. He took another, to confirm that they were beyond good. "Move on to the part where you ask me to do something. That's why you're here isn't it?"

"Actually, I came here to eat your lemon tarts," Harry said, finishing with a sigh of pleasure the one he had just taken. "What I'm thinking is that both Franklin and Soñadora would be safer if he was not in Salvamento with her. Is there any chance of getting him into Haven House?"

"We do have children in there from time to time, but they usually come with their mothers," Rowena said, putting down her cup. "I don't recall our ever having a ten-year-old boy with no mother in the house, not that something couldn't be worked out if it was necessary."

"That's a relief," Harry said.

"Now comes the hard part," she told him.

"Soñadora?" he said.

"Have you talked to her about this?"

"No, I haven't been calling."

"That's what she told me. What's wrong with you, Harry?"

Although in her benign moods she wore the demeanor of a female Friar Tuck, she was formidable when roused.

"I was trying not to do anything that connected me to Salvamento," he protested.

"Did you ever hear of a public phone?"

"I never thought of it."

"What does that tell you?"

"Early onset of the big A?"

"It's not funny, even though I laughed," she said, trying to get her scowl back. "When are you going to start treating her the way you should and want to?"

"As soon as I leave here?"

"Another trip into denial-land," Rowena said dispiritedly, then rallying. "It may be too late, but you'll find out when you talk to her; and a word of caution, Harry. She is not going to want to part with Franklin."

"I thought that might happen," Harry said. "Somewhere under all that armor, there's a warm and loving person. At the same time she's going through hell over her father. Do you know about that?"

"Yes, we've talked about it."

Harry nodded, knowing that's all Rowena would tell him.

"If she'll part with Franklin, will one of your people pick him up?" he asked.

"I'll arrange it, and, Harry, what about Carla Rodriguez?"

"I think she would be safer with you."

"Talk to Soñadora about it, and you watch yourself. Remember, you're not immortal."

Harry promised that he would, thanked Rowena, and left, thinking how irritating it was having people tell him he was mortal and in imminent danger of having it proved.

Driving out of Avola in the last of the daylight, Harry stopped at a Marriot and called Soñadora from a phone in the lobby.

"I thought the coyotes had eaten you," she said.

"They may yet. How's Franklin?"

"I think he is bored, being stuck here with me."

"Give him a few years and he would think he'd died and gone to heaven."

"It is clear that not every adolescent male thinks so," she said coolly.

"Zinger number two," he said. "Rowena had to remind me of public phones."

"Why were you talking with Rowena?"

Harry decided there was no easy way to say he wanted to move Franklin.

"I think Franklin and Carla Rodriguez would be safer in Haven House than they are with you. She said she would take them."

"Why?" she cried.

Harry heard it all in that single word, and he hated doing what he was doing, but he was certain it should be done.

"A lot of people know about our connection. Ernesto has told me that someone, posing as a relative of Carla's, is offering money for information about the location of Rodriguez and Franklin. It is only a question of time before someone suggests Salvamento."

"No one in my organization would ever give such information," she said angrily.

"Perhaps not, but would you bet the life of two people on it?"

"What is gained by transferring them to Haven House?"

"There are no obvious connections between you and me and Haven House. The inquiries are being made in the Latino community. Almost no one there would think that either Franklin or Carla would seek refuge in Haven House."

"Have you forgotten Rigoberta Quirate?" Soñadora demanded.

"It's not likely I will ever forget her or Hazel or the night you and I rescued them," he said, "but that was a long time ago. If I remember correctly, Rigoberta was the only woman in the house who wasn't an Anglo."

"I want to think about this," Soñadora said.

"How do you like having Franklin to look after?"

"I like it," she said. "He is a very nice boy; and unlike you he is a . . . *caballero*."

"Gentleman," Harry said. "I like him too. Think hard about my suggestion. I'll call you tomorrow."

"Harry," she said before hanging up, "be careful."

It was dark by the time Harry turned onto the Hammock bridge, disappointed that clouds had obscured the moon. Seeing the moon in Puc Puggy Creek always made him feel better about coming home alone. As usual, as the Rover clattered over the two loose planks on the Hammock end of the bridge, Harry told himself that tomorrow he would drive in the spikes that had loosened. At that same instant, a rabbit leaped out of the weeds on the left side of the track, and plunged straight under the Rover.

Swearing, Harry gambled and spun the wheel to the left, hoping the tire would miss the rabbit. At that same instant, the windshield exploded into pellets that rained down on the hood and inside the cab. That crash was accompanied by a burst of automatic weapon fire. Harry killed his lights, switched off the engine, opened his door, and slid out of the cab onto his knees in the sand. Another burst from the shooter sizzled through the Rover, taking out the remaining glass.

Gripping his CZ, Harry slid backwards into the brush, then began crawling and stopping to listen until he had reached a place opposite to where he thought his assailant had done his shooting. The clouds had passed over the creek, and the moon was pouring light onto the white road which lay bare and empty.

A moment later, he heard one of the loose planks creak as whoever had stepped on it removed his weight. Reversing direction, Harry crept back to the Rover with the same care he had used in moving away from it. Having worked himself into a position from which to observe the bridge, he settled down to wait. Gradually, the night sounds, silenced by the Rover crossing the bridge and the rattle of gunfire, returned; and a kind of fragile, moonlit peace, dimpled by the tuning notes of locusts and crickets, settled on the creek and its surrounding jungle.

Ten minutes later, a powerful automobile engine barked into life and later roared away in a screeching of tires in the direction of Avola. Harry stood up and slowly slipped through the bushes and out onto the road. Easing the safety on, he put away the CZ and took out his cell phone.

"Soñadora," he said. "Someone just shot the windshield out of the Rover."

"Are you all right?" she asked.

"Yes."

"Where is the person who shot at you?"

"He drove back toward town. If the Rover will still run, I'm coming in. With the windshield gone, I'll have to drive slowly because of the bugs."

"No, Harry," she said loudly. "You must not drive on that road tonight. You will make a perfect target. Whoever tried to kill you may expect you to do just that. Promise me you will not leave the Hammock. Take every precaution!"

Harry had been walking around the Rover as they talked. Reaching the front, he heard the drip and dying gurgle of liquid leaking onto the ground.

"The radiator is drained," he said in disgust. "I'm stuck. Now, listen. Get yourself and Franklin into the most secure room in the place and one you can get out of fast in case of fire. Are you listening?"

"I'm already making the preparations," she said.

"You still have your revolver?"

"Yes, I have it and plenty of bullets. Don't worry. You know I can use it."

"Turn all of the inside lights out."

"Harry, you are not remembering," she said sternly, "I have known all this since before I was twelve years old."

"If he hasn't come by sunrise, I think you're safe. Promise

me you won't do anything rash."

She laughed.

"The stove is calling the pot black."

"Pot and kettle," he said.

"What?"

"Never mind."

Harry found he did not want to break his connection with her. He did not want her left alone with Franklin. He did not want to be stuck helpless on the Hammock with her in Avola.

"Harry," she said and then said something rapidly in Quiche.

"Translate."

"No. It is just something I wanted to tell you. Go with God."

And she was gone. What he had heard he had heard her say before, but where and when he couldn't remember.

Harry found, as he began walking toward his house, that he could not do it. He could not stand to spend the rest of the night not knowing what was happening to her and Franklin. He stopped and dialed a number. Jim answered.

"It's me," Harry said and told him quickly what had happened and that he was worried about Soñadora and Franklin.

"Did you get a tag number or the make of the car?"

"No, it was parked on 19. I was on the Hammock side of the bridge."

"I can't do more than have one of the deputies on night duty check on her place a couple of times."

"Not enough," Harry said. "If I can, I'll get a taxi out here to take me to the Salvamento."

"You won't get one to drive out where you are after dark. Hang up. I'll call you back."

Harry's shadow fidgeted on the white sand until his cell rang.

"There's a deputy a few miles from you on his way back to the station," Jim said. "He'll pick you up if you think it's safe to stand out on 19."

"I'll be there."

Harry asked the deputy to let him out of the cruiser a block from Salvamento and called Soñadora.

"I'll be at your front door in about three minutes. If anyone's with me, shoot him."

"How did you get here?" she demanded once she had Harry inside and the door locked and barred again.

The work room in which they were standing was in darkness; but the outside lights filtered into the room, allowing them to see one another. She was fully dressed in a black shirt and slacks with a wide leather belt, her revolver in its holster at her back. Harry wondered what the chances were of finding her in a nightdress and robe, indulging his delight in finding her safe by making a private joke.

"I ran, swam part of the way, and hitchhiked the rest," he said, still gay with relief.

She was walking past him toward the inner part of the building when he answered her. Spinning around and, putting all her weight into it, she struck him on the chest with the flat of her hands, sending him backward into the door with a loud crash.

"One of these times," she told him, fists on her hips, "I will kill you."

"Why did you do that?" he demanded, rubbing the back of his head where it had hit the door.

"Because I am *mestizo* and lack all *mesursa,* and you are a *blanco idiota.*"

"Are you two fighting?" a very tentative voice asked from the darkness.

"No," Soñadora said, reaching out and catching Harry by his free hand, pulling him along with her as she walked toward the voice. "If we were fighting, he would be lying defeated."

Franklin put on the light and let them into the kitchen, then closed the door behind them. The windows in the room were covered with heavy drapes.

"Why did you push Harry into the door?" he asked Soñadora.

"It's because she likes me," Harry said, getting in first. "Haven't you seen girls at your school punching the boys they like best?"

Franklin laughed.

"Oh, for shame!" Soñadora cried, her face flaming. "He gave me a ridiculous answer to a serious question, Franklin. He was being punished."

"Some of the girls are very strong," Franklin said seriously. "It is no joke when they punch you."

"You're right," Harry said. "Feel the bump on my head."

"Enough," Soñadora said. "Harry, have you had any supper?"

"No, but first," he said, "I want you to show me over this place. It may be possible to see where it would be easiest to break in."

They left Franklin watching television and with Soñadora leading, set off together. The windows at the back of the building had been built with iron grates set into their frames, and the two entrances had metal doors with locks, heavy dead bolts, and cross bars.

"He's not coming in this way," Harry said.

"I think not," Soñadora agreed. "It is more probable that the two windows in the office area at the front are most vulnerable."

"OK," Harry said when they had finished their tour. "You and Franklin are set up in the first guest room off the kitchen, and I think I will settle out in the work area where I can have a wall at my back and face the windows."

"When Franklin is asleep, I will join you. I am sorry I pushed you so hard. I did not wish to hurt you."

"I almost believe you," Harry said.

She gave a low, soft laugh and, taking his hand, said, "Come and eat," setting off for the kitchen with long strides.

"Soñadora has been teaching me Spanish," Franklin said while Harry ate. "I like it."

"That's good," Harry said. "Did you know she also speaks Quiche?"

"What's that?"

"A primitive language," Harry said with a straight face.

Soñadora was sitting across the table from them, nursing a cup of tea, watching them and listening with interest.

"Believe nothing this *gringo* tells you, Franklin," she said. "Quiche is a Mayan language and was my mother's language, the first language I learned. My father taught me English and Spanish."

"What does Quiche sound like?" the boy asked, finishing his baked apple.

She spoke rapidly for a moment.

"That sounds hard. What did you say?"

"That the Mayans are an ancient people who once had a great civilization that was destroyed by wars and probably starvation and pestilence."

"The remnants of their cities can still be seen," Harry said. "You may have seen pictures of them."

"I have," Franklin said. "I would like to see them myself someday."

"Then I'm sure you will," Soñadora said, glancing at her watch. "It's bedtime."

By the time she came back from seeing Franklin into bed, Harry was sitting in a swivel chair behind one of the dozen or so desks in the room. He was sitting facing the windows but far enough back from them to be out of their light.

"He is a good boy," Soñadora said with something in her voice Harry had not heard before, but he knew what it was.

Katherine had it in her voice when she spoke of the children.

"When my children were little," Harry said, "I thought that when they grew up, I would no longer worry about them. It turned out not to be so. Sometimes it seems I worry more about them."

"I have always thought I did not want children," she replied in a guarded voice, "but Franklin is a pleasure to have with me. I think I could easily come to love him."

"I'm sure you could," Harry said and left it there.

He saw no point in telling her that loving a child was the easy part. Bringing one up was where the cost came in.

They went on talking quietly with periods of easy silence. There were even periods when Harry thought she might be sleeping. He hoped that she was. She worked extremely long hours, and even when she was not working, the people whom Salvamento served were always in her mind.

He thought that he had been consistently alert through all of the dark hours, but Soñadora's voice jumped him out of a sleep.

"Harry," she said, "something's happening."

Above the screen of bushes across the front of the yard, he saw the cab of a large pickup truck moving slowly along the street.

"Let's get down just in case," Harry said.

They slid off their chairs and crouched behind the desk, peering over its top. Harry had drawn his gun and, glancing at Soñadora, saw that she was holding hers in both hands, intently watching the windows. The truck turned toward the building, its headlights shining through the hedge.

"Is he going to ram us?" Soñadora asked in a tight voice.

"If it comes through," Harry said, feeling that boost of spirits danger always gave him, "shoot out the lights and then try for the driver."

At that moment the truck's engine exploded into a roar, and

the pickup crashed into the hedge, bulling its way through the shrubs and gaining speed, driving straight at the window to the right of the door.

The explosion of the impact and the rending shriek of metal being hammered through the stucco, wood, and plaster wall were momentarily deafening to Harry; and as the truck bucked half its length into the room, the nerve-rattling noise was instantly followed by an astonishing silence, broken by the double blasts of Harry's and Soñadora's revolvers. The flaring lights of truck behind its steel bumper died, plunging the room into darkness.

"The driver," Harry said. "Up together, fire and drop on two. One, two."

They came up together and fired into the cab. Nothing.

"I'm reloading," Soñadora said. "Then you."

Instantly, a blast of automatic weapon fire left the top of their desk in splinters. Harry grasped her arm and, pointing at himself and then to his right, slithered away with almost no sound until the toe of his sneaker caught on the leg of a chair which turned on its caster and banged on its desk.

With a yell, their attacker fired a burst at the sound, ripping the back of the chair to shreds and sending the shattered frame careering across the floor. Responding instantly to the blast, Soñadora sprang up and fired three shots at the muzzle flame then dropped to the floor and snaked away to another desk.

The shooter returned her fire, giving Harry a target. On his knees, he fired behind the tongue of flame that flared from the shooter's gun. There was a grunt of pain followed by a clatter as the weapon smashed into the floor. Harry fired again, and the shooter fell with a loud thud.

"Stay down," Harry said loudly, to be sure Soñadora heard him.

Pulling off his sneakers, Harry moved in a crouch towards

the fallen man; and when he was close enough to see the man, sprawled facedown on the floor, he slowly stood up.

"You bastard," someone said out of the darkness and fired at him from less than ten feet away.

Harry's right shoulder felt as if he had been struck with great force by a white hot poker. His CZ fell out of his hand, paralyzed with the pain. He tried to move, to do something, but his body did not seem to be responding. Then his legs gave way, dropping him in a heap on the floor. He was not aware of falling; but with a surge of regret he decided he must be dying.

There was a second shot, closer than the first, but instead of feeling the bullet strike him, he heard a dull groan, followed by another shot.

Then silence. After a moment of absolute silence, during which he believed he was dead, Soñadora shouted, "Harry! Harry! Where are you?"

How odd, he thought, vaguely annoyed; but, making a great effort, answered.

"I'm here. Wherever here is."

29

Harry woke to a foggy scene, containing a smiling face surrounded by red hair peering down at him while fiddling with something attached to his arm.

"How did you get here?" he whispered.

"On shank's mare," she said with a grin. "What's my name?"

"You used to be Alice Saunders."

Harry's vision began to clear, and the hospital room slowly came into focus, but the face had vanished.

"I still am," Alice's disembodied voice said cheerfully. "Who are you?"

"Harry Brock. Am I alive or dead?"

"What do you think?"

The fog rolled in again and speaking became an effort.

"I thought I died, but I can't remember why."

"You were shot, and here comes another one."

"Something stung somewhere."

"Hey!" he muttered.

"Sleep," she said.

He heard the voices before he saw the faces.

"Harry, wake up."

He opened his eyes. Soñadora was bent over him. He was immensely relieved to see her.

"What happened?" he asked, concern replacing his relief when he noticed that her left arm was in a sling.

"It is nothing, a scratch. How are you feeling?"

"I don't know. Franklin . . ."

"Is fine. He is with his uncle."

"He drove through the wall," Harry said, his memory dribbling back. "I thought I'd stopped him, but he shot me, twice, I think. I was sure I had died."

"It was a close thing, my friend," a loud voice said as Hodges's moon face loomed over Soñadora's shoulder. "You just about bled out. You've had a bad couple of days, but it looks like you'll make it. I'll say one thing, you've got more lives than a cat."

"Frank!"

Jim's voice came from behind Frank.

Harry laughed, but that was a mistake, and the sound ended in a gasp.

"Now see what you've done?" Jim protested. "Come away from there."

Complaining that he had more to tell Harry, Hodges's happy grin was replaced by Jim's somber face.

"Welcome back. Frank and I will see you later. Ms. Asturias is staying. She'll fill you in; and, Harry, she is one brave woman."

"Captain, it is not necessary . . ." Soñadora began, but Jim was already hustling Hodges out the door.

"Are you sure you're all right?" Harry asked when they were gone.

"Yes, but I can't stay bending like this. The weight of the sling . . ."

"Sit down, sit down," Harry insisted. "I'm really glad to see you."

She pulled a chair toward the foot of the bed, positioning herself so that Harry could see her without putting a strain on his right side.

"I can't remember all of it," he said. "Tell me."

"First," she said, "there were two of them."

"Two!" Harry said, astonished.

"Yes, Michael Rhinelander and Rita Kronsky. It was Kronsky who shot you."

Harry struggled to remember the sequence of events.

"Then I did shoot Michael."

"Yes, he is dead."

"And you shot Rita after she shot me."

"Yes. She, too, is dead. I'm sorry that I was not quick enough to keep you from being wounded. I blame myself."

"It was pitch dark in there, Soñadora!" Harry said, contradicting her. "I didn't see her, and she must have been standing almost in front of me. The truck hit the wall and blew the outside lights, and we shot out its headlights. After that, I was shooting at muzzle blasts."

"Yes," she said. "So was I."

"Did she shoot you?" Harry asked.

"She must have. I think she was falling when it happened."

They sat without speaking for a moment; then Harry asked, "Carla Rodriguez?"

"She left with her daughter the day before yesterday."

Harry paused. "Time lost, but I'm not surprised."

"Nor am I."

Alice came in at that point.

"OK, lovers," she said, winking at Soñadora. "Crocodile Dundee needs his beauty sleep."

Harry was kept in bed three days and allowed to drift around the hospital for another twenty-four hours before being discharged with detailed instructions on dressing the wound. His right arm was in a sling and immobilized against his stomach. Therapy for the shoulder was to begin in a week.

Jennifer came once; but although she asked all the polite

questions, there was so much chill in the room, Harry almost asked for a second blanket. The visit confused and depressed him. He had been glad to see her, but the visit was so painful, her going was a relief. What was he to make of the failure? He didn't know.

The first day he was mobile, he went to see Cooper. There was no deputy at his door, and he found Cooper sitting in a chair, reading the paper.

"Hello, Harry," he said with a broad smile. "I am very glad to see you. You had us worried."

"This is an improvement," Harry said, putting out his hand. "Welcome back, but go easy when you shake that hand. You know your filing has been approved by the judge."

"Yes, I can't say I'm surprised."

"I've got a suggestion. Talk with John Kringle. You may be able to avoid a lot of lawyer work."

"I want it established beyond a reasonable doubt," Cooper said.

"I know. Talk with him anyway."

"If you want to be, you're still on my payroll," Cooper replied.

"Thank you, but my work is done. That doesn't mean I don't want anything more to do with you."

"All right. If next week I still remember who you are, I suggest we have dinner."

"If you'll cut my steak, you're on."

Cooper laughed and lifted his doubled fist. Very gingerly, Harry bumped it.

"Tucker's going to look in on you," Jim said as they drove away from the hospital. "I don't know how you're going to like this but he's also arranged for Doreen Clampett to come in and 'do' for you, as he put it."

"Oh, my God," Harry said and groaned pitifully.

"Didn't she look after Tucker when he had that trouble with his heart?" Jim asked with a grin. "I think I remember seeing her out there."

"You would certainly remember Doreen," Harry said. "Titian would have worshipped her, but she can talk the hind leg off a donkey. I won't get a minute's peace."

"There'll be some compensation in just looking at her," Jim said wickedly.

"Well, that's true," Harry said, "and she's got a heart of gold, but a greasy frying pan is her weapon of choice when it comes to cooking. What's the situation with John Kringle?"

"We've done everything but run over him with a disc harrow," Jim said with relish, "and our conclusion is that what he says is true. Although he didn't turn a hair at learning what his half brother and sister had done, he had no part in the murders. I must admit to being surprised. Do you know he asked after you every day we grilled him."

"I'm glad you cleared him," Harry said. "If he hadn't made that comment to me about keeping my eyes on the two coyotes, I don't think I would have pushed as hard as I did—not that I ever guessed that Rita Kronsky had played a role in the killings."

"I forgot to mention that the soil tests from her tires came out positive," Jim put in. "The same was true for Rhinelander's wheels, but the tests came back too late to be of any use."

"And that leaves Cooper," Harry said. "Have you seen him since he recovered his memory?"

"No, has it really come back?"

"It has, but he's not going to be of much use to you," Harry answered. "His last recollection of Sophie is stepping out of the elevator with her on the way to his room, laughing at a joke she'd just told him. From that point, to his waking up knowing who he is, his mind's a blank; but he's the same as ever he was as near as I can tell."

"He's going on with the effort to get himself declared Lilly Rhinelander's son?"

"Oh, yes. He wasn't at all surprised to learn that the judge had approved his suit, and he speaks warmly of Persephone."

"I wonder why his mother wanted to talk with him?" Jim asked.

"We'll never know," Harry said.

"Probably not," Jim agreed with a laugh. "I almost forgot. Kringle said he planned to offer Cooper a DNA sample if he wanted it. 'Anything,' he said, 'to get this f-word will settled.' He swears worse than Frank Hodges," Jim added in a shocked voice.

Tucker, accompanied by Sanchez and Oh, Brother!, was waiting in the yard when Harry and Jim arrived.

"You're in good hands, paws, and hooves," Jim said, stopping under the live oak.

"Then it's over," Harry said, pausing before getting out of the car.

"Two more cremations should do it," Jim agreed.

Tucker pulled open Harry's door.

"Can you make it on your own?" he asked.

"We're about to find out."

Henry David Wylie and Franklin called on Harry three mornings later and would not have made it beyond the screen door if he hadn't called to Doreen and told her it was all right, which he did not do right away because he was having too much fun listening to Henry David trying to convince her that he was a friend.

"Your housekeeper is very protective," Wylie said after Doreen had made them sit down on the lanai, practically lifted Harry into a chair, and gone back in the house.

"She is strong, even stronger than Soñadora, who throws a ball like a man," Franklin added, his admiration shining through his words.

"They are both good, strong women," Harry said, leaning forward to give Franklin's shoulder a welcoming shake. "How do you like being home?"

"I like it," he said, glancing at his uncle, "but you and Soñadora were really good to me," he added quickly.

"It was good having you here."

"I have come to discuss something with you, Harry," Wylie said.

But before he could go on, Doreen appeared with a tray loaded with a coffeepot, mugs, a plate of oatmeal and raisin cookies, and a glass of milk.

"My husband Wetherell could no more talk on an empty stomach than a horse could fly," she told them in a loud voice while pouring the coffee. "So go on and eat and drink, and if you run out, holler. There's more."

She turned to Wylie and said, "But don't you worry him none, or you'll answer to me."

"For a really good-looking woman," Franklin said in a whisper when she was gone, "she's some scary."

Harry laughed and paid the price, but managed after a moment to say, "A woman who doesn't scare you once in a while, Franklin, isn't worth chasing. Now, Doreen can be scary; but she's warm-hearted, generous, and kind; and having her in the house makes the world seem a whole lot better place. Now, let's hear what your uncle's thinking about."

"How would you like some Hierba Altos for neighbors?" Wylie asked.

"What do have in mind?"

"You know there's a problem with drugs and poaching in the back corner of the reservation, bordering on the Stickpen. That road running into Fillmore Wiggins's place has been a conduit for all kinds of mischief, as we've all just seen. The Council is talking about buying that property if it becomes available and expanding the buildings into a fully outfitted research station, inviting scientists to visit and work, providing them with laboratories, dormitories. We're thinking of opening it to the public, expanding his orchid collection, and making it the focus of the project. If the property falls into the state's hands, it will be auctioned off and broken up."

"Airboat rides, alligator wrestling, gift shop, bar, and hillbilly music?"

Harry's voice had grown cold. Wylie's face stiffened a little, but his voice remained calm.

"Absolutely not. The aim is to run it as an educational and research center in such a way that we and our visitors will learn more about what we have here and how to preserve it for our children and our children's children."

"And maybe persuade your white brothers to take better care of what surrounds you?" Harry said, with the warmth back in his voice.

"An important talking point, I must mention it to the Council," Wylie said with a straight face, but Franklin laughed.

"He has been spending too much time with the white-eyes," Wylie said, ruffling the boy's hair.

"Why are you telling me about your plans?" Harry said when they grew serious again, although he thought he knew the answer.

"Good question," Wylie said. "As warden of Bartram's Hammock and the state's official representative in this area, we won't get beyond the initial filing without your support."

"That may be giving me more influence than I really have, but if the plans when they're drawn up reaffirm what you've told me so far, I'll give all the help I can."

Doreen came onto the lanai, to see them on their way, and when Franklin praised the cookies and Henry David the coffee, she blushed and smiled a little but didn't say anything.

"The boy's a love," she told Harry as the car was driving away, "and for an Indian, Wylie's not too bad looking or would be if he was fed up a little." Then she put her arm around Harry's waist and pulled his good side against her and said, "Don't I have all the luck? Here I finally got you all to myself, and you're all busted up."

30

A week later Harry and Soñadora met at Jennifer's office, to review their sworn testimony regarding the deaths of Michael Rhinelander and Rita Kronsky. Jennifer went over the depositions with them then closed the file on her desk and said, "Ms. Asturias, you're in the process of becoming an American citizen. Is that right?"

Thanks to the efforts of Jim and Harley Dillard, the press release by the sheriff's department had indicated by omission that Harry had done the shooting.

Soñadora, no longer wearing her sling, said that she was and hoped to be through the process by December. She had been icily polite throughout the meeting.

"And here you are involved in a shootout, growing out of a desperate attack on your place of business," Jennifer said. "You and the marginally respectable man sitting next to you resolved the issue by shooting two people dead."

"Two people who were intent on killing a ten-year-old boy and Harry and would have killed me and nearly did," Soñadora replied.

"Whose gun were you using?"

"Where is this going?" Harry asked.

"Stay with me," Jennifer said, not gracing him with a look.

"The gun belongs to Salvamento," Soñadora said. "A lot of people do not like what we do."

"And you shoot them?"

"No, but the women working with me feel safer knowing the gun is in my desk."

"Why your desk?"

"I know how to use it."

"Is it licensed?"

"Yes, but not in my name."

Jennifer continued to stare at the woman for a moment, but Harry could not read the expression on her face.

"OK," Jennifer said, pushing away from her desk and standing up. "If Immigration shows up, stick with that story. They may swallow it. I think we're finished with you two. I'm sorry about your building, Ms. Asturias."

"Is there going to be problem with the gun?" Soñadora asked, once she and Harry were in Harry's rented Mustang.

His right arm was in a brace but he had limited use of it.

"I hope not," he said. "Harley Dillard will go on doing his best to keep Immigration off you. Have you been thinking about your father?"

She leaned back, resting her head against the seat, and closed her eyes. Harry thought she looked exhausted.

"He has asked me to come. He knows he is dying and says he has things to say me that must be said with me beside him."

She rolled her head back and forth on the seat, clearly in distress.

"I can't go. The work on Salvamento has begun. Someone must be there to make decisions."

"That's true," Harry said, "but it doesn't have to be you."

"Why are you pressing me to go?" she demanded, suddenly twisting toward him.

Harry was not sure whether the question was an appeal or a challenge.

"Because if you don't, you will never forgive yourself," he told her without hesitation.

"Is that the only reason? Do you want me to go away?"

Her voice had risen. Harry was not sure how to answer her. What was she asking? Why was she asking it?

"You know better than that," he said quietly.

"Perhaps I do. Perhaps I am too tired to know what I think."

"If I buy you a return ticket," he added with a smile, "will you be convinced?"

"You are a *picaro*," she said with a shaky smile.

"Good news," he said, starting the car, "I've progressed from an idiot to a rogue."

That night, Soñadora called him.

"Harry," she said, "I think I must go. I'm not sure it's the right thing, but you are right. I cannot live with myself unless I do. But it will take me a long time to pay you back."

"Neither of us will worry about that. *¿Claro?*"

"*Sí.*"

"Good. How soon will you go?"

"As soon as I can assemble the money."

"It's all 'assembled,' " he said suppressing a grin. "When do you want to go?"

"I cannot take more money from you," she said resolutely. "It is not right."

"Fine," he told her, "it will be a loan, and you will pay me back when your ship comes in."

"I have no ship," she said, alarm tightening her voice.

"OK, you can return it when it's assembled."

"Why do you keep saying *assembled?*" she demanded.

"Small joke. When do you want to go?"

"I have not said I will accept your offer."

"You don't have to. It's yours without your having to say anything. Now, when do you want to go?"

"I could leave in three days. I am already beginning to be

frightened that he will die before I get there."

"Tell him you're coming. He will wait for you."

"How can you know?"

"I trust him. I'll call you as soon as I have the ticket. Make sure your papers are in order."

The next morning Harry bought the ticket and gave Soñadora's office manager the date and time and said he would drive Soñadora to the airport. The woman thanked him with relief brightening her voice.

Shortly after putting down the phone, Jennifer called and asked a bit stiffly if Harry was free for lunch. He said he was. Since Doreen had taken a slightly tearful farewell, nearly putting him back in the hospital with one of her full-body hugs, he had been drifting through the house like a restless ghost, strong enough to get around but still too weak to do much of anything useful.

"Things are winding down," Jennifer said formally after they had ordered.

She had chosen the Canary Island Club, a place near her office that only opened for lunches and was always packed. Harry thought the place had about as much character as a pencil.

"I've noticed the autumnal light," Harry replied. "Cooper tells me he has made his and Kringle's lawyers unhappy by accepting Kringle's offer of a DNA sample that he is certain will establish his claim to being Lilly Rhinelander's son."

"What about the estate? Will Cooper file for a piece of it?"

"Crazy as it sounds, he and Kringle are working to resolve that out of court as well," Harry said. "Maybe there is a Santa Claus."

"Ha!" Jennifer said with a sharp laugh. "And maybe lollipops grow on trees. How are you feeling?"

Their unremarkable sandwiches arrived, just after the diet

water that Harry was restricting himself to.

"I have a statement and a question," Jennifer said after eating a quarter of her sandwich in two bites.

Harry put his sandwich down and waited.

"You're not going to marry me, are you?" she said, giving him a gimlet-eyed stare.

"Well?" she asked when he made no response.

"I'm waiting for the statement."

"I'm going back to Jacksonville tomorrow. Harley's done with me, and I've learned he's not going to accept a judgeship for at least four years because the one he wants won't come vacant until then. He plans to take the time remaining to gain support for his campaign."

"The question first," Harry said carefully, aware that he was entering a mine field. "Are you proposing?"

"No."

"I thought not. As for your question, I'm not moving to Jacksonville. That said, I'm going to miss you."

Even as he said it, Harry realized that while he was telling the truth, he had meant what he had said and nothing more. It was a surprise to him to discover that he wasn't particularly sorry that she was leaving, and he was reasonably certain that she wasn't all that ripped up about going.

"It was fun while it lasted," she said. "Finish your sandwich."

On the morning he was to take Soñadora to the airport, he found Sanchez sitting on his lanai step, observing the antics of the two raccoon cubs, who had escaped their mother again and were rolling around together on the scanty grass, squealing and chewing on one another.

When Harry opened the door to let the dog in, Sanchez hesitated, looking from the cubs to Harry.

"You're right," Harry said, following the dog into the kitchen.

"They're delinquents. I feel sorry for their mother."

As he took out the Milk-Bone biscuits and gave Sanchez some water, he went on talking to him and not noticing that he wasn't carrying on a conversation with a person. While Sanchez was enjoying his snack, Harry read the note from Tucker that had been rolled up in the dog's neck scarf.

"Good news!" Harry said. "Jane Bunting has come home and has brought two kittens with her. Tucker has fixed up a box for them under the kitchen stove."

Sanchez looked at Harry.

"Oh," Harry said. "Not good news."

He looked back at the note.

"Tucker says you're sleeping out in the barn with Oh, Brother! for the time being. I gather she's a little overprotective."

Harry wrote something on the note, rolled it back up in the dog's neck piece and said, "I've told him I'll be over later in the day to have a look for myself."

Sanchez finished his biscuit and went to door, where he paused to look at Harry again.

"Don't worry," Harry said, letting him out. "I'll stay away from the stove."

Harry got Soñadora to the airport on time, helped her check her bags, and accompanied her to the gate. The line was short, and the moment came very quickly when they had to say goodbye.

"Are you coming back?" he asked her after wishing her good luck and a safe trip.

"Is it a return ticket?" she asked with a twitch at the corners of her mouth.

"Yes," he said, trying to decide if he should give her a kiss or a hug or both.

"Then I'll be back. I have to go now. Goodbye, Harry."

Kinley Roby

That did it. He astonished himself by pulling her into his arms and kissing her on the mouth. She threw her arms around his neck and kissed him back, then pulling back slightly, said those words in Quiche that he had heard her say before.

"What did you say?" he asked her, hoarse with emotion.

Taking his face in her hands, she kissed him again, then said in a whisper, "If you're lucky, one day I'll tell you. Promise me you will take care of yourself, Harry."

"I will. You do the same."

And she was gone, pulling off her shoes as she went. He watched her progress, returning her final wave as she was slipping into the crowd. Turning away, he recalled that last lucid moment after he had been shot when he thought he was dying and experienced that powerful surge of regret.

He stopped and looked back at the teeming gate, knowing suddenly that the cause of his regret was that he would never see her again. For an instant, the pain of it overwhelmed him a second time, but with his eyes stinging he fought it off.

"Idiot!" he said aloud. "She's got a return ticket."

A young man with a day's dark growth of beard, crowding past him as Harry spoke, grinned at him and said, "Hang onto that thought, pal. Hang onto it."

ABOUT THE AUTHOR

Kinley Roby lives in Virginia with his wife, author and editor Mary Linn Roby.